THE ICE QUEEN

Book One of

The Azure Syndicate Trilogy

HENRY STOKES

First published by Lulu Press Incorporated 2014

Design by Henry Stokes © Henry Stokes

Cover image Leona Lee, www.behance.net/LeonaLee © Henry Stokes

Editing by Louisa Cardinale,

www.linkedin.com/pub/louisa-cardinale/53/773/393

Typeset in 12/16 Times New Roman

Printed and bound by Lulu Press Incorporated

National Library of Australia Cataloguing-in-Publication data:

Stokes, Henry, 1987- .

The Ice Queen/Henry Stokes,

978 0 9925485 0 6 (Hardcover Format)

www.henrystokes.org

ACKNOWLEDGEMENTS

Publishing this novel was my dream, and I could not have achieved it without the help of so many others.

Thanks to all my Kickstarter backers: Simon Herd, James Beauchamp, Martin Hablitzel, Ben F, May Kim, Alex McGill, Jimmy Northwood, Alan Stokes, Anne van der Sanden, Russell Stokes, Michael Cratt, Andrew Arquilla, Dave Burrows, Matti Hiob, Julia Nesbit, Josh Allan, Revek, Diego Munoz, Mad Jarvis, Jason Flanders, George Bajuscik, Nathan Broadfoot, Derek Freeman, Wes O, Jessica M, Andrew Johnson, Wanda Budzyniak. Special thanks to Donnie, Tania Nesbit and Jeremy Leis; I was truly humbled by your support, and I will always remember it.

The biggest challenge to finishing this novel was the editing. I was incredibly lucky to meet Louisa Cardinale. Thank you so much for saving this project. You're an incredibly gifted editor with a keen eye for detail, and an intuitive gift for storytelling.

To my cover artist Leona Lee, thanks for being so patient.

To my friend Camellia Yildirim, many thanks for the guidance, support and information throughout the publishing process. I cannot tell you how much it helped and how much I appreciate it.

To my partner Anne, thanks for your support things got tough. I love you.

Thanks to my family for their support: To my father Alan, to my mother Susan, to my grandmother Yvonne, and to my grandmother Joan. To my brother Oliver, thanks for being my best friend.

DELPONT COMPANY CHART

Key people at Delpont during the final days (As researched by Will)

Chief Executive Officer: Morgan Docker *(formerly Paul McDermott)*

Chief Operating Officer: Andy Ling *(formerly Morgan Docker)*

Chief Financial Officer: Lew Noble

Trader: Warren Francis

Trader: Steve Socek

Trader: Andrew 'Shark' Hunter

Chief Accounting Officer: Kristen Worthington *(formerly Andrea Beaufort)*

Head of Investor Relations: Kelvin Anderson

Head of Human Resources: Murray White

CEO, Delpont Property: Michael Blake

PROLOGUE

There were no lights on this stretch of Wakehurst Parkway. It was deserted as far as the eye could see, surrounded by woodlands. He scratched his short trimmed beard as he contemplated what he needed to do. From his vantage point he could see cars approaching around the bend further up the road, and also had a clear path to the road directly below. He took a slow, deep breath as he ran a hand through his medium length dark blonde hair.

He ignored the car approaching from the other direction. He knew his target would be coming from the south, after a meeting that would have finished around 9pm. So, he should be coming past any minute. He replayed the plan in his head making sure he was prepared. Having followed his target for months he was certain the man would be alone.

Lights appeared over the horizon and he pulled out his night binoculars to get a better look. It was the wrong make and model, not the Mercedes he was waiting for. He put down the binoculars. A few minutes later he watched as the car passed by. He heard loud music and saw a bunch of teenagers drinking. Not his problem.

He'd kept tabs on his target for some time, and had a good idea of what he was like. Kelvin Anderson was a private and shy man, whether at work or with his family. There was a lot about his life that he kept hidden from both parties.

He pulled his leather gloves tighter and retied the laces on his sneakers in a double knot. Scanning the path to the road in front of him, his eyes having adjusted to night vision. He had already walked the path a few times clearing rocks and sticks that could pose a trip hazard, keeping low to avoid being seen by passing cars.

He saw another set of headlights approaching from around the bend. He pulled up his binoculars to check the car. It looked the right colour and the shape was definitely a Mercedes. It looked to be the right model as well. The headlights made the plate partially visible. He strained to see it, squinting and focusing the binoculars until he could see. It matched up.

He felt an instant adrenaline rush. He had a window of one minute. Sprinting down to the roadside, he checked for traffic coming from the other direction. Nothing. All clear to go ahead. He ran back to the trees, grabbed the large log he had left there with both hands and started dragging it onto the road. It was heavy but he was still able to haul it onto the road quickly. He saw headlights coming around the corner. The car would be in full view in a few seconds.

Satisfied it was in position, he sprang back off the road and retreated behind the cover of the trees. As soon as he reached them he saw headlights illuminate the log. That had been close.

He was sweating and breathing faster, trying to take deep breaths to slow it down. Crouching low he watched as the silver Mercedes approached the log and slowed down, coming to a stop. The engine was left running.

There was a moment of silence. Aside from the car's engine, all he could hear were trees being blown in the cold night wind and the chirping of crickets. He took a deep breath, his breathing now almost back to normal. The door clicked and opened. He saw the man emerge from the vehicle on the right side.

'Fucking hell … what is this?' His target Anderson said, irritation heavy in his voice. He was in his sixties but could pass for being in his forties, even though he was a bit out of shape.

'This road is a bloody menace.' From the trees he could see the man shaking his head as he lumbered towards the log.

He drew his knife from his pocket.

Keeping low, he moved quickly but silently, not wanting to make any noise. He made his approach by going around the back of the car, so that he could come up on Kelvin Anderson from behind. Anderson started tugging on the log and groaning. It was only in that moment where he showed his age.

He approached his target from behind, his blade ready in his right hand.

'Over here,' he called out with a smirk.

His target jumped and turned. He said nothing at first, seemingly too startled to talk. Then he noticed the knife in his hand.

'Who are you?' The fear in Anderson's voice came through.

He ignored the question.

Anderson took a step backward, raising his hand to cover himself.

'Stay back!' He shouted. Though the words felt weak, without any real confidence in their effect.

He rushed forward and plunged the knife deep into the man's chest, deliberately making the incision low and ripping upwards. Anderson fell to the ground slowly, blood pooling at his feet. There was a moment of silence as he coughed and stared up at him. Anderson took a few shallow breaths. Then the life left his body.

He withdrew the knife and looked down on Anderson, his eyes fixed open even after life had left them. Somehow, looking at him up close for the first time, it didn't seem right. Whatever he had been in the past, he was an old man now. A dead old man. Somewhere out there was a family, now without a husband and father.

He sighed and drew back. The body fell limp, lying face down. He lifted up Anderson's left palm and made a few quick and light swipes at them with the knife, giving them defensive wounds. He put it back down, lifted the other palm and did the same.

With the body taken care of, he pulled out Anderson's wallet from his back pocket. He looked at the ID. Kelvin Anderson. Born 1950. He breathed a sigh of relief. While he had felt confident it was the right person, he felt better knowing with certainty. *It was dark; anyone could make mistakes.*

He pulled out the wad of cash from the wallet, needing to establish a reason for the crime, and flipped through the notes; five hundred in fifties. It wasn't enough to justify a planned robbery. He turned the man over and took off the slim gold neck chain he was wearing, and unhooked the expensive watch as well. There would be another five hundred or a thousand dollars worth in those two pieces. When the police asked the family, they would notice these things missing. Meanwhile, he would sell them off quickly in two separate pawn shops, without cameras, several kilometres away. They would turn up in a few weeks through the police investigation, but he would already have the cash. He felt the motive of robbery would look convincing.

He took one end of the log and began dragging it towards the forest; it would raise too many questions. Better to leave the crime scene as simple as possible.

Having moved the log, he grabbed a small branch with lots of leaves at the end and used it as a broom to sweep away evidence of his footprints as he backtracked towards the trees. He left the car engine running to further a robbery motive. Someone would drive by soon enough and slow down when they saw the lights, then the body.

He went back to his vantage point, sweeping his footsteps away as he did and staying low, moving as slowly as he could, just in case a car passed by. He looked back at the crime scene that was now a hundred meters away; he could barely see it.

He picked up the shoulder bag, and following one last look over his shoulder, started walking through the bush, parallel to the road, sweeping behind him as he went.

After five minutes of walking he saw a pair of lights coming towards him. He didn't think it would be so soon. No matter. He ducked low as they passed by, but he was far enough from the road, invisible to the driver. After it had gone past, he kept walking, brushing as he went. He took off his dark canvas jacket and put it in his shoulder bag, already feeling warm with the exercise.

After twenty minutes or so, he heard a police siren in the distance. By this time he was in an elevated position, looking down on the road, he could see the headlights far away through the trees. The siren got louder as it passed and then faded away. He kept walking.

He hiked for a further five minutes through the bush before finding the path he was looking for, and proceeded to make a move east along the walking trail. In the distance he could hear another police siren from the road, but he was far away by now and could no longer see the road. The walking trail continued to climb. It took him another ten minutes to reach the top before pausing to catch his breath before starting his descent. Within another ten minutes he had reached the start of the walking trail near Cromer and the beaches. His shirt was covered in sweat from his walk, and the night air had gotten colder.

When the street was in view, he set down the shoulder bag, and pulled out the change of clothes he had prepared. He took off his sneakers, got out of his dark jeans and black tee. Finally, he stripped off his underwear and socks, to be thorough. He rubbed himself down with the towel he had brought, wiping off sweat and dirt.

Having cleaned himself up, he laid down the towel and stood on it like a bath mat. He shivered in the light breeze as he put on clean underwear and socks, then put on blue denim jeans and light green branded t-shirt. He slipped on the casual shoes he had brought and laced them up. Finally, he put on the stylish biker style leather jacket that had set him back a couple hundred dollars. It was one of the last objects he owned from his former lifestyle. Recently, it had paid back its weight in gold in terms of cover disguises. Back in street clothes, he packed away the dirty clothes and everything else into the shoulder bag.

He looked around for any sign of people. It was now past 10pm, he had walked for forty minutes from the crime scene and was now far away, separated from any police in attendance by the large national park. Satisfied there was no one else around, he walked into the streets. His car was parked in a dark street two blocks away, far from any houses.

Once he reached his car, he opened the boot, stashing the small shoulder bag under the spare tire, just in case the police stopped him. It would pass a quick check. Even if he were stopped, he doubted they would suspect him.

He got into the driver's side of the car and waited a nervous moment before turning on the police radio. He listened for a few minutes to the police chatter; all of it was about the body found by the Mercedes. Forensics had only just arrived on scene. It would take some time before the police started searching the area. He sighed in relief. They were focused on checking traffic up and down the road. He started the car and pulled out, driving along the coastline. From there, it was a short drive to the highway and his trip back to the city.

THE JOURNALIST

Will frowned as he looked around the room, wondering how he must seem compared to the rest of the people at the party. He was average height with light brown eyes and short dark hair standing in a room full of blonde haired and blue eyed models. Having grown up coming to galleries such as this, he should be more or less used to it by now. The artist crowd that he belonged to and yet was never comfortable with. He had put on a black t-shirt, dark denim jeans and a black leather jacket. He couldn't find his friend and he didn't know anyone else there. Uncomfortable with waiting, he scratched at the cologne on his neck and adjusted the laces of his blue Vans shoes.

He frowned thinking about how he had ended up at this party. Being a journalist had brought him close to this crowd, since the media and the artists in Sydney usually ended up in the same circles. Artists and those in the media usually had similar jobs; an interior designer or a foreign correspondent, a photographer or a cameraman, a graphic designer or a journalist. The romance that once existed in journalism had all but been lost, save for a few select journalists where the adventure still remained. Unfortunately, Will was not part of that lucky cache. His writing was purely economic.

Normally, he wouldn't have come, he didn't know anyone there, but his friend was back from overseas and he wanted to see her.

It was only when he checked outside on the balcony that he found Isabelle. He couldn't help but smile when he saw her.

As always, she carried her camera with her. She was snapping a few pictures of the outside of the bar. It was a hole in the wall bar, with nothing but a black door to distinguish it from the outside.

When she turned and noticed him, she waved and shouted. He laughed. She was little but had a big personality and an even bigger voice.

She looked different than when she had left. Her skin was more tanned, her hair had gone from jet black to dirty blonde with streaks through it. She was dressed in skinny blue jeans, a colourful scarf, purple singlet and burgundy shoes. Her scarf partly covered the tattoos on her arm and shoulder. Despite her different look, her big smile and bright green eyes had not changed. She threw her arms around him and squeezed.

'How are you, darlin'?!' she asked energetically, a big smile on her face.

'Yeah, going alright,' he nodded to the camera, 'Still constantly looking for something to catch?' He teased.

'Always,' she laughed. 'I can't help it'

'Can I have a look?'

'Sure thing,' she passed him the camera. 'Feel free to take a few.'

'You know I have no eye for that sort of thing,' he laughed, looking through her photos. 'These look really good. I like them. You've gotten so good.'

'Thanks. The course helped. But mostly it's just been practice. I've been getting a better feel for it.'

He nodded, 'That's good to hear.'

They chatted for a while about her flight from Barcelona and how she was doing before heading inside. Together they walked down the narrow staircase to the bar below. As the old wooden stairs creaked underfoot, he wondered what the building was designed for. From the size and structure he presumed it could have originally been someone's house. There were a few people hanging around the bar, but it didn't take long to order a bottle of white wine to share. From experience he knew it wouldn't last long. They would be on their second within an hour.

They walked through the underground bar and outside to the smoking area. Due to the slope of the hill, the balcony overlooked the street below. There was a wood barrier surrounding the courtyard, and the wooden pavilion overhead that was interlaced with vines. They sat down on a couch by a square table. Iz took out a pack of cigarettes from her clutch and lit up a cigarette.

'Do you want one?' She raised an eyebrow at him.

He considered it but shook his head. 'I'm trying to quit. So, what will you do now that the course is over?' He poured a glass of wine for himself and another for her, making sure to pour tall glasses.

'Ah, I don't know,' she frowned, sipping at her wine. 'I don't think I'll study again. I want to do something. I liked the course but I was frustrated by the end of it.' She puffed at her cigarette and tried to wipe the smoke from her eyes. For the past two years she had been living in Barcelona doing a design course. Despite the distance, their friendship had remained strong.

'I can understand that. What do you want though? Do you want to work now?'

'No, not now.' She pursed her lips. 'I want to get a few exhibitions. Get my work into galleries' She smiled and looked at him. He could feel her confidence coming through her voice. 'I think I can do it. I've been working on getting a website set up and making up some business cards. Being pretty professional about it.' She grinned.

He smiled. 'That's awesome. I'm really proud of you.' He pursed his lips and looked up at her. 'Are you thinking of doing that here?'

She shrugged. ‘I think so. I’m not sure yet. I’ll talk to people here and see how I go. I’ve met a few people with contacts at galleries so I have to meet with them and show them a portfolio.’

He grinned, ‘Sounds pretty promising.’

‘Thanks!’ she beamed. He already knew she was aware of the uphill battle she would face. Getting into that world was hard to do, to get noticed. But he didn’t doubt how badly she wanted it, and that she wouldn’t give up.

Frowning, he cleared his throat. ‘So do you think you’ll stay this time, or go back to Barcelona?’

She frowned. ‘I don’t know,’ she said softly, looking at her glass. She shook her head and smiled, changing the subject. ‘Anyway, how’s everything with you going? How’s the life of my successful economic writer?’ She teased.

He winced when she mentioned the word ‘successful’. ‘Don’t say it like that.’ He said softly, sipping his wine. ‘I was writing at the right time on the right issues. I got lucky.’

‘Oh, come on! That’s bullshit. It wasn’t luck, it was talent! That book you wrote about the global financial crisis. It was really successful!’

‘Yeah,’ he sighed. Admitting to himself that for a moment he *had* been successful. ‘The first book. And you know I put all that money back into the second book, and no one read it.’ He frowned and took a large gulp of wine. ‘All that money is gone now Iz’

‘Pfft,’ she scoffed. ‘So what? You still have that Crows Nest apartment you bought! And that place is sweet.’ She said, encouragingly.

‘Yeah, but that’s all that is left. Whatever money I had is tied up in that. And I can’t sell it because the price went down so much.’

He sipped his wine slowly. *Sometimes I wish I had the money instead of that unnecessary apartment.*

'What was that first book about anyway?' she asked with a frown, changing the subject.

He raised an eyebrow. 'You never read it?'

She shrugged. 'I gave it a go.'

'Alright then.' He laughed and shook his head. 'It was all about how dangerous CDOs were.'

A frown formed on her face. 'What are CDOs?'

'Well,' he sighed. 'It stands for collateralised debt obligations. It basically means investing in mortgages belonging to a group of people.'

'How can anyone make money off that?'

With a shrug, he replied. 'When people make repayments on their mortgages.'

'How does that work? Most people struggle to pay their mortgage back?'

'Yeah, exactly … Maybe you should read my book?' he suggested, teasing.

She glared at him.

'But that's partly why they were so dangerous; no one understood them. Even the people investing in them.'

She scrunched her face. 'Why would anyone invest in something they didn't understand?'

'At the time the business magazines and financial journals were all recommending them. All of the big banks and trading firms were encouraging them as well, though that might have been because they were betting that the mortgages would fail.' He sighed deeply, thinking of the inequality.

'Oh right. Anyway, do you still have that job with the paper?' she asked, changing the subject.

'On a freelance basis,' he said, sipping his wine with a frown. 'It pays for groceries. But that's about it.'

'Must pay for your addiction to sitting in cafés as well, right?' she said with a cheeky grin.

He laughed. 'Of course. One of the few benefits of being stuck with that apartment is that there's a café right down the bottom.'

She laughed so loud a group turned to look at them.

'Hey, there's a few people I have to catch up with here. Do you mind?' She said with a sigh.

'It's fine.' He smiled. 'Go catch up with them. I understand. I mean shit, you literally just got back.'

'Yeah,' she said, eyes wide and groaned, 'I'd kill for a good night sleep.'

She got up and crossed the room to a group of her other friends. When she reached them she was all high energy again. She greeted them loudly and excitedly. He laughed. He could hear her voice from the other side of the room.

As he sat at the table he thought of the book Iz mentioned.

It had started with a Masters thesis that no one had wanted him to write. He was one of the only people who had written about increasing risk in financial markets before the 2008 crisis. He tried argue that CDOs were a largely unregulated and misunderstood market, and had tried to draw comparisons with the bursting of the dot com bubble and similar speculative busts.

His economic professors had tried to explain how he was wrong, and they had essentially viewed him as a heathen for doubting in the power of free market economics. He had written the thesis anyway. Through a stroke of fate, his thesis had come out just before the 2008 boom, and then the bursting of that bubble. Will and other similar academics had been vindicated, and with the benefit of hindsight, were able to say they had seen it coming and in the fallout he had been hailed as an 'expert'. It always felt false to him.

I got lucky, he thought to himself as he sipped his wine slowly.

Following that he had been approached to publish a book version of the thesis, which ended up selling successfully. He got his five minutes of fame. Then he put what money was left after buying the apartment into a second book. It had been more speculative, about applying economic theories to reducing crime.

The key theory he had developed in the second book had been the spiral bankruptcy theory of criminality. It was a radical idea; police focusing on arresting the lowest levels of criminal organisations. In theory, there would be lower supply of criminals for hire, increasing the demand for workers and the amount they'd need to be paid. If this pressure were kept up, then criminal organisations wouldn't be able to pay increasing wages of workers, and would go bankrupt.

Regardless of how proud he was of his work, the book had not drawn as much attention as the first and had, in fact, barely sold. His moment of success had passed and the money from his initial success had dried up quickly. But the more he was exposed to the world of journalism, the more he missed the work he had done as an academic.

He submitted some articles to newspapers, a simplified version of his academic publications. Most were focused on inequality, but also dealt with financial markets and other economic issues. Based on the success of his first book, he had been offered a freelance writing position. It was the perfect situation for him, but for the most part he was living pay check to pay check.

He left the table, shaking his brain out of his thoughts, and crossed the room, thinking how welcoming the inside of the gallery was. The tea lights that adorned the dark brick walls around the outside courtyard made everyone look like strangers. Under the warm, bright lighting inside the gallery everyone looked more recognisable. The light seemed to accentuate the yellow in all colours. People's skins seemed to glow and their eyes sparkled. Perhaps it was why this lighting was so common in this environment, it made everyone seem more glamorous.

He snapped out of his thoughts, noticing a woman arrive at the gallery. He'd never seen her before but something about her caught his eye.

She moved across the room, touching a man's arm as she passed. Laughing, she threw her hair back lightly, her long golden curls rippling over her shoulders. She had a svelte figure and wore a dark blue dress, which fit perfectly and cut off at the knees. Her high cheekbones lifted as she smiled and enchanted the room. All were helpless to her. Her smile, her style, her grace. No one could blame them. It seemed any room she went would be lit up and brightened by her presence.

I've seen girls like her before, he thought, sipping his drink with a frown. The beautiful ones, the charming ones, the ones with a commanding presence. The bright lights of the gallery illuminated her light bronze skin, softer than smooth.

'Stop staring Will,' Iz snuck up behind him and giggled.

He turned and glared at her as she laughed. He felt foolish for being caught fixating. He hated to be like the other guys in the room, caught admiring this gorgeous woman.

The woman walked over and greeted Iz.

'I don't think you've met each other yet,' Iz said.

The woman slowly tilted her head to face him, a smile forming on her face. He looked at her as her eyes turned to him. It was all over when they made eye contact. Her big, bright, ocean blue eyes that sparkled under the lights; warm and inviting.

He had always been a sucker for eyes.

She was beautiful. She looked like a princess, or a queen, but definitely something regal. There was something ethereal and unreal about her. She lightly took his hand and they shook while Iz made introductions. But he was not paying attention.

'Will, this is Amber,' he absently heard his friend say.

For the first time in a long while, he couldn't quite figure out what to say. He wished he had a cigarette.

THE DETECTIVE

The train doors slid open. There was a drawn out hiss and a low ringing sound signalling the station. The voiceover announced the stop but the speakers always seemed to muffle the sound, it was impossible to figure out where you were in this city from sound alone.

As the hydraulics released, Aoki Sun stepped from the train to the platform. She scratched her black hair, tied back, and concentrated as she stepped over the slight gap between the train and the platform. It wasn't much of a gap, but every day she found it required her attention. Despite the money in Sydney, simple things like that never seemed to get addressed.

The cool night air rushed to meet her as she disembarked. While she was wearing a dark purple wool cardigan, she wished for a heavier jacket. She almost always forgot it in her rush every morning. Underneath she was kept warm by only a black top and tan pants, with black flats on her feet.

It was nearly half past eight and there were only stragglers drifting home from work. The figures exiting the train were illuminated only on one side by the lighting at the station. The other side obscured. There was no talking and no sound save the hiss of the train doors and the shuffle of scuffed soles.

As she left the platform, she suddenly realised that her eyes were watering. She wiped it away with the back of hand. It sometimes happened to her, a by-product from her constant fatigue and days spent in front of the computer.

Her mind was still racing. She was always wired after work and on edge. Most of her colleagues forget about work the moment they walked out the door, though she suspected they weren't really thinking about it while they were there either, just going through the motions. For her, the work followed her and was always with her. She was always thinking about the cases she was working on at the moment. Occasionally it led to moments of brilliance, where a few pieces of information and inferences came together to create a significant realisation.

Mostly however, it meant a lot of sleepless nights and mornings spent longing for more sleep.

As she left the lit area of the station she thought about a case from that day; a man who had murdered his girlfriend. It was a crime of circumstance. They had been a happy couple, there were obvious signs of a fight at her apartment, and he had left a lot of evidence. He'd been the first suspect and it hadn't taken long to arrest him. Once arrested, he hadn't talked much, merely covered his face and looked at the ground. There was no fight in him. The signs of remorse were there.

Aoki couldn't stop thinking about why he had done it. A woman's life was lost and he would have to contend with killing the woman he still loved. Though, for all that, all the evidence proving he had killed her, she still felt sorry for him. She felt as though he would take it all back if given the chance. On one of the few occasions that he looked her in the eye, she saw in them a life that had now lost all meaning. She really did feel sorry for the man.

Because of this she felt sick. The man was a murderer, and had murdered someone who loved and trusted him. Her partner on this case had been content enough that it was wrapped up with knowing who the murder was. He wasn't too concerned with the reasons behind it. Though to Aoki, behind every case there were always motivations.

Her partner wasn't an uninterested man, he cared about their cases. He cared about the justice and wasn't relishing the prospect that this man would suffer in imprisonment, but anything beyond that was irrelevant. She, however, couldn't help thinking about it. As she walked briskly from Stanmore station, on the narrow sidewalk in the dimly lit street, she decided that next time she had a chance to talk to this man she would come out and ask him why he did it.

Aoki adjusted her cardigan that had become dishevelled from the handbag tugging on her shoulder, and found herself impulsively pulling a cigarette from her bag. She paused for a second as she lit it. She heard footsteps behind her, and subtly but swiftly turned her head.

Nothing.

Just a mousy woman reaching her hatchback, heels clicking as she traipsed back from the station. This woman was one of the many who had various stages in their commute to work. Clearly, she had driven close to the train station and then caught the train from there. This habit had always confused Aoki. She never understood why these people didn't just live on the train line, or catch a bus. Rents in Sydney were expensive the closer you got to the city, and she understood that, but when she considered all the additional costs of tolls and petrol she wondered whether the costs wouldn't balance out at some point. *Plus the entire practice of driving to work is harmful to the environment,* she thought with a frown, *let alone your wallet.* She decided to shrug it off, if it were one of her friends then she would have challenged them, but if not then there was no point dwelling on such issues.

Inhaling the last of her cigarette, she reached the outside of her apartment. Through the window she saw one of her two cats, lying across the windowsill, and felt her mood lift.

She waved at it with a big smile on her face. The cat looked at her, then turned away and jump down from the windowsill. She listened to the sounds of her partner, Rick, in the kitchen. He was always ready with food when she got home. She turned her key in the lock and opened the door.

'Hey!' She called out, closing the door behind her.

He popped his head out of the kitchen and smiled, 'Hey love. How was work?'

'Yeah,' She grumbled with a sullen face, '… alright'.

He chuckled and pointed to the stove, 'I did you up some pasta. It's pretty terrible but at least it's free'.

She smiled as she chucked her bag on the floor. He was a clear foot taller than her, lean and handsome. She'd noticed those exact things and in that exact order when she had first met him. She had felt only attraction to him at first, until she learned that he truly had a kind heart.

He had large green eyes, which was rare considering most of his family were Italian. At her insistence, he had trimmed his permanent five o'clock shadow that he had favoured in his single days. He conceded to having a trimmed goatee. Aoki thought he looked more handsome with it.

She gave him a cuddle as she walked into the kitchen. He wasn't the best of cooks, or the most adventurous, but he always put the effort into making sure she came home to food when she worked late, and always tried to cook her things she liked. It was the small things like that she appreciated. They made her days a little more bearable.

'How long have you been home? How was your work?'

'Meh, wasn't too bad, got home around … four, I think? I had training today, we had all that motivation bullshit,' His mouth curved into a frown. He had recently started work in an HR company, the first job he had in a few years that was related to his management degree. What he had found out quickly is that management and human resources were soft sciences, and referred to as bullshit by the income generating areas of companies.

'Yeah? You alright?' She said, feeling the brush of the cat's fur through her work pants. She bent down, kept her gaze on her partner, as she stroked the jealous feline. His back raised and eyes closed as he purred over the attention he was now getting.

He sighed. ‘This isn’t what I want to do. But it’s good to have a regular pay check again.’

For a moment she thought he would talk about going back to studying, and was glad he hadn’t mentioned it. While she truly did want the best for him, it had been so stressful for both of them when he was studying full time. He had only been able to work sporadically, and there were periods where he wasn’t working at all. Between their living costs, and their ongoing mortgage payments, she had been sick with stress at times. Needless to say she had been smoking a lot during that period. She wasn’t excited to go back to those dark days of worrying how ends would meet. While he said that the new job wasn’t too stressful, she knew it wasn’t what he thought the industry would be. In his first job after university, he had been responsible for assisting in identifying which employees were not business critical, and then arranged for their retrenchment, a window dressed term for laying someone off. After several rounds of cuts, he found himself on the other side of the desk, as he was no longer needed. The irony was not lost on her.

She rubbed his shoulder to reassure him, she could see from his expression as he focused on cleaning up that he was still having a crisis of faith. She hated seeing him like this, and she knew that at some point he would need to get out of this industry and retrain himself.

‘We had to break into the motivation groups again today.’ His voice faded away and he avoided eye contact, frowning.

‘Oh, I’m sorry.’ She knew exactly what kind of day he would have had. Part of their motivation strategy was to have the teams break into ‘motivation groups’. She had found out it was exactly as pretentious as it sounded. Each group had a name like ‘success’, ‘teamwork’ or ‘initiative’ and so on. They then had to each speak for several minutes on why this name was so important to their team, and what they would do to improve their team's performance.

She had to stifle a laugh. His modern corporate torture would be hilarious if it weren't forced on them in such an Orwellian fashion. There were usually several directors or executives present, watching and taking notes.

She changed the subject and discussed plans for the weekend to try and cheer him up. He brightened a fair bit when she reminded him it was Thursday.

Aoki finished her dinner and tumbled the bowl into the sink. She saw Rick scrunch his face at the clunking and scraping sounds, instantly remembering how it annoyed him. She felt a little guilty.

Her weeknights always seemed to go quicker after dinner, and followed predominantly the same routine. The two of them slumped together on the couch, watching a few episodes of her favourite shows from her hard drive on the TV. He would usually go to bed after an hour, having to get up early for work the next morning. She was a nighthawk and would usually stay up late watching TV, always going to bed far later than she anticipated.

After another night gone by too fast, she took a moment before bed to have a cigarette outside and reflect. As she lit the smoke and dragged on it, work started to come back to her. She rubbed her face and sighed, partly due to exhaustion and stress. It did no good though. When she closed her eyes she saw the woman's body again from today, she saw the boyfriend's eyes as he looked in and saw his guilt and remorse. Try as she might she kept thinking on how the relationship between victim and suspect had ended, and thinking about her and her kind hearted man. She felt sick and upset with herself for thinking like that, but she couldn't control her thoughts sometimes; a side effect of her job she'd found, always thinking the worst.

She managed to finally put all thoughts of work out of her head around 2am. Suddenly feeling tired, she stumbled to bed and crashed. As she fell asleep, one final thought snuck over her before sleep took hold; she realised she would have to do it all again tomorrow.

Her eyes closed and she drifted into darkness.

THE MAN IN THE SHADOWS

He wore all black. Dark jeans the only exception. The night sky was darkest here, away from the central hub of the city. Night time around Kings Cross was mostly a world in blackness, a few car lights flashed passed occasionally. The streetlights were mostly broken or dimmed, providing only a faint yellow outline of the surroundings against the backdrop of darkness. Remaining unseen wasn't a problem. This part of town wouldn't see much expenditure on repairing them as, despite being so close to the city centre, it was largely ignored by police and government. It was the centre for drugs and prostitution in the city and for the most part the authorities turned a blind eye to crime in this area. No one ever said it, but the authorities believed it was better to leave crime in that area rather than risk it coming into their neighbourhood. He was a few streets away from the main busy strip, in the quiet area.

As he walked, he passed a few addicts on the steps of buildings, occasionally a dealer on the odd corner, but as long as he didn't make eye contact they were unlikely to remember him. He stuck to rules like this to remain undetected as long as possible.

Rule number one: Never be seen.

A convenience store presented an obstacle. There was a small low resolution camera at the door, designed to catch people as they walked in but it would also catch part of his image as he walked past. He crossed the wide street without looking, there were no cars in this part of town at this time. By avoiding alleys and the people on corners, he was able to avoid any of the criminals that would cause trouble. *Any of the other criminals*, he supposed. His shade of justice he always knew wasn't understood. Doing the right thing wasn't always legal. All he could do was avoid detection and avoid attention. This part of town was a perfect hunting ground, it was a rare opportunity he couldn't pass up. He'd come as soon as he found out his target would be here.

The apartment building was around the corner. He hoped his timing was right.

As he turned, he saw a light on the third floor across the street. There was only one car in the block that was less than a year old, the others were twenty to thirty years out of date. There was a driver sitting behind the wheel waiting outside the building, ready to pull away. There were a few glimpses of shadows from the apartment, the slight hum of muffled bass that could be faintly heard from the street. If he had figured right, that's where he would be.

He picked his spot. An alcove on a building across the street that looked abandoned. He approached it slowly and calmly so as to not draw the attention of the driver. The door was broken in and hadn't been repaired in a few years. There were no noises inside. He immersed himself in the shadows by the doorway. He wore a black hooded jumper and a faded black leather jacket over to conserve warmth. A black beanie was keeping his head warm. At the same time it obscured his features. For this target he had chosen to look more haggard. He looked more the part.

He focused his attention on the building across the street. Whatever had brought a man like that to this part of town was something dark and best left unfound. It was unusual for people like this to liaise directly when they needed things done or obtained. There was usually a go between or a mule that could do it for them. It must have been something important to have his target here in the middle of the night.

He plotted his route, counted the steps and figured out the timing. Checking one last time for people in windows, cameras anywhere or any lights that could jeopardise his chance, he assessed no threats and readied himself. In his childhood in Northern Europe he had been told about the power of visualisation. A positive mindset was key to anything. *I assume they would at the least frown upon how I chose to utilise this mantra*, he thought with a smirk.

There was movement and what sounded like a conversation in the building. Silhouettes moved past the window. The car across the street turned on, silently. The lights were left off; the driver was trying to draw as little attention as possible. The first figure out of the door was the bodyguard, checking the coast. He held a hand up and made a signal. Then *he* emerged. Navy blue suit, white silk kerchief, black polished leather shoes, even in the shadows and dim light he could see the taught flesh on his face, tortured with fake tans and plastic surgery. Lips that were unseemly inflated, his thin hair tightened back, whiteness matched only by the unnatural gleam of the fangs that bore through. In the darkness they seemed incandescent. *His choices have made him a grotesque caricature of a man.*

He went over his plan one last time; 16 paces, stick to the wall, draw at the fifteenth.

He set off, moving quickly.

On the thirteenth pace the guard turned. He drew at fourteen. The guard spun as he was knocked down.

He cornered on his target and locked eyes with him. The grey eyes widened suddenly. Panic and terror. Evil regressed back to a child. At some level, no one ever escapes from being that scared child they were, afraid of the world. They hide it better, deny it to themselves, but there is always something that can bring out this terror. Something that can shock them out of their façade. The barrel of a gun being pointed at your face is one such thing.

Sixteen. He shot; noise muffled by the silencer. The grey eyes turned white. The guard went to draw, but a shot to his right forearm crippled him. The guard shouted and dropped again.

By eighteen he was back in the darkness, moving along the wall, avoiding the street lights. He turned into an alley, turning again quickly to exit into a different street. He crossed the street, sticking to the exit route he had planned.

Within a minute, his target was legally dead. The guard was only just calling for an ambulance. The man in the shadows was gone and impossible to distinguish from any other person on the streets.

WILL

He first read about it when he logged online in the morning. The article described how Marcus Docker had been shot just outside the central business district in Kings Cross. The details surrounding the incident were few and far between. Only a few released the suburb and many didn't mention that he was shot. For what he could tell, Will assumed that some details were being deliberately omitted.

Looking away from his laptop he looked out into the mid morning view coming through his living room, thinking about the implications of such a high profile killing. In his articles he had often mentioned the decisions made by Marcus, especially after the economic downturn of 2008. Marcus had personally overseen a wide range of cuts in several sectors, and while this made sense for a business losing money, Will had been critical of where those cuts had come from. Typical to many of the large banks, the cuts were mainly from support services, such as human resources, marketing, the retail staff and also cuts in facilities and maintenance. There had not been similar cuts to the investing side of the banks, much the same as the other banks in Australia, and the same could be said of banks worldwide. While there had been sweeping cuts in terms of graduate and entry-level staff and a complete cut in graduate intake, the existing staff in equity, derivatives and commodity trading suffered no substantial retrenchment.

The point that Will had tried to make, was that these were the industries which had by and large caused the crisis of confidence of the downturn, and yet they seemed to be the industry which were least affected. His arguments in papers and in academic journals had been largely criticised as being far too liberal, interestingly enough this had been by the most devout deregulation writers and politicians.

Still he had to think about whether it was necessary for him to make a statement about Marcus. He had publicly named him among several key figures responsible for widespread cutbacks in the economy, which he viewed to be the most harmful thing during any recession.

He showered to take his mind off it. As he got dressed afterwards, he cleaned up the apartment as he went. Picking up empty coffee cups from his desk that overlooked the harbour views and national parks. Behind the couch he found a two dollar coin, and added it to his coffee funds clattering around in his pocket. He could always see any speck of dust floating in the air, partly because of all the natural light. The living room and kitchen area had glass windows on three sides. As he looked over his cleaned apartment he smiled, but then winced. *I got lucky,* he thought. He wiped a drop of sweat from his brow. The windows in the living room were a double-edged sword; they allowed great views of the harbour, but made often made the room uncomfortably hot.

For the most part the apartment life suited him quite well. Whenever he felt like the company of a crowd, he could walk downstairs and go to the café at the base of his building for his morning coffee. It was a relatively small café, and by the time he usually left the house around ten or eleven when the early rush was all gone. It suited him fine, he wasn't much of a morning person. He preferred to take his laptop out and work on articles he was in the process of writing. The background music of slow jazz that always played helped him relax and write. He needed the sound of life around him to focus on his work properly anyway. Without the sound of talking and laughter of the people in the café, he went crazy writing in his apartment, and would usually stare at the screen. He would end up spending most of the time having little to no idea what he was meant to do with his articles.

Thinking back on the issue with Marcus, Will decided that it was most appropriate to stay silent. Being a wealthy man, who held a senior position with such a large bank, there would already be a flood of condolence press releases from prominent members of the industry, contemporaries and also politicians, who were always keen to weigh in with their opinion in areas that didn't fully concern them. Amidst the flood of superfluous tributes, his silence would not be missed. He thought that it would be more disrespectful to publicly comment and offer his own condolences to the family, given that he had been publicly critical of him.

For what it was worth, he truly felt bad for what he had said of the man, considering the end he had met.

Realising that he needed to get out of the house, Will scooped his keys, wallet and phone from the granite top kitchen counter. He left the apartment in a hurry, otherwise he would be overcome by an overwhelming urge to spend the day on the couch. Not that he was a lazy man, though to be fair he wasn't the most active, but if the interior design of a living room is done well, there is no man who could find the motivation to leave the couch.

Despite the natural light in his apartment, the rest of the building was quite dark. Especially the stairwell to the street. Entering the small café, he sat down at a free table free and put his bag down. The only other customers were one lone man reading the newspaper, waiting for his coffee, and two elderly females, sharing a morning tea and swapping stories. From what he could hear it was a relatively anxious discussion about how it wasn't safe to walk the streets nowadays. He stifled a smile and ordered at the counter.

Satisfied with a cappuccino and a cake for a healthy start to the day, he sat down on the couch and opened his laptop.

The waitress brought his coffee, he thanked her and stirred it as he contemplated his work. The article he was working on at the moment was a short piece for a newspaper. He took a sip of his coffee. Still a little too hot to drink, but he could immediately savour the soothing bitterness. For his article, he had originally suggested a piece about the difficulties being experienced by university and college graduates, and the wider economic impact. However, that article hadn't been too popular with his editor John

Leech, a crotchety old man. Every conversation he had with the wiry and miserly man angered him.

John had made veiled references to the recent protest in Melbourne city against an amendment act that had substantially reduced rights and compensation for casual and low-income earners. The protests had lasted almost a full week and there had been several clashes with police. The bulk of these protestors were students.

As a result of these protests, his editor Leech viewed that inciting further unrest was inappropriate. The grumpy editor stated it was declined, in a matter-of-fact way. It wasn't a well-kept secret that the middle-aged editor was staunchly conservative. And like other conservatives of the world, served only the interests of rich old white men. He resolved to challenge this again when next he saw the editor, if only to irritate the miserly old man. With any luck he might be able to ruin Leech's day.

The café wasn't too noisy, save for the background noises of the coffee machine and grinder, the hum of the refrigerator and the chatter of customers coming and going with take away coffees. He heard the bells tingle gently as someone entered, and impulsively looked up.

When he looked up this time it was to see Amber walk into the café. He felt his heart beat faster. Her shoulder length blonde curls seemed to bounce as she walked. She wore a white top that ended at her shoulders, a silver belt just below her breasts, dark blue jeans that fitted her perfectly, and navy suede boots that ended just below her knees. The jeans revealed her long, slender legs, making her seem demure, but at the same time it made him take a deep breath. He felt flustered just by the sight of her, but perhaps the half drained coffee cup was also a factor. She looked around and caught sight of him, giving him a gentle smile and a wave. He smiled back, trying to ignore his nerves.

‘Writer in a café? I never anticipated you would be one to obey to stereotypes,’ she teased. Her ocean blue eyes illuminated as she smiled.

She strode gracefully to his table and reclined into a spare seat opposite him.

His left eye twitched. *She's beautiful, and out of my league.* ‘The adage is relatively accurate then.’ He replied.

‘Which one would that be?’ She asked, an eyebrow raised.

‘That stereotypes and clichés often exist because there is some basis in reality.’

She laughed. ‘That statement as a defence is somewhat of a cliché in and of itself, isn’t it?’

He smiled, but found himself feeling defensive that she found him predictable. He thought of himself as someone that usually stood out, for better or worse.

‘So, is this the lifestyle of a successful economic writer?’

He winced but didn’t correct her as she smiled at him. His moment had passed but he didn’t want to tell her that.

‘More or less,’ he answered, ignoring the compliment. ‘I’m just writing an article at the moment. So what brings you to my part of town? I thought you lived in Mosman?’ he asked, changing the topic before she could ask him for any specifics about it.

She narrowed her eyes and smiled, ‘Good memory,’ she said, a hint of reserve in her voice. He realised his error quite quickly, she hadn’t told him that, it was something he had found out from her Facebook. He wasn’t proud of it, but he found himself looking through her photos when he was bored. Her looks truly were regal and captivating. She gestured to the waitress with a hand raised and a smile. Despite the polite intention of the request, her presence made it seem commanding. The waitress made her way to the table.

She ordered a glass of water and a flat white. Soy milk. No sugar.

As the waitress left she furrowed her brow and locked her gaze with his. There was something unexpectedly intense in the look. 'You're reading about this Marcus Docker killing?'

He frowned. Quite put on the spot and slightly confused.

Her face relaxed into a smile. 'Your screen, Will.'

He glanced down and grinned.

'Only just before. I woke up late. But what I read was a bit of mess, not much detail. And the things that were being revealed seemed to be largely contradictory…' He paused mid sentence, realising he had responded as a writer and a critic. He worried that he must seem unsympathetic to her. He looked back at her, if she thought that then her face revealed nothing.

He continued, 'But yeah, I mean it's a really tragic way to go, the poor guy. I'm just thinking about his family right now, and what they must be going through.'

Her face warmed a little so he figured it was the right answer. 'Mmm, it is really quite sad. I haven't spoken to my father yet but he must be taking it quite badly.' She spoke softly.

'Your father?' Will wasn't sure of the relevance.

She looked at him quizzically and laughed, 'Sorry. Paul McDermott?'

He felt embarrassed; he had not put that together. It made sense now why she was at that party when they met. Her father was the former CEO of Delpont, which was Australia's largest diversified financial bank prior to the scandals. It was the type of thing he should have known.

‘You really didn’t know?’ She teased with a laugh. ‘I always thought you were the type to be thorough in your research. Maybe I should double check the references in your articles?’

‘I know, I should have known that.’ He said shaking his head. *It’s the truth.*

‘It’s fine,’ she said with a wicked grin. ‘I’m teasing’

He smiled warmly then cleared his throat. ‘From what I know though, they were quite close?’

She nodded, ‘They were very close. Marcus took my father’s former position when he left Delpont.’

He frowned. He had always had doubts about the timing of McDermott’s departure from Delpont. The man had left the company only a few months before the corruption and fraud were revealed over a decade ago. McDermott had avoided jail time because he had assisted in the investigation. However, many people still questioned his innocence. He put the thoughts aside.

‘Have you had a chance to talk to him about it yet?’ He asked, gently.

‘No, not yet,’ she shook her head, cleared her throat and paused, her face suddenly more serious. It seemed to him that she was weighing up whether or not to tell him something. ‘I overhead something last night though.’

Intrigued, he looked at her and waited for her to continue. She looked away for a fraction of a moment. When she turned back her mood had changed, she was smiling, but there was a hint of sadness to it.

‘But, oh well. I’ve found it best not to dwell too much on such things. What was it that Thatcher said about legitimising acts of violence by focusing attention on them?’

‘Something along those lines,’ he was only half familiar with the statement in question. Political history outside of economic relevance was always a weak spot for him.

She proceeded to ask about his work, some questions about what his plans were for the week. He couldn’t help but notice the subtle changes in her voice, it seemed like she was engaging in pleasantries and small talk. They talked for a while about friends and mutual acquaintances. He wanted to get the topic of conversation back to what she was about to tell him, he could sense that there had been something serious on her mind. There was no opportunity to do this, however. She was going through the motions of polite conversation.

‘Mm,’ she sipped her coffee with both hands. Staring down, she savoured the taste in silence for a moment, before resting the cup back on the table. ‘I should be going, I have to be somewhere shortly. But it was good to see you.’

‘Likewise.’ He paused for a beat. ‘You don’t have work today?

‘I’m working from home, as it were. I’m quite lucky, my boss isn’t too strict with coming into the office.’

‘Interior design, isn’t it?’ He couldn’t help but be genuinely interested. Women with artistic aptitudes always seemed more attractive. Architects, painters, graphic designers, interior and fashion designers. He found himself drawn to them.

She smiled. ‘Yes. I’ve been loving the work at the moment. Working on a big renovation.’

She rose and picked up her handbag. She left ten dollars on the table for a three dollar coffee. It was almost an after thought to her.

‘I’m sure I’ll see you soon. It was good chatting. We should meet up again.’

'Yeah I'd like that,' he replied. He decided to go out on a limb. 'Did you want to get a drink tonight? I've got some free time.'

She paused and looked him in the eyes. 'Would that I could but tonight I promised a friend I would get dinner with her. That would have been nice, though.'

'Yeah, sure thing.'

'Another time though, for sure! I'll see you soon,' she said with a smile and turned.

He watched her leave the café. The sound of traffic passing by brought him back to the present. He looked at his screen and realised he hadn't written a word in the hour that he had been there. He swore and put his head in his hands. It was going to be a difficult article. As he contemplated the work that was ahead of him, he considered the hint that she had seemed to drop him, that there was something else to the passing of Marcus Docker. He wanted to investigate further.

AOKI

She snuck into the office. She felt flustered and stressed and she clutched her handbag as she walked with a purpose. She was about two hours late and had intended to come in early. As she entered the office, she tried to slink in quietly.

'Hey Aoki!' Someone said with a wave and a smile.

'Heyyy Aoki!' Another girl called out.

She had been found out. She replied briefly but kept her gaze down so as not to draw attention. It was too late, though. She had the office's undivided attention.

Everyone in turn proceeded to greet her and say good morning.

'Morning guys,' she responded flatly and politely.

She couldn't tell whether people were being friendly or condescending when they greeted her when she came in late. She suspected it was about half and half. Her supervisor, Lawford, had mentioned to her previously that he was getting complaints about her late starts. But at the same time, he didn't personally have a problem as he knew she stayed late to catch up, and also stay on top of her work. This morning, it seemed, would pass without a warning. For that she was grateful.

One of the other detectives, Hannah Moray, gave her a dirty look. Despite the warm smile on her pretty face, she was a two faced bitch. She was friendly with most detectives, but the two of them had never gotten along.

She sat down at her desk and logged into her computer, not looking forward to seeing her inbox after the morning's activities.

There was a lot of buzz around the office this morning. She noticed it when she sat down. A quick glance through her emails revealed why.

Last night there had been a shooting of a high profile banker not too far from the city centre. She always suspected there was more to the situation when it involved those people from the financial world. Their activities always seemed to flirt with criminality. She remembered a similar case a few years back. A property developer in a rich suburb had been shot. There had been rumours that it was because of dodgy deals, however the case kept getting pushed back, and as it wasn't her area she didn't have much access. She felt that there was something else going on in the case. Her impulse said that it was probably someone from a competing company, or even someone within his own company, and sensed that it would be an interesting and challenging case, despite no one talking to the police. The biggest difficulty for whoever investigated would be dealing with a contingent of lawyers. Whatever 'career making' possibilities to a case like that, she was honestly glad she wasn't involved. There would be a lot of media attention placed on her, close attention from her superiors, and in general a lot of drama. She didn't want that kind of stress in her life, she knew she couldn't handle it.

Looking through her emails though, anything looked better than the two cases she had just picked up. A detective receiving more than one case in a hit was yet another benefit of working for a police department running on a tight budget. It was the same for most stations in the state.

Both of them were pretty much the same case. No identification, found dead in public places and appeared to be homeless. Both had a layer of dirt on them, seemed undernourished and had a few cuts, bruises and scars. The only difference was that one was an elderly man, his skin withered, and the other was a relatively young man who couldn't have been more than thirty. When she started as a detective, the crushing weight of so many homeless deaths felt like it was going to destroy her. Everyone else seemed so callous and indifferent to it; they viewed cases like these as a burden.

She smirked, realising that she now felt the same. She felt guilty, but she knew she always cared once she actually got into the case. These situations were tragic, but she had come to realise it was a reality of the city. A lot of people fell between the cracks. Many of the reasons were the typical factors spouted off by conservative politicians; drugs, alcohol, gambling and so on. But the real causes were difficulties anyone could encounter no matter how hard they worked. Things like a husband going through a divorce, not having money to pay rent, being in between places and short of friends and not being able to find a place to stay. Running through what money they have on hotels, then finding themselves out of a comfortable financial job because they couldn't perform anymore.

Tragic things like a daughter losing both parents, not having any other family and so turning to a guy who offers her a place to stay. Not being able to stay in school because she has to work, and then losing the guy. Needing a job she can live off, and so winds up selling herself. Once they're done with her, she ends up losing them too.

It's a slow transition to the street, and it's one of survival. All of these people tried to survive after such setbacks and all of them refused to give up and take an easy way out. And yet, they were all cases she had come across. People who had tried to survive and keep going, to get their old lives back, and yet had fallen short and passed away on the street. *No matter what happens to the people, the city will always be the same*.

She was brought back to reality when the phone rang.

'Hi, this is Aoki speaking,' she said timidly. She knew it was impractical to answer like that, but she wanted to be polite.

'Hey, this is Jason Liu calling from forensics.' She could hear his pronounced accent.

‘Yes!’ She replied more excitedly. He was calling about a case she had been stuck with for a few weeks. Not because it was difficult, but because it was obviously a natural death. ‘How did you go?’

‘Yes, ok, good,’ he replied tentatively. Despite the fact her family was Korean and she detested racism, she always got agitated herself when people couldn’t speak English properly. ‘We’ve got currently report available, full report is done, but primary decisions is it’s the natural causes.’

Despite her guilt, small grammatical errors tended to irritate and annoy her. ‘Thanks so much, I’ll be down later to pick it up. Will it be in the pigeonhole?’

‘No, see Mindy at front desk, and she make it available to you.’

‘Ok. Thanks for that. Bye.’ She replied quickly, eager to get off the phone.

With the report from forensics, she had essentially everything she needed to clear that one and get onto others. She felt a little better knowing that she could focus on other open cases. She might even be able to close one or two of them. Even then though, with the two she had just picked up, she had her work cut out for her. She started to think about everything she had to get through. She rubbed her face quickly, stressed out.

‘Kiki!’ She heard a call from behind her. She already knew it was her partner.

‘Morgan stop calling me that,’ she chuckled and shook her head. ‘You know how much I hate that nickname.’ The nickname was bad enough, but he could have teased her much more if he knew the truth of her name. In an attempt to reconnect with their roots, her parents had chosen ‘Aoki’, believing it was Korean. It wasn’t until years later that they realised it was actually Japanese, and also a boys name.

‘Yeah, I know.’ Morgan Kerr laughed and sat down, lounging back in his chair with a smug grin on his face. He ran his hands back through his short dark blonde hair, accentuating his widow’s peak.

Their desks were opposite each other so they talked often. She was glad for their seating arrangement, because he was her best friend in the team. She could always talk honestly with him about things that bothered her, mainly because the same things bothered him. When they first met he didn’t strike her as police, much less a detective. Mainly, because he was so good at networking and had an aspect of casual confidence. He seemed better suited to the corporate world. There were always laughter lines around his dark brown eyes, and his smile was always cheeky, as though he were mucking around. He was dressed as always in corporate clothes; grey pants, blue checked shirts and a plain black tie. He had a stocky build, and a slight belly. The shirts he wore were always tight around the waist. He frowned as he read through his emails, and scratched his stubble. He was rarely clean-shaven. He had casually slung his grey three quarter length jacket near his desk. He leaned back in his chair and relaxed.

‘Pretty crazy about the banker, hey? I heard Moray and Bay are on it.’ He said with a smirk and sipped at the cup of coffee he had presumably gone out to buy.

‘Yeah, what a surprise right.’ She said sarcastically. Referencing an in-joke of theirs from earlier that Carl Bay and Hannah Moray were being groomed for more senior roles.

He sat further down in his chair and lowered his voice so that no one could eavesdrop. ‘Carl I pretty much figured would get it. He played for it. I mean, he’s a friendly guy, a bit dopey but he is friendly.’

‘Noo. Really? He’s actually pretty good!’ She rebuked. ‘I mean he puts in the effort.’

'Yeah yeah, whatever,' he waved it off. He spoke quickly and energetically as per usual. 'I mean, he's alright. But he's cluey. You saw how he was with the lieutenant? They were mates for ages! He played golf with him.'

'True. What? You think he planned it?'

He shrugged. 'Maybe. I mean, he doesn't come across as much of a threat. But I think he is smarter than he lets on.'

She frowned, considering it. 'Hannah I don't get though. She fucks up all the time.'

He laughed. 'Oh come on. It's not *that* hard.'

She scoffed. 'Fuck you. It's not about that.'

'Seriously. She's cunning. She flirts with everyone but she's got a very convenient excuse of, "Oh I'm sorry. I have a boyfriend",' he said while doing his impression of her. She tried to stop herself from laughing. He was good at it. 'I mean, it's perfect!'

'Bullshit. I don't think she is like that.'

'It's kinda irrelevant,' he shrugged, talking quickly. 'I mean she can tease the guys, give them attention and they love it. The other cops, the forensics guys, the senior guys. And all along they can keep thinking she is just a ditz and when she is single they can take a run at her.'

She winced. He could be so crass sometimes. But thinking about it, she'd thought similar things. The 'boys club' culture was still very prevalent.

'And all the while, they do little favours for her. Give her some leniency here and there, a report prepared for her a little sooner in the queue. There's nothing essentially wrong with it…'

'Well, there is,' she cut him off with a frown. 'Protocol is pretty clear about the priority of forensic and ballistics reports.'

‘Yeah, whatever. My point is that it’s a grey area.’

She sighed, and focused back to her work. She didn’t want to talk anymore. Sometimes she would just stop talking when she was done with a conversation. He realised it pretty quickly.

As the day drew on, what they talked about started to bother her more and more. Not what he said, but the whole situation. As it became dark and the office started to empty, she brought it up again.

‘Hey, how come it isn’t us?’ she asked, breaking the silence.

‘What?’ He looked up from his screen, genuinely confused.

‘Why *they* get cases like that. Never us.’

‘It really bothers you?’

‘Why? Doesn’t it bother you too?’

‘Not really. I mean it’s a lot of extra work. And it’s a risky move.’

‘Risky?’

‘You remember those cases a couple of months ago? About the shooting in the Western Suburbs?’

She nodded. Already starting to see his point.

‘I mean those guys were dragged through the media because they got that thing wrong. And I mean it wasn’t a massive error either. The guy they charged sued the force.’

She nodded slowly with a sad smile. ‘I was actually thinking like that earlier. About all the extra attention.’

‘What from the media?’

‘Yeah,’ she paused, ‘But also supervisors in the office and further up the chain. I mean can you imagine that kind of scrutiny on everything?’

‘So why are you thinking it should be us?’

‘I dunno,’ she said with a sigh. She didn’t have a good answer, but it bothered her. ‘I mean, shouldn’t we be doing those sort of cases? Getting on to more serious stuff?’

‘Career cases? I think it’s riskier to go for those. There is a lot of potential to go wrong.’

‘If you do things right, though.’

‘If you do things right then yeah, obviously. But most of it is out of your control. I mean, what if you can’t get a suspect and there’s a roadblock and no further evidence? What if a witness statement turns out to be wrong and you’ve gone after the wrong person?’

‘Don’t you want to move up though?’

He grinned smugly. ‘I will. Trust me. The key to progression is the same no matter where you are. In government, in business or in the police, it’s always the same thing. It always comes down to politics. Playing the game.’

He always liked his speeches. She tried to hide a grin. He was not an unconfident man.

He rose and put on his grey jacket, the office was almost empty now and the day had flown by for her.

‘Are you staying back for long?’

‘Um, probably. I have a lot still to do.’ She scratched her head. She always did when she was stressed.

‘What with?’ he asked, frowning.

‘I’m still trying to make sense of that hit and run from a few weeks ago.’

‘The courier? Was that the one where they robbed him of his delivery?’

She nodded. ‘Yeah, that was him. When the paramedics found him he kept muttering about whether the laptop he was carrying was ok. They didn’t have the heart to tell him it was broken.’

He shook his head. ‘That’s fucked up.’

‘Yeah. I was going to call the sister and talk to her, it’s too late now though.’ She said with a sigh. It was a problem she dealt with every day. There were always people she needed to talk to, but when she eventually got time to call them it was too late in the day.

‘Alright, well don’t stay back long. Get out of here and go home!’ He teased.

‘Yeah, sure thing. I know’.

She watched him pack quickly and threw his three quarter length jacket over his shoulders. He slung his gym bag over his shoulder and waved as he walked out the door. No matter the situation, he always had the same walk; quickly and with a swagger in his step.

She looked at the screen and the mountain of work that awaited her. She was stressed and needed to smoke before getting on with it. She sighed and scratched her head. She decided to start with the case she was most familiar with. Even then, she would most likely stay back in the office for another three hours.

ANDREA

The taxi stopped at the front of the building and Andrea paid with a twenty, telling the driver to keep the change. She pursed her lips, aware of her accent. Despite her best efforts to keep her accent non-regionalised, it was subtly British from her first twenty years living in England. She got out of the car and straitened her black knee length skirt and her sky blue silk blouse. Her blonde hair was cropped back. She held her agenda under her arm and focused on the appointment ahead. She'd been out of work for six months and needed this. Work had been hard to come by for executives since 2008. At the age of 45, she had handled other downturns, and believed there was always work there despite the adversity. In interviews she focused on her skills, her experience, and she thought about all the times people had challenged her. She drew strength from it. They had challenged her skills and her insecurities, and despite what they had said she was still there. She had always been a successful person; she wouldn't ever let that be taken away from her. She focused and repeated her mantra; *'I will be the best.'*

The building was new. The architecture was from after the millennium. But it was ambitious, so she thought it must have before the bust of 2008. There were glass revolving doors and a large lobby that utilised marble. So the cost would have been extravagant. As she walked in she ensured to come across as she belonged there, she didn't want to portray even a moment of weakness. She scanned the lobby for the plaque, found the level she was headed for. Level 44. The lift was quick and smooth. She reached the floor and did her best to blend in, searching around and getting her bearings, looking for where she was meant to go. She approached the receptionist who smiled to greet her.

'My name is Andrea Beaufort,' she said confidently with a straight face. 'I'm here for a meeting at 3pm.'

‘Hmm,’ the receptionist furrowed her brow and scanned the screen. She looked up with a big smile. ‘Yes, I have you here. I’ll just let them know you’re here. Please take a seat.’

She was left to wait. She sat by the coffee table near the entrance and overheard the receptionist on the phone. She turned her thoughts to her preparation. Thinking of the questions they always ask, she prepared thorough answers, even when asked about her weaknesses she made sure to end on a positive. Turning a weakness into a strength in a professional manner, she found, was perhaps one of the most effective interview techniques. It demonstrated the ability to be challenged, to handle it with poise and to solve challenges while remaining positive.

The receptionist approached and ushered her in. She rose and gathered her belongings before moving, she hated carrying clutter with her. With her agenda in hand, she strode through the corridors and met the two men outside the room. One man introduced himself as Charlie Arnaud, the man she had been talking to over the phone.

She made quick introductions and smiled politely, she always hated to fake being friendly. Both men were in their fifties, and gave her a friendly smile but she saw them looking her over. She ignored it and walked into the room. While they started asking her questions she ensured to keep her back straight and look them in the eyes, legs crossed and hands in her lap. As they asked their questions she automatically went into interview mode, going through the motions. Sometimes she responded so quickly and instinctively that she felt like an observer, like someone else had taken over. She found it hard to blame herself, the questions were routine for the most part. They asked her about her previous experience, what separated her from other applicants. But as always the questions ended up back at the same point.

Her time with Delpont.

She knew the questions were coming and after more than ten years she had plenty of experience dealing with them. With time she had found a way to turn it into a positive. But the questions were always a challenge. No amount of time could fully take away the damage that those years had done to her. The dot-com era had led to a lot of executives at a young age but an equivalent number of careers that would forever be tarnished. She wasn't the only one who found it hard to get another job after. She hadn't found a stable job since. She had spent a few years of the past decade out of work. But regardless, she was quite fortunate, as she had left the firm a year before the fallout. Her record was technically clean; she hadn't been involved in any of the fraud or conspiracy. Regardless, people always viewed her through a filtered lens. She could see it in their faces when they viewed it on her curriculum vitae, but to leave it off would be dishonest.

They asked the questions and she spouted off the usual answers, about how it had been a challenge to work in such an environment, how she had personally found issues with it and had decided to leave the firm after it didn't respond to the issues she had raised. She stated she had no knowledge of the corruption or fraud. Her movements and level of involvement backed her up. She shouldn't have known, and the fact she left so early spoke well for her. The majority of Delpont employees had never known the account records were so fabricated. They had been swept away in the love affair the stock market had with the company. The dizzy highs of perpetual profit and growth were broken sharply with the inevitable bust. She ended up presenting herself as a moral compass in interviews, but that made her feel worse because the reality was different. She resented getting credit for things she hadn't done.

The questions then moved on to examples of when she had demonstrated leadership and when she had succeeded in the face of adversity. She dealt with those questions easily. She always had a few examples she could draw on.

As their questions ebbed, they moved onto the section where they asked if she had anything to ask them. Always the section where people say they have nothing to ask, she ensured to always ask questions about the position and the responsibility. She could see when interviewers were taken aback. Interviewees generally did not take advantage of this section, however it was always a time to distinguish herself from the other candidates and put the interview on her terms, challenge the interviewers and show she was not one to be intimidated.

She narrowed her gaze confidently, gaining the control of the interview. She had spent a few years at the beginning of her career as a recruiter and had learnt small lessons like that. They always helped to distinguish her. As she wrapped up her questions, they discussed the next steps and she asked when she would be contacted if successful. They spent a few minutes on small talk and pleasantries, and then started walking out. She shook their hands, thanked them for her time and gave her warmest smile, which was still frostier than most.

She had done well.

Out on the street, she pulled a phone from her bag and typed a number in from memory. The call was answered on the second ring.

'Hey there, sex kitten. How are you?'

She smiled. He always had a way of joking around with her that she loved. 'Hey, handsome. I just got out now. Are you still free?'

'Sure thing, I'm just at home doing a bit of work. Come by!'

'Try and stop me. Do you have anything to drink?'

'Maybe a bit of rum. You'll probably have to get something for yourself.'

'It's fine, I'll have to drive later so there is no point.'

'Forget that. Get a cab and drink. I love you drunk, it always makes you get so wet.'

'You are such an asshole! You'll pay for that.' She said pretending to be offended. She smiled and bit her lip, feeling herself getting excited.

She heard him laugh on the other end of the line. 'Can't wait. Hurry up.'

'Fine, but I'm driving.'

'Yes, miss. Whatever you say.' Mockingly, he taunted her. He never seemed to listen to what she wanted, and when he did he would never make much of it. It both infuriated her and drove her wild.

'See you soon, love.'

She hung up and got in her car. The drive over always made her a little giddy. She could already see his smile and feel his touch tickling her skin. She thought of his eyes as he laughed. She felt her body yearn for him.

When Hank opened the door for her she was already ready. He smiled. His dark blonde curly hair was pulled back, his greyish green eyes wrinkled as he smiled. He always had stubble with flecks of grey, despite being only a year shy of 40. He wore his usual uniform of a flannel shirt and jeans, the benefit of working as a sculptor.

'I missed you, gorgeous.' He said as he pulled her close and kissed her passionately.

He slid his hands around her waist and undid her silk blouse, feeling her breasts as she slipped her heels off and then unbuttoned his shirt. He started to pull her to the bedroom, but they only made it to the living room couch. They undressed each other quickly before she pulled him inside her, she wanted to feel how deep he went and moaned as he entered her.

She closed her eyes and felt him gently bite her, then sink his teeth deeper as she gasped and dug her nails into his shoulders.

His pace quickened and she felt herself go flush. She gave herself to him and let go, her orgasm washing over as she felt her lover's seed shoot inside her. Her skin was warm and sweaty. She felt his body tighten as she caught her breath, then he relaxed and gently held her, his face nuzzled in at her neck. Both of them were breathing fast and were relaxed, bodies melted into each other. She ran her fingertips up and down his back. She truly loved this man. His cum warm still inside her and she loved the thought. In moments like these she felt truly like she was his.

She lay there in his arms, feeling his warm skin and running her hands through his sweaty hair. She wanted to stay in this moment so she tried to block out the thought of returning to her husband.

She reflected on the man she was married to, whom she had been with since she was twenty-three. When they had met he was thirty-five and at first she had loved him because she had thought he was powerful. His wealth and his self-confidence. But a lot had changed. She hated him for being so old, for not being able to keep up with her. But she had been a foolish girl, she hadn't even had the simple ability to do the math and realise he would be an old man while she was in her peak.

Every time he touched her it felt like a lie. She cringed at the thought of his touch, the man she had married and been with for so long. At the same time, though, she knew that she *did* truly love her husband, despite all that.

She bid adieu to her lover and promised to spend longer next time. Reaching into her bag for her real phone, not the supermarket phone with the prepaid sim card she had used to phone her lover, she phoned her husband to tell him it had went well, but was unable to reach him.

'Hi dear. Just got out of the interview, it went quite well. I'll be home soon, just on my way now. I'll see you at home. Love you'.

She straightened her clothes and fixed her hair and make up, and made the journey back home to her husband. Home to the man she had made a life and a home with, a man she still loved. He was a good man.

THE MAN BEHIND BARS

He rose with the sun. His cell faced east and as soon as dawn broke it became too bright in the room. The first few months had been too hard to sleep, he'd had only a few hours sleep between his paranoia and the feeling of him losing his mind. He still felt like that. Most nights he would cry in anger and hit himself, shouting in a whisper so as not to be heard. He wanted to let it out like nothing else but didn't want to make himself a target. He was enough of a target already.

He'd found that prison was largely what he expected. He had walked in pale as a ghost, trying to stop from shaking as he walked past much larger men who chuckled and told him he was fucked as he walked to his cell. His shaking hands had confirmed to them that he knew it.

For any man, going into prison was the end of his life. The man that he was when he entered was not the same as when and if he leaves. The crimes of Lew Noble were firstly fraud, but he had also been charged with insider trading, making false statements to investors, intimidating witnesses. There was not a day that went by that he didn't hate the world for all this. He hated himself because he knew that when the investigators had picked him up that he was cooked. He remembered feeling a sinking sensation when they walked towards him. He had accepted it, in that moment, because he knew they had him, and he couldn't fight them.

But for all that, he could never let go of the hatred that had built in him since and the anger that he held to with every waking moment. For he knew that others had done worse and hadn't been caught. During the dot-com boom every company had cooked their books. There were so many that had lied about business and booked profits that they never received. He had been targeted because their company was the biggest. It was his face over every news article for months. It still sickened him to think about how they looked at him now, with shame and disgust.

Lew wasn't meant for this. He woke up every day thinking this was a nightmare. During his heyday he had felt the best. Being able to hold big functions, getting awards, the company doing so well. Everyone had needed his attention and his business. He'd had power to negotiate. His beautiful wife, whom he had met at university, at his side and his two young kids at home. Now he was stuck in a cell every hour of the day. He left for exercise and other things, but he had been dead inside for a long time. When he entered the prison he had longed for the opportunity to kill himself but they watched him closely. He'd given up on that hope some time ago.

He was now nearing fifty. He was still tall, but much thinner than when he came in. He hadn't seen a mirror in a while, but he assumed that his face still looked as ungainly as it did when he entered; narrow face with his wide nose, still crooked from being broken so long ago. He hadn't been a handsome man even in his youth. But when he had been somebody, they had described him as a tall successful man with dark hair and dark eyes. He'd been happy and content. He'd been a lot of things. Now there were just the crimes that he'd committed.

As he rose from his lumpy, uncomfortable bed and was greeted by a paper left by the door. He looked but there was no sign of who had left it or how long it had been there. He sat up slowly and stiffly, leaned over from his bed and picked it up. His joints felt sorer than he could remember. It was a local paper and below the crease of the page was a small article. Marcus Docker, a chief operating officer, had been gunned down in the downtown area. The article had been circled in red marker by someone. Underneath it was scrawled; 'This is what happens to rich bitches.'

He recognised the name as colleague from Delpont, someone who had been around during the good times but had changed sides when things had started to turn. He'd emerged from it with his reputation unscathed. It was unlikely any of them would know the two had worked together. Most likely it was just an attempt to upset him, threaten him by showing what had happened to another rich man. But he honestly couldn't care what happened to some colleague he had once worked with; he could hardly remember the guy. He was more interested in who had left the newspaper and what it could mean for him. He needed to look after himself first. Survival of the fittest.

It was probably one of the guards. He assumed they were new. The other prisoners had not been too bad to him. He had expected a lot worse but his position and the wealth his wife still owned had counted for something. The threat of litigation against the prison had forced many of the guards to crack down on prisoners attempting to beat him. Though, he'd noticed that the guards hated doing it. He could tell that they wanted him to get beaten. Somehow that made him enjoy it so much more. He chuckled at the thought. This new guard could get targeted for harassment with such an act. He reminded himself to mention it to his lawyer when next they spoke. He might even be able to get a reduced sentence. He felt a stir of hope that he might even be able to get out soon.

He rose as the doors buzzed and opened for the day. He put the paper next to the book he was reading at the moment, a history book about the story of the Roman empire. He'd been truly fascinated by it. The paper was safest in the open. If he tried to hide it then it would be found straight away. Short of removing a small section of wall and reattaching it, there were no places to hide things. Under his mattress was the only accessible spot and that was checked almost every day. He hoped that they would think nothing of the paper and leave it be.

Over breakfast he sat by himself, at a table of others who sat by themselves. They had sat together for close to three months, this group of six people, and not a word had been spoken. He didn't recognise any of them, so he assumed they weren't in for financial crimes. They hadn't hassled him, so there was little to be gained by finding out their story.

Since the day he had come in there, eight years ago, he had not spoken to anyone in the prison. Not a guard, not a prisoner, not a soul, save when he asked for a book from the library. He'd had conversations with his lawyer often, and for the first few years his wife had visited, he had even seen his kids twice in the beginning. But he'd lost them too. Last he heard his wife had remarried, and his kids were too young to remember him. They were so gorgeous, though. He remembered little Robbie with his blonde hair, chubby face and big laugh. Always running and breaking things. His wife had lost her temper, but he had always found it funny. He smiled for a moment, then came crashing down when he realised his son was 13 now. His daughter Sarah would be 11 in November. As he sat at the table with these strangers, he had to bite the inside of his cheek to keep from crying again. He felt a lump in his throat, but continued to force food down.

After breakfast, there was usually an hour or two outside. The grass was mostly torn up out of inmate frustration. But all he wanted was to feel the sun on his skin again. He was lucky today and the sun was out, the summer weather was holding up, for what it was worth to him. He silently skulked across the yard and found a spot near the fence, away from where people could hear him. He sat down and lifted his chin for the first time all day. For a moment he was free, the sun on his face lifted his spirits.

For a moment he remembered a day ten years ago when he and his wife and spent the week in Fiji for their anniversary. She had to drag him to use the jet skis one day. It was a beautiful hot and humid Fijian day at the Hilton and he had just wanted to drink cocktails and lounge by the pool. She had convinced him to do it, though, and they had set off.

For the first part she had driven the jet ski while they made their way to an island, he held onto her as they had agreed to take it in turns. They had gone snorkelling on the island, and it had been fun. But on the trip back, he had been able to drive. It was a memory he clung to. As soon as he figured out how it worked, he had watched the rest of the group fly away. His wife had yelled at him to catch up. So, he floored it.

He could feel it now. The deafening sound of the engine. The rocking feeling as they flew over the ocean, whatever waves he rode over were small, and felt like ripples. The wind had flown at him and he heard shouting and cheering. It had taken him a few minutes to realise that it was himself. Any doubts he ever had were gone, he finally felt like he was the person he was born to be. The water seemed a brighter, more luminescent blue than before. The sun cast down a beautiful glow. The trees and the islands seemed greener and more beautiful. He wanted to stay there. Stay around the islands, riding on the jet ski and fishing and lazing around all day. This was where he wanted to live.

He kept pace with the group and had quickly caught up to them. They gestured and cheered at each other, despite being strangers. It was only then that he realised his wife was screeching at him to slow down, swearing and calling him a fucking asshole and that she was going to fucking kick his ass when they got to land. He turned slightly and caught her eye. He had started laughing, but with his whole body. He felt truly happy. After a moment his wife had started laughing too, she had warmed to him for the first time in months. He then felt her wrap her arms around him from behind and she held tighter than he could ever remember. This was what he wanted, his wife and this jet ski.

They screamed over waves and laughed as one. He swerved and jumped waves and she cheered him as he did. The group was doing the same. All around him he could see the beauty of these islands. A few tall impressive mountains that would have originally been volcanoes, now covered in lushness and green. Still there were also smaller islands, dotting the horizon. This beautiful world surrounding them as they soared over the waves, the water so azure blue and clear they could see the reef below. He remembered getting back to the hotel room with her, they had laughed the whole way, wrapped around each other.

When they got back to the room, they jumped straight into the shower and tried to get the salt water off, but in undressing he found himself looking at her as he had forgotten to. He wrapped his bare body around hers and kissed her, her skin tasted of salt but he didn't care. She had smiled warmly and they had made love like when they had first met, a passionate young couple.

He felt suddenly cold and opened his eyes. A cloud had passed, obscuring the sun. Coming back to the present, he felt even colder, and the sinking feeling came over him again. Those good memories were now so painful each time they came to him, each time it hurt more to think on that happiness that he once had. It wasn't the woman he missed, though he missed the feel of her body. He had come to hate her for moving on and forgetting about him. What he missed was the freedom. He spent the rest of the day in a daze.

At night, he was moved back into his room. He checked the shelf and found that the paper had been taken away. He didn't care anymore. He had died a long time ago.

AOKI

She stood outside their North Shore police station, smoking and watching the traffic go past. Their station had a unique view in that there was a court right across the road. Often they saw people going into cases and families leaving. It gave her some perspective to her work; every win for her was a loss for someone else. A loss for a family.

The midday sun warmed her face and made her feel slightly better. Back at her desk there was a mountain of work waiting, things she had intended to do the next day one week ago. It was hard to focus at the moment, though. There was infighting in the team, people playing politics, and talking gossip about promotions. Out here she could just be on her own and leave the job behind. She found it easy during the day, at night it was harder.

Stubbing her cigarette out, she made for the lift. As she walked through the lobby, she felt the cool hit of the controlled air-conditioned environment. There were always a lot of conversations going on at the entrance, the sound of them all blended in together to create an indecipherable background noise.

She got into an empty elevator and pressed her floor. As the doors closed someone stuck their hand in and they reopened. A nervous looking guy butted into the lift and smiled at everyone. She ignored him. He pressed the button for a level a few below hers. It was typical; whenever she got into this lift someone always had to go to a floor below hers. It was a minor inconvenience that became a daily hassle. People who butted into her lifts always irritated her.

The office was a mix of quiet discussions and unspoken excitement. There was agitation amongst the team. The ‘dynamic duo’ on the murder of the trader had not turned up any clues so far. Media pressure was mounting. She put her things down at her desk. When she looked up and saw Morgan was back, and quickly walked over.

'Did you hear about Moray and Bay, and their case?' she asked in a hushed voice, looking around to make sure no one could overhear.

'Yeah. Dead end,' he smiled with a wink. 'Media's starting to get restless. What did I say?' He said confidently, grinning.

She crossed her arms. 'Yeah, you called it. That's weird though, right?'

'What is?'

'Just the lack of information. All they've found is a partial footprint. No weapon found anywhere, none of the cameras on the street caught anything.' She spoke quietly but felt excited. There was something strange about the case.

He frowned. 'Yeah, I guess. It doesn't seem like a random crime to me. It almost has the feel of a professional hit.'

She thought it over. 'It's not likely.'

'It's a possibility. I mean, the getaway was remarkably clean. It was a clean shot too. A one kill shot through the centre of the neck.'

She laughed and then quickly covered her mouth. 'I knew it! You're interested too!'

'Of course. It's hard not to be. But I mean, all that drama?' He shook his head and grinned. 'No way is it worth it. Have you seen how stressed Hannah is?'

She nodded slowly. Hannah had looked stressed. The past few days had been too much for her, especially with no real media training so far.

‘She’s in over her head. And Carl, fuck,’ he said in disbelief, ‘That kid is basic.’

She stifled a laugh. But she felt guilty for finding such a mean comment so funny. ‘He’s done some good casework, come on.’

‘Yeah, with other people. As a lead though? Law and order are doing their utmost to make sure this case remains unsolved.’ He laughed at the thought.

‘No, I don’t think so,’ she said gently. ‘They made a mistake putting those two on, I think I know what they’re going to do, though.’

He turned to her, confused. He crossed his arms and narrowed his gaze. He always crossed his arms when he was thinking. ‘Yeah?’

‘Well, they’ll have to bring someone else in. They’ll have to change one of them. Or expand the team. Say the case has become more complex. They can’t leave the two of them on their own, or with each other. It’ll make way too much attention if there aren’t any results soon.’

‘You might be right. They’ll have to do it carefully tho…’ he stopped mid sentence, his gaze firmly planted on his computer. ‘Fuck, I just got a lead on that domestic abuse case. The one where the guy did a runner?’

‘Yeah?’

‘Want to come for a drive? One of his cards was just used. It might turn out to be too late but still? Could be fun.’ He said jokingly, a wry grin on his face.

She groaned. *I’m so behind.* ‘Like I have a choice.’ She muttered as she ran her hands through her hair and then rubbed her face.

He laughed.

WILL

'Declined due to budget?' Will tried as hard as possible to remain sensible.

'Yeah, leave it until the next budget review meeting.' John Leech muttered absently.

'That's not for another two months?!'

'There's nothing I can do.' Leech said with a tired voice. All the old man could think about was his budget. He was so miserly he'd be hesitant about spending even one cent.

Will exhaled deeply and fought the urge to throw everything off his desk. 'So, how much time can I spend on this story?' he asked sarcastically, referring to the piece he had proposed.

It was an article on the continued downsizing in Australia. Corporations were reducing the size of their workforces despite increasing profits. His preliminary research had found a common occurrence emerging for organisations to not raise the salary of staff each year. The implication of this, as a result of continued inflation, was that employees were now earning relatively less than before. The boom had been getting more publicity lately but he knew that costs had been cut, the effects of the 2008 recession had lead to downsizing in every industry, including the profitable ones.

'None. It's not a critical story. Go back and do some more preliminary research.' Leech said with an uninterested voice. It was the same response he always used. It made it seem like something was being done, but all he was doing was biding time, hoping the story went away. This man would do anything to avoid a cost.

'Fine. I'll be off then.' Will said between clenched teeth. He rose to get out of there as soon as possible.

'Before you go, do some work on what I'm sending you now.'

Will rubbed his face and tried not to lose it. He knew it would be a useless article.

'Get started on an article on the proposed changes to the tax system, in particular the 'wealth tax'. Look at the negative effects for businesses and how that will affect working families. Argue that it'll be disastrous.'

Will's assumption was right; it was a wank of an article. There had been a series of changes proposed about a restructure of the tax system. Essentially, it reduced low income and medium income taxes. Part of it, however, was a proposed increase in taxes on high income and luxury goods. It was largely theoretical, and while he supported the idea, he expected it to be shot down. It already had garnered a lot of negative media attention. There were even talks that the 'wealth tax' could be the death knell for the current government. The opposition had run a widespread fear campaign, and while their arguments were incorrect, they had convinced a significant portion of the public.

'Yeah I'll try,' he said, walking out the door to avoid any further conversation. He assumed that Leech had probably been given the order from someone higher up in the media conglomerate. It was common knowledge that the owner of the media company was doing backroom deals with the leader of the conservative party. The media billionaire would give the party millions in campaign donations and in return the conservative party would reduce corporate taxation, high income tax and make other changes that benefitted only the wealthy. If economics were a game, it would be played with loaded dice.

He needed to get out of the office. He headed outside knowing that everyone would just assume he was working from home again today.

Heading to the train station, he reflected on Marcus Docker. A colleague of his had written the article for their paper and had been talking to the police. So far, they had not made any breaks and it had been a few days now. None of the articles he had seen were well written. All had played up the death to a point of tragedy for the country.

It was the same thing when any of these rich people died. There was always a lot of attention paid in the media, nightly news discussing the life and showing photos of the deceased. Death is only ever a tragedy for the family, everything else is just loyalties and politics. The newsrooms play long tribute stories out of obligation. When someone so rich passes they are bound to have a stake in some media outlets who will run the piece. He thought of an especially wealthy man who had owned another media network a few years back, the man was worth billions, but when he died he had been given a state funeral. It was disgusting. He'd given little of his money to charity, had been a misogynist and a sexist, and had been involved in who knows how many dodgy deals. Several of his mergers had been in violation of corporate and media laws, yet they had gone ahead anyway.

He swiped his ticket at the gates. The interior of the upper floor of the station was new and clean. Once he got down to the platform though it was another story. Soot and pollutants lined the walls of the train tunnels. The tiles were old and yellowed. The vending machines dated from the nineties. He stood on the platform and looked at the screen showing what time the next train was. It was a crappy old screen, like a refurbished 80s computer. It was almost embarrassing how poorly funded the transport systems were. The problems weren't entirely an issue of funding, though.

The city had originally been set up around a hundred and thirty years ago. It had mostly been designed for horses. No major infrastructure changes had been made since. It was a mess of a city. Will had found ways around this. He always lived close to a train station, and he always lived close to bars and cafes. That way, if he needed to do anything at night he could just walk somewhere. Taxis and driving were too expensive. He had the necessities close by; caffeine and alcohol.

He heard the screech of the train, the tracks had no real work done to them since they had been laid down and it was a constant side effect whenever they entered or exited a station. As he entered the train, he saw a familiar face. He smiled, surprised.

'Don?!'

His university friend looked up and gave a big smile. 'Will! Hey mate! How are you going?' he said warmly. Whenever they spoke Don was always friendly and encouraging. He had always been gifted at making friends with people and networking. He was wearing a black suit, white business shirt and light blue tie. His dark blue eyes were as friendly as ever.

The two hugged and patted each other on the back. They hadn't seen each other in some time. 'Good, usual bullshit with the paper.'

'Yeah? That's no good,' Don said sympathetically with a narrowed gaze, to show concern. He was always sympathetic. Partly because he was so good at making friends, but it was also because he genuinely cared. 'How's everything going on the book front? How does it feel to be a successful economist?' He teased with a smile.

Will winced. 'Going ok. Might publish something else sometime. How are things with you?' He asked, changing the subject quickly. 'How come you're heading home so early?'

'Not feeling well. Couldn't stay any longer. So sick at the moment.' He said, a frown on his face. He hated being sick, and was rarely ill. He had always been a high achiever. In school, he had been captain and a natural leader. He'd been picked up straight out of uni for his leadership experience and good grades. He went into a job as a trader in one of the big financial organisations and he had excelled.

Don laughed as the two sat down. 'It's been too long. How are things going with Nicole?' he asked warmly.

Will shook his head with a smile. ‘We split like six months ago.’

‘Really? Fuck, I’m sorry.’

‘Nah, it’s alright. She moved overseas and we’d grown apart. I’ve seen a few girls since. Nothing too serious, though.’

‘Yeah? Sounds good.’ He said positively.

Will frowned. It had been more lonely than good. ‘How about you? How are things with Kelly?’

‘Not, ahhh … Not going too well,’ Don said sarcastically and laughed. ‘We broke up a few months ago.’

‘Fuck, sorry. It’s been way too long, then.’ Will laughed.

‘Yeah, I know. I’ve been so flat out. Sorry, man.’ Don ran his hands through his hair and sighed. ‘The past few weeks have been no good. I’ve been doing accreditation exams. I’ve been flat out on weekends. Most nights I’ve been working until eight, as well’

Will shook his head. ‘That’s bullshit. They shouldn’t be working you so hard.’

Don frowned. ‘There’s so much to do. But honestly, it gets to the point where it’s 5pm, and everyone will just sit staring at their screens watching each other.’

Will frowned. ‘What do you mean?’

‘No one wants to be the first to go.’

He smirked. ‘Are you serious?’

‘Yeah. No one wants to be seen as the first to go. But once one person goes everyone will start to leave.’

Will sighed. ‘Fuck.’

‘Yeah, it’s pretty crazy. Especially since the first person doesn’t usually leave until 8pm or so. Maybe you should chuck that in one of your business articles.’ Don joked.

Will raised an eyebrow, though. It actually might be a good article. Presenteeism was a serious issue in some organisations, especially those without set shifts.

‘Anyway,’ Don said, changing the subject. ‘We should do something soon, though. Yeah?’

‘For sure.’ Will replied.

‘What’re your plans this weekend? Are you going to Chris’ birthday?’

Will smiled and shook his head. ‘I didn’t even know that was on. Fuck, I haven’t seen him in so long.’

‘Yeah. I haven’t seen him in months either.’ Don shook his head with a smile. ‘I only found out about it from Facebook. Without it I swear I would even forget family birthdays.’

Will found that hard to believe. Don and Chris had been friends since primary school. They’d done everything together, school, university and even surfing.

‘Anyway, it’s this Friday. It’d be a good chance to catch up.’ Don ran his hand through his hair. ‘Otherwise I’m flying out in a few weeks’.

‘What do you mean?’

‘I got a job interview over in New York.’

‘Really?’

‘Yeah. I don’t really have a chance with it. It’s a long shot. But I get a free trip to New York.’ He laughed. Don had always loved to travel. During university he had gone overseas whenever there was a semester break.

'You never know. Good luck with it, anyway.' Will said, but frowned as he contemplated the prospect of his friend living overseas. 'I've always wanted to do something like that.' He said softly.

'Something like what?'

'You know,' Will shrugged. 'Just leave one day. Run away overseas'

Don laughed. 'What do you want to run away from?'

Will grinned. 'I dunno. I just always wanted an adventure. Start over, you know?'

'Yeah, totally.' Don smiled. 'You should do it!'

'Nah, I could never do that.' Will shook his head and smiled. It wasn't something he could do. He liked to go on holidays but his life was here. He wouldn't be able to leave.

There was an indecipherable muffle over the train speaker system as the train emerged from a tunnel. Don straightened his jacket and picked up his shoulder bag.

'This is me, sorry to cut our catch up short, but see you Friday, yeah?' Don smiled.

'Yeah, for sure,' Will agreed. 'Seems like the only time you're free. Things really sound crazy for you at the moment.'

'Yeah, you're not wrong.' He sighed. The train slowed and screeched as it pulled into the station. As it came to a sudden stop, Don and Will were lurched forward. 'We'll talk soon! Take care mate.' Will watched his friend walk out the doors.

Will's stop was the next station and when he got off the train he reflected on how things with Don had changed. As he'd gotten older he had found himself growing away from his friends from university. They'd gone in different directions and had been living their own lives, and the time between each catch up had become longer.

He was almost home when his phone rang. The call was from a private number. It could be almost anything.

He cleared his throat as he answered the phone. 'Hello, Will speaking.'

'Hello, Darling!' He recognised the energetic and friendly voice on the other end.

He smiled straight away. 'Iz! Hey, how are you?'

She laughed. 'Good, good! How are you?'

'Yeah, all good. Just went into work.'

'Oh, right. How was it darling?!' She asked.

He groaned. 'Don't ask.'

'Fuck, that's shit. Anyway! I have to tell you something!' She said energetically.

'What's up?'

'I'll be staying here!' She said energetically.

'Really? That's awesome.' He grinned, glad his best friend would be staying this time. The two of them had been through all kinds of break ups together, and their friendship had always survived.

'Yeah, I can't wait to see everyone more often. I love you all so much!'

'I miss you so much, can't wait to hang out again. Hey, I didn't get time to ask the other day. But, how was the design course, anyway?'

'Really good. Really difficult but really good.'

‘Yeah? How so?’

She sighed. ‘Just pretty demanding. They also really try and challenge you, like get you to work in mediums you aren’t necessarily used to or experienced in. That part of it has been a challenge.’

‘Yeah that sounds challenging. Sorry to hear’ he said comfort gently. ‘But that must have been rewarding too? Challenging yourself to develop as an artist?’

‘Yeah, definitely. It’s been good and bad. A good opportunity to develop, for sure. I’ve grown a lot.’

He smiled. ‘Glad to hear,’ he paused and wasn’t sure whether to ask his next question or not. ‘So what about everything with Olivier? What will you guys do?’

She went quiet for a moment. ‘Things aren’t working out.’

He was genuinely surprised, they had been so happy a few months earlier. ‘What? What happened?’

‘He changed so much when I went over there. He got really clingy and jealous. We haven’t been talking. He just sends me messages and a few passive aggressive calls now.’

‘Fuck.’

‘He’s a dickhead. I’m over him.’

‘That’s rough. Are you alright?’

‘Yeah, I’m doing alright, babe. Part of me still loves him, but,’ she sighed, ‘I’ve been really miserable lately with all his drama.’

‘I can understand, that’s terrible.’ He was upset to hear her like this. She was usually so happy and positive. She was the most fun and friendly person he had ever met.

'It's alright. But hey!' Her voice was animated again. 'We can party again soon!'

He laughed. 'Sounds awesome. Hey you remember Chris?'

'Nah, don't think so. Have I met him?'

'I dunno. Well, anyway,' he said slowly. 'It's Chris' birthday this Friday, he's organising something for it. You want to come with?'

'Hell yeah!' she said. 'Hey, by the way, I saw you talking to Amber a lot the other night.'

He grinned 'Oh yeah?'

'Yeah. Have you been seeing her much?'

He was confused. 'I ran into her the other day. I don't know her too well. How do you know her?'

'Only through other people. I went to school with her.'

'Really?'

'Yeah. She was two years above me. I was never friends with her, but I know her.' Her voice was quieter than usual.

'Oh ok.'

'Yeah. Listen, be careful around Amber. She's a piece of work.'

His left eye twitched. 'How so?'

'Just some things I heard. I get a bad vibe from her.'

He laughed. 'A bad vibe?'

'Shut up. It's hard to explain.'

'Well, I don't even know her that well'

'Yeah, but she is your type. I know it. Blonde, blue eyes, tall, artistic.'

It was true, she had him. 'Yeah, fair enough.'

'Her art is shit, by the way.'

'I haven't seen it yet.'

'Well it's shit. She only got into interior design because of her dad's money. He owns her business.'

'What?' He was genuinely surprised.

'Yeah, he started it up for her. She essentially gets paid by her Dad. Anyway, just watch out around her.'

'I will,' he tried to ease her concerns. He knew his friend hated to see him get heartbroken. She always told him to be careful when he got involved with someone. It was deserved, though; in the past he had a tendency to dive headfirst into relationships.

'Will you take some time and see family before you settle over here?' He asked. Both her mum and her dad had moved over to Europe.

'Nah, I'm broke as. Mum's coming over for a visit though! I actually haven't seen her in about six months.'

He laughed. 'No way.'

'Yeah, the last night I saw her was my farewell.'

'So I've seen your mum about as much as you have.'

She laughed. 'Yeah, very funny.'

'Tell her I said hey, by the way.'

She groaned. 'Very funny.' Her tone was rich with sarcasm.

'Tell her if she is single again soon to call me, yeah?' He teased.

‘Shut up.’

He laughed.

‘Hey, PS, if you hear anyone looking for work let me know!’ She said energetically. ‘Hook a sister up!’

He laughed. ‘Alright, will do. What are you looking for?’

‘I dunno, yet,’ she said with a sigh. ‘A friend hooked me up with this photography gig with a paper.’

‘Oh really?’

‘Yeah, just getting photos for articles and things.’ She said, uninterested.

‘That’s really good!’ He encouraged.

‘Meh,’ she replied. ‘It’s not much money, and it’s not often.’

He exhaled. ‘Yeah, I can understand. Alright, I’ll ask around for you’

‘Thanks! Hey love, I have to go. We’re heading out now.’ He heard her talk to her friends. ‘Alright, chill out! I’m coming!’ She pulled the phone back to her ear. ‘I’ll talk to you soon, babe! Can’t wait to hang out again. I’ll talk to you soon.’

‘Sounds good. Have fun, bub. Talk soon.’

He heard her disconnect and suddenly realised he had been standing outside his apartment building talking to her.

THE MAN IN THE CAFE

He was out of his usual territory. Daytime took away the shadows he would usually blend into, but still, he found other ways to blend in. He knew this world well. After all, he should have been a part of this world. The indoor café at the base of the commercial building, large glass windows and a large open plan, industrial design ensured as much natural light came in as possible. People in suits, tightly cropped short hair, faces sucked tight through liposuction. Wearing a three thousand dollar suit but carefully budgeting whether they could afford a twenty or fifty cent tip for the barista on minimum wage, then deciding against leaving one altogether.

A tall man with short black hair entered the café. He bounced as he walked, no doubt a side effect of his lanky gait. He was dressed professionally but without a suit jacket or tie; his style was formal casual. This was the Taylor Sheeran from his research. The tall man gave a big smile to the person sitting at the table next to him. The man sitting down was short and stocky. It looked like he was balding but with that baby face he couldn't have been more than thirty. The short and stocky man then stood to greet the Sheeran.

He watched from a table nearby while Sheeran and the stocky man greeted each other, careful not to pay them too much attention.

'Taylor, good to see you. How was your flight?' The stocky man said politely.

'You too, Shane. Yeah, flight was fine. Can't complain.' Taylor said, forcing a smile. 'I hope you haven't been waiting too long?'

'I just got here myself.' Shane said with a tight smile. It was a lie. The man had been there for twenty minutes. He had called his partner and complained about how he was waiting for 'some wanker', using his own words.

The corporate world runs on these perpetual lies and illusions that everyone gets along. From his table nearby he sipped at his coffee as he eavesdropped on the conversation between Taylor and Shane.

'Alright, so did you have any concerns over that spreadsheet I sent out?' Taylor sat down and pulled out his laptop from his shoulder bag.

'Just a few minor queries, vis-à-vis the rollout moving into the next quarter.' Shane pronounced each word deliberately and pretentiously.

He could sense the type already. *Someone not too bright who managed to learn a few buzz words.* The type of person who would spend all day worrying people would learn he wasn't intelligent, yet every word he spoke betrayed him.

'Ok, well at this stage we're trying to go live by March next year. We've budgeted to shut down existing operations in Australia in the months leading up to March.'

'Right, and you mentioned when we spoke on the phone that the additional expenditure occurred …'

Both he and Taylor cringed at the error of getting 'occurred' confused with 'incurred'.

'… during the transition period?'

'The expenditure would be *minimal*, correct.' Sheeran nodded, making direct eye contact with Shane. 'Operations in Australia would shut down at 6pm on the Friday, operations in Bangalore would start at midday. The transition period would only be six hours.'

'So we would only be doubling up for a few hours?'

‘Paying wages in both countries? That’s correct. Additional expenditure would be minimal.’ Taylor said, emphasising the last word.

‘And the *feasibility* of transferring trading operations overseas?’

‘We have found in similar such transitions that quality reduction has been minimal.’

‘And English skills?’

‘The loss of client satisfaction due to minor language discrepancies has not been significant.’ Sheeran spoke with a blank face. *Translated from corporate speak; the English skills were not great.*

Since the millennium, moves such as this were common. Jobs shipped overseas to cut costs, massive losses to employment, especially jobs that would generally be staffed by youths and university graduates. The entry-level jobs were always the first to get cut.

Shane pursed his lips. ‘Hmm very good.’ He paused. ‘Just in regards to the potential cost effectiveness of the entire project, at this stage what are the anticipated savings?’

‘Your current operations in Australia employ a staff of twenty six university educated staff for market analysis, the wages for these staff are fifty five thousand a year. That totals one million, four hundred and thirty thousand a year. In wages alone.’

‘Correct.’

‘Currently, we anticipate that we could run the centre with forty staff.’

‘Is the additional staff count is to compensate for the fact that they’re unskilled?’

'Well,' Taylor appeared stumped. 'They are given all the training they need in market analysis, there is a thorough introduction course, and they are trained to follow templates provided …'

'But they are not technically university educated?' Shane cut him off.

There was a pause. 'Correct.'

'Hmm,' he said stroking his chin. This seemed to give Shane cause to reconsider. 'I hadn't considered this.'

'But in regards to reduced cost of the new centre,' this brought Shane's attention back. 'It would run with a staff of forty. The wages of each would be six thousand US dollars.'

'Six thousand a month?' Shane was on the brink of shouting. 'That's almost double what we pay our current staff.'

Taylor grinned widely. 'Not a month. That's their annual salary. Times forty is two hundred and forty thousand a year.'

Shane's jaw visibly dropped. 'Six thousand dollars a year per worker? Two hundred and forty thousand for the entire division a year?'

Taylor nodded. There was a moment of silence and Shane looked away, thinking. He frowned.

'Is it legal?'

'Is what legal?'

'To pay these workers so little? I mean, we are a multinational corporation. Aren't we required to pay the comparative wage we would in any other country?'

'Correct. This is the average wage for the country, though. Living costs are considerably cheaper, rent is lower, but the key factor is that the population is obscenely high and so there's an oversupply of cheap labour,' Taylor paused, realising he had used the word ‘cheap’. He continued when he realised it hadn’t fazed Shane. ‘And so, because of the over supply workers are willing to forego salary.’

Shane mulled it over. ‘Two hundred and forty thousand. A year.’

‘It’s a considerably saving. It would mean your division would have an extra one million dollars a year.’

Shane’s eyebrow perked up.

‘Hmm. I suppose that would make room for increased expenditure in other areas.’

‘Or a round of bonuses? It has been a hard few years.’

‘True,’ Shane chuckled. ‘I think after something like this I would deserve a big bonus.’

Taylor smiled. He knew he had him.

The man at the nearby table hadn’t been noticed by Taylor or Shane. Nor had he been noticed by anyone else in the café. There was no reason he would have been. Wearing a suit, typing on his laptop; he looked like the other clientele. He appeared normal and unremarkable. The man sitting at the table nearby decided that Taylor fit the profile perfectly.

ANDREA

Her eyes opened suddenly and for a moment she forgot where she was. Her phone was vibrating on the wooden floorboards. She had put it on silent but the vibrate mode was so strong it always woke her violently. Shifting to the side of the bed, she reached for it. The call was from one of the men that had interviewed her from the Securities and Investments Commission.

She rolled out of bed and pulled herself up while the phone continued to ring. Ducking into her ensuite, she ran the tap and splashed cold water all over her face, feeling herself being shook awake.

She cleared her throat and slapped her cheeks. The phone was still ringing and she hurriedly dried her hands to answer the call. She lifted the phone to her ear and took a deep breath, calming and focusing herself.

'Andrea speaking.' She said in the clearest and most professional voice she could muster.

'Hi there, Andrea, it's Charlie Arnoud. We met the other day? How are you doing?'

'Hi Charlie. Good to hear from you again. What can I do for you?' She dodged the question about her wellbeing. She hated wasting time on formalities and trivialities such as that.

'I wanted to thank you for meeting with me the other day. We were really impressed with both you and your experience.'

Crap, she thought, *not again.* She needed this.

'And we would like to offer you a position.'

Urgh. Typical. She rolled her eyes and was glad it wasn't a face-to-face conversation.

‘Sorry for the misdirect,’ she heard laughter on the other end. ‘But congratulations!’

‘Thank you. That is great news.’ she said calmly.

‘We were impressed with the range of your experience. We thought it really fit with the requirements of the role.’

She frowned. His last comment had confused her. ‘From what I understood of the role, working in the prosecutions team seemed like it was a straight correlation to my legal experience.’

‘That’s true. You would be an excellent fit for the prosecutions role. However, there is another opportunity at the moment.’

She was intrigued.

‘In the past few months ASIC has been working on a new department. It’s still in the development stages at the moment, but the primary task would be drafting up new legislation.’

‘I thought ASIC already had a division that looked dealt with legislative advising?’

‘Yes, that’s correct,’ he spoke slowly, sounding a little frustrated. ‘But this new division would be more effective, it would be more proactive than reactive.’

‘Oh. Okay.’

‘It’s essentially trying to prevent similar circumstances as other large scale cases of fraud or deceiving investors.’

‘It sounds like an interesting project.’ She said slowly.

‘We thought that your background and knowledge would be a good fit for the project. With your experience in legal and accounting,’ There was a bit of a pause, ‘and we also thought that you would be able to provide a unique insight.’

He paused. She understood what he was referring to. ‘Oh, ok.’

‘Yeah. We thought with your previous employment provided you with a valuable perspective, which would otherwise be difficult to obtain.’

She tried to stop herself from laughing. It was the first and possibly only time that her time with Delpont would be an advantage to her.

AOKI

She was glad for the day off. The past few days had been long and busy and there was a lot to catch up on. She was actually happier to take the day off during the week, it was easier to get around and a lot less busy.

'Hey, I'm off now.' Rick called from the other room.

'Alright, I'll see you tonight.'

'Enjoy your day off, I know you need it.'

'Yeah, I'm pretty drained,' she sighed while pouring the cats food into the bowl.

He laughed.

'What?'

'Whatever you do. Don't go into work again.'

She laughed loudly. 'Ahh, fuck you! That was one time.'

He smiled as he packed some snacks into his backpack. 'It wasn't. You've done it on five days off in the past year.'

'Yeah yeah. Don't worry, I won't. Work is last place I want to be right now. It's so stressful at the moment, way too busy.'

He sighed. 'Yeah, I'm sorry, it's no good.' He slung his pack over his shoulder, 'Alright, well I'm off!'

'Did you want a lift to the station?'

'Nah, it's fine, just relax on the couch. I know you don't get too many days off like this. Take advantage of it!' He said with a warm smile.

'Yeah? You sure?'

'I'm sure,' he nodded. 'I'll see you tonight. Let me know if you want me to bring something home. I probably won't feel like cooking anything.'

'Sure thing.' She knew what he was trying to do. He didn't want her to cook tonight because it was her day off. She grinned and shook her head. He was too cunning sometimes.

He gave their cat a stroke on the way out the door. It raised its back and purred as he did, then it cocked its head in confusion as he walked out and closed the door. It could never comprehend why the proper attention wasn't paid to it sometimes.

She lay back on the couch and went back to her tablet, checking her emails and Facebook. She sent a few messages to friends, trying to organise dinner over the weekend.

After catching up with messages, she reclined and tucked her knees up on the couch, she already felt relaxed after only a few minutes of down time. She needed a cigarette, though. She reached across the coffee table and groaned as she tugged the ashtray towards her. It was a dark blue metal with gold trim, with 'Bali' written in stylised font around the edge. A souvenir from a trip they took many years ago, before they purchased their first house. She slipped out a cigarette and lit it. As she inhaled her body relaxed and she collapsed back into the cushions. Her eyes wandered to the window and she stared outside. Being at home at 9am was a novel moment for her. She wasn't usually awake this early on the weekend, and during the week she was usually at work, or still asleep and running very late. Despite being a weekday she was struck by how remarkably quiet it was. Probably a side effect of living in the suburbs. The only noises were the morning calls of birds in the national park nearby and trains pulling in and out of the station up the road.

The sky was clear blue and the cool morning air came in through the window. She felt truly relaxed for the first time in a long while. She knew to make the most of this moment, there wouldn't be too many more like this for a while. Things seemed to be getting busier and busier.

She opened her tablet and pulled up a book. She'd taken to reading some classic English novels in her free time. One advantage was that they were so old that they were part of the creative commons, and could be downloaded for free. Though her patience with them was severely limited. If they weren't driving her crazy for being so grand and romantic, then they were causing her to tear her hair out for their confusing and archaic language. All in all it hadn't proved to be as relaxing and enjoyable as she had anticipated the exercise would be. She'd tried it for a few weeks now and was about ready to give up at any point.

After trying to relax amidst period romance for half an hour, she sighed, and tried to fight the urge to throw the tablet across the room. She stood up, rubbed her face and exhaled. Calming herself down from frustration at the language in the book. She decided to quickly check her work email and see if there was anything important.

She crossed the room to her laptop and opened it up. She'd received a mountain of emails, and even though she had remembered to set up an out of office reply, she knew that they would still be sitting there needing action taken on them when she returned tomorrow. She regretted checking them instantly. As she slumped on the chair and sighed, realising there would be no enjoyment from her day off now that she knew exactly how much work was sitting there. She knew she had no choice. Heading into the kitchen, she made herself a cup of tea and prepared herself to focus on the work at hand.

Her first step with managing her inbox was to go through and delete any internal emails; anything referring to standard of ethics, equality, training courses, or any other organisational emails. They were essentially junk mail. She felt they were just for show and useless to her. Despite wanting to get more involved in training courses initially, she had found that the courses were very basic and not very informative. Additionally, she'd found that the organisation was not keen to spend money on too many sessions given her low position. They were mostly for more senior staff and, whether intentionally or not, had become useful only from a networking perspective. She'd seen a few promotion opportunities form during these courses on the rare occasions she had been allowed to attend.

Once these were all deleted, she went through and sorted out any emails from members of her team which weren't work related. There were always a few funny emails or pictures sent around, but she didn't understand the sense of humour of her team. The things that she found funny or witty didn't get much of a reaction from the others. In addition, she found their humour pretty basic and crude. She'd given up on relating to them on that level a few months back. There weren't too many today so she gave them a quick look before deleting. There wasn't anything too remarkable in most of them. However, flicking through she discovered a gem.

Someone had forwarded her team an email trail that had been going around the department between an officer and a gentleman trying to report a theft. This person had seemed very intent on reporting the theft of personal belongings while he was at the gym. Someone had stolen only one item from his locker; his pants. It turned out it wasn't the first time it had happened, and eventually confessed he never locked his locker. The officer has resolved the issue by saying that they couldn't invest police resources to investigate the theft of pants if the victim had not made the items secure, as in locked away. After reading all the way through she was laughing and astounded by the ridiculous exchange. She grinned and shook her head at the image of this dejected man making his way home in a business shirt and suit jacket, business shoes and a pair of gym shorts. It wasn't the first time that she had seen a request for something so ridiculous. There was usually something like this sent around the team once a week.

She saved the email for future reading.

Skimming through the other items, a particular exchange caught her eye. It was an exchange between her team talking about the case of Marcus Docker. Despite not being on the case, all detectives were being kept in the loop. She suspected it was in case any additional detectives needed to be assigned to the case. The seniors had become increasingly frustrated at the lack of progress and they were beginning to turn on the two young detectives assigned. The message informed the team that Docker's security had not been able to make a positive identification. The bullet had not provided any leads. The investigation into close contacts and Docker's family had not revealed any probable suspects. However, the most surprising aspect to her had been the lack of video footage.

There had been a thorough sweep of the area and footage had not revealed anyone approaching on foot or any cars fleeing the scene. She couldn't understand it. There was usually some small piece of footage that at least revealed something, however, so far there had been nothing.

It frustrated her. There had to be some stones left unturned. She knew that there was some record of the person arriving and leaving the scene of the crime. However, with no motive so far there appeared to be growing pressure to write this up as a random act of violence, or a murder gone wrong. She was infuriated by the idea. It was obviously premeditated. She closed the laptop and sighed.

She couldn't get her mind off the Docker case. It was driving her crazy because she had her own cases to work on, but she hadn't been able to focus properly on them. She'd been able to resolve a few, but there were many more that she'd been given. She was going to get a warning to take action on them soon, she knew it.

She got up from the couch and paced the room, trying to walk off some of the stress. After pacing for a few moments, she decided to make a cup of tea and enjoy the rest of her day off. Although, she didn't truly believe she would be able to.

WILL

When he reached the top of the stairs, he looked out over the view. The sun was setting over the harbour and he had a great view of the Sydney skyline from the balcony of this rooftop bar. The setting was perfect; down by Circular Quay with the sun setting to the west. The red glow reflected off the water and the glass of the buildings. He'd spent the past few days having to rush through the article John had given him. He was sick of the paper and was glad it was Friday, so there was no reason or need for him to go into the office tomorrow. He felt a cool breeze coming in, a welcome relief from the warm day. Summer had only just started but the change was quite rapid, the unseasonably cold nights that had lingered in spring were long gone. It was a beautiful moment and a welcome change from the bullshit at the paper.

'Are you sure I can be here?' Iz asked, slightly apprehensive. He didn't often see her intimidated.

He laughed. 'It's fine. Chris and Rebecca are old friends of mine.'

She nodded. 'So, how come I've never met them before?'

'I'm not sure,' he frowned. 'Chris and Rebecca are usually busy with work.' *Is that the only reason?* He wondered.

'Chris started working in a bank right after uni. And Rebecca, well, you know the story about Delpont right?'

She rolled her eyes. 'Not as much as you.'

He laughed. 'Well, after uni she started out as a journalist. She actually did the initial article saying there was something wrong with their reports.'

'Really?!' Iz went wide eyed. 'Yeah, shit, I know about that. Far out. She must have been young?'

He shrugged. 'She wrote it when she was studying accounting and journalism. She had a part time job as a journalist.'

'Fuck.'

'Yeah. Anyway,' he laughed. 'Don't bring it up with her. She got famous almost overnight. There was a lot of attention on her.'

'Really?'

He nodded. 'In the end it got too much. She dropped out of journalism and stayed with accounting.'

Iz frowned. 'That's shit.'

'I know,' he sighed. 'She was good at it. Anyway, the point is, don't bring it up.' He exhaled. He didn't want to go into the details. It was a long story.

Rebecca had become famous overnight after uncovering the story about the dot com era of corruption and fraud. Her investigation had started when she was doing an article on Delpont, which had given her access to their accounting information. As soon as she looked at it her accounting degree had come in handy. It didn't make sense to her. When she had asked questions, the executives at Delpont had quickly shut it down. They told her she was wrong but she didn't buy it. She did her own research and released an article that was the beginning of Delpont coming undone.

As they walked inside Will noticed Chris and Rebecca standing by the bar. Mostly, he noticed how different Chris looked. He was still tall and good looking, but what was becoming a lifetime of working for a bank was starting to take its toll on him. Where before he had been bulky from the gym and surfing, he was now pudgy and starting to develop a belly.

Rebecca still looked much the same. Slim and slightly taller than Will. She had light hazel eyes and long dark brown hair. When they saw Will they excused themselves from the conversation and came over to say hi.

'Will! It's been ages.' Chris beamed. He swaggered a little as he walked over. He was a big man with a big physical presence, however his mannerisms were almost childlike. He wore a dark grey suit and polished black leather shoes. His shirt underneath was white with light blue vertical stripes. He had a goofy smile and walked over with his gaze down.

He smiled. 'I know, guys. It's been too long.' He said with a sigh.

'I know, hun!' Rebecca agreed warmly. As always her voice was energetic and husky. She smiled widely with her high, wide cheekbones as she wrapped her arms around him. She wore light blue jeans and knee high black suede boots. Over the top was a three quarter length black jacket tied around her waist. Rebecca always dressed casually whereas Chris would usually wear business casual.

When she stepped back she played with the black scarf around her neck. 'Hi, I'm Rebecca, by the way.' She said to Iz.

'Hey! I'm Iz.' She grinned.

'Hi, I'm Chris.' He said with shy smile.

Will grinned. *Maybe her tattoos intimidate him.* 'Yeah, sorry, I'm terrible at introducing people.' He apologised with a shrug.

'Don't worry,' Rebecca said to Iz. 'He's always been pretty forgetful.' She said with a playful grin.

'Very funny,' Will said with a sarcastic smile. 'Shit! I think the last time I saw you was at Don's twenty fifth birthday?'

'No way. I can't believe it's been that long.'

Will shook his head. 'What have you been doing with yourself? Still with the bank?'

'Meh,' he shrugged, in par with his laidback nature. 'Work is work. I'm pretty much always busy though, I've been doing a masters course part time, started at the beginning of the year, and finished up my accreditation course last year.'

'I don't know how you have time for that.'

'I don't,' Chris said light heartedly with a laugh. 'How about you? Sounds like your books are going well? Though working for a bank I might have to ideologically disagree with your argument.' He teased.

He winced at the comment about his books. *I was just lucky*. 'That's fair enough, I can understand.' Will laughed, then exhaled. 'But yeah, the book part of it has been good. I'm pretty much over the paper, though.'

'Really? It sounds like a sweet deal you have there. Walk in, walk out.' Rebecca said with a smile. Fussing with the black scarf around her neck.

'Yeah, true.' Will had forgotten the benefits of his agreement with the paper as of late, obsessing over the frustrations. 'I just don't have much control, a lot of my articles get knocked back.'

'That would be pretty frustrating.' Chris paused, hesitating. 'Hey, I'm just going to grab some air, you want to come Will?' he asked, looking down and scratching his head.

'Uh, yeah. Sure thing' Will replied with a frown.

'I won't be long.' he turned to Rebecca.

'Don't worry about it.' She grinned widely, waving away the apology.

‘There’s something we need to talk about.’ Chris said, as they pulled away from the others. ‘I, uh. I think there’s something going on.’

‘Yeah, sure,’ Will spoke gently. He could hear concern in his friends voice, something he hadn’t heard before. ‘Are you ok? Is Beck ok?’

‘Nah, it’s not like that. We’re both fine. It’s just …’ He trailed off.

‘Can you talk about it?’

‘Not here,’ he said, looking around. ‘We should probably meet up. Is that alright?’

‘It’s alright. I’m here to help.’

‘Thanks, mate.’ He smiled. ‘Sorry, I know it must be frustrating for you.’

‘Little bit.’ Will laughed. ‘I trust you, though.’

‘Look it might be nothing. I might be imagining something. I just figure it’s best you know about it.’

Will frowned. *It doesn’t sound like relationship or career problems.*

‘I should probably get back to the party.’ He laughed wearily. ‘I’ll get in touch.’

‘Sure thing. Let me know.’

His friend nodded and walked back inside. *Well, that was strange.* He frowned. If he was honest with himself, he had never really had an in depth or intimate conversation with his friend. The two had always kept it superficial. Talking about university, work and their shared friends. The two had barely talked even when going through break ups, and they had only become further estranged since uni.

He leant on the glass railing around the balcony and exhaled deeply, lost in the view. He looked out over the horizon and thought about what Chris had mentioned.

A loud laugh from a conversation by the bar shook him out of his moment of peace. He sipped his beer and looked across the harbour. He could hear the sounds of the birthday party he hadn't been aware of before; the low key music, glass rattling, inaudible indistinguishable conversation. Inside, he could see Iz rapping along to the music, and dancing energetically with a group of people. He chuckled and shook his head. The wait staff were being kept busy and looked stressed covering a fifty person function with only five staff, he doubted that a bar like this would really need to worry about keeping costs low.

'Here you are. Couldn't find you anywhere.' Don came up and leant on the rail next to Will.

'Yeah, just wanted to head outside for some fresh air.'

Don laughed. 'Fresh air with some tobacco in it?'

Will smiled and looked down at the cigarette in his hand. 'Always helps.'

'You never smoked much in uni, did you?

He shook his head. 'Just when we were drinking.'

'Yeah. True,' he laughed. 'You remember the first time I tried one?'

Will chuckled. 'Yeah, you started coughing straight away.'

'The first and last time I ever tried one.' Don smiled confidently.

'Far out, that was funny. That was back when you were seeing Sandra.'

Don smiled. 'Yeah, that *was* a while back. Those university days.'

‘They were the best days,’ Will said, reflecting. He remembered those days well. Back then he, Don, Sandra, Chris and his girlfriend Beck had been inseparable. They hung out every other day, any excuse to go out to dinner or drinks.

‘They were good. Things are pretty good now, though.’ Don said encouragingly.

‘This is true.’ He said with a smile. *It isn’t true though.* He raised his glass. ‘Cheers!’

The two fell silent and looked out over the harbour. The sun was almost fully set now. One half of the city was dark, the other still reflecting the dying sunset.

‘So, how are your articles going?’ Don asked.

‘Well, for the most part. Working on a bit of a joke one at the moment.’

‘Oh yeah? What is it about?’

‘Something my editor has been pushing me for. Trying to talk about the effects of the ‘wealth tax’ and how it is going to harm the economy.’

‘Sounds interesting.’

Will turned, his face puzzled. ‘How so?’

‘Well, it’s true. Any increase in taxation on income always leads to decreased demand. Given how tentative things are at the moment it makes no sense. I mean, consumption is already at an all time low.’

Will exhaled, irritated. Sometimes he forgot that Don was on the other side. He was not the student he had gone to university with. He was now a trader working *for* the banks. This was not his best friend.

‘It’s not like that, though. Prior to the eighties the wealthiest percent were always taxed. Then Reagan came in and reduced taxes on the wealthiest incomes, primarily through reduction of property tax and tax breaks for investment.’

‘So it’s a return to that?’

‘Essentially, yeah.’

Don smirked and scoffed. ‘Yeah, so what happened after Reagan introduced those changes?’

Will frowned. He could sense the bait. ‘Yeah I know. Widespread growth. The most rapid growth of all time. But that’s a different story. It was in combination with widespread deregulation, new forms of technology and investment. It would be hard to say it was because of any one factor.’

‘Valid point.’

‘Besides, it was a bubble. At the same time as that growth, inequality skyrocketed. Wages went up, but only with gradual growth. Annual income by the top percentage skyrocketed far quicker. Inequality has gotten so much worse since then. It still is a massive issue.’

Don shook his head, frowning.

‘Prior to the 1980s, average CEO pay was less than 50 times that of the average worker. Now, it ranges between 200 and 300 times that of the average worker’ Will said, slowly. He smiled and thought of his own bait. ‘So, what else happened since the eighties? What else occurred through the eighties, nineties, two thousands? Maybe something in 2008?’

Don frowned and shook his head. He sipped at his drink quietly. ‘Those were a few bad apples. Everyone always talks about them.’

‘And yet they keep happening?’ He muttered.

Don turned. Will looked him in the eyes. He saw something he hadn't seen before. He saw resentment in his old friend. Then Don sighed and the moment was gone. He smiled. 'Anyway, good luck on the article. I'm going to head inside and catch up with a few people. Are you keen to come?'

Will heard the friendly gesture, but at that moment the words sounded cold from his friend. 'I'll stay out here a little longer. I'll see you in a bit.'

'Sounds good. I'll see you inside, then.' Don said with a smile. He turned and left.

Will watched his friend walk away. He turned and squinted as he watched the last of the sunlight fade. *What just happened?* He asked himself. They'd never had a disagreement like that before, they'd always had the same opinions.

Iz ran past Don as she came outside. She looked excited.

'What's up, pumpkin?' He teased her with a smile.

'Hey, I'm really, really sorry!' She said, fumbling through her bag and putting her scarf on. 'But I have to go!'

'What?' He frowned.

'Yeah, I'm really sorry, babe! I just got a job though!' She grinned and clapped her hands.

'Oh, serious?' He smiled.

'Yeah! With the paper. They need someone to get photos for an article, but I need to leave like, right now pretty much!' She laughed energetically.

He shook his head with a grin. 'You're a bundle of energy, sometimes.'

'Shut up!' She slapped his arm playfully. 'I'm really sorry, though.'

‘It’s fine,’ he insisted. ‘I understand. Now get out of here!’ He waved her away teasingly.

‘Aye aye, captain.’ She mock saluted him, then turned and half walked and half ran out of the bar.

He laughed and shook his head. As he turned to walk inside, he was greeted by a warm smile.

‘Will.’

‘Amber? Hey, how are you?’

Her smile was warm and her eyes welcoming. She opened her arms and hugged him. ‘Good, sweetheart. How are you?’

‘Going well.’ He warmed at the thought of her calling him ‘sweetheart’. She wore a sleeveless white top and blue jeans with light heels, her thin arms showing and her blonde curls falling to the right side of her face. Her big blue eyes looked into his, a crystal blue. They were blue as the water in the travel advertisements for island holidays, as the perfect waters of the Maldives he would never see.

She ran her hands through her hair after it had been messed from their embrace. ‘How is the writing going?’

He laughed. ‘Don’t ask.’ Thinking about the conversation he just had.

‘That bad huh?’ She said with a smile.

‘Pretty much.’

‘Why don’t you write more things like that article a few years back, the one about redistribution of income? ‘Wealth is a crime’?’

He looked at her genuinely surprised. ‘You know about that article?’

She smiled. 'I read it when it came out. It was quite interesting, and I tend to agree with it.'

He was surprised for two reasons. Firstly, that she had even read it, as it wasn't that well known. Secondly, he assumed she would be opposed to it.

'I'm surprised you agree with me, I would have thought you would be against it as an idea?'

'Well, I'm not saying it is a crime but I do agree with the general idea of relative wealth.' She narrowed her gaze.

'Yeah, well we live in a world of finite resources. So naturally, if someone's nominal wealth rises and even if it stays the same for everyone else, then the relative wealth of everyone else will still go down. Their purchasing power is lower.'

'Yeah, that part makes sense. Why you consider it a crime though is where you lost me.' She said with a laugh.

'Yeah,' he said, sighing slowly. 'It was a suggestion made by an editor to draw in more readers. Personally, I would have preferred to use the term 'immoral'. I think it's 'immoral' to have excess wealth and not give back to society. I did explain that side of it in the article.'

'But you still left in the part saying it should be considered a crime?' she asked with a raised eyebrow.

'Yeah,' he exhaled. 'I couldn't decide.'

'From what you're saying, it sounds like you should have said 'wealth is a responsibility, not a right'?' She teased with a smile.

He grinned. 'Where were you when I needed someone to edit?'

'Very funny, but back to what I was saying, if you take away incentives like income then what is stopping everyone from working retail jobs outside of school? They would be earning the same as people who finished a university degree?' She shook her head. 'Wouldn't everyone just work in an ice cream shop, then?'

'Speaking from experience?' He teased.

'You know what I mean.'

He shook his head. 'That's taking it to the extreme, though. I never advocated everyone being paid the same, incentives are important. I just wanted to argue it should be more equal and less disparity.'

'Even then, how do you ensure that people continue to work the jobs that are difficult and need to be done? Doctors, nurses, teachers, scientific researchers?' She asked with a straight face. He was no longer intimidated by just her looks.

'Yeah, but I mean, are they paid so well at the moment?' He asked sarcastically. 'You know as well as I do the richest people are those working in accounting firms, in financial markets, as lawyers. Doctors and teachers and scientists are continually paid less and less and put on the backburner. They aren't paid nearly what they deserve. So are you suggesting that the most important people to society are the traders and lawyers?' He asked bitterly.

He realised he had been too harsh as soon as he said it. He winced when he remembered her father was formerly CEO of one of the largest trading companies. It wasn't a great way to make friends.

He looked her in the eyes and saw the sutble hint of a glare. It wasn't something he expected to see. The lapse was momentary. She smiled quickly and laughed, the moment was gone. 'Touchy on this topic, are you?'

He laughed. 'I prefer to use the word 'passionate'. Anyway, I haven't done writing like that for a while. Nothing I've really been too 'passionate' about I guess.' He joked. 'Anyway, how has everything been for you lately?'

‘A little busy. A lot of things on. I’ve been working on a big renovation lately.’ She stated with a smile. The way she said it felt rehearsed to him. She looked out over the horizon.

‘I remember you saying. How is it going, anyway?’

‘Of course.’ She smiled and shook her head. ‘Sorry. It’s a great project. It’s a 1930s home. Quite a large place, originally constructed as a mansion. The aim is to extend it and continue in the original style. Trying to convert it from 1930s extravagance to 1960s simplicity.’

‘Like the case study houses.’

She smiled and looked him in the eyes. ‘Exactly like the case study houses. How do you know about architecture?’

‘I’ve always been interested. I used to want to be one.’

‘Really?’ She smiled, then frowned. ‘That’s so surprising.’

‘Thanks.’ He teased.

‘How come you aren’t doing something creative, then?’ She crossed her arms.

He winced, a little offended. ‘Journalism isn’t traditionally an art form. But it requires imagination, interpretation. You need to be able to find out information from people and sources. And then you need to take all those influences and put it into something well written. How then does it differ from writing a screenplay or a novel?’

Amber smirked. ‘Point well made, Mr Martec,’ she leaned closer and spoke quietly. ‘I like you when you’re angry.’

He laughed. ‘I’m not angry. I’m just telling you the truth.’ He looked her over while she was drinking her white wine. Her lithe, svelte figure was so delicate. Maybe it was the alcohol talking but he just wanted to take her, to get lost in all her flowing golden locks and that big smile.

'Either way. You are right.' Her warmth suddenly cooled as she continued. 'Anyway, I have to be up early tomorrow for work.'

'On a Saturday?'

'Unfortunately.'

He sipped his drink and sighed. 'That is unfortunate.'

'It was great to see you again.' She said as she wrapped her arms around him.

'Always a pleasure.' He gave her a kiss on the cheek as they embraced. There was a tingle from the feeling of her body against his. Her hair smelt of subtle perfume, the scent reminded him of lemon and the smell of summer. Her skin was warm and he could feel it through her sleeveless top. It was a brief moment and far too fleeting.

And then she was gone. She turned and smiled as she waved goodbye. Then she disappeared inside and out the door.

And suddenly everything was normal again. He was brought back down to earth, left to wonder who she really was, and how she had such an effect on him.

THE MAN IN THE DARKNESS

As the sun was setting, he made his move. Hanging low and keeping to the walls, he slipped over the wall and stuck to the bushes around the large house. On any normal street this would have been an entire block, but in this suburb it was only considered big enough for one house. He didn't have time to move slowly for this target, he had a very narrow window of opportunity.

The family had just driven off and he was home alone. His target hadn't activated the security system. He had found these people only did so when they were all out or when they went to bed for the night.

He slipped over the balcony railing, pulled himself up to the second level and crouched low on the balcony. He checked his leather gloves for any cuts or damage from the climb. Adjusting his shoulder bag, which was out of place after his ascent, he stopped just outside one of the bedrooms. He could see his target in the study two rooms away. One of the rooms had been left open. He reached through and opened the door silently.

He had to move quickly. He kept low to the ground, getting out of the room, down the hall and into the study. Taylor Sheeran turned suddenly and made a move to get up, completely shocked with the sudden intrusion. Before he was up, the man had raised his arm and swung it down, and the knife had been buried into Sheeran's chest. The movement was quick and the blade was sharp, it only took one quick motion. The blow pierced the heart. Taylor coughed blood and fell back. He was dead before he hit the ground.

It was too easy.

He needed to change the rules of the game. Without attention, this mission of his was pointless. This wasn't about death; people needed to change. He needed to communicate with the people chasing him.

The dramatic way to send this message would obviously be to write it in blood, scrawled on the wall. He wasn't one much for clichés himself, though it did have advantages in terms of how effective it would be. There was certainly no shortage of blood on hand at the moment. But he was on a tight time limit. He reached into his shoulder pack and took out a can of red spray paint. It had been paid for in cash, from a small store far away with no cameras. It would be a dead end.

He decided on the wall next to the door. That way people would see the body first, and would only see the message when they turned around. It had a certain dramatic tension to it. He wrote the message.

Once he was satisfied with his work, he left the scene and checked there were no footprints left in the blood pool.

He made his way out of the house quickly and out into the night. He still had a few minutes before Taylor's wife returned from dropping their kids off for a sleepover.

AOKI

Her eyes instantly opened at the sound, she bolted upright and looked around. She realised the sound which had woken her was her phone and relaxed a little, but she was instantly awake.

'Aoki speaking.'

'Hey, it's Morgan, did you get the call already?' He spoke even quicker than usual.

Her body was up, but she realised her mind was still in a dreamlike state. 'Call? No. Yours only. Why?'

'There's been a crazy murder around Mosman. Everyone's moved pretty quickly, called in our department.'

'Wait why? It's not our area.' she frowned. It was a ritzy suburb home to bankers and lawyers.

'Yeah. But it's going to be pretty high profile. No one else wanted it, and we drew the straw. Apparently we have less cases.' He said with a hint of sarcasm.

'You and me?'

'It's 'You and I', but yes.'

'Alright, I'll get ready and head over.'

'I'm on my way now, I'll see you soon,' he paused and added. 'And by the way, don't eat before you get here, it's pretty fucked up.'

AOKI

The block was a chaotic clusterfuck. Normally a quiet street in a wealthy and secluded suburb, it was 2am and there were film crew vans everywhere. Choppers were passing overhead, more likely to be media than police. There were floodlights everywhere. Local residents were all standing at their doorsteps, watching the insanity. They watched in the same way the darker side of human nature compels one to slow down when driving past a car crash. Amongst the throng, the police accounted for the minority. There were six patrol cars at the scene, but the officers were mainly on crowd control.

She saw Morgan wave to her from near the gates. The mansion took up the entire block, and was barred on all sides by an eight foot stone wall. The iron gate had been deliberately rusted in order to look authentic and the hinges creaked as they ducked through. There was a cool breeze blowing over; she couldn't tell if it were due to the night air or the helicopters screaming low overhead.

'Did you find the place alright?' Morgan greeted her with a grin. It was forced, and betrayed how nervous he was.

'The one advantage of getting a call at 1:30am is not having to fight traffic. I made good time.'

'Yeah, I can imagine. I'm not too far so it honestly only took me ten minutes to get here.' Morgan said with a smile. Sometimes she forgot that he lived around this area. He had grown up on the Lower North Shore and had gone to private schools, so she always teased him for being a rich kid. She wondered again why he had joined the police.

'I hate you.' She groaned, thinking of her long drive over.

He laughed and shook his head. It seemed to relax him.

They walked past the main gate where a junior officer was standing. She had a few reporters hassling her for details.

'No comment, guys. Please get back.' She nodded to the two detectives as she saw them approach.

'Any problems Sasha?' Morgan asked gently.

Aoki smirked. The officer was young and pretty. Morgan would flirt with any attractive girl he met.

'Plenty of them Morgan. One of which is you.' She teased back. Morgan laughed.

'This is Detective Sun.' He said, taking a break from flirting.

'I'm Sasha.' She smiled at Aoki before waving her through.

'Good to meet you. Don't let them get to you.' Aoki said with a smile. The officer nodded as they walked past.

Through the gates they walked up a pebble driveway, the centrepiece of which was a roundabout with a low cut box hedge. The outside of the large mansion was well lit and the mansion itself was well designed and well kept. It was hard to see much of the upper part of the house, the lights around the driveway were bright and felt blinding. Walking along, she felt the pebbles crunch under her shoes, but couldn't hear the sound because of the rabble in the street.

'Things are crazy here. It's out of control.' He said quickly. He took a deep breath, and seemed to relax as he moved away from the noise.

'How the fuck did the media manage to get here before me?'

'Dunno. They got here around the same time I did.'

They walked inside and away from the crowd and bright lights. Once they entered the door, they were immediately greeted with a reprieve from the insanity at the gate. Although once inside, Aoki realised she would prefer the intensity of the crowd.

Every room in the house was large and spacious, but felt cold and empty. The only lights that hadn't been left off were those in the study and hallway upstairs. It had been furnished as best as possible, but the house was too extravagant and the decorating too elaborate. The effect polarised just how impersonal the mansion was.

'This place creeps me the fuck out.' Morgan commented under his breath, mirroring her own thoughts.

'It's too big,' she nodded. She often found that the richest people lacked the most in their lives. Without hardships, they lost the fight that she felt defined so much of human nature. 'I'd prefer my apartment any day.'

'The wife says she got home just around eight. Went upstairs and found him in the study'

'Eight?!' She asked with a raised voice, frowning. 'What the fuck? When did she call it through?'

He let out a small chuckle and shook his head. 'Not until after midnight.' He said in a hushed voice.

Her eyes widened.

He squinted and spoke even quieter. 'She was in shock. Couldn't process it. Go easy on her. She wasn't talking for a long time.'

'Alright. I'll keep it in mind.'

'And also,' he sighed and stopped her to have a quiet word. 'I hate being the one to say this to you, but be really delicate about this.'

'With her?'

‘Yeah. She’s uh …’ His voice trailed off as if he didn’t quite know how to put it.

She knew where he was going. ‘Well connected?’

He nodded with a frown. ‘Pretty much. About a minute after I got the first call from dispatch, I got a second call from Gary Tackett.’

She groaned. Gary was a notorious micromanager. He was one of the seniors in the state police, responsible for budgeting and media and all that other senior bullshit. However, he took a personal interest in getting involved in minute details. In a situation like this, it was quite understandable for him to talk to detectives directly. It wasn’t out of the best interests of the police force; it was because he wanted to protect himself from any fallout. She had met him a few times and he had always given her the creeps. He was short and skinny, in his late forties and always wore suits so poorly cut it seemed they were wearing him. None of this was helped by the fact he had decided to grow a moustache. She shuddered at the thought of the creep.

Regardless, if he were paying attention to this case she would be under particular scrutiny. When they reached the door, he turned and looked at her before heading inside. Aoki thought of how careful she would have to be on this case.

Immediately she saw the body, still unmoved from where it had fallen. He was slumped with his face on the ground but still kneeling so the man must have fallen to his knees after being struck, and then fallen forward. There was something so undignified about the position that made her uncomfortable.

There was a pool of blood from the wound, which had spread across the floor now. With the exception of the blood pool and the body, there were no signs a crime had been committed. There were no scuffmarks on the floor, no blood trail, no furniture overturned or items broken. There was no sign of a break in to the house and there were no signs of a struggle in this room. It was clean. She took a deep breath and frowned, taken aback.

'Weird, isn't it?'

'I know what you mean.' He replied.

'It's just …' She stumbled. 'There's no mess.'

'No entry signs, window on the balcony and the open door in the other room implied he came through there. No signs of a fight. It's almost professional.' He said slowly. For once it seemed he didn't know what to do. There was something about the clinical and clean crime scene that disturbed her as well.

'Or personal.' Aoki said with a frown. 'Have you spoken to the wife yet?'

He shook his head. 'Tried to. She hasn't said much, she mumbled a bit.'

She looked at the cupboard to her side. She noticed now how clean the house was. No clutter, very minimalistic. No paper waste or scattered books, magazines, dvds, cds; any of the usual clutter that accompanies real life. 'It could be professional but the lack of a fight might imply he knew the attacker?'

He nodded, understanding the implication. 'Possible, yeah. I don't think so, though. She is really in genuine shock. Her reactions all seem genuine. She's shaken up. If she were in shock then it is unlikely she planned it.'

'That's true. There'd be some kind of sign of a struggle.'

He smiled and looked her in the eyes. There was a bit of wickedness to it.

'What is it?'

'Well, it conflicts with the other evidence, suggesting ulterior motives.' He said confidently. He no longer seemed so subdued.

She furrowed her brow, confused.

He was smiling smugly. 'Isn't it interesting how when people first enter a room they look directly ahead? When walking they only watch where they are going?' He said, the question asked with feigned sincerity.

She looked around the room, to her sides. She turned to look behind her and saw it immediately.

A message was scrawled on the wall in crude red spray paint. It read; 'Wealth is a crime'.

As soon as she saw it, she felt fear in the pit of her stomach. A wave of panic rose over her, realising she was in a completely different crime scene to the one she thought. She could tell it had been done quickly and the writing was messy. She realised her heart was beating fast.

'Fuck. That scared the shit out of me.' She said nervously.

'Me too.' Morgan replied with a grin.

'You are such a dick for doing that.' She said as she slapped his arm.

He dodged with a smug grin.

She breathed a deep sigh of relief and laughed. It took away from the tension.

'Sorry, I couldn't resist.'

'I see what you mean. This is seriously fucked up.' She said, shaking her head.

'Surely implies something about motive.'

She paused. Looking it and the scene over again. 'Do you think it could be a misdirect?'

‘As in, to draw away from something else?’

‘Yeah. Maybe something personal, maybe something to do with his business?’

‘Maybe.’ He said slowly, scratching his stubble. He crossed his arms, considering it, narrowing his gaze and inspected the writing again.

‘What information have we got so far?’

He shrugged. ‘Not much. Just what we could get off his driving record, two minor infringements for parking and speeding but tickets were paid promptly. No criminal record.’

‘Any investigations on him before? Any instances where he was a person of interest?’

He shook his head. ‘Nothing’s come up yet.’

Aoki thought everything over. She wished she hadn’t taken that call. She didn’t want to work something that would have so much attention paid to it. She already felt anxious about it. Sydney wasn’t a city that saw many shootings. When it happened it was usually in the western suburbs. It made front page news that day and was then forgotten a few days later. In a suburb like this, though, a shooting had only happened one time around ten years ago. It had made both front page and national news, and had gone on for ages. When she considered that it was some kind of ideological statement against wealth, it seemed too sensationalist to her and too much to deal with.

‘Can you imagine what would happen if the whole story were released?’

Morgan nodded. His otherwise confident nature seemed somewhat subdued. *He must be as anxious about this as I am*, she thought.

From outside they heard a commotion as two officers burst through the doors. The one who walked first seemed to be in charge. He was average height and stocky. His hair was short with dark blonde hair, and he had dark green eyes. There was a scowl on his face and he was shaking his head. The other officer stood timidly behind him, looking down and scratching his head.

'Hey, you're the detectives they got?' The older man asked them with a scowl. He couldn't have been over thirty but even his questions seemed like orders.

Morgan nodded. 'Yeah, what's up?' He asked casually.

'I'm Luke Wade.' The older Constable put in, then gestured behind him. 'This is Probationary Constable Ryan Hislop.'

'Tell them what you told me' He barked at Ryan.

Ryan sighed. 'I found someone on the crime scene.'

'What?' Morgan frowned. 'Now?'

'Five minutes ago.' Luke stated.

'I couldn't see them too well,' Ryan continued. 'They were taking photos from the balcony. Of the crime scene. They must have climbed the fence.'

Aoki felt her stomach tighten. *Not the media already.*

'Anyway, I chased after them but they got back over the fence. I mean,' he exhaled, looking at the floor. 'This kid was quick.'

'Kid?' Aoki asked, blank faced.

'Yep' Luke shook his head. 'Some kid with a big camera snuck over the fence.'

Morgan exhaled and shook his head. 'Fuck,' he swore under his breath.

‘Do we know if they actually got any photos?’ Aoki asked quietly.

Luke shrugged. ‘Probably. We can’t be sure. They didn’t have much time.’

‘You see where they went?’ Morgan asked.

‘Yep.’ Luke nodded. ‘Walk with me, I’ll show you.’ He spoke firmly.

Morgan grinned at Aoki, ‘Bossy, huh?’ He whispered.

She tried to hide a grin.

‘Alright, I’ll head with these guys and check it out. You alright to have a look around here?’ Morgan asked her.

She nodded.

When the three of them walked out of the room, she exhaled deeply. Glad to have some privacy to think. She rubbed her face and started to look around the room with greater attention on the details.

Other than the dead body, the pool of blood and the open window, the crime scene revealed precious little information. She had been looking around for half an hour and hadn’t found much. So far, there was nothing but a few partial footprints, which might provide some sort of a lead, though there was nothing in the way of fingerprints. Forensics had found nothing on any of the windows, railings around the balcony, or anywhere in the office. They had done a pretty solid sweep and they’d not found any hair fibres, nothing. Everything suggested it was a professional job. There was nothing personal about any of this crime scene; no struggle, no resistance, no mess. She highly doubted the wife had done it.

The woman was a wreck. She was sitting out in the corridor against the wall, her knees tucked under her elbows. Her eyes were still wide and her hand appeared to be shaking, but it was difficult to tell as the woman was rocking back and forth slightly, staring straight ahead at the wall. Altogether, she was emotionally unstable. A junior officer had been keeping an eye on her. As Aoki approached, he nodded and walked away, giving some space to talk with her.

Looking at her outside of the context of the current circumstances, Aoki could see the typical tells for that type from this area. The woman was slim and slightly taller than average. Her clothes fit her perfectly. Whoever she had been when she was younger, she had accepted and embraced her role as a yuppy mum. The tightness of her body told Aoki that she kept to a strict fitness routine every day, most likely yoga or going for a jog. She was still wearing the clothes she had found her husband in; designer jeans, which were stylistically faded, shin high black leather boots with heels, a light white cotton top and a tight black leather jacket. Thinning blonde hair, thin frame face and taught cheeks, her lips slightly too large and her forehead that was subtly stretched tight, she'd obviously had work done, especially around her eyes.

It was pretty common for women in this area to get plastic surgery. Aoki had never understood the appeal herself. It always struck her as a vain attempt to cling onto fading beauty, a futile act of insecurity against something truly inevitable. It was impossible to do. She preferred the look of those who accepted the ageing process and handled it with a smile and a sense of grace. She realised though she was still young and had good skin. In ten years time, she might feel differently.

The woman had spoken to police frantically when they had first arrived on the scene. She had appeared in a condition of mania, excited and agitated, stressed and needing to tell them everything. Her speech had been erratic, telling them how she had been out dropping her kids at their friends. She told them the exact items she had purchased at the supermarket, going so far as to show her grocery list to the officers on scene. She eventually told them how she had come into her home and searched for her husband. However, the officers said they noticed a sudden change once they were set up in the study. She had frozen and slumped down in the hall once the equipment had been set up. They said they had no clue what caused it, none of them had said anything. However, Aoki thought she could understand what was going on.

She approached the woman and knelt down next to her. 'Mrs Sheeran? Hi, I'm Aoki.' She said gently. It wasn't the first time her soft-spoken nature helped; a gentler touch was often needed in moments like these.

The woman stared ahead, seeming not to notice the fact that Aoki was talking to her. Her big brown eyes looked glazed over. The woman was staring at the blank white wall with unblinking intensity.

'I'm with the detectives division. I know you must be going through a lot right now and I'm sorry but I need to ask you a few more questions.'

Still no response, she's definitely in shock.

'I know you spoke to the other officers when they arrived, is there any way you could talk to me too?'

The woman blinked and shuddered slightly, cradling her knees a little tighter, but her focus remained unbroken. Aoki realised she would have to try a different tact.

She gently put her hand on the woman's arm. Her gaze suddenly flicked to Aoki and she could see into her eyes. She could see the panic. 'I know why you aren't talking.'

The big brown eyes softened slightly in their intensity.

'When they first got here it was different, they came to your house and you were in control. You told them what happened, you showed them through.'

The woman hesitated but nodded slightly with a sad smile.

'But once you saw them set up in your husband's study, once the equipment and the lights and the forensic techs were going through there, it became a crime scene. It was a crime scene in your house. That was the moment it all sunk in'

The woman nodded but suddenly regressed, she stared back at the wall and started to shake slightly.

'Hey. Hey, it's ok. It's going to be ok yeah?' Aoki said warmly, reassuringly rubbing the woman's back.

The lack of a response suggested the woman disagreed.

'We're going to catch this guy. We will get him. But we need your help. Can you help us? Do you want to find the man who did this?'

All she needed was something small, a little nod, a smile, anything. She could take that and work with it, get the woman to open up. But she would have no luck it seemed, the woman had completely frozen up now. Helping her to understand why she had frozen up hadn't seemed to help at all. It had been a futile effort. Maybe this is why Aoki had never succeeded as a psychologist. She stayed with the woman for a few more minutes before deciding it was hopeless.

'Alright, I'm going to take a look around, but if you want to talk then just let me know, yeah? I'll be right around here.' She got up slowly and sighed.

She felt terrible for the woman but right now she was no help to anyone. If she were truthful, Aoki felt she was being selfish having this reaction. Mrs Sheeran was a wife but she was also a mother, her kids hadn't been told yet and they'd need know to soon. This woman was now all these kids had. As much of a tragedy as it was for this woman, it wasn't just about her. She needed to rise to the occasion and be there for her kids. She could sense the type now; someone who had always been in control of things, but only because of good fortune, either she had inherited wealth, married into it or possibly both. This was most likely someone who had never been outside her comfort zone. When faced with an actually challenging situation, they were not equipped to handle it.

Looking around the actual desk in the study, she realised for the first time how well decorated it was. It struck her as odd since the rest of the house was well designed with complementing colours, organised and efficient. The majority of the house was simple and subdued. The study, however, was well designed in a more ostentatious manner; louder colours like a lot of red, complemented with balancing black elements. The choice of decorations such as lighting, decorations, vases and so on was definitely daring yet it seemed to work. It struck her as odd because it was most likely the husband had done it himself. The study seemed like his zone. The lock on the door suggested it was a private and personal space, even from his wife.

She needed to know more about him. She wondered whether the attack was actually because of some business gone bad, and had been dressed up to look like the act of a mad activist. The alternative was that it was truly the result of a social vigilante on some sick personal vendetta. She didn't know which made her more worried. She looked at the closed laptop by his desk, opening it up and turning it on. Once it got to the account login screen she realised his personal account was locked. Password required. Instantly defeated, she realised it would take the technicians some time to get access to his computer, which could prove difficult to justify.

She frowned, noticing the objects on the desk and realising something else. On his desk was a Mac desktop, however, the laptop was a PC. It was unlikely that someone would have the two opposing systems for personal use. This man travelled a lot for work, with a position that was well-paid and most likely included bonuses. Bonuses such as a laptop. She continued with this train of thought. Assuming this was a company computer, most companies required their workers to change passwords every other month because of sensitive information, some even required it to be done every month. In times like these, most people ran out of passwords they could remember automatically. Aoki herself had a different password for her computer, her facebook, her work computer, her email, her online banking, and so on and so forth. However, changing passwords all the time could be difficult to remember, and most people were worried about getting locked out of their accounts.

She rummaged through the desk drawer, looking behind the screen of the desktop. Nothing. Of course, he travelled a lot, he wouldn't leave it here. She opened the laptop bag and rummaged through the pockets, she found odds and ends, cards, pens, napkins, sanitary towels. She pulled the cards out and flicker through them. One of them was Taylor's business card. She turned it over and found 'Portugal91' written on the back. She typed it in to the laptop and then watched the system load up. She smiled, feeling proud of herself. It was all available to her; emails, notes, documents, financials. Searching through the emails she smirked, realising the irony; what one man had done to increase security had inadvertently made it incredibly easy for her to access his information. Corporate security made insecure due to the element of human error.

Everything she looked through seemed pretty standard. There was nothing incriminating. Aoki glanced over her shoulder nervously, and kept an ear out for anyone coming. She couldn't afford to get caught looking through these files without a warrant. Nothing she found could be used in court, but she needed information to understand where to look. The emails were pretty boring, mostly talking about budgets. This man seemed to be a penny pincher. In most of his sent emails he would tell someone that they needed to cut the budget to a lower target, and then a month later would set an even lower target. The man screened his emails to folders based on contacts. There were thousands of unopened emails. People complaining that their teams were falling apart because of under funding. In one of his teams a university graduate had committed suicide because of being overworked and under paid; Taylor hadn't even read the email. Aoki was starting to be glad the man was dead. He seemed like a bastard. The more she looked, the more she felt he deserved his fate on the floor.

She looked through the trash folder, which had been emptied recently. All of the other folders had nothing incriminating or revealing. It was looking like it was a dead end. She decided to try the drafts folder in a last ditch attempt. There were a few unfinished emails discussing drafts and some that were not addressed to anyone. There was a confusing email that was not addressed to anyone and read only; 'What happened to the blue drive?' . The subject line was a question mark and an exclamation mark. She frowned and made a note of it, then kept looking. Next she decided to look through his sent items.

She raised an eyebrow when she opened an innocent enough email. Or at least, she thought so. It was a graphic description and explicit exchange between Taylor and another man. She shook her head as she made a note. Not that she disagreed with the lifestyle; a lot of her friends lived it. But what she couldn't understand was that the man would keep it a secret. She thought of his wife and frowned, it was likely she didn't even know.

WILL

He woke relatively early for a weekend. By 9am he was out of bed and by 10am he was showered and dressed. So, his mind was awake when his phone rang.

'Will speaking.'

He heard the sound of a dry raspy voice, a man clearing his throat. 'Hello, Will. It's John here. I need you to come into the office.'

Will rolled his eyes. 'What for John? It's my day off.'

'I know that,' he could hear the irritation in his voice, 'I can't talk about it over the phone but there's been a murder. I need you to draft up an article on it.'

'I don't do front page, though.'

'It's your area. I just need a short section on the background of the victim.'

'Why? Who was he?'

John paused. 'Haven't you seen it on the tele? It's all over the shop. The murder on the north shore last night, wealthy businessman.'

Will frowned. 'Far out. No, I hadn't heard about it. Alright, I'll head in for a bit.'

'Rightio. Cheers. Bye.' John hung up quickly. He was as sparing with his conversation as he was with his money.

Will instantly flipped open his laptop and looked up the story. There were already some major articles about the death. They were all over the front pages of all the major Australian news websites. Given the exposure, he figured it must have come in before 2am or so last night otherwise it wouldn't have made it to the front page articles of so many. He assumed there would be a corresponding length written in the print news today. Someone at his paper must have dropped the ball or they too would already have something in the paper.

What he read was pretty crazy. He hadn't heard of Taylor Sheeran before, but apparently the guy worked in financials. The reporter had suggested it was a robbery gone wrong. Police weren't releasing much information, but that hadn't stopped the reporter from focusing on all the drama at the crime scene. Most articles were poorly written. The introduction 'It was like something out of a movie' had been used in the majority of the articles.

'Lazy writing.' Will muttered, shaking his head.

After reading for a few minutes and getting precious little information about what had actually happened or who the guy was, he decided to head in.

The drive over was pretty quick. There wasn't much traffic around this side of town on weekends. There was precious little to do around these suburbs, except for the few businesses that worked through the weekends. It was a warm day, and he knew that the roads going to north would be congested from all the beach traffic. He reflected on how fortunate he was to not be a part of that, albeit somewhat sarcastically; he faced an easy drive to go into work, they were facing a traffic jam but would end up at the beach.

He parked near work without difficulty. Before heading in, he decided to grab something to get his mind into work mode. Unfortunately, this part of town was all but closed on weekends. It was a less populated business hub; packed during the week with workers, but dead quiet on weekends as none of those workers lived near the area. His favourite café at the base of the building was closed. Looking across the street, however, he saw that there was still a small corner café open. He walked over and into the familiar café sounds. Coffee grinding, radio barely audible in the background, baristas exchanging orders. No matter where they were or what time it was, for some reason he always found cafes relaxing. Though, that could have just been because of the smell of ground coffee beans.

Having ordered a small cappuccino, he sat down and read the arts section of the paper, looking for a movie to watch or a new gallery exhibition to check out. There wasn't much on at this time of year.

'Small cap, two sugars.' The barista called out his order. He got up and collected the coffee, saying thanks as he left the café. He left a few silver coins as a tip.

When he got into the office, he saw it was still a busy day for some people. A few sports writers were busy doing a big piece on some transfer. There seemed to be one of these every week. He didn't have much in the way of respect for the sports team; their writing was terrible. Furthermore, they seemed to write the same article every week. It always seemed to be over some bad call a referee had made that had cost a team the game and they would always use the term 'heartbreak' in the title with a picture of some player looking down with his head in his hands. To be fair, there was only so much one could do with that source material. Sport was an excellent topic for people who were otherwise unskilled at making engaging conversation.

He looked around at the desks and saw Leech had already called several temps in.

'Will. Good to see you finally turned up.' Leech said in his tired pompous voice.

'What are the temps doing here?'

'They got here before you. I'll have to pay them for a minimum of four hours for their casual shift. So, there's no need for you to work.'

'What?'

‘You were taking too long, Will, I needed to get this written as soon as possible.’ Leech said dismissively. ‘And besides, this isn’t your area.’

Will scoffed. ‘What about the economic piece you needed? The background?’

‘Doesn’t appear to be much need for it. We did a bit of background search and there isn’t much to him. He made a good living, some excellent money, but his actual career was quite quiet.’

Will nodded, his teeth clenched. Leech had thrown a bunch of junior writers in the deep end, and wanted to keep his budget tight so wouldn’t ask for Will to help. ‘Well, I’ll go home then.’

‘Alright. Thanks for coming in, anyway.’ He said in a disinterested voice. Even when saying thanks, Leech still sounded ungrateful.

‘What angle are you going to run, anyway?’

Leech shrugged. ‘There isn’t too much information. The only things we can talk about are the reaction from people in the suburb, how this sort of thing never happens there, and then look at what the police should have done to avoid it, or how they can prevent it from happening again.’

Will shook his head. ‘How can we slam the police on this if we don’t know what the back story is?’

Leech shrugged and said nothing. Will knew the answer to his question before he asked it, though. The billionaire owner of this media company had friends in the opposition political party, and wanted them to get re-elected. If this were to occur, they would introduce taxation cuts on the wealthy and reduce protections of workers. It was the wet dream of a rich man; more money in and fewer rights for workers. He had even gone so far as to make a declaration to an office of staff that they were to make personal attacks on the current prime minister as often as possible, as he wanted the opposition to get elected.

'Who is handling it?'

'Sally is writing the article and Seth is helping with research.'

Will nodded. Sally was a good writer, young but passionate. She did have a tendency to be too political, which he thought was a liability. Seth was a bit of a mess, though. Awkward and untidy, his clothes were always shabby and he seemed to forget to shave most days. He stuck out like a sore thumb most of the time, and was often late. He didn't know the topic too well, either. It was a bad situation; these two kids shouldn't have to deal with it. It was a delicate article and, while Sally would be able to write it, she wouldn't get the research she needed from Seth.

'Alright, I'll leave them to it then.' Will turned, shaking his head. 'Fuck,' he swore under his breath. He could have really used that article. He needed grocery money.

Leech turned away, no longer paying attention.

Will sighed and shook his head, tired of having to deal with Leech.

He sipped at his coffee as he walked back to his car, thinking about the death of Sheeran. He could have used the money, but was quietly glad he didn't need to write the article. *The media always glorifies the dead, whether they deserved it or not.* He frowned, *I would have been expected to do the same.*

By the time he reached his car the coffee was well and truly cold. He pulled open the door of his car and ducked inside, tucking the cup into the car door. Something about the Sheeran murder was bothering him. He exhaled deeply. *Is it because it was so violent?* He shook his head, thinking to himself. *No, it's something else. It doesn't seem like a robbery.* He started the car and pulled away to head back to his apartment. He sighed deeply, feeling the coffee take over. It energised his thoughts, but also his sense of unease.

He was wealthy, he was probably just involved in some dodgy deals, he told himself. *That's all it was.*

He was still thinking it over when he reached the front door of his apartment, and found his friend curled in a ball at the front door. Her head was buried between her knees.

'Iz?' He scrunched his face.

She looked up at him quickly. There was a wild look in her eyes.

'What's going on?' he asked cautiously. 'It looks like you're living on my doorstep.'

She winced. 'I didn't want to call you about this,' she said softly, staring at the floor. 'I figured you'd be back soon'

Something's wrong. 'What is it?' He asked gently.

'Alright,' She sighed and stood up. 'Well, remember that job I got last night? How I had to leave the party?' she asked, ruffling her hair.

'Uh, yeah.' He asked, frowning. 'What about it?'

'Well,' she pursed her lips. 'I got there right, and this place is crazy. I mean,' she shook her head. 'Fuck, there were cops everywhere.'

He felt a sinking feeling in his chest. *Ok, something is worse than wrong.* 'The job was to get a photo of the Sheeran killing?' he asked slowly.

She looked up and narrowed her gaze. 'Yeah.'

'Ok,' he nodded. 'So, why are you acting like you've got bad news?'

She groaned and rolled her head back. 'Alright, well,' she sighed. 'I got there and it was really crowded. I mean, I couldn't see anything. But the contract was to get a front page photo. And I had nothing.'

'Iz,' he prompted softly.

'Alright, alright,' she said irritated. 'I'm getting there. Anyway, I climbed the fence.'

He rolled his eyes. 'Right. And now you're in trouble?'

'What?!' She scrunched her face and laughed. 'I wish. That would be easier.' She exhaled.

'So, I got a photo of the crime scene, and well. It's probably easier if you just have a look at it.' She shook her head. She reached down to the case and pulled her camera out. She looked intently as she flicked through the photos.

What does this have to do with me? He shook his head.

'Uh, alright,' she said timidly, holding the camera to him. 'It's this one.'

He took held of the camera and read the display. His chest tightened as he read the words. *Wealth is a crime*. He shuddered, but couldn't look away.

'That's from your article, right?' she asked gently, pursing her lips. 'From that article you wrote?'

'Uh,' he went to reply, but no words came out.

He cleared his throat and kept staring at the screen. His heart started to beat faster.

'Yeah, it is.'

AOKI

Her hands were trembling as she made the cup, scooping two teaspoons of coffee and another two of sugar into her mug. She used the boiling water dispenser in the kitchen to half fill the cup and then put in a quarter of milk. She liked it strong and sweet, and in her current state it would take anything to keep her awake. It felt like she was running on a cocktail of fumes and adrenaline. She'd lost count of how many coffees it had been that day, and how many hours it had been since she last slept. It was close to 1pm and things had been a blur since leaving the scene.

She reflected on what had happened at the crime scene. There had been nothing conclusive on Taylor's computer and at the time she'd been the only one in the study. Once her moment of privacy passed, however, she hadn't had a moment to breathe. They had spent a little longer at the house before leaving forensics to carry out a detailed analysis. They'd needed to run from the front door to their cars out front, dodging both public citizens and reporters. By the time they left, it had been nearly light out and the crowd had grown considerably.

When Morgan had driven back to the station, she had lain in the back seat. There had been a moment of peace in transit, away from the crowd at the scene. The sunrise had been breaking over the horizon, and the cool fresh morning breeze had come in through the open windows. As the tensions of the night dissolved, she had instantly felt herself let go of the anxiety and the stress. For a moment at least, she had been able to let go and relax. She'd felt herself dozing off and knew she could comfortably sleep for an entire day. Her mind faded to black and she was gone.

She'd been woken with a shake and was bolt upright. They were back at the station. Morgan was in her face and she'd felt frightened. She had known her body was in shock. She needed sleep and was being denied it. She had experienced a similar sensation when travelling, being jetlagged and sleep deprived had wrecked her body before. Morgan had smiled but she'd known her face was blank, and her eyes wide and alert. Morgan had told her she had only been out for twenty minutes. She remembered nodding to him but it hadn't registered at the time.

If she'd known that momentary nap would be her only rest for the next twelve hours, she probably would have crawled up into a ball and cried until someone let her go home. She was optimistic at the time, however, and had thought she would only be needed at the station for an hour or two. She sighed, thinking how incredibly wrong she had been.

Since the moment she had gotten in someone had been calling her, emailing her, trying to find her, trying to tell her something, trying to ask her something. She had barely had a moment to sit down, let alone get any sort of rest. The whole situation had blown out of control. The station was chaotic and there was frantic movement everywhere. With her bloodshot eyes and killer migraine she was in no condition to handle it. Somehow, she had managed to get her work done but she knew there would be a cost once it was all over.

A few hours in she had found a place no one looked for her; the staff kitchen. It was her own personal refuge, her momentary sanctuary.

She was somewhere between five and ten coffees down, and had neither water nor any food save for the kitchen biscuits. She would crash hard when the adrenaline and caffeine ran out. The only question was whether that would happen before she was able to get out of the station.

At that moment, Morgan came around the corner and entered the kitchen.

'There you are! I've been looking for you everywhere.' He spoke quickly.

So much for her temporary safe zone. 'Yeah, hey. Just making coffee. Do you want one?'

He shook his head. She looked at his eyes. They were wide and as bloodshot as hers. Moreover, his skin was pale white as opposed to his usual subtle tan. His hair was a mess and his shirt had sweat stains under his arms. He'd probably had too much coffee too, he tended to get anxious and sweat when he did. He looked like he might be in even worse condition than her. She had seen him in similar states when he had come into work severely hungover and on no sleep. To his credit, he usually managed to make it through the entire day.

She was never more grateful to have him as a partner. He had carried their partnership through the day by running admin and having conversations that she wasn't able to have. Even so she had still been inundated with people chasing her. Without him or with anyone else she wouldn't have been able to cope.

Aoki looked at Morgan. 'Are you doing alright?' She asked gently.

He shook his head. 'Nah. Not really. This whole thing is fucked.' He said with a sigh, looking down. She had rarely seen him so worn down.

She nodded.

'I mean, this is typical of the department now. That whole attitude of 'doing more with less' is bullshit. It's moments like these we need more cops to assign and spread the workload.'

'We're tasked to capacity.'

'Yeah! And that is when things are normal!' His voice was becoming agitated. Management issues like this got him angry often. After knowing him for so long she knew he needed to vent. 'When things go bad or get crazy we're always understaffed. Fuck! It's bullshit!'

‘I reckon. Today is fucked.’

He nodded. ‘Definitely,’ he sighed, seeming to relax a bit. ‘Anyway, I actually have some good news. El Capitano just told me they’re all prepped up and won’t need us around much longer. They’re changing over shifts now, so they’ll get two other detectives to handle anything that comes in relating to this. I think one of them is Hannah. We just need to brief them properly.’

It was unorthodox, but necessary given the high profile nature of the case. She sighed, relaxing already at the hope of finally leaving.

ANDREA

She rolled over and woke herself. It was late in the day, she could tell because she felt so rested. It must be almost midday, and though it was her last weekend before starting this new job, as far as she was concerned she was spending the time exactly where she wanted to be. She opened her eyes and looked to Hank, still asleep. She ran her fingers lightly over his chest, and slowly nudged up against him. She extended her bare leg over his, feeling the warmth of his skin against hers.

She'd gone out with friends last night. That much her husband knew. But after a few drinks she had decided to stay at their apartment in the city. Her husband had purchased it several years ago when they had both been working in the city, to be used when either of them were required to work into the late hours of the morning, so that they could at least get a few hours sleep before going back into work the next day. When her girl friends had decided to call it a night, she had been too drunk for the hour trip home.

She'd walked to the apartment from the bar, fortunate that she had the spare key still on her keychain. When she collapsed into bed she had felt like slept, but something had been tormenting her. She was being driven wild by the thought of Hank. She knew he was out in the city and couldn't stop thinking about him, but she had also worried about him being with another woman if he got too drunk. In her inebriated state she had texted him, asking him to come to her apartment. He had been there quickly. As soon as she opened the door for him he'd greeted her with that smile of his. She'd felt herself get wet as soon as he embraced and kissed her.

Looking at him now and thinking of last night got her excited again. She pulled herself closer to him and rested her head on his chest. At that moment he stirred. Groaning and squinting he looked around the room, and then to her.

'Morning, gorgeous.'

She smiled and moaned. 'Morning, handsome.'

'We're in your apartment.'

'Yes, we most certainly are.'

He paused and smiled. 'You've never invited me back here before. You've always come to my apartment.'

'I know. But I had to have you last night, darling.'

He smiled. 'I'm glad. It was fun.'

'It always is.'

'No, not that. I mean, having you *here.*'

She raised an eyebrow. 'How so?'

He spoke slowly and softly. 'It just turns me on. Having you in the apartment your husband bought for you.'

'You bastard.' she hit him playfully. 'But I know. I enjoyed it so much more like this too.'

He was quiet for a moment, considering something.

'What is it? Is something wrong?'

'Just thinking.'

'Care to share?'

He paused. 'Have you ever had anyone else back here?'

She pulled away from him a bit. Sitting herself up in the bed. 'What do you mean?' She couldn't help hide the defensiveness in her voice.

'I'm just asking if I'm the first person you've brought back here.' he spoke flatly and calmly, he never got fazed when she got assertive. He never backed down. She found it uniquely frustrating.

'No, I'm not a whore.' She felt herself get irritated. 'My husband bought this. I have more respect for him than to do it here.'

He tried in vain to hide a grin.

'Other than this time of course.' Her voice softened a bit. 'But it is different with you Hank. You know that I love you.'

He narrowed his gaze and smiled warmly. He pulled her hand close and gently kissed the back of her hand. 'And I love you, m'lady.'

She smiled and closed her eyes as she felt his touch and his kiss. She felt herself lose her breath. She sighed and rose on top of him, tilting his head up so she could kiss his neck. She looked into his eyes, shook her head then turned away.

'It's never felt like this with anyone before Hank.'

He nodded. 'I know what you mean.' He gave a low growl and leaned in, kissing up from her hipbone, kissing slowly up her stomach and to her breasts. 'God, you just excite me so much. I love the way you move, the way you kiss and touch, you are a total sex kitten.'

She bit her lip and enjoyed the moment. The way he said it with his low calm voice was driving her wild. He paused and slowed down the affection.

'Were there others before me though? While you've been with your husband?'

She shook her head. 'No, Hank, I've only been with you and him.'

She could see him look slightly pained at the thought of her with another man. 'But we've been married over twenty years, Hank. Things haven't been right with him for a long time,' she ran her hand through his dirty blonde curly hair, stroking it softly while she talked. 'I was unhappy for a long time before I met you. He stopped making love to me a long time ago. He just fucks me now, it's all for him.'

He nodded. 'I'm sorry. I can understand.'

'The past few months with you have been incredible. I haven't felt this happy in so long.'

He smiled warmly. 'I'm glad. It sounds like you need it.'

She held him close and kissed him tenderly. She was hesitant about saying the next part, but decided it was time. 'I haven't been with anyone since we met.'

They locked eyes. She could tell there was a softness in her gaze she usually avoided. He smiled. 'I haven't been with anyone else either.'

She laughed. Then looked at him, sighed and exhaled deeply. 'God. I was so worried about it. I know we never talked about it but I couldn't stand the thought of another woman with you.'

He nodded and kept kissing down the side of her neck as her arms wrapped around him. She just wanted to stay like this, in bed with her lover. She couldn't stand the pressure of needing to work, the thought of her and her husband running out of money. *This is the only thing in my life I really enjoy*. Even at drinks last night she hadn't been able to enjoy seeing her two best friends, Melissa and Katrina, because her thoughts were wrapped up in this man. She hadn't been able to tell them about him yet.

She couldn't tell Melissa at all. She had worked with her husband and the two were best friends, as well. Her friend thought he was the kindest man. She would have been able to understand a discreet love affair. After all, Melissa had done the same to her husband several times, so to judge would be hypocritical. But this was different. Andrea could not stay with her husband any longer. She loved Hank and needed to be with him. Melissa would view this as a betrayal. At his age, there would be nothing left for her husband. He rested his hopes of children and a family with her. She felt a sinking feeling as she thought of reality again. She loved her husband but could never have kids with him. She had never thought of herself as being a mother, but being with Hank now she was excited by the thought of having children with him.

He rose and pulled himself out of bed. 'We should get up. It's getting late and I'm starving. Do you want to get lunch before you head home?'

She sighed, thinking of going back to the empty house. 'I could definitely go for a coffee, at least. I think I had too much wine last night; I doubt I could stomach anything heavy.'

He chuckled. 'Speak for yourself, missy! I need bacon and an omelette. With feta and zucchini.'

She scrunched her face. 'I don't know how you can eat that on a hangover, darling.'

He laughed, crossed the room and heading to the bathroom. As she rose from the bed she could hear the shower running. She needed to clean up the apartment before leaving. She wrapped her light blue silk robe around her and tied it tight. There were clothes scattered everywhere, the sheets messed up, and two bath towels used. If he visited the apartment, it would be obvious to her husband that she had been with someone. She found two used condoms next to the bed. Why they used them was beyond her, they always ended up doing it without protection regardless. He loved the feeling of her against him, and she loved being able to feel him inside her. She picked the two of them up carefully and found an empty plastic bag to put them in.

She checked for any additional evidence, and scanned the area thoroughly. Finding nothing either beside the bed or underneath it, she then proceeded to take all the linen off the bed and put it in the washing machine. She put it on a short cycle so she could start drying it before leaving. She checked the area again, and felt satisfied with her work.

Only then did she realise she had forgotten to check if her husband had tried contacting her. She picked up her phone from her bedside table. Three messages and a missed call. *Fuck.* She remembered sending a message before Hank had arrived, letting him know she was staying in the city. He'd messaged back saying it was fine, but reminding her they had lunch with a good friend of his and his wife at midday. *Double fuck.* He'd then sent a message telling her he could pick her up. She felt suddenly panicked realising he could arrive at any moment, but his last message said that he assumed she was hungover and he had gone to lunch without her. She breathed a sigh of relief. That could have been disastrous.

She decided to call him. It went straight to voicemail.

'Hi. Sorry, dear, I only just woke up. I'm so sorry. I completely forgot about lunch. Tell Greg and Liza I say sorry. You must be driving. I'm really sorry. Call me later.' She hung up, and felt terrible. The thought of him going to such an awkward lunch while she was naked in bed with her younger lover made her feel shit. At the same time, something about humiliating him appealed to her.

She had been drawn to him at first because he was powerful and stern. Now he was just weak and old, she felt angry at him for not being able to keep up with her. He would never come on walks or do anything outdoors with her. He had always been lazy but it had gotten much worse as he aged.

She put aside the unpleasant and uncomfortable emotions of her relationship with her husband, and put aside her guilt that she had missed lunch with him. She didn't want to waste the time with her lover.

Hank was still in the shower. She entered the bathroom, dropped her robe to the floor and snuck in behind him. Gently kissing his back. He turned around, the two embraced. They made love while the water washed over their bodies.

WILL

His mind was working overtime as he looked through the titles on the cupboard in his office room. *Wealth is a crime?* His stomach turned.

'Will?' Iz asked gently. 'You ok?'

He shook his head slightly. He flicked through the books in his cupboard, looking intently for the one he needed. He kept all printed work archived on his shelves.

'You're starting to worry me,' she said timidly. 'You've barely said anything.'

'I'm trying to find the book.' He said absently, scratching his jaw. *Can I handle this?*

She exhaled. 'Look, Will. Maybe I'm just imagining it, alright.' She said, slightly irritated. 'Just relax. You're freaking me out.'

'Iz,' he turned quickly. 'How would you feel if you thought someone died because of you?' He blurted out.

She shook her head. 'It's just one sentence. Wealth is a crime.'

He winced at the mention. 'How long before someone blames me for it, though?' he asked softly.

She sighed and walked over to him. 'Chill, babe.' She said soothingly, hugging him. 'This isn't on you.'

He exhaled. 'I wish I didn't have that coffee earlier.'

She laughed as she let go of him. 'It's not helping?'

'Not at all,' He turned back to his bookcase. 'Still, could this killing be because of me?'

She shrugged. ‘I dunno, but I doubt it. What was the article about anyway?’ she asked with a frown.

He turned and looked at her curiously. ‘You didn’t read it?’

She held her hands up. ‘Hey I was busy alright! I read like, parts of it.’

‘Which parts?’ he asked with a grin.

She shrugged. ‘The summary.’

He laughed, starting to relax. He was glad she was there. He took a deep breath. ‘Alright, well I wrote just after I finished uni’ he said with a shrug. *When I was fresh and ambitious*. ‘The article was basically saying that wealth wasn’t a good thing.’

She fell silent and pursed her lips, looking at the floor. ‘Alright. So what did you say in it?’

‘I dunno’ he sighed. He felt tempted to hide from the situation. *I’m responsible for it though*. He shook his head. ‘I mean, it was a long time ago. I didn’t even want to call the article that. It was my editor’s idea.’

‘Ok then’ she replied quietly. She rubbed the tattoo on her shoulder.

‘I mean, yeah’ he thought out loud. ‘I guess I wanted to make it dramatic.’

‘Why?’ she asked, scrunching her face.

‘I wanted people to pay attention’ he admitted. ‘I just assumed no one would care. For the longest time, well’ he cleared his throat. ‘For too long the main economic arguments assumed that being wealthy was a good thing. My view was different. I only wanted to argue the point so dramatically to try and create a shift in paradigm.’.

‘Paradigm?’ she looked at him strangely.

‘Ah, yeah’ he shrugged. ‘It basically means like a way of thinking.’

She nodded and narrowed her eyes. ‘Cool word.’

He grinned and shook his head. ‘I guess. Anyway’ he sighed. ‘The attempt to gain extra attention was in vain. The paper didn’t draw any real attention’ he said with a wince. He scratched his cheek and looked at the floor. ‘It didn’t lead to any serious debates on a rethink on the idea of wealth.’ *Now it’s being used to justify murder*. The idea weighed heavy on him.

‘Hey,’ she said gently. ‘Don’t worry. We’ll figure it out.’ She assured him, putting her hand on his arm. ‘So what are you looking for anyway?’

‘The article.’

‘Why?’

He exhaled. ‘I have to see what I wrote.’

‘But why?’ She asked again, slower.

He turned and looked at her. ‘Because I have to know,’ he replied softly. ‘I have to know whether I encouraged this.’

She nodded. ‘How can I help? Where is it?’

‘That’s what I’m trying to remember,’ he replied. He narrowed his gaze on a title. ‘The first time I talked about it was in this journal,’ he said as he pulled it out of the cupboard. ‘But I only talked about it briefly.’

‘And you talked about it somewhere else, as well?’

‘Yeah,’ he replied. He put his head in his hands and sighed, trying to focus. ‘I remembered spending a chapter in a book discussing the same idea in more depth, but I don’t which book.’ From memory he believed he had put the section somewhere it didn’t belong. He had wanted to develop the idea, however it didn't fit with the book he had been writing.

He opened his eyes and squinted, remembering. 'Shit.' He said with a smile, as he pulled the thick volume from the shelf.

'What is it? Something wrong?' She asked with a frown.

'No, nothing. Except maybe my memory,' he grinned and shook his head. 'It was in my first book!' He said, clearing his throat. 'The book was all about increased risk leading up to the 2008 recession. I wrote about worldwide regulatory changes over the financial industry since the Reagan government of the eighties,' he thought out loud, flicking through the pages. 'There had been widespread deregulation of the industry, less rules and restrictions for them to abide by. My argument was that it had encouraged reckless lending and risky investments. It wasn't a popular argument in the years leading up to 2008, when I originally published it as a thesis paper.'

'How come? Because all those bankers were making money back then?' She asked, trying to look over his shoulder.

'Yeah. And they made money hand over fist. At the time no one had believed that these investments were risky or volatile.' He said with a grin. *At the end of 2008 and 2009 however, my argument had been met by a different reaction.* He was one of the 'experts' who could say he had seen it coming. Since then, he had republished the argument as a book, and received critical acclaim and recognition. His career had been forever changed because he had argued the right thing at what would later prove to be the right time.

He looked up at his friend. He realised she was staring at him, and that he was lost in the history behind the book and the sense of pride he still felt over it. He winced. *I got lucky, that's all.* It was still a bittersweet memory. He took a deep breath and scanned the pages, still unaware exactly where it had been.

‘Will,’ she said, waving her hand in front of him.

‘Yeah?’ he looked up with a frown.

‘I’m going to make a coffee while I wait,’ she said with a frown. ‘You’re pretty distracted right now.’

He laughed. ‘Sorry.’

‘Sometimes I swear you’re off in your own world.’ She sighed and shook her head. ‘You want one?’

He rubbed his face, trying to focus. ‘Nah, I’m ok.’ *I can’t handle any more nerves right now*, he thought to himself. He flicked from chapter to chapter; skim reading to find the section he was after. He reached the end of the book without finding what he was looking for. He sighed. It would take some time to check properly. He seated himself at his desk, gave himself proper lighting and set about getting to work.

LEW

Sunday morning greeted Lew unpleasantly. His body felt stiff. Waking up was starting to get harder. With each morning his body seemed colder, muscles starting to feel dead with lack of stimulus. He tried to pull himself up to a sitting position. He grunted and groaned but gained no ground. All he wanted was more sleep. He wanted to go back to the darkness, back to his dreams to where he could feel freed. A passing guard told each cell to get up and head to breakfast. *I won't get the luxury of fantasy this morning.*

For some reason he missed his brother, wanting to just talk to him like when they still lived at home. Despite being several years younger, the two had always been close. He sighed. *It all changed.* In his late twenties he started earning more money, and his brother was working as a nurse in low paid jobs. They had started arguing as their views began to diverge. That was the beginning of a void between them that only got worse. His brother hadn't even come to court when he had been convicted.

At breakfast, he looked around as the others ate their meals in silence. They sat in quiet acceptance of their situation. Their gazes averted. Usually, he would do the same, but not today. He wanted trouble for once. *Anything to feel alive again.*

He looked from person to person slowly, scanning the room, staring from left to right and back again with cold calculation. He got a scowl from some middle aged skinhead with a long forehead and grey stubble. He kept eye contact despite the rising nervousness he felt. After a few minutes he saw the man slowly shake his head and return his attention to the food, which was apparently more interesting. When he locked eyes which a chubby bald man with a weak face he got a look of fear. The little bald fat man hastily lowered his gaze and ate his food quicker. There was a nervous panic to his actions, the man had no nerve.

He stared around the room for a while longer before giving up on his efforts. There would be no trouble for him today. He exhaled and thought of the harbour views from the corner office he once had.

He found his mind wandering to a morning almost fifteen years ago to the day. It had been a similar morning, a coolness and dampness in the air, but a bright and warm sun in the sky. Everything else had been different, though. It had been when he was still actively working in the markets floor, before becoming an executive. His life had been trading and research. He had been up all night in the office, planning and rereading everything, preparing for battle. When trade opened at 10am he already had his exit point planned. It was the culmination of half a year of work. At the time, he had been managing an account of twenty million and at these early stages he invested a relatively modest five hundred thousand on this speculation.

Over the months, all results he found confirmed his speculation, and he became more heavily invested. By the open of trade on that morning around ten million of his then twenty five million portfolio was invested in this company. His instincts had been correct; there was a major press release that morning. Shares in the company had been rising over the months and, when before trade was at just below two dollars a share, almost a ten fold increase from his entry point. By midday the share price peaked at ten dollars a share, a twenty fold increase from his initial investment. However, he had also diversified into put and call options in the derivatives markets. At the end of the day the ten million dollars worth of investments he had started the day with were now worth one billion dollars.

He smiled and felt warm inside thinking of the pride he still felt over his biggest coup. The trading floor had been a zoo that day; everyone at his company had ended up a winner. After that, he had become the biggest player in the firm. That day had made his career, and he had won through putting in hard work, doing the time researching and winning the mental game of trading; it had been pure talent and a little luck.

His smile turned to a cringe as he came back to the present. After that day, so many years ago, he had risen quickly through the company, becoming an executive and eventually chief operating officer by virtue of his portfolio. That had been the beginning of when everything had become so confusing, when the lines had started to blur. Legal and illegal had been replaced by 'getting away with it' and 'getting caught'. *That morning had been probably the last victory due to my talent alone.* He wished he could go back to that moment, his final real win before they had started rigging the decks. *I want to prove I could have done it all without the information advantage*, without what had been smeared as a breach of the law.

He felt angry knowing that his team would have achieved the same wins regardless. In his heart of hearts he knew they had been better than the other traders; smarter, quicker and more determined. His reputation now had been destroyed long ago and people were already starting to forget about the story of Lew Noble. The history books would not be kind to Delpont; the fallen empire which at one time had ruled the world.

ANDREA

It was only midday on her first day, but she had already noticed attention from half the men in the office. They were subtle moments. Momentary glances at her body during conversation, gazes suddenly diverted when she looked over her shoulder. It hadn't taken long to remember why she hated working in offices. *Still*, she sighed, *it's not as bad as the corporate world.* When working in corporations she would constantly be flirted with or leered at by the bankers, and she'd overheard herself being called the 'eye candy'. *At least here they have they are polite*.

Despite the attention though, it seemed like a good job. They hadn't micromanaged her, she had mostly been left to her own devices. They had given her a gradual explanation of everything she needed to do. There was a pretty laidback attitude. The other workers seemed in a good mood. *They're a bit dull, but at least they're smiling most of the time*. There was no conflict, but at the same time wasn't too much interaction between staff. She assumed it was relatively indicative of government work. She smiled. *This would do nicely for me*.

She noticed Charlie Arnoud walking over to her desk. He had the kind of gentle smile only capable by harmless old men. He was average height, around fifty, balding and had a chubby face. A kind face, but a chubby face.

'Hi Andrea, here is an old document we had about the process here. Sorry we don't have anything more current, we don't get too many new staff.'

'I thought this was a new department, though? Isn't everyone new?'

Charlie smiled sadly. 'Unfortunately, no. They essentially created this team by moving over an already existing team. Plus a few additions.'

That was a bad sign. It made it sound like a puppet organisation; set up to make it seem like something was being done, but really it was the same thing as before. 'Ah. Ok, that must be helpful, having so many people who already know the processes?'

'I'm glad you can see the positive in it.' He said with a casual shrug and a relaxed grin. He had a relaxed confidence that she did not expect. 'By the way, we keep things pretty casual around here. You don't really need to dress so professional. It's pretty much smart casual. Half the guys don't even wear ties, let alone jackets.'

She had already noticed this. She had worn a black jacket and skirt with a light blue silk blouse. She felt a little overdressed. 'Thank you, Charlie. Duly noted.' She smiled warmly and genuinely. He had been friendly to her but not overly, and was one of the few men not to flirt with her. She was glad she had built rapport with at least one person in the office who didn't see her like that. She felt rather guilty for having been so formal thus far. She appreciated his help.

As he turned to walk away, she decided to take some initiative in making a friend. 'Have you been working in government for long?'

He turned back, leaned against her desk and furrowed his brow, as if in reflection. 'It's been almost fifteen years now. It feels a lot longer. Things move pretty slowly here,' he chuckled. 'I suppose it's good and bad. I worked as a trader in the eighties, then retrained as an accountant in the nineties, after one bust too many.'

'Really?' Try as she might, she couldn't imagine Charlie as a trader. 'That's quite interesting. This must be a good fit for you with your previous experience?'

'Hmm. It was easy to move into. Nowadays though, I spend most of my time trying to keep up with regulatory changes,' he chuckled. 'Markets have changed a lot since I started.'

‘That is true. They must be almost unrecognisable now.’

‘The humanity behind them hasn’t changed. A lot of people wanting to make a quick buck and not many willing to invest for the long term. Since the inception of markets, traders everywhere have thrived on the ignorance of those investing their money.’ He said with a shrug.

She smiled and narrowed her gaze. Impressed by how wise this man was. Despite his looks, he spoke with conviction. He was sure of himself. ‘That’s very true. The turn of the millennium must have been a crazy time?’

He sighed. ‘They definitely were. I moved over to the side of angels in the mid nineties, right as the internet kicked in. Everything changed. Suddenly, everyone was an investor. And you know how that old saying goes; when everyone is saying to get into the market, that is usually the best time to get out.’ He said with a laugh, shaking his head.

‘That must have been right before the dot com boom . Oh!’ she exclaimed. ‘You must have been here when Delpont went under then?!’

Charlie frowned a little. Like he was surprised she was so open about her past.

She had accepted her involvement and responsibility some time ago, she had not been personally responsible. She had been unashamed of her time with the company for some time now.

‘Yeah, that’s right,’ he shook his head with a frown. ‘They were bad times for us. Everyone was saying we fell asleep on the job. The fallout was unbelievable. I mean our investigators had been looking over their books for years. None of us had seen anything wrong.’

‘I can empathise,’ she said gently. She felt guilty, having brought it up. She hadn’t considered the impact it would have had on the careers of those outside the company. ‘Take it from me; there were a lot of good people working there. I was there day in and day out, we just thought we were better than everyone else, and that was why we were doing so well. We were looking right at it, and none of us saw it.' She said sadly. She thought of her former colleagues, and the shock and disbelief in their faces when they found out the company was rotten to the core. It was a bitter memory. Made no easier by the fact she had left years before things had gone bad. She had left when Delpont had been king, her record was cleaner than most.

'That is true. The corruption ran deep. Lew Noble fooled a lot of people.' Charlie said, shaking his head.

'It wasn't just Lew. There were a lot of people behind it,' she spoke softly. Andrea winced at the mention of Lew. In the fallout they demonized Lew and blamed the whole thing on him. Despite never liking him, she felt he didn't deserve how he'd been portrayed. 'A lot of people were complicit in it. Lew Noble became a fall guy.'

He stared at her, squinting. He seemed to be determining the veracity of her statement. 'I hadn't thought of it like that. I suppose that is very true.' He said slowly. 'I didn't mean to keep you. Just have a look through the procedures document and let me know if you have any questions.' He added with a smile. Perhaps he sensed the topic upset her, and that was why he changed the subject.

'Many thanks, Charlie. It is much appreciated.'

'Don't worry about it, Andrea. We'll ease you into the role, make sure we don't throw you into the deep end. If you have any questions let either myself or one of the other members of the team know.'

She smiled. 'Will do. If there is anything you need me to do just let me know, I'm happy to assume greater responsibility as needed.'

‘Love the enthusiasm,’ he laughed. ‘But feel free to take it easy. Things are pretty relaxed around here. Feel free to check Facebook or Youtube if you have got everything done. I’m not too fussed.’

Andrea laughed. ‘Sure thing, Charlie’

He turned and walked back to his little office. He put his reading glasses back on and went back to squinting at his computer. She was lucky to have found such a good boss. She already had a good feeling. Everyone else in the team seemed to have clear direction and a good work ethic. She found that people worked best when they were respected. Being too critical and angry with staff usually resulted in resentment, and poor performance. The irony was that seniors usually confused management with bullying, trying to control people, and ended up losing the engagement of their people. She felt like one of the team already. Maybe in this department she would be able to do some real good for once. She felt like this could be an opportunity to contribute and make a difference.

AOKI

She looked across the office at Hannah, laughing and flicking her hair to one side, flirting with the seniors. They all seemed to love her. At first, she had been pissed off that they'd gradually moved Hannah Moray closer to the Sheeran case, while moving Aoki off it. She was already back to her regular caseload, which had gone unattended. Hannah was a lithe little thing, big puppy eyes and the ability to charm almost anyone. She gave Aoki the shits. Partly, because she was so useless. She noticed Morgan walking towards her, his head in his hands.

'She's doing my fucking head in.'

Aoki smirked. It was about the only good thing to come out of this situation. The only person who could stand Hannah less than herself was Morgan.

'I just don't get it. Is she doing any work? She never interviews anyone. She's rubbish at finding evidence but spends most of her time standing next to whichever cop is being interviewed.'

'Yeah, I'm glad I don't have to deal with it.'

'Her records are terrible. She never files a single thing.'

Aoki laughed. One of the perils of working with attractive and vain people is they tended to be so used to other people doing things for them that they forget how to do it themselves. 'I've never worked with her so I can't comment. How is she on the case though? Does she know how to think it through?'

He shook his head. 'I can't tell. I've got absolutely nothing to go on so far. It is so random. We've checked out absolutely every contact of Taylor's and found nothing.'

'Yeah? So what do you think about the social activist angle?'

He glared and hushed her. ‘Not this again. You’ve got to stop talking about it.’

‘But did you look into it?’

He sighed. ‘Yeah, fine. I did.’

‘And?’

‘And I don’t know,’ he shrugged and lowered his voice. ‘I looked up that ‘wealth is a crime thing’, but I couldn’t find anything with that exact statement.’

‘Oh.’ She pursed her lips.

‘Except for this one article,’ he frowned and scratched his scalp. ‘But it was about economics, nothing to do with this.’

She scrunched her face.

‘Aoki,’ he rolled his eyes. ‘I’m sure. The kid who wrote it was just talking about theory, about consumerism and stuff like that.’ He shrugged. ‘There weren’t any militant or violent implications to it.’

She frowned.

‘Anyway,’ he sighed. ‘We buried that as much as possible. You’ll get yourself into trouble if someone overhears you talk about that statement.’

She scoffed. ‘Why? It’s the truth.’

‘Yeah, well,’ he scratched his stubble. ‘No one wants word of it to get out.’

‘I know,’ she rolled her eyes. ‘No sign of that photo anywhere yet?’ She asked with a raised eyebrow.

He shook his head with a frown. ‘I don’t understand. That photo would be worth a lot.’

‘Maybe they didn’t get a photo of it?’ She shrugged.

‘Maybe.’ He said softly. ‘Look, don’t mention that ‘wealth is a crime’ stuff. You’ll just bring trouble on yourself.’

‘So what?’ She exhaled. ‘I want to know.’

He sighed and rubbed his temples. ‘I mean if not for yourself, do it as a favour to me.’ He put his hands together as if praying.

‘Whatever.’ She grinned and shook her head. ‘It was there. It’s evidence whether it’s true or false.’

He nodded. ‘I know. And I don’t care.’

‘How can you say that?’

‘Because I don’t.’ He shrugged. ‘Look, even assuming this guy was murdered as a part of some grand plan, I don’t care. He sounds like an asshole.’

‘Morgan!’ She scolded him with a frown.

‘There are more important cases than some privileged rich boy.’ He sighed wearily. ‘I just need to get off this fucking case.’ His voice was lowered. ‘And I need to get away from that ditz’.

She tried to cover up a chuckle. He was getting so irritated working with Hannah. In addition, Morgan believed it was a career case, and viewed it as too much of a risk.

‘Besides. You should to be the one looking at it.’

‘They moved me off it. It was out of my hands.’ She said quietly.

He shook his head and spoke softly. ‘That’s bullshit and you know it. Look, we need to talk about this. I know what happened.’

She glanced up at him hesitantly. ‘I don’t want to talk about it.’

He sighed. ‘You can’t keep doing this to yourself. You are a better detective than half the guys here. You know how to solve this, I know you do. You can't keep doubting yourself.' He spoke passionately and convincingly. *It seems a waste he didn't go into the business world.*

'I know,' she paused. 'I just got scared. There was so much pressure,' she ran her hands through her hair. She still felt the pressure she had been under not too long ago. 'I couldn't deal with it.'

'You could have. You were doing better than most on this. Look, just trust yourself.'

'Yeah. Yeah, I know,' she said, deflated. 'It was just a lot. All at once, as well. I just—I didn't know what to make of it. I was so flat out I didn't have time to think. It doesn't matter now. I'm off the case now.'

His voice was resigned with defeat. 'Yeah, I guess so.'

'Besides you can't talk. You want off this case as much as I did.'

'Yeah, well, there's a difference,' he turned to walk out of the office. 'I don't stand a chance of solving this.'

With that he slung his coat over his shoulder and smiled glumly, waving goodbye and making an inconspicuous exit. The case had taken its toll on him over the past few days. Aoki hadn't been off the case for long, but already she was feeling better. She had been so stressed with the workload that she hadn't been able to sleep. The copious amounts of caffeine hadn't helped either. Regardless, she was glad she could now do the work that had built up over the past few days.

Her current case was a dunker. It was a messy crime and was clearly personal. There had been a spate of shootings throughout the western suburbs and she had picked up one of them. The victim had been shot outside the front door of his house. He was in his mid twenties, had tattoos on both arms and his family background was eastern European. The parents had yelled at her when she first arrived on scene, saying it was the fault of the police that it had happened. A cursory examination of his bedroom had found drugs and a gun hidden in a secret closet compartment. Her first instinct had been gang related. So far it had felt right.

They had also found another gun two blocks away, dumped into a storm water drain. They had cleaned it up and found fingerprints easily.

When the lab results come back this suspect will be locked away within a day or two. She picked up her bag and headed for the elevator. *If only the Sheeran case were the same.* She exited the foyer and made her way to the entrance. She plucked a cigarette from her bag and lit it, her lighter hissed and she inhaled deeply. As the tobacco hit her system she felt the world dissolve away. The sounds of traffic and the hustle of city stress at midday faded away. She was unaware of the sounds around her, her mind was clear. Even her thoughts went silent.

Some time passed before she realised her cigarette had gone out. She must have been in a trance like focus for several minutes. Taking a deep breath, she headed back into the station.

She thought about how this case that had been so easy to solve, compared to the murder of Taylor Sheeran. With a frown, her mind wandered to Marcus Docker. Simple cases like this had amateur mistakes, made usually because of arrogance or ignorance. Marcus Docker had been something else. The precision of the attack had been almost surgical.

Suddenly, it came to her. She walked with hurried footsteps, turned the other way and went back to her desk at double time. She logged onto her computer, quickly pulled up her files on Marcus Docker and printed them out. Despite not being on the case, it had been bothering her for some time. Something was nagging at her, in the back of her mind, but she couldn't articulate what it was.

She left the office quickly and left for the train station, heading for the crime scene. Her mind was working overtime on the train ride. Aoki flicked over the files. In particular, she looked at the witness report from the guard, and the notes from Detective Constable Bay about lack of footage.

The crime scene wasn't too far from Central Station. She got out and walked. She wouldn't consider doing this if it weren't daytime, in a few hours it would be dangerous. The government had put a lot of welfare housing in this area to try and assist, but their efforts had been at most half of what was needed. The result was that a lot of desperate people were simply being moved closer to the city without any additional support. Crime had increased by a factor of ten in this area over the past ten years.

When she reached the street, she stopped for a moment and took stock. She lit a cigarette and took a deep breath. She was standing exactly where Docker had died.

She read over the report. From the guard's account she determined where the car had been, and from where the attacker had approached. *It must have been from the other side of the street, there were a few covered alcoves there but precious little on this side*. She looked up; there were also two street lights directly outside the entrance to the building. If he had approached from this side of the road they would have been alerted early without a doubt. She crossed the road, staring left and right impulsively for traffic. She stopped in her steps. It was daytime now, as busy as this area would get, and still there were only a handful of cars around. At night there would be even fewer. It was a perfect spot for something like this. She went over Bay's account of how difficult it was to get footage. He tried both convenience shops on the street and found nothing. Aoki looked at where the shops were located; there was one about fifty meters from where the shooting happened, there was another about a hundred meters up the road in the other direction. She walked slowly, up and down the street, looking at all the terraces. One of these houses would have had a street facing security camera. It was her only hope at this point.

After walking up and down the street for twenty minutes, she noticed three private security cameras that both previous detectives had missed. She finally had a fresh lead.

WILL

He hadn't slept much the past few nights. His mind had been preoccupied with all the Sheeran drama. It had been all over the news, but nothing had mentioned the writing on the wall. He'd been able to relax a bit after reading through his articles, convinced he had not advocated it. He still felt responsible, but didn't feel he had suggested murder as a solution.

He rubbed his face to wake himself up. His living room was stuffy. It was a hot day outside so he had left the blinds closed. Unfortunately that meant there was no fresh air coming in. He had been writing for most of the day, and was starting to crawl the walls.

He was writing an article about two individuals he had interviewed some time ago. They had come to him anonymously from a cleaning company, mainly contracted for large commercial buildings in the city. One was an Australian and the other was an Indian on a student visa. Their company was employing workers that had arrived in Australia on student visas, and they had signed the contracts not knowing the laws. The company had then put them on a different contract to the Australians so they were hired on a contract basis, not as employees. As such, they didn't get any normal employment protections. The Australian was paid fine, and had no idea what was happening to the overseas workers. He only found out because they became friends. The implication had been clear; it was a race issue. The overseas workers were vulnerable; they had signed contracts that they couldn't get out of but at the same time it was very easy for the companies to get rid of these workers.

The result was that they were given projects impossible to do in normal shifts and only paid fifty dollars a day to clean big office buildings. So they had to stay late and work long hours, most working ten hours a day. Will had felt angry at that. Cleaners being paid five dollars an hours working in commercial buildings where company employees would be paid over one hundred thousand a year and still complain about it. Inequality happening in plain view. Two people could be meters from each other but would always be worlds apart.

They overseas workers were not able to speak to the authorities because they were in breach of their student visa restrictions. On that visa they could only work twenty hours a week, but most were working ten hour days for four days of the week. Those that had challenged the bosses disappeared; they were kicked out of the country quickly.

The recording was still playing in the background. He heard the voice of the Australian, 'It's happening. Right now. In every building in the city, in every city on Earth. Big businesses have been doing this over the past ten years, it's gradually gotten worse. They genuinely believe that they can move everything to this system. This is their business plan for the next hundred and fifty years. Some of these people owning these companies don't even understand what damage they are causing. Even if they knew, I don't think these suits would care. Their only goal is profit. I've seen some of them. They think it's their god given right to make money, no matter the impact on other people. They think they are somehow better than everyone else.'

'Yeah, I know the type.' Will heard his own voice on the recording.

He sighed, and thought about people he had gone to school and university with. For some it was their aim and goal to start their own businesses and become rich. He wondered how many of them would pay the same human price in order to make money. He wondered how many would care as long as they could live the lifestyle of mansions, expensive cars and yachts.

After thinking about the situation of the overseas workers, Will felt very differently about the murder of Taylor Sheeran. Based on this exploitation, and what he knew about relative wealth, it seemed the lifestyle of wealth was only possible because of the human cost paid by the lowest income earners. There were traders being paid millions working in expensive corporate offices, the same offices kept clean because exploited immigrants earned below minimum wage. He had forgotten there were so many unseen people working every moment of their lives but stuck incredibly poor.

The murder wasn't a priority to him anymore. He'd looked into the industry and had found nothing on the issues with contract work and foreign workers. There had been no news articles about this either. Everyone was worried about the death of one rich person, and yet it went undocumented that there was living death experienced by millions of unseen people every day.

He sighed, frustrated at being indoors all day. He needed a break.

He headed to the bathroom and took a quick cold shower, giving him a moment of relief; a fresh change from the heat outside. He dressed comfortably. Despite not being a fan of shorts, he had no option but to wear a pair of khaki ones and a white t-shirt. His one consolation was that there was still a light breeze.

Exiting his apartment block, he picked up a cappuccino from the café at the foot of his building. The service was quick, perhaps due to the fact that it was a Wednesday afternoon and there was no one else around. Regardless, he made his way from the cluster of cafes around his area and headed to a nearby park.

As soon as he passed through the ring of trees that circled the modest park, he already felt like he was in a different city. The noise of the traffic faded away, blocked by the tree line. The warm sun took on a different light under shade; the uncomfortable heat of before was suddenly replaced by a relaxing cool. Will felt like he could breathe again. He picked out a spot under a large pine and sat down on the grass. He leaned back, rested on his elbows, and took a deep breath.

Only once he sat down did his mind start to slow down.

He drifted off into a daze, only to be woken by his phone vibrating in his pocket. He didn't remember lying down on the grass, but he woke up in that position. Groaning, he rubbed his face. *I must have needed a nap.* Squinting at his phone, he saw a call from an unknown mobile number. As his phone buzzed silently, as Will usually left it on silent, he debated whether to take the call or not. At the third ring he felt like letting it go to voicemail. By the fourth his curiosity had won out, and he answered.

'Hello, Will speaking.'

'Will. Hey It's Chris.' He heard the familiar and gentle voice on the other end.

'Oh,' he frowned. 'Hey mate. How're you going?'

'Yeah,' he could hear him shrug over the phone. 'Can't complain. Hey, uh, remember that thing we talked about the other night?'

'Sure do.' Will replied hesitantly.

'Well, reckon it's about time to catch up over a drink?' Chris suggested with a chuckle.

AOKI

She sat in one of the conference rooms, with the case files sprawled over the table, her head bent down low. She felt defeated. Her hopes of finding a fresh lead were dashed. None of the cameras had held any new footage. She had even expanded her search to a few hours before and after the attack. On her laptop she viewed through each of the footages time and time again, hoping to find a glimpse of something. There was nothing there.

After several minutes of feeling sorry for herself, she regained her composure and looked at the files again. She knew she hadn't missed anything, she had been thorough but there was simply a lack of evidence.

'What're you looking at?' Morgan walked into the room, peering over the table. 'Oh, the Docker case. Why are you looking into that? I would've thought you'd be more interested in the Sheeran case?'

'I can't explain it. I keep thinking about it.' With a shrugged, she breathed deeply. 'There's something bothering me about the case.'

'But there's nothing there?'

She looked at him in the eyes. He was right. There was nothing there. Her eyes widened as she took a deep breath. She realised what the problem was now.

'There should be something here, though, right? Especially with the street footage.'

'Yeah, it's been doing Reikhart's head in.'

'Reikhart?'

'Yeah, they dumped it on him. They said Moray was all tied up with the Sheeran case. So they palmed it off on him. Pretty bullshit, if you ask me.'

She paused for a moment.

'You're pursing your lips. You've got something, haven't you?'

'Maybe,' she said slowly. She moved to her computer, leaned over and started searching the web. Morgan waited on the other side of the room, arms folded. Her focus was on the computer the entire time, her gaze unflinching. When she finally looked up after sending the image to the printer, she saw him smiling his smug grin. She scoffed. 'You look so arrogant when you smile like that.'

He laughed. 'Whatever. I love to see you in the zone.' He walked across the room to the printer, picking up the A3 size sheet. He frowned. 'What is this? A map?'

'Yeah. It's a map of the area around where Docker was shot. Now check this out,' she picked up the map from him and took it to the whiteboard, using a few magnets to pin it up. 'Around here, there were two shops with cameras.'

'But nothing on the footage.'

'Exactly. I found another three cameras in the houses surrounding. Again, nothing on any footage. Now have a look at this,' she grabbed a handful of coloured button sized magnets, putting two on specific points on the map.

'These are where the shops are and this is the range of the cameras,' she used a marker to indicate, colouring in the area on the map. 'Now, take into account the private cameras, located here, here and here,' she said slowly, placing magnets over the respective locations, and scribbled in blue marker. 'And this is their field of vision.'

She stopped talking and looked over at Morgan. His eyes had visibly widened. The coloured market had blocked out one side of the footpath and street at three points, it had blocked out the other side of the street at two points.

‘Fuck.’ He swore, a curious look on his face.

‘No matter what, this guy didn’t approach or flee using just one side of the street. He must have crossed tactically a few times.’

‘Yeah, you’re right. He must have. I mean, he must have known where those cameras were. He must have scoped out the area in advance.’

She paused. Took a step back and looked at the whiteboard from a distance. For the first time since the case began they had an actual lead.

‘Whatever this guy is,’ said Aoki. ‘He is a professional at something.’

WILL

Chris smiled and waved as he entered the bar, swaggering over with an awkward smile on his face.

'Hey, buddy.' Will said with a grin. *Seeing that awkward grin again reminds me of Chris's good heart.*

'Hey, Will. Sorry, I'm running a bit late. Rebecca dropped me off.' He said as he lumbered into the seat.

'Oh, how is she?

Chris shuffled. 'Yeah, she's well. It's kind of because of her that I'm coming to you.'

'Yeah, ok,' he frowned. 'What it's about?'

He sighed. 'I should just tell you.' He sighed, glancing over his shoulder. While scanning the room, he drummed his fingers against the table. 'There's no sense messing around and drawing this out. I should tell you now while I have a chance.'

'What do you mean? Why wouldn't you have a chance?' *Is he even talking to me?* Will wondered. *Or just himself?*

'I mean, in person.' He shrugged. 'I don't want to have a phone call and have it recorded. Will, this can't come back to me. Right? This didn't come from me.'

'Sure thing. But just tell me what is going on.' Will was taken aback. This conversation had escalated quickly. This was not what he was expecting.

'Alright,' Chris exhaled. 'You know those two killings, Docker and Sheeran?'

'Yeah, of course. I've actually been following them pretty closely.'

Chris nodded. 'Me too.' He looked Will in the eyes, pausing before continuing. 'I think they might be linked.'

Will frowned. 'How so?'

'I talked to Beck about it. I think they might be linked to something that happened over ten years ago'

'How so? You think they were committed by the same person?'

Chris glanced around the bar, scanning the room. He nodded. 'Whatever's happening, Beck thinks there's something else going on. She isn't sure *what exactly* is happening, but she has an idea what it's about.'

Will felt increasingly nervous. Everything that Chris had told him was a total shock. *I don't know if I'm ready for this.* He resented himself for feeling like that. *I shouldn't be afraid, my friends clearly need help.*

'I'm meeting someone tonight whose agreed to be a source for you. We need to keep it private, though. If you come they can tell you the full story.'

Will nodded. 'I'll be there.'

Chris nodded and smiled. 'Thanks,' he rose, squinted and scanned the bar. He exhaled deeply, looking at the floor. 'I thought I was doing the right thing when I joined the banks a few years ago.'

Will waited for him to continue. There was something he wanted to say. However, the moment passed in silence and Chris said nothing. He got ready to leave. *That was a quick visit.*

'What time tonight?'

'It'll have to be just before midnight. That's the only time they can do it.'

The smoke and mirrors seemed overly dramatic. It was frustrating Will. 'Who?'

‘I can’t tell you yet, I need to talk them first. Just come. I’ll call you when I figure out exactly what time.’

Will nodded. His friend turned and started to walk out. As Will started to pick up his things, trying to make sense of what happened, he saw his friend stop and turn back around. Chris looked him in the eyes.

‘Will,’ Chris paused and cleared his throat. ‘This whole thing is tied up in Delpont. It’s all got to do with the fallout from the company going under.’

‘Delpont?’ Will frowned. ‘That was ages ago. Most of those guys are either behind bars or dead. Besides,’ he sighed. ‘In terms of fraud it was minor league compared to the fallout of 2008—’ He stopped and looked down, realising that he was sounding insensitive. He shouldn’t be questioning his friend like this. It was clearly difficult for him to say this. Regardless, it hadn’t seemed to affect Chris. He continued gently. ‘Why would anyone need to kill over this? Why now?’

‘Because,’ Chris said slowly. He sighed in what seemed like frustration. ‘The full story of what happened at Delpont was never told.’

ANDREA

It had been a long day. She was glad it was Thursday and almost the weekend. The initial excitement of working a new job had worn off after only a few days. She was already tired of the routine. She walked out of the office, the soles of her feet aching. She longed to kick her shoes off when she got home.

As she entered the elevator, she pulled out her phone to find a message from her husband. He would not be coming back from his business trip tonight and he needed to be there tomorrow as well. Almost instantly she felt relieved and excited. She had not been looking forward to him coming back after a few days away; whenever that happened they usually had sex. After working all week, the last thing she wanted was to be on all fours while her husband used her like a pornstar. The satisfaction was usually one sided.

'Night, Andrea.' One of the younger guys in the office smiled and waved in the foyer.

'Bye, Aaron.' She smiled back, heading to her car in the opposite direction to the 5pm migration that was occurring. She assumed they were going to the train station.

Once she was far enough from the office and out of earshot of anyone she worked with, she pulled her phone out and called her lover. It rang a few times before going to voicemail.

'Hi, darling. I just found out I'm free tonight and I've got a free house. Call me back, handsome.'

She continued on to her car, parked on a small street ten minutes walk from work. Despite the fact that her work was in a small commercial hub, this spot was residential and was only a few minutes walk. It was quiet here, she couldn't hear any of the noise she had heard only moments earlier. Passing traffic and a hundred different conversations competing with each other at the same time. The agitation she had felt during the day had started to fade away. She rolled her head, releasing the tension in her neck.

A few minutes had passed; Hank hadn't called her back. She double checked her phone to make sure she hadn't missed anything. There were no messages or missed calls. She sighed and put it back in her small black leather handbag. From memory it had been a gift from her husband, one of the rare times he had chosen something she liked.

Her drive home was quick, there wasn't too much traffic and she was fortunate to live in an area where she could avoid main roads. She kept looking at her phone sitting on the passenger seat. She was desperate to see him. She wanted to be touched and held, going a few days without that affection made her frustrated.

While looking at her phone, she almost didn't notice the light turn red. She braked hard at the last moment, coming to an abrupt stop over the line. The car behind her honked loudly. She glared at them in her rear mirror. As the pedestrians crossed the street they had to move around her car, making their way either behind or in front of it. She squinted, focusing on the traffic light ahead, avoiding their disapproving stares. She refused to feel embarrassed. When the light changed, she was gone in a hurry.

She was home within twenty minutes. As soon as she walked through the door she took her clothes off and headed for the shower quickly, desperate to freshen up and feel clean again. She put her phone on the counter above the sink, just in case he rang.

While washing and cleaning herself, she kept an eye on it. As soon as she got out of the shower and was dry, she sent him a message. She typed up essentially the same message she had sent to him by voicemail, in case he hadn't received it. Freshly showered and dry, she was ready to go out and do something. She was ready to see him. She exhaled deeply. Pacing the room while picking out clothes, Andrea could feel herself becoming increasingly frustrated and agitated. She started to worry that he was with another woman. She shook her head and pushed the thought aside, it was a crazy thought.

To pass the time waiting, she went to the kitchen and made herself a quick and simple pasta dish. As the water started to boil, she stirred the creamy cheese sauce. She poured herself a glass of white to relax, deciding on one of the sauvignons blancs she had chilled in the fridge. She smelled the drop, took a small sip. She hadn't tried this before but it was smooth and sweet.

She zoned out while eating and after dinner realised she had drunk half of the bottle. She checked her phone again. Nothing. She felt a mixture of nerves and frustrated lust. She called Hank again but it rang out and went to voicemail, *again*. She was becoming anxious, starting to worry that something had happened to him. He could be flaky and take time to get back sometimes, but usually not this long. She looked at the time on her phone; it had been two hours since she tried calling him. It was getting late, and she was running out of time to see him.

An hour passed. She watched the news and played on her iPad to pass the time. She alternated through websites and mind training apps. Her mind wandered while reading an article about Marcus Docker.

Something about the article reminded her of one particular time. She remembered seeing him celebrating on a day they'd made a couple hundred million.

Marcus, Lew Noble and a few others had broken open a few bottles of champagne at close of trade. She had seen the labels and knew they must have been about a thousand dollars a bottle. The other hundred or so traders on the floor had been given boxes of champagne that must have been at least a few hundred each. While the junior traders celebrated and got drunk on the lower level, the seniors partied on the upper level, overlooking the floor. Within fifteen minutes, plates of cocaine started to get passed out to everyone. She'd been invited by Marcus to party on the upper level, the invitation was delivered with a wide, coked-up smile on his face and a hand cupping her behind. Her face had remained cold as she looked him in the eyes, took his hand off her and turned him down. She remembered the look of resentment on his tanned, wrinkled face. He wasn't used to being turned down. Within a minute, he had shrugged and moved on to a slim and busty blonde graduate, whom Andrea was relatively sure had been hired out of a modelling academy.

Andrea watched the party escalate out of control; nervous new employees gradually becoming more comfortable as the cocaine and champagne hit their system. She hadn't joined in these parties for a few months since they had gradually become wilder and more closely resembling an orgy. Andrea paid face time until she knew her departure wouldn't be commented on, knocking back a few glasses of champagne to blend in. She tactically avoided whenever the plates of coke came around so that she wouldn't have the uncomfortable situation of turning it down. After another fifteen minutes the hook ups had started. This had been occurring more and more recently. She wasn't surprised by the younger staff; it could be expected of young people in a highly adrenaline packed and competitive environment, where lines between risk and reward were blurred. Adding alcohol and illicit drugs to the mix had exacerbated the situation. What surprised her was how senior staff had not only tolerated this culture, but had actively encouraged it. Her memories of Delpont were always dominated by that image of Marcus and the other boys watching the party from the upper level, co-workers making out with each other over desks, cheering each other on as the clothes started to fall off. Grown men carrying on in a drug induced stupor, fuelled on by their arrogance, behaviour more animal than man. As Andrea decided it was time for her to leave, before it got any worse, she watched as Marcus hiked up the skirt of the blonde graduate he had invited up, unzipped his fly and entered her as she laughed and the other seniors cheered them on. Whether the girl thought this would get her promoted, Andrea couldn't tell, but she knew that this company would chew her up and spit her out.

That was the beginning of the end for Andrea, the parties had never gotten that reckless or brazen before. From that point on she could no longer identify with the culture, it had morphed over the years and had become something she could no longer recognise. Within a few weeks she had left the company. A year later the company had fallen apart and most of those in charge were preparing to stand trial. She would, however, always remember that image of Marcus Docker, always think of him as that ravenous animal out of control. As far as she was concerned, that was who he truly was underneath.

Her phone buzzed and she came back to the present, forgetting all about Delpont and Marcus Docker. She began to feel nervous again, still hoping Hank was able to see her. She opened his message and read; 'Hey, sorry. I only just got your message. I'm with friends tonight, I can't do anything. Sorry, gorgeous.'

She tried to control the anger and jealousy, for a moment. Then she flung her phone across the coffee table.

WILL

He had waited all night for the call from Chris. He had fallen asleep on the couch watching an architecture show at around 1am.

Will woke to his phone buzzing. He groaned and tried to open his eyes. His neck was stiff from sleeping in an odd position. His phone was buzzing against the table and he reached for it but it was out of reach from his supine position. He missed the call. He laid back down and almost fell asleep again, only to be disturbed by another buzz. The caller had left a voicemail message. He exhaled deeply and pulled himself up. He yawned and felt his eyes water, feeling like a zombie.

He looked at the screen. The missed call was from Chris. He slid his phone to unlock and listened to the message.

'Hey, mate, it's me. Sorry for taking so long, can you meet us here now?' Chris was speaking loudly, talking over the waves breaking against the rocks. 'I'm sorry for getting you into this but I didn't want to do with this.' A strong wind screamed through the phone. 'Just come meet us by the rocks we used to smoke at. Remember that spot?'

His voice was anxious, speaking quickly in stark contrast to his usual slow and relaxed manner. Will remembered that he was meant to meet up with him now. He decided to hurry and skip the shower, trying instead to straighten out his hair. Maybe stop it from looking like the birds nest it had become from sleeping on it.

He tried calling Chris to tell him he was coming now. It went to voicemail. He sent a text to tell him instead.

The drive over felt surreal. Whether it was purely due to his current state of mind, he couldn't tell. The night was dark and the streets were deserted. The only things he heard were streetlights changing and the sound of his own engine coming in through the open windows. The only sights were the passing lights. They blurred as he drove past in his exhausted state, the cool air rushing in was the only thing keeping him awake. On the entire drive over, he didn't run into a single other car.

The waves crashed against the rocks. Clouds covered the sky, grey and overcast. One side of the sky was slowly lightening, the other still the darkest blue. It was early morning and the dawn was still breaking. The winter morning chilled him to the bone. Mist from the breaks reached his face as he walked along the rocks, moving slowly so as not to fall. The shore was still wet from high tide and he made his way around the base of the cliff, the sand still damp. The wind whipped all around and howled in his ears.

As he walked around the cliff base and the rocks area came into view, he found the man he had come to meet.

The man was no longer alive.

He lay tattered against the rocks, his woollen jumper soaked and weighed down, cuts to his hands and arms with his face in a shallow pool of salt water. Chris' face was hard to recognise in between the blood and the damage done to it. He could smell only the salt air otherwise he would have retched at the smell of the body.

The man who had asked him to meet him here an hour ago.

His body had been in the water for some time. All around was the stench of salt and seaweed. The seagulls cawed as they flew overhead.

He felt a chill run up his spine. Whether it was the cold or the scene in front of him, he didn't know. He only just noticed how quickly he was breathing.

He tried to calm down, to keep his cool. He took deep breaths. Tried to think it through. Whatever was going on right now went over his head. He thought about the voicemail he had received. It was only an hour ago. He could not imagine how it had happened so fast.

He realised that someone must have overheard Chris' phone call. Closing his eyes, he thought back over the past few weeks, and how he had ended up in this situation.

AOKI

By the time she got to the scene the sun had come up. She had been called early, and left home before it was light.

The crime scene wasn't what she had expected after her last callout. There were no crowds and was only one member of the press. She walked around the ambulance parked by the lifesavers clubhouse on the north side of the beach. The two paramedics were standing around waiting, most likely for forensics to be done with the body so they could take it away. The car park ran all the way to the building, and on the other side were steps down to the beach. There were waves today but no surfers. It was a cold morning. She looked out to the coast, out to the heavy surf and grey sky. She was rugged up in a heavy waterproof jacket, half asleep without her morning coffee.

As she walked down the steps, she saw Morgan waiting at the bottom. She perked up and smiled; he had brought coffee.

'I figured you would need it.' He said with tired grin.

'Thank you! I'm dying,' she took one of the cups and cradled it between her two palms. It was still hot. 'Seriously. Thanks a lot.'

'All good. You grab the next one.'

She fumbled through her pockets, rummaging to find her smokes.

'Nah. No need to pay me back.' He waved his hand dismissively.

'Oh, I was getting a cigarette.'

He grinned. 'Right.'

She stopped in her steps to light it, turning her back to the wind to protect the flame. A strong wind had kicked up during the morning. He turned and waited for her to catch up.

‘Have you checked the scene out yet?’

‘Nah. I only got here just before you. I saw your car pull up and figured I would wait down here.’

She nodded and sipped her coffee.

‘Any more major breakthroughs since yesterday?’ She couldn’t tell whether he was teasing or not, but it hit a nerve.

‘Very funny,’ she shook her head. ‘I’ve been thinking it over and over but I’ve got nothing else.’

‘It’s all good. You’ll figure it out.’

‘I dunno about that.’

‘What do you mean?’

‘I just—I’ve just been feeling frustrated. I keep thinking, maybe figuring that out yesterday, maybe that’s as good as I get.’ She frowned and looked at him. ‘I’m worried that I won’t be able to think of anything else, you know what I mean?’ She sighed.

He paused. ‘Hey, I was only teasing. You know that right?’

‘Nah, I’m serious, it’s not that. I’ve just been worrying about it.’

He put a reassuring hand on her shoulder and spoke slowly. ‘You’re a great detective. You are incredibly smart and I’m sure you’ll figure this out.’ He paused and made eye contact with her. ‘Don’t doubt yourself.’

She stopped and frowned, looking him in the eyes. She was taken aback. It was oddly sweet and sincere coming from him.

‘Thank you,’ she said uncertainly. ‘It means a lot.’

He nodded in acknowledgement and smiled, then cleared his throat and looked away. He got a little uncomfortable when talking honestly about his feelings, though it was rare.

The two kept walking along the beach. Their shoes sinking into the soft sand as they walked. She was glad she had chosen runners. Judging by the uncomfortable grimace on Morgan's face, he was regretting wearing his good leather shoes. He must have forgotten to read the full message again, and probably didn't realise the crime scene was physically on a beach.

As they made their way around the last stretch of rocks, the crime scene came into view.

The dead body was sprawled on rocks. Two forensic techs were investigating the deceased, and two officers were patrolling the scene. One of the officers was with a man sitting on a rock not too far from the body. He was hunched over with his head in his hands. He kept alternating between scratching his hair and rubbing his chin. He looked on edge. The man looked respectable enough; short brown hair and reasonably well dressed. He wore dark jeans, blue vans, grey jumper and a black three quarter length jacket.

'Who's this?' she asked with a frown.

'William Martec, the writer.' Morgan explained. 'He was the one who found the body and called it in.'

Aoki looked at him quizzically. 'I've never heard of him. Does he write like detective novels or something?'

'Nah, more like a journalist. He writes for a paper and has some books. Business type things. I don't really know him too well.'

'Oh, ok. What time did he call?'

'He says he got here about five, he called it in ten minutes later.'

'Five? What was he doing here at that time?'

'As soon as I asked him that he clammed up. Since then, he hasn't said too much.'

'Alright, then,' she frowned. She noticed he had a sneaky smile on his face. 'What is it, Morgan?' She asked, arms crossed.

He made eye contact with her. 'You remember the other day, we were talking about 'wealth is a crime'?'

'Ah, yeah.' She replied hesitantly.

'I told you I found one article about it?' He grinned. 'Well,' he said as he gestured towards Will. He didn't finish the sentence, the implication was clear.

'Wait what? Really?' Her eyes widened. 'No! Really?'

He laughed. 'Yeah.'

Aoki frowned, looking at the witness suspiciously. 'Have you considered him as a suspect?'

'Nah,' Morgan shook his head. 'Nah, I checked it out, he was still at home when this Chris guy died. By the time he got here, he would have already been dead a while. His story checks out with his phone records, and he stopped for petrol on the way.'

She squinted at Morgan.

'There's a receipt from when he stopped, I checked it,' he rolled his eyes. 'This guy isn't our suspect.'

'Alright, fine.' Aoki sighed. 'But I mean, the Sheeran crime scene, this death. Do you think they're connected?'

Morgan narrowed his gaze on her. 'I don't know,' he replied, uncertainty in his voice. 'I fucking hope not.'

She looked over at the suspect. He seemed shaken up. 'He's involved somehow.' She muttered what her inner voice was telling her.

'Yeah, but—'

'I don't mean as a suspect,' she cut him off. 'But I've got a feeling. He is involved in both deaths somehow.'

'Yeah, maybe,' Morgan shrugged. 'Look, his friend has just died. We can bring him in for questioning, but maybe let's do it later?' He suggested gently.

Aoki nodded. 'Alright. I'm going to go chat to him.'

'Sure thing.' He shrugged. Morgan walked over and knelt down next to the body.

Aoki walked over to the witness.

He looked up, realising she was there to talk to him. He looked nervous. *This man isn't a murderer*, she thought. *But he is trying to hide something*.

'You're the detective?'

'I'm Aoki. You're the journalist?'

'Will, yeah.' He sounded defeated, and kept looking away.

'The officer said you got here at about five, is that right?'

'Yeah. I called the police after I checked him.'

'How did you end up here so early?'

'He, uh, he called me, asked me to meet him here.' He shook his head and looked at the ground. 'When I got here he was already—' He shook his head again.

'Ok. Did you see anyone else here? Any other cars around?'

He shook his head.

'So, did you know him well?'

His mouth twisted slightly. 'Chris. His name is Chris.' He said slowly. 'I met him about eight years ago. At uni.'

‘You were close?’

‘Yeah. We are. We’d fallen out of touch for a bit.’

‘No conflict between you two? No disagreements?’

‘No,’ he said with resentment in his voice. ‘Not at all. He’s my friend.’

She realised he was still talking about his deceased friend in the present tense. She also noticed that he was trying *not* to look at the body. Everything suggested to her that he wasn’t the killer. He was clearly upset.

‘I’m sorry.’ She spoke softly.

He nodded slightly, still looking at the ground.

‘So, why did he ask you to meet him here?’ She asked gently.

He shrugged, shaking his head. It seemed as though he had shut off to her questions. She had made him defensive.

‘Do you know what he wanted to talk to you about? Did he say anything?’

‘I don’t know.’ He said dismissively.

‘Why would you leave your house in the middle of the night to meet him and not know why?’

He shook his head and sighed. ‘I’m not entirely sure what is going on, but he called me to talk about something. He didn’t say what it was exactly. It seemed like he was in trouble though.’

She studied his body language. It seemed right.

‘I, uh, have the voicemail he sent me. If you want to listen to it.’ He added, looking up at her.

‘Yeah, that would be helpful.’

He dug into his pocket, pulled his phone out and dialled his voicemail. It was only then she noticed his hand was trembling. He was looking through but struggling to use his phone. He gave up and handed her the phone. 'It's the only message on there.'

She put the phone to her ear and listened to the message.

'Hey, mate, it's me.' The recording said. The voice was gentle. 'Sorry for taking so long, can you meet us here now? … I'm sorry for getting you into this but I didn't want to do with this … just come meet me by the rocks we used to smoke at … Remember that spot?'

She paced back and forth as she listened, paying attention to any cues. She frowned after the first playback. He had given no hint as to *what* he wanted to talk about. She sighed and played back the message a second time, blocking her other ear to pick up any background noise, but it was too noisy by the rocks with the waves so close.

'Is there any way you could send this to me? I just want to have a better listen to it later.'

He cleared his throat, thinking for a moment. 'I do have an app. I use it for writing articles when I need to do phone calls. It lets me record straight from the phone.'

'Yeah, that would be great.' She said uncertainly, handing him the phone back. She didn't want to try and figure it out.

He focused on the phone. She saw him get out of voicemail, open an app and press a button. He then went back to the call and played back the message. 'How do you want me to send this to you?' He said looking up at her. Having one task to focus on had seemed to calm him.

'Email is probably best.' She handed him her card. 'That's really handy.'

'Yeah. I use it a lot.'

'I'm going to go take a look at—' She stopped herself from saying 'the body' to refer to his friend. 'The crime scene over there. If you think of anything else I'll just be over here, ok?'

'Sure thing.'

As she turned, he spoke. 'He has a partner, he's been with her for about five years, she's probably worried sick about him.' His voice was starting to choke up. 'Can I tell her first?'

Aoki felt her own throat get tight. *This body on the rocks was the man that someone loved*, she thought. *Someone had wanted to make a home and family with him. All their hopes and dreams for the future had been lost with his life, and the love shared between them was gone*. Her mind drifted to thoughts of what would happen if her own love went missing. How she would deal with it if she had that conversation. She felt upset even by the thought. 'Of course. I'm so sorry,' she added gently.

'I should go see her now. I, uh, gave the officer my details if you need anything else.'

'If *you* think of anything else, here's my card.' She said as softly as she could.

He nodded glumly, looking at the card.

She turned and walked away to Morgan. When she turned back Will had started walking back to the car park. His shoulders were slumped and his steps slow. He was defeated.

Walking towards Morgan and the crime scene, she could feel herself breathing quicker. She made sure to take slow and deep breaths to calm herself. She wasn't sure why this case was affecting her so much. She was usually able to distance herself from crime scenes, to view them less as people and more as bodies. She knew it was cold and clinical, but it felt natural to her by now. Though in moments like these, she was reminded that there were real lives affected by what she saw. It had only happened to her a few times, usually when the victim reminded her of a friend, a family member, or in this case, a partner. She sniffed and wiped her eyes, glad that Morgan hadn't noticed. Not that he would be insensitive, but she was uncomfortable showing emotions like these to her partner. She took one last deep breath and composed herself as she got close.

'How are you going here?' She asked him.

He looked at her closely. For a second she was worried he could tell. He turned back to the body and gestured. 'Not much here. The time in the water has taken away any fingerprints. Forensics have already checked. The friend from over there—where has he gone?'

'He wanted to go tell the victim's partner.'

'Oh, fuck.'

'Yeah.'

Speaking gently, Morgan crossed his arms. 'We should be doing that though.' His gaze was fixed on the ground.

'Yeah, I know.' She frowned. 'We'll give him an hour, then we can go talk to her. If it were me; I would prefer a friend telling me, rather than a stranger.'

Nodding slowly, he exhaled deeply. 'We, uh, got the ID from the friend and the wallet says the same. Chris Collins. Age 29.'

'Any criminal history?'

'Not even a parking ticket. This guy is a clean, upstanding citizen. This definitely looks like a murder to me.'

'Yeah, agreed. His body is mangled, his face especially looks like a fall from the cliff face above.'

He looked up. 'Yeah, that is what I was thinking.'

'Soaking wet clothes, though.'

‘Yeah, definitely spent some time in the water. Tide was probably higher then and just washed over the body.’

‘Suicide?’

Morgan smiled. ‘That was my first thought but check this out,’ he walked in close to the body. ‘It’s hard to see but right there, that looks like bruising on the neck.’

She knelt down next to him and watched where his fingers were indicating. There was a fine blue line around the neck. ‘You’re right. That’s definitely bruising. It looks like ligature marks, consistent with strangulation.’

‘That’s what I’m thinking.’

She stood up and took a deep breath. In her mind, it was definitely murder.

‘But he called his friend and told him to meet here.’

Morgan frowned.

‘He left a voicemail on the writer’s phone. It would have been about an hour before we found him.’

‘So, he was still alive at what? Like 4am?’

‘Yeah, about that. He said to meet ‘us’ here.’

‘Plural?’

‘Yeah. So, where’s the other person that guy, Will, came here to meet?’

Morgan smirked. ‘Good question, detective.’

WILL

He couldn't have stayed for any more questions. He wanted sleep. He was scared and overwhelmed. Chris was dead and he'd felt dizzy since he found his friend. At that point, Will couldn't remember calling the police.

He got into his car and took a look at himself in the rear view mirror. He was pale and his lips were dry. His eyes were bloodshot and the outsides of them were red and irritated. No doubt due to stress combined with a lack of sleep.

All he wanted was to go home and get back into bed. But every fibre of his being knew that he needed to find Rebecca. He needed to do this for his friend. In that moment, though, he could only think of his own pain, he could not bring himself to tell her. He felt ashamed. He wished he were a stronger man.

After a few minutes of doubt, he came to his senses. He took a deep breath and knew what he needed to do. He put his key in the ignition, pulled his car out and made his way towards Chris and Rebecca's apartment.

The drive went by in a blur. The whole way over he thought about what to say, how to tell her, how much to tell her. He wondered how much she knew of what Chris was up to. He became lost in his train of thought that he didn't notice the drive had passed. Before he knew it, he was parked out the front of their apartment.

As he got out of the car his heart started to beat faster. With each step he took towards the front door he kept seeing images of her, memories. In every one of those memories Chris was by her side. He didn't know what to say. He sighed and tried to slow his breathing. He couldn't help but think about all the times he had walked into this same apartment block to see Chris and Beck. Walking up the stairs to their floor, he remembered the times he and Chris had carried each other up the stairs late at night.

Walking past apartment 304 and smiled thinking of the time that Chris had tried for ten minutes to open the door to that apartment one time after a night out, thinking it was his apartment, 504. Will had stayed on their couch that night, and had been able to convince the owner of 304 not to call the police after thinking his house was being broken into. Will was about to laugh but his throat choked up, remembering the image of his friend strewn over the rocks.

He knocked on the door to 504. He heard footsteps and then saw the eyehole go dark. The door opened quickly.

Rebecca was standing waiting, her eyes red and her skin white, as though she had been crying all night. She looked at him expectantly. He thought of what he had decided to say.

Her voice was faint. 'Chris? Where is he?'

He bit his lip. He looked her in the eyes for the first time. His face betrayed him.

'No, no,' her lips trembled, her brow creased. 'No, please, no.' She dropped to the floor and started to cry, face in her hands. It was silent at first, her body shaking quietly. He could hear her sobbing and then she finally broke down into tears. It was only then that he noticed he was crying, too.

Beck shut the door on him. He kept knocking on the door and calling to her for another half an hour. Eventually, he realised she wouldn't let him in and he had decided to go home. He was falling asleep at her doorstep.

As soon as he got home, he pulled his clothes off in a daze and then stumbled into his bedroom. He was asleep as soon as his body hit the bed.

The next thing he felt was wind blowing in through the open window and heard the sound of curtains rustling. He slowly opened his eyes and looked towards the curtains, bright light was coming in from outside. He reached for his phone to check the time. It was past 3pm. He groaned.

There were no messages on his phone. He had hoped Beck would have gotten back to him. He sent her a text, telling her to call him so they could talk. Though at the same time, he felt she needed a moment to get her breath. As much as he wanted to be there for his friend, he knew she dealt with these things on her own. He remembered when her grandfather had died, years ago, and how Chris hadn't heard from her for at least a week.

He showered and pulled out a pair of blue jeans and a plain white tee. As he put them on, his phone rang. He reached for it quickly, hoping it was Beck.

'Hello.' He answered, his voice fast.

'Hey, fuck, it's me.' He heard Iz's voice on the other end. 'Fuck, I heard about Chris.' She said gently.

He sighed.

'I'm so sorry, babe. I can't believe it.' She said softly. 'Are you ok?'

He exhaled. 'Not really.' He muttered, his heart beating quicker.

'Fuck,' she swore again. 'That's a stupid question, I know. I'm sorry,' she sighed. 'I'm really shit with these conversations.'

He chuckled and shook his head. *She's trying*, he thought to himself. 'It's ok, I understand.'

'Is there anything I can do?' She asked.

He frowned. 'Maybe. I dunno, I really need to get out of the house now. I want to stay at home and recover, but I need to get out of the house.'

'And away from your own thoughts?' She suggested gently.

He sighed. He needed to be around other people, around the sound of chatter and music. It was dark and depressing in his apartment, and eerily quiet. Even then, he was torturing himself and unable to get the image of Chris' body out of his head. 'I need some help with something. I need to find out more about Delpont, but the prospect of doing that inside and alone is pretty daunting.'

There was silence on the other end for a moment. 'Delpont?'

'Yeah,' he sighed. 'I'll explain later. Want to meet at that café at the bottom of your street?'

'Alright.' She replied hesitantly. 'Yeah, that's fine. Meet there in two hours?'

'Sounds good.' He replied. He was about to hang up, then frowned. 'Thanks, by the way.'

'Of course. I'll see you soon.' She replied before hanging up.

ANDREA

She was glad she'd decided to call in sick. It wasn't a great start to her new job, but she was feeling frustrated already. The routine was difficult to adjust to after having so much free time. She woke at her usual time of 7am but didn't have the energy to face her routine. After a quick call to Charlie to say she would not be coming in, during which she pretended to be sick as much as possible, she had fallen back into bed and went straight back to sleep.

She remembered running through the halls, someone chasing at her heels. Her heart was pounding and she feared for her life. She turned and saw the wild eyes and evil grin of a demon in animal form. She screamed but no noise came out. She screamed as loud as she could. She shouted with her whole body. She was about to die.

She jumped up from the bed, sweating and screaming. She breathed deeply realising it was all a dream. Her heartbeat still erratic, she forced herself to slow her breathing. She counted to ten and breathed slow and deep, feeling the sweat over her chest and the back of her neck. She had no idea why she had the nightmare. She was lucky no one else was home. Her husband always freaked out when she had them. She sighed, calming herself. She needed to get out of the bed. Her sheets were covered in sweat.

She sighed deeply again, calming her nerves. That nightmare had brought up old feelings. It felt personal, but she couldn't understand why. She walked to her ensuite and washed her face at the sink with cold water.

Despite the hours of extra sleep she had gotten, she felt more tired than ever. Her movements were sluggish and slow, she felt her age for once. Being honest with herself, she felt older than her age. Lately, she had been feeling as though she wasn't as quick as she once had been, problems seemed to take longer to solve, things she tried to remember were often forgotten. On days like these she would rather be dead. She would hate for anyone to see this side of her, she was so competitive; needing to stay active and feel as healthy as ever. The older she got, however, the more she realised that the ageing process was unavoidable. With each day she felt she became less capable. She looked at her reflection in the mirror and widened her eyes, checking the whites and the colour of her pupils.

She showered and presented herself. With everything cleared up she decided to get out of the house and away from her thoughts. She was preoccupied by thoughts of failing at this new job, and also an increasing feeling of guilt in regards to the cuckolding of her husband. Lately, her relationship with Hank had her feeling conflicted.

It was only then that she realised she was hung over from last night, she had forgotten how much wine she had drunk. The harsh bright light of the bathroom brought out every flaw she had ignored for some time, the lines around her eyes which showed she was in her forties, the wrinkles around her exposed cleavage. She remembered what she had looked like at her best over ten years ago. The person in the mirror seemed to have flaws where those same perfections once existed.

She hit the mirror closed, shaking her head bitterly. She closed her eyes. When she opened them she decided to ignore these encroaching thoughts, too much was going on in her life, she needed to stay positive. She focused on her makeup and applied a light layer. Going for the look between completely natural and full make up, but subtle enough to suggest she still wasn't wearing any. The final result looked natural. She had come to learn the importance of subtlety as she became more mature.

She dressed casually for a change; jeans and a light white blouse. It was raining outside but she wore her brown leather jacket and grabbed her umbrella on the way out. The first thing she needed was breakfast, as the house was bare. She got in her blue hatchback and made her way to the shops. It was quiet in her suburb on a weekday, and a quiet day was exactly what she needed.

As she parked her car she thought about Hank. She was still feeling angry with him for not seeing her last night, but also for taking so long to get back to her. At the same time, she was aware she had overreacted by assuming he was with another woman. He loved her and she should be able to trust him. She felt bad for momentarily doubting him. She had been instantly reassured once he had sent a message letting her know where he was. He seemed to be seeing friends more and more often though. She missed how he had treated her at the beginning of their affair. Missed the days when he had paid complete attention to her.

'Andrea?!' She heard a shrill voice behind her.

She turned.

'Margaret.' Andrea replied, caught off guard. She wasn't prepared to see the former receptionists of Delpont. She cleared her throat, and smiled politely. 'It's been years. How are you going?'

'I've been well! You know, things just going along as usual,' she laughed with her energetic voice. She was now a petite, mid fifties woman with short blonde hair, she had worry lines etched in her brow. From her voice, however, Andrea could tell she was still the little bubbly woman who always had too much energy. She was a little hard to handle for most people as she was so intense. 'I've had a few jobs since back in Delpont, though. Moved around a few places doing reception.'

'That sounds good,' she replied briefly. 'Where are you at now?' She asked, going through the motions of conversation. With anyone from that world, she felt she needed to maintain polite decorum.

'Just this small real estate agency. It's pretty close to where we live so it's easy to drop the kids at school.'

'They must be teenagers by now?'

She laughed. 'Yeah, teenagers now. I miss when they were kids, though. They talked back a lot less!' She giggled. 'So, how about you? Do you and your husband have kids now?'

Andrea cleared her throat. 'No. Not yet. We've talked about it but haven't made the decision.'

'Oh. I'm sorry.'

'No. It's fine.' Andrea frowned. It bothered her when people had that reaction, assuming the decision not to have kids had been made by her husband, and assuming that Andrea was upset by it. The truth was that neither of them wanted kids, at least not right now. She had only ever thought about kids in the back of her mind. She changed the topic. 'It has been quite a while. Have you seen anyone from Delpont lately?'

'Oh, god, no. I didn't keep in touch with any of them. The men were all a bunch of animals.' She said, laughing still.

'I tend to agree with that.' At least on that point, the two were similar.

'Oh, I did see them all a few weeks ago at Kelvin Anderson's funeral.'

Andrea's eyes widened, confused.

'Oh, you didn't know?' Her voice lowered. 'I'm so sorry.'

'I had no idea. What happened?' She asked, frowning.

'Oh, it was pretty tragic. Some punk robbed him.'

'What?'

'Yeah. Held up his car, killed him and then left him there on the road.'

Andrea felt her stomach turn. She let out a deep breath, and felt her hand start to shake. It sounded so violent. She had always liked Kelvin. He was a big kid but a kind old man. He would have been in his sixties now. 'That's so awful. He was always so lovely with everyone.'

She smiled again. 'Yeah, despite everything it was a lovely funeral. I mean the wife and kids were distraught but everyone only had kind things to say about him. After Delpont, he was volunteering full time, collecting food and clothes for the homeless. Things like that.'

'Really? I didn't hear about that.'

'Apparently, he was pretty private about it. Someone told me he felt guilty how so many people had been affected by Delpont.'

'He was lucky he avoided jail.' She said out loud, instantly regretting letting it slip.

'True. Anyway, apparently he didn't let too many people know about it. One of his friends told me he didn't want to be seen as doing good.'

Andrea frowned. 'That's terrible. Why would he do that?'

'Oh, I dunno,' she laughed. 'I just talked to his friends at the wake. I didn't get a chance to talk to his family. They were the ones who told everyone about his volunteering during the funeral.'

'I guess they wanted people to know the good side of their husband and father.'

'Yeah. It was really touching. I would have thought you would have gotten an invite?'

‘Oh, I fell out of touch with everyone. I just didn’t hear about it.’ She felt slightly bad for not being there. The invitation was probably in one of the emails from old Delpont people she had deleted without reading.

‘Oh, god, this conversation got a bit morbid.’ She giggled as she attempted to lighten the mood. ‘Anyway, I’ve gotta run. We should catch up soon, I’ll send you an email!’

‘That would be good. It’s been too long.’ She replied politely, smiling. She doubted Margaret would email her, and she doubted even more that she would respond to it.

‘Agreed.’

Margaret turned and continued with her grocery shopping. Andrea quickly grabbed some food to cook and left in a hurry, not keen to run into Margaret again. She hated those awkward moments when she said goodbye after catching up with someone in a supermarket, only to run into them again. She always seemed to run into people she knew at this supermarket. She might need to find a new one to go to.

She left the supermarket and went to a small café in the parking lot. She ordered a cappuccino to go. As she sat at the table waiting for her order, flicking through the paper, she reflected on the news about Kelvin’s death. She frowned.

When she got home she read over all the articles about it. What she read made her feel increasingly suspicious. It felt as though there was more to it. She was frustrated reading the articles, as though something were missing. She needed to talk to someone and get some answers.

WILL

It was an overcast day outside but it wasn't meant to rain, so he'd opted for his leather jacket. With his MacBook in a laptop bag, he drove down to the closest beach. It should be quiet there on a day like today. It was a small harbour beach in one of the most expensive suburbs in the city. High-end sports cars littered the street, interspersed with luxury four wheel drives favoured by wealthy mothers. The beach was visible from the road that went right up until the sand, separated only by a concrete path and a strip of grass.

When he got there he remembered that this suburb was never quiet. Despite being a work day, the area was crowded with white haired couples in their sixties and groups of mothers. He had forgotten that no one in this suburb needed to work. Most could comfortably retire at forty, however, they ended up holding a position with the company and only coming in once every few weeks. For the hour or two of their time, they usually earned a couple hundred thousand a year. Trading companies loved to reward those who were loyal and towed the company line. Most of these people, however, would have inherited their wealth. From all his research and time spent studying economics, he had learned that most wealth resulted from inheritance in one way or another, due to lump sums of cash or the better education and networking opportunities available to those in the comfortable minority.

He parked on a backstreet at the northern end, and proceeded to walk the strip of shops. He found a café towards the southern end that had a few free tables outside and wasn't too noisy. He ordered a burger with fries and a cappuccino to wake him up. He paid with a twenty and tipped the rest.

He felt slightly better as soon as he eased into the red and white wicker chair outside. The tabletop was faux marble, the dishes were plain white and the salt and sugar shakers were stainless steel. The lounge music was quiet and soothing. The murmur of conversations interrupted only by an occasional round of laughter, or the quiet clatter of coffee cups and cutlery.

He had a look around at the café crowd. It provided a pretty typical representation of the area. A middle aged wealthy woman with her elderly mother. A couple in their early fifties wearing their sports gear and baseball caps along with expensive sunglasses and jewellery, stopping on their daily walk for coffee and muffins. The woman had puffed up lips and taut skin indicating plastic surgery. Their dark brown, stretched tight skin was suggestive of excessive time spent in tanning salons under UV lighting. The only other person in the café was a man in sports gear with a big belly and a similar UV tan, eating lunch with his pale blonde teenaged daughter who wore designer sunglasses and clothing. He sighed deeply, resenting the area already. The only bright side was it had good food and better views of the harbour.

He could infer a lot from the dynamics of the café crowd. The cheap clothing of the elderly woman implied that she had not grown up with wealth, in contrast to her middle aged daughter. The daughter had most likely achieved this wealth during her lifetime. The woman of the sporty aged middle couple was being overly affectionate towards the husband. A hand on the lap here, a stroke of the arm there. She was either cheating on him and paying extra attention to compensate, or more likely the two were lovers and married to other people. The father and daughter upset Will the most. The teenage daughter seemed shy and reserved from her father. The father had been on the phone the entire time talking business while the daughter sat patiently with her head bowed. The waiter delivered their food while the father kept talking. When he finally got off the phone, he made an awkward attempt at talking to his daughter, trying for the obvious topic of school. Before long, his phone rang again and the father was lost in business talk while the daughter sat quietly. Will sensed she was one of those girls who would trade the comforts of that money for a more present father. If that were the price of wealth, he would be happy not to pay it.

His own food arrived quickly and he thanked the waiter with a smile. He set it to the right side of the table, pulled out his MacBook and opened it up to his left. He needed to understand more of Delpont. *Whatever Chris had wanted to tell me was tied up in the company.* He needed a better understanding of the people behind the fallen empire.

He looked up the article that Beck had written and read through it. In another window he created a mind map. He wrote down the key people and how they related to the company. Some more research on *Wikipedia* found a simplified version of the corporate structure at the time of the collapse. Finally, he looked through the media coverage of the scandal and also the trials.

He spent nearly and hour reading over all the articles and information and making notes in his mind map. The articles discussed crazy things. Will hadn't heard many of these stories before. Traders were taking cocaine and drinking while recklessly gambling with millions of dollars. Interns were being hired by modelling agencies, paid over a hundred thousand a year to essentially file paperwork and act as eye candy. There were also widespread stories of traders having sex with each other and interns in full view of other people, sometimes even being cheered on.

The company had appeared incredibly generous, ostensibly giving away tens of millions of dollars. However in the years since, it had been found out that the charities belonged to the wives of traders and senior executives, and the wives were often paid salaries of half a million dollars. There were lots of articles about how the legal department had tried to shred all the paperwork just before the authorities moved in. There were countless embarrassing photos of the legal team being caught walking around with boxes of shredded paper when the police entered the room.

However, it was the human cost that upset Will the most and it was also the topic that had been reported on the least. The regular workers were encouraged to invest their savings and wages into company stock, considering it had been doing so well. Many of them had even foregone wages for bundles of company shares that had been worth more at the time. Some had even gone so far as to invest their retirement superannuation in shares. When things had been good, they were all doing incredibly well. Employees who had been with the company for five years were sitting on retirements of six hundred thousand to a million dollars at the peak. When things turned, however, they were left with nothing. There were tragic stories about employees in their sixties getting ready to retire and live comfortably, only to have the company go bust and all the money they'd saved, evaporate. Will swallowed hard at the thought, thinking about his own father now in his late sixties being in that same position.

When he felt like he had read enough, he sighed deeply and stretched.

He felt arms wrap around him from behind. His eyes widened. 'Are you doing ok, babe?' Iz asked gently. Her hair tickled his neck.

'Fucking hell,' he swore. 'You scared the shit out of me.' He laughed nervously and scratched his neck.

'Oh, sorry.' She said, pulling back.

'Nah, it's ok. Sorry. I was just off in my own world.'

'Yeah, I can understand,' she said, her gaze moving from him to his screen. 'That's Amber's father.' She stated, pointing at a photo.

He narrowed his gaze on the photo of Paul McDermott. The man had thinning white hair, a narrow face. There was a tight, forced smile on his face. It was a stock corporate profile photo. He wore a suit, behind him a view through the office window over a sunny harbour day. It had been taken from a high level, and you could see much of the city skyline in the background. *Every businessman in this city has the same photo*.

'He looks older than his age, except for those eyes.' Will muttered. Paul had bright, blue eyes.

'Yeah, sparkling eyes.' Iz said hesitantly. 'I don't know if they do it in a good or bad way, though.'

He grinned and shook his head.

She slumped down in the seat next to him. 'So what does this have to do with Chris?'

He frowned. 'He wanted to talk to me about Delpont.'

'When you went to meet him?'

He nodded. 'I don't know what, though.' His words trailed off. *I don't want to talk about Chris right now.*

Iz seemed to pick up on that, and she dropped the topic. 'So how did you go looking into it?'

He shook his head and sighed. 'It's a mess.' He cleared his throat and spoke calmly. 'I mean, at the centre of the scandal was the fraud. That was the start of all the corruption. The blackmail and everything else had been just to cover this up.'

'Alright,' she frowned. 'They were making up profit. I remember talking about it at school with a friend, after Amber ran out of that assembly.'

Will's left eye twitched, thinking of Amber in that situation. 'Poor girl.'

'Whatever.' Iz shrugged.

'But, you're right,' Will cleared his throat. 'The key crime was falsified accounting information and profit and loss statements.

The company was booking business that never happened through a complicated net of puppet companies, which had been created by someone who reported to Lew Noble, the chief financial officer. All the articles made Lew out to be the bad guy. He was the one who was punished most severely for the crimes of Delpont'.

'But you don't think it was him do you?' She asked, eyes narrowed.

He grinned. 'You know me too well. It wasn't just him. Pretty much everyone at the company was involved.'

She nodded. 'Figured.'

'Listen to this, though,' he said excitedly, clearing his throat. 'The company structure took me longer to figure out; it was somewhat of a mess. At the time of the trial, Marcus Docker was at the head position of Chief Executive Officer. But Paul McDermott held the position until two years before the collapse. McDermott wasn't charged with anything. It looks like he was the lead witness for the prosecution.'

'Fuck,' Iz swore. 'Sounds like a piece of work.'

Will smiled. 'They all tried to save their own skin. Docker cooperated from the beginning, he pled guilty and testified against others. For his cooperation, he escaped with house arrest for five years. And that was later reduced to two years for good behaviour.'

She shook her head.

'The second in charge was the Chief Operating Officer, Andy Ling. Ling got the harshest of sentences, over 50 years in prison.'

'Yeah, that's right!' She said, loudly. 'But he died before he went to jail.'

Will furrowed his brow. 'I haven't heard about that before.'

'Oh, really?' She scrunched her face. 'It was all over the news a few years ago. There were all those conspiracy theories about it. The circumstances were suspicious as well. Ling was driving his sports car, heavily drunk. Anyway, he drove it off a cliff by the beaches and his car exploded and burned on impact.'

'Right before trial?' He asked.

'Yeah, something like that. Anyway, regardless of the suspicions, the cops did a full investigation, and they found nothing.'

He sighed and moved on. 'I can see why people would be paranoid, though.'

'Yeah,' she raised her eyebrows. 'I reckon.'

'Anyway,' He cleared his throat, reading from his notes. 'At the next level down were five people reporting directly to the COO; chief financial officer Lew Noble, chief accounting officer Kristen Worthington, head of human resources Kelvin Anderson, head of investor relations Murray White, and CEO of Delpont Property Michael Blake.'

'Give me a look,' she shook her head and leaned over to look at his screen. 'I can't follow it with you reading it out to me.'

'Fine,' he said, pointing at the organisational chart on his screen. 'Delpont Property was a sub company that carried out projects and development. Of those five; Noble, Worthington, White and Blake had been sent to jail.'

'Yeah, but they all got let off.' She said absently, looking through his notes.

He nodded and scratched his scalp. He cleared his throat as he read through the charges. 'Anderson assisted in testifying, and wasn't accused of being directly involved in the fraud or falsified accounts. Worthington also cooperated and was given a reduced sentence of three years minimum security. White was viewed to have purposefully misled investors and was given a twenty-three year jail sentence. Blake had been working directly with those falsifying accounts, and was booking large projects through falsified companies. He was given a thirty year sentence.' Will said with a laugh, reading through the notes. 'He also acted like a prick during the trial.'

'Guess it didn't help him.' She muttered.

'Noble was the main guy, though. He got the second longest sentence of forty-five years. He had gone to jail straight away. After all, it was the trading teams reporting to him that had taken unnecessary risks and lost the majority of the money.'

Iz sighed, and rested her head on her right palm, supporting herself. 'Alright, then. But most of them didn't go to jail?'

'Pretty much.' He frowned.

'If they'd gotten caught selling drugs though, they all would have gone straight to jail. But no, all they did was take millions of dollars.' she muttered bitterly.

He grinned. 'True.'

'What about the traders?' She asked with a frown. 'Did any of them get in trouble?'

He exhaled and read through his notes, scanning for anything related. 'There were three core trading teams reporting to Lew Noble. The equities team led by Warren Francis, the commodities team led by Steve Sosek, and the most notorious of them all was the derivatives team led by Andrew Hunter, nicknamed 'Shark'.'

She scrunched her face. 'Seems fitting for trader.'

He grinned. 'By most accounts, it was Shark who came up with the original idea. He was the one who had created all the fake companies, and he was the one who had falsified all the profit. Sounds like this guy went after any suspicious accountants with unmatched tenacity. Any accountants brave enough to ask questions were subjected to intimidation by him. You know, Beck once met Shark?'

'Really?' Iz narrowed her gaze. 'When she wrote the article about Delpont?'

'Yeah,' he raised his eyebrows. 'When she wrote her article, she raised questions over the accounting practices. Anyway, she had been sat down by Shark, Noble and a few other traders and warned her to back off. She'd been pretty young at the time and new to journalism, the intimidation would have been overwhelming. She managed to hold it together while they were yelling at her, but she had broken down into tears as soon as she got to her car.'

Iz exhaled deeply. 'Shark sounds like a real piece of work.'

'He got a twenty-five year jail sentence. To his credit, he hadn't bothered appealing.'

'Fair enough.' She sighed, crossing her arms. It seemed she was waiting for him to keep talking.

'That's everyone, by the way.'

'Ok,' she nodded slowly. 'Yeah, fuck, I mean all in all it's a crazy story.'

'Yeah, I know.' He shook his head. *And we've only just skimmed the surface.*

'But still, even with all that you just told me, I still don't see what any of that has to do with Chris getting killed?' She asked bluntly.

Will frowned, she had him there.

'It was ten years ago, Will.' She shrugged. 'It sounds like it's all history.'

Will narrowed his gaze on the screen, unable to come up with an answer. 'I have no idea. I mean, if what Chris said was true, a lot of the story hasn't been told yet.'

'Alright, I guess,' She pursed her lips and crossed her arms, leaning back into her chair. 'But I mean, think about all these insane things that are already out there. I mean, fuck. Think about how easy it was for you to find it.' She said, gesturing at his screen.

He looked at her and frowned. 'What do you mean?'

'Well, you know,' she shrugged, mussing up her hair. 'Considering everything that's already public knowledge, just how bad are the things that haven't been told yet?' She spoke gently, uncertainty in her voice.

'Considering there are people willing to kill to keep it that way.' Will muttered with a frown.

AOKI

She woke herself up as she rolled over. Yawning, she cuddled back into the pillow and tried to get back to sleep. She felt exhausted. It was light out, though, and she wondered what time it was. She rubbed her face with her free hand, the other was under the pillow, and reached for her phone, next to her bed. It was 11am. She squinted and looked again. She realised that she must have had more sleep than she realised. Suddenly, she didn't feel so tired.

She inhaled deeply and then let out a deeper yawn, glad it was Saturday and that she could sleep in without getting in trouble at work. Her eyes were half open as she stumbled into the living room. Rick was busy cooking in the kitchen.

'How come you didn't wake me?' She half said and half yawned.

'Seemed like you needed it. I only got up an hour and a half ago, though.'

'What is this?' She said, sliding in next to him and looking at the dish in progress. She ran her fingertips up and down his singlet over his back.

'I'm doing up some omelettes.'

'Is that feta?'

'Yup. There's also some honey ham and spinach.'

She smiled and clapped impulsively. 'I love feta.'

He chuckled. 'I know, bub.' He squinted as he focused back on the hardest part, flipping it over. 'Hey, Denny called just before. He's doing mid afternoon lunch with Jules at that small bar we went to last week. They invited us, if you're keen?'

‘Hmm,’ she rubbed her eyes thinking. ‘I thought we were seeing your brother?’

‘No, that’s tomorrow!’

‘Oh really? Oh.’ She laughed. ‘Sure. Sounds fun.’

‘It’ll probably turn into afternoon drinks knowing them.’

She nodded and groaned, agreeing.

He finished cooking and slid the omelettes onto two plates. He handed her one and they crossed the room to their small dining table. She put her plate down and went back to the kitchen. ‘Iced tea?’

‘Please and thank you.’

She poured iced tea into two coffee mugs. They were constantly out of glassware. No matter how much they bought, it always seemed to break. She left his cup in front of him and set into her food. They ate quickly and in silence. He had always had big breakfasts since she had met him. He was always hungry in the mornings. Whenever she ate breakfast with him she found herself adopting his habits, as opposed to her usual tendency to skip breakfast.

After her meal, she stretched. She yawned, still waking up. He cleared his throat and then cleared their dishes. She lay back on the couch and played with her iPad, flicking through design ideas. The cat jumped up next to her, eager for affection. She stroked her furry companion as he purred with an arched back.

‘Hey, I’m going to grab some coffee, you want one?’ He asked.

‘That would be amazing. You sure you want to? I can go?’

He waved his hands dismissively. ‘Nah, it’s fine, I feel like a walk. It’s so close anyway. It’s almost like walking downstairs.’

She smiled. ‘Can you get me a Cap?’

‘One sugar?’

‘Yep.’

‘Done.’

‘Are you getting Chai lattes still?’

He ran his hand through his hair. ‘Yeah, I’ve been feeling better since I stopped having so much coffee and started having tea.’

‘That’s good. I’m glad.’ She said encouragingly. ‘I’ll just shower and check my messages.’

‘Sure thing,’ he said as he took off his singlet and put on a t-shirt. He was never fussed with showering before going out. She loved how relaxed he was, it always mellowed her out. He picked up the keys and his wallet. ‘I’ll be real quick.’

The door slammed heavily behind him. She was definitely awake now. She yawned as she walked to the bathroom, kicked her pyjamas off, and immersed herself in hot water. She wasn’t able to wake up and feel civilised until she had a hot shower. She used the lavender scented body wash with her loofa. It always left her feeling brand new.

With Rick out of the house her mind always turned back to cases. The body by the rocks had been on her mind lately. Something about it seemed particularly cruel to her. She frowned at the thought. All murder was inherently cruel. She corrected herself and rephrased her thoughts; everything about it seemed as though it was intended to hurt someone, to send a message. Everything suggested that the body was dumped at sea, but she believed they wanted for it to be washed ashore. Especially, when she thought about that voicemail the journalist had received. An hour before he was found, he would have been waiting more or less in the same spot.

She finished her shower and dried slowly, appreciating that she had the time to enjoy showering as opposed to her weekday experience. She dressed in jeans and a silk shirt.

When she was all done she checked her phone, looking for messages from work. She had a missed call from Morgan while she was in the shower. She frowned. He usually didn't call her on weekends. She hoped it wasn't another dramatic murder. She needed a day off. Just as she was about to check the message her phone started ringing. It was Morgan. She slid her screen to answer.

'Hey, Morgan.'

'Hey. Fuck. Sorry for calling you on a weekend.'

'It's all good. What's up?'

'Alright, so I was looking into that guy Chris—'

She cut him off, her voice excited. 'I've been thinking about that case, something seems—'

'Off! I know. Thank you!' He said talking quickly and excitedly. 'Alright, I'm glad it's not just me.'

'It feels like something else.'

'I think it might be.'

'How so?'

'Well, it might be nothing, but I checked him out and he lives with a girl called Rebecca Fulton. They've been living together for like two years or something.'

She frowned. She didn't understand what he was getting at.

'I went and saw her yesterday, she was all kinds of messed up. The journalist had just been over at her house and broke the news to her. She was pretty nice to talk to me but she was broken down.' He sounded insensitive, it was irritating her.

'Of course! Her fucking partner just died.'

'Yeah I know!' he said defensively. 'I was very gentle with her.'

'Alright. I'm glad.' She sighed.

'I did a pretty quick check on her, she's pretty clean except for a few parking and speeding tickets. But it turns out she used to work as a journalist too.'

She took a deep breath. *Will didn't mention that.*

'So I ask her about it, just making conversation. She had been very helpful up until that point. But as soon as I ask why she changed she totally clammed up.'

She felt excited. He was onto something.

'Anyway, I wasn't able to get too much out of her after that. She seemed pretty upset. So, I go home and look up her articles, it was very easy, guess what her last article was about?'

She was getting irritated at his games. 'I don't know! Just tell me!'

He laughed. 'Alright, her last article was about Delpont.'

Aoki suddenly breathed in, she knew her eyes had widened.

'So, this girl, Rebecca Fulton, it turns out she is the first journalist who broke the story about Delpont. She found out all about the fake bank accounts and falsified profit. All of it.'

Aoki realised she had audibly gasped.

'This girl pretty much brought Delpont down, man.' he said proudly.

Aoki was suddenly excited. She had a burst of energy on this case and real motivation to get into it now. Her mind was working overtime. But then her critical mind kicked in, and took the wind out of her sails. 'Hang on, wait. It doesn't make any sense. Why would the boyfriend get killed? More importantly, why now? It was like ten years ago.'

She heard him sigh over the phone. 'Yeah. I know. I haven't figured it out yet. Like I said, it's a stretch. But it just seems like a coincidence given the death of that Delpont guy a week ago.'

She looked up into imaginary clouds, as she was often prone to do when thinking over something. 'So, maybe he was killed by the same guy? Or he was killed in retaliation for the other death? Like two separate groups warring with each other.'

'Yeah, it does seem too gang-like.' He replied tentatively.

'Doesn't really fit.'

'I don't know how it fits in but I just wanted to tell you.' He sounded deflated now. Maybe she had shot him down too quick.

'No, it's really good! I'm glad you called me about it. I've been thinking about it.' All of what she said was true as well. That was sometimes the best way to cheer people up.

'Mmm. Well, anyway, have a think about it. We'll have to look into it some more.'

'Yeah, well, at least we already have plans for Monday.'

He laughed over the phone. 'Agreed. Something real like this almost makes me excited for Monday.'

She groaned. 'Oh god. I hope I never get to that point.'

He laughed loudly. 'Alright, well have a good weekend anyway! Say hey to Rick for me.'

'Will do. Hope it's a good weekend.'

‘I have a 21st tonight with a tall, thin, leggy blonde. My weekend will be fantastic.’

She smirked. ‘Terrible. Have fun.’

‘I always do.’ He said cheerily, and then hung up.

Aoki’s smile faded as she got off the phone from her friend and partner. The full implications and possibilities of what he said started to sink in. It was only when she got off the phone she realised there was something she wanted to ask him. *What about Martec’s article? Is there a connection with Fulton’s?* At that moment Rick walked back in the door with her coffee and his chai. He looked at her, as she was biting her lip with her arms crossed. He frowned instantly.

‘You got a call from work, didn’t you?’

She laughed. He had a knack for knowing.

‘No! God damn it!’ He said, trying to hide a smile. ‘Your mind always stays on work afterwards. Can you at least try and enjoy lunch today?’

She smiled and nodded. ‘Deal.’

WILL

He sat at the dark brown table and drank his beer. He was already a few in, but only then did he take a proper look around the bar. The Foxtrot was a narrow bar with lots of dark browns and blacks in the interior design. There was a graffiti mural on one wall of the room, the original brickwork on the opposite. The lighting was soft and low, candles on each table and lining the back bar. It was a warm environment. Will could appreciate it, but he had spent the day lost in his own thoughts.

He kept thinking about Chris and Delpont. It was all a mess and he had spent all that day and the day before looking for some link, some more information. He couldn't figure out how his friend fit into the picture. It had something to do with Rebecca, and the article she wrote about Delpont, but he didn't understand why Chris and not her. More importantly, it didn't make sense why this would happen now. He sighed and put his head in his hands. Chris had definitely said that these killings had something to do with Delpont.

He sighed deeply, his thoughts drifting to Amber. With everything going on, he wanted her so badly. Thinking of her big blue eyes and wide smile. He just wanted to nuzzle into her neck as she cradled him, wrapping her arms around him. He was drunk and exhausted. His body was drained and he had been wrapped up in guilt over the passing of his friend. He kept thinking what would have happened if he answered his phone, if he had talked to him. He shook his head. He should have stopped Chris at the bar. He should have talked to him then while he had the chance. Maybe his friend would still be alive. He felt bitter and regretted his own indecision. He felt that Rebecca probably blamed him, so he felt maybe he should too. He swore under his breath. He just wanted Amber, wanted to make her his. He just needed affection at this point.

He looked around the bar. He had been lost in his own thoughts so much that he didn't realise how crowded it was. He realised he must have looked crazy, drinking on his own and swearing to himself. He felt self-conscious, hoping the bartenders weren't looking at him. Somehow, he could tell they had other things on their minds, though. There was a throng around the bar, the two male bartenders looked under duress and were rushing to fill all the orders. He saw two attractive women in their early thirties at the table in front of him. One made eye contact with him, he smiled sadly It was the best he could do under the circumstances. She looked back at her friend and seemed to dismiss him. He felt stupid for trying. Mostly, it was just guys out with their friends, getting drinks. He felt a hit of regret, remembering times where a group like that had been him, Don and Chris. He still hadn't talked to Don about it, or even Rebecca. She hadn't returned his calls. He wondered if Don even knew yet. The thought made him tear up. He was a drunken mess, but he couldn't go home. He couldn't face being alone that night.

He looked around the bar again, glancing behind him. There were three tall and thin attractive girls in short form fitting dresses. He looked closer at the blonde one in the royal blue knee high dress with her back to him. He frowned, thinking it must be Amber. She turned to look at the bar and he saw her face. His heart beat faster as he realised it was her. He got up and walked to her, her back was turned to him but he could tell she was laughing with her friends. He tapped her shoulder.

'Amber?'

She stopped and turned slowly, squinting at him. He could see it was her. 'I'm sorry?'

'Amber. Hey, it's me Will.'

'What?' She paused and looked genuinely confused. She was starting to look less and less like Amber. 'You've got me confused with someone else.'

‘Oh,’ he said dejected. He was confused himself. ‘I’m sorry.’

She turned back to her friends but kept her eyes on him suspiciously. He couldn’t see Amber in her anymore, only a stranger. Her friends were looking at him and trying not to laugh. As he turned away he heard them giggle about the drunk fool that had tried to pick up their friend. He realised that it was probably time for him to go home, but he also knew he needed a drink after that embarrassment.

The crowd around the bar was still there, seemingly unchanged. He took a position in the queue behind a brunette with short hair. When he got to the front of the line, the bartender went to serve him before her.

‘Hey mate what can I get for you?’

‘Oh, no. She was first,’ Will replied, he turned to the brunette. ‘You go first.’

‘Are you sure?’

‘Yeah it’s fine. You were in front of me, anyway’

She smiled. ‘Thanks. That’s nice of you.’

‘Don’t worry about it.’

She placed her order with the bartender. He disappeared for a while to prepare her drink. ‘This place is so crowded tonight. I usually love coming here.’

‘Same here.’ Will was struggling to maintain conversation. In journalism and usually his personal life he could get people to open up, asking active questions to find out more about them. In his current state of inebriation and duress, all of those skills were gone. ‘So, what have you been up to tonight? Just been here?’ He was on the borderline of shouting to be heard over the music and other conversations.

‘No, we were in the city before. We headed back here for one of my girlfriend’s friend’s parties.’

‘Oh, ok.’ He couldn’t tell whether she meant girlfriend in the sense of her female friend, or her partner. He could be wrong but he felt like she was hitting on him. ‘Which one is your girlfriend?’ He asked in an attempt to get some clarification.

She stood up on her toes and looked to her right, trying to locate her. She pointed and said ‘Over there. The tall girl with the bright red hair.’

Will looked. His vision was a little blurry over distances in his state. He could, however, see a redhead glaring at him.

‘Oh, yeah. I see her. How long have you two been seeing each other?’

‘About six months or so now.’

Will nodded. He realised that he had been incorrect about her hitting on him. He frowned, confused as to why she seemed to be interested in him.

‘I’m Kelly, by the way.’ she smiled.

‘Nice to meet you Kelly, I’m Will’

‘That’s a nice name.’

‘Thanks.’ He smiled and looked down.

‘So are you on your own?’

‘Yeah, just needed to get out of the house.’

‘Oh, that’s no good.’ She said soothingly. ‘Hey, you should come and have a drink with us! You can meet my gorgeous single straight friend.’ She said with a laugh.

Will impulsively raised his eyebrow. ‘Sounds good.’

The bartender returned with her cocktails. Will, then ordered a beer while Kelly waited. He gave her a hand carrying the cocktails back to her friends. When they got to the group, Kelly's partner and another girl gave him suspicious looks. The third girl gave him a smile, however. She had long brown hair and light hazel eyes. Will figured that she was the single one. Kelly introduced him to the group. The friendly girl sitting down was Samantha. Will sat between Kelly and her.

He didn't remember much of what happened after that. He chatted and put some questions to Samantha, or Sam as her friends called her. It turned out she was studying design, she was a painter and graphic designer. They talked about their favourite artists and movements. He asked her what she wanted to do in design. She asked him about his books and his articles, and what he wanted to do next. After a while everyone got up and went to the dance floor. Her friends gave Sam a wink and they all went for a walk at the same time. When they did she moved in and danced close to him, leaning into his neck. He looked down at her slim body in the loose dress. It flattered her curves. He swallowed. The attraction was mutual. He slid his palm in and cupped behind her ear. Her eyes looked into his and they kissed slowly. It was a long kiss and she introduced tongue first. He could feel her pull herself close to him. At some point the kiss crossed the line into making out. Suddenly, she pulled back and straightened her hair. He turned and realised her friends had come back.

Will leaned over to whisper in Sam's ear. 'Did you want to get out of here?' He said calmly, despite the excitement he felt.

She looked up into his eyes. He could see she was breathing faster. She smiled and nodded. They ducked out of view of her friends and made their way through the crowd. When they got outside there was a small crowd out front smoking. They made their way around them and walked down the row of bars. As they walked down the road, she slipped her arm around him and they walked hand in hand. He could feel the warmth of her body against his.

When they reached his apartment, they started making out again but without restraint. While kissing her neck, he bit hard and she gasped. She pulled his hair, a wry smile on her face. He grinned, slipping the straps off her dress and watching it fall down. She tugged at the buckle of his belt and his pants fell.

He felt the warmth as she kissed his neck. He pulled up his shirt and yanked it off, taking a deep breath as he kissed her exposed skin. She wrapped her arms around his head and pulled him close to her chest. He held her by the hips as they moved towards the bed. They kissed and ran their hands over the others bodies, slipping off each other's underwear as they fell onto the bed.

LEW

He lay on his bed, looking at the concrete ceiling. Half the day was already gone. For whatever reason, he had no energy. He got up and looked at the small mirror in the corner of his cell. He scratched at his neck and rubbed his nose. Looking over his features, he realised he had gotten considerably slimmer over the past few weeks.

‘Hey, Noble. You have a visitor today.’

He pulled himself up from his bed slowly and looked at the guard. The guard stared back at him blankly. It didn’t seem like he was fucking with him. ‘Who is it?’

‘Dunno. Some lady.’

‘My wife?’

‘You have a wife?’ The guard looked confused.

‘Ex-wife.’

‘Right. Well, she didn’t say. Some blonde.’

Lew frowned. ‘Did she say her name?’

‘I don’t fucking know, rich boy. I’m not your fucking receptionist. Now either get the fuck out of your cell and see the bitch or don’t. I don’t give a fuck.’

Lew shook his head. He opted to see her. The guard unlocked the door and led him out to the visitors centre. There was a room full of visitors and prisoners, but one empty table across the room. He knew the blonde sitting at the table, but she was one of the last people he would expect to visit him.

‘Hey there, blondie. Come to visit me now that I’m not married? Make up for lost opportunities from back in the old days.’

Andrea frowned at him. ‘Charming as always Lew. And no. I would rather fuck a coffee table. It would be more charming and much more useful.’

He winced. She was always quick witted, and still a knockout. Tight blouse and knee high skirt that hugged her curves. He had always wanted to have a fling with her, but at the end of the day, he wouldn’t have done it. He had preferred his wife. That wasn’t a going concern anymore, but he got the feeling he didn’t have a chance. He had always enjoyed getting her worked up though. ‘Then why are you here?’

‘I see you are as blunt as ever. It is refreshing.’

‘No problems.’

‘I’ll be similarly frank. People have been dying Lew. Delpont people.’

He sighed. She always greeted him and every other guy in the office with a cold reception. That was also unchanged. He shook his head. ‘I know. I saw the article about Docker. So what?’

‘There have been others, as well.’

‘Do I look like I care, blondie?’ He gestured around the room. ‘I went to jail for those bastards. If they’ve got issues they can sort it out themselves.’

She rolled her eyes. ‘Nice attitude, Noble.’

‘What do you expect, darlin’?’ He asked sarcastically, a twisted grin on his face. ‘That I’d help you? Why don’t you sort your own shit out?’ He waved her off dismissively.

Her face flushed red with anger. ‘People have been dying Lew.’

‘Like Sheeran?’

‘What?’ She looked at him quizzically.

He frowned, realising his error. 'Never mind, who did you mean?'

She frowned. It didn't seem to register for her though and she dropped it. She mustn't have heard about that yet. 'Kelvin was killed a few weeks ago.'

He frowned at her. 'I didn't know about that.' He exhaled deeply.

'I'm sorry to be the bearer of bad news.' Her eyes softened, almost sympathetically. She frowned.

Kelvin didn't belong in with the rest of them. He had taken part in the fraud but he had fought them on it initially. 'He was pretty regretful over everything that happened. I heard he spent his time after Delpont volunteering.'

'He did. The family only told people about that at the funeral. How did you know?'

He shrugged. 'He came to visit a few times. We talked over everything. He felt pretty guilty for the first few years. He said he found real happiness with the volunteer work.' He said with a smirk.

She glared at him. 'It sounds like he was quite generous.'

He shrugged. 'How did he die?'

She cleared her throat and looked away. 'There was an incident. He was driving back from work at night. Someone stopped his car and robbed him. He was stabbed in the process.'

'Fuck.' He swore softly. He shook his head bitterly.

'I agree. It looked pretty suspicious. Whoever it was, got away clean. From the article I read it didn't seem like there was any evidence.'

There was a moment of silence while he thought it over. 'Why now though?'

'I'm sorry?'

'Why would anyone target us now?'

'Excuse me? Us?!' She raised her voice, her tone hostile.

He smirked. 'Oh, don't give me that princess. At the end of the day you went home with the money just like we did.'

'Go fuck yourself, Lew. I didn't make any fraudulent statements. I most certainly did not create any fraudulent companies. And I most definitely did not make profit while others suffered.'

'Yeah.' He grinned widely. 'But you knew about it all, didn't you?'

She glared at him. In that moment it seemed like she wanted to kill him.

He smiled. *I'm glad I can get under her skin.*

She spoke slowly, her voice full of venom. 'You can go straight to hell, Lew.'

'It's true, though. Isn't it, princess? I bet you haven't told anyone since just how much you knew, did you?' He laughed.

'That is none of your business, Noble.'

'The only reason I'm in here and you aren't is because you could plausibly claim you didn't know anything about it.'

'You think what you want to.' She glared at him, crossing her arms.

'Well, I'll think what I know is true. Because you were in the exact same meetings I was. You heard and participated in the same conversations I did. We all knew what we were doing.'

She was silent. Her look of spite had softened. Andrea's ice blue eyes betrayed her.

He smirked. *She's afraid.* 'So, before you walk in here giving me the moral high ground, maybe think over your own involvement. At the end of the day, you are the same as me. I made money off it. You made money off it.' He smiled at her. 'Our positions right now could have been very easily reversed.'

She shook her head bitterly. Her teeth were clenched. She fell silent for a moment, looking off lost in her thoughts. Finally, she turned back to him and smiled tightly. 'So, how does it feel to know the woman who was once your wife is now fucking and married to another man?'

He glared at her. He considered whether it was worth the harsh punishment to spit in her bitch face. 'Fuck you, Andrea.'

'I saw her wedding photos. She looked seriously happy, you know?' She was smiling smugly.

He sighed. 'You can't rile me up. She's not my wife anymore. I don't care what that bitch does.'

She furrowed her brow, trying to tell whether he was saying the truth or not.

'And no matter what you say about me, I never cheated on my wife. Can you say the same of your marriage?'

She glanced at him quickly. Her eyes widened. She was silent for a moment, looking at him. 'What are you talking about?'

He grinned smugly. 'I hear things.'

Her eyes widened, she seemed worried. There was an unexpected softness in her normally cold gaze. 'You're lying.'

'Well, if I am, then surely there's no harm in me passing this on to your husband?' He asked with a smirk.

She gave him a death stare.

'You know, I never saw you break your marriage vows during the hedonistic days of Delpont, why afterwards?' He asked sarcastically.

'I will end your pathetic life in here, Noble. How about I tell all the guards you're a rapist? Maybe pay them a thousand dollars to spread it to all the other prisoners?'

'We both know you don't have that kind of money.' He replied dismissively. 'At least, not without asking your husband. He is still your husband, is he not?' He asked tauntingly.

'Do the world a favour and kill yourself Lew!' Her voice was louder.

He smirked. 'You can't get rid of me that easily. But, I mean, I get that you don't want to talk to me about it. Maybe I could use my time in here to write your husband a letter? And ask him these questions?' He asked mockingly.

She stared at him with malice and a look to kill. She said nothing.

'If you can judge me so easily, then how about you take a look at yourself. You were just as responsible for the crimes of Delpont as I was. At least I'm honest about who I am. I am serving time for the crimes I committed. You lied every step of the way since Delpont, your life of wealth and privilege is a lie, too. Fuck, even your marriage is a lie. I'd even wager that he was completely faithful to you, as well.'

She shook her head. Her lip twitched.

'So while you were out fucking some stranger in an office or in a hotel room or maybe even in his apartment, think about how he was probably sitting at home waiting for his wife—'

'That's none of your business.' She cut him off. Her voice was surprisingly soft.

He had never seen her so vulnerable and weak. Suddenly, he didn't feel like the one who was trapped. He leaned in close to her, a grin on his face and asked softly. 'Did you ever even love your husband?'

Her voice suddenly choked. She covered her mouth. 'I love my husband.' Her eyes looked as though they were starting to tear. 'Fuck off.' He was starting to feel sorry for her.

He shook his head and sighed. For a moment, the two were silent while he leaned back and she sat there with her arms folded. He was about to apologise, when finally she shook her head and stood up.

'I don't even know why I bothered to come here.' Her hand was shaking. He couldn't tell whether it was from rage, or because she was upset. 'I don't know why I expected I could get help from you. It was my mistake.' Her voice started to raise in anger. 'You were, are and always will be a cunt, Lew Noble.' She shook her head and sighed. When she went to speak again her voice was clear and calm. 'You belong in here. From the bottom of my heart, you truly deserve what has happened to you.'

He swallowed hard and looked down. He put his head in his palm. At that moment all the animosity towards her went away. He no longer wanted to scare her or make her cry because at the end of the day she wasn't the person who he hated. He sighed and blinked, hiding that he was tearing up. He was vaguely aware that she was walking out of the room. She was right. She wasn't the one he hated. It was himself that he truly hated.

ANDREA

She stormed out of the jail in a hurry and headed to her car. It had been a colossal waste of time trying to talk to Lew. She felt like a fool for going to see him. Whatever information he had about what was going on, she doubted he would ever share it with her. He had always been somewhat of a dickhead, but she was taken aback by how cruel and angry he had become since she last saw him. He wondered if Lew had just been trying to get to her. *He couldn't have known about Hank. It's not possible*. She sat behind the wheel of her car in the parking lot, calming down. She shook her head and sighed. She supposed it was to be expected given everything.

On her drive home she thought about Hank. After the experience she had just been through, she needed some comfort. They'd been texting for the past few days but hadn't seen each other for a while. When she pulled up at a red light she sent a quick text to him, asking what he was up to that night. She didn't expect a reply too quickly. She was surprised when she got one shortly after the light turned green. She wasn't able to check it with her attention focused on the road and the traffic.

Andrea thought anxiously about what it could say. Lately, she had been increasingly anxious whenever she heard from him, more so after periods where he seemed to disappear and she didn't hear from him for a few days. She had been worrying lately that he might be ending things. By the time she reached another red light and was able to check it, she was breathing faster from nerves and felt anxious when reading it. She breathed a sigh of relief. All was fine. He was at home and wanted to see her. She smiled and took the next right to detour by his house.

She parked across the road from his apartment and made her way up the building. She checked the street to see if any cars had followed her. It was dead quiet, no cars had come into the street with her. She felt a little paranoid but her husband was wealthy. If he suspected anything it would be easy for him to have her followed. She had always been careful about covering her tracks. It always hurt to delete the texts her lover sent her. Some of them were quite romantic and touching, she would have loved to keep them to read over later. It was a chance that she was unwilling to take though.

She knocked on Hanks door. She waited a minute and there was no answer. She knocked again and heard movement inside. He opened the door and greeted her with a smile.

'Hey. Sorry, darling, I was out back listening to music.'

'That's fine. God, I needed to see you.' She kissed him, then wrapped her arms around him and held her close to his chest. He held her back and stroked her hair.

'Everything alright?' He asked when they pulled apart. He held her gently by the shoulders as he studied her face.

She shook her head. 'It's fine. I just ran into someone I used to work with. It wasn't pleasant.'

He frowned. 'I'm sorry to hear.' His gaze softened. He smiled and gestured to the kitchen. 'Well, I have wine. That will fix pretty much anything.'

She smiled. They walked together and he poured her a glass. She frowned into her wine. This felt so unnatural. He usually pounced on her as soon as he saw her. She started to feel anxious again that something was wrong.

She tipped her glass back and finished off her red. Before she put her glass down his arms were wrapped around her and he was kissing her neck. He kept kissing her neck as he leaned back and started undoing her buttons. She exhaled and smiled. Her world made sense again. She bit her lip as he kissed down her neck, lightly kissing over her collarbone and down her breasts. She grabbed his hair tight and closed her eyes.

He stopped kissing her and smiled as she looked at him in frustration. He held her by the hand and led her to the bedroom. She pushed him onto the bed when he had his back to her. He laughed as she pulled herself on top of him and the two undressed each other. She exhaled deeply when he pulled her bra off and started kissing her breasts. He was playing that game he liked where he slowly kissed towards her nipples. He smiled as he teased her. How could she have thought he was seeing someone else? When he was here with her she felt truly loved, his entire attention focused on her. She fell onto her back as he entered her. She closed her eyes and enjoyed the moment, feeling the comforting warmth of his skin against hers and the affection way he ran his fingertips lightly over her skin.

After he spilled his seed in her he lay down next to her and she rested against his chest. She ran her fingertips over his chest and felt how warm and sticky he was with sweat. After a few minutes, he got up and cleaned himself up in the bathroom. She frowned. Usually, he stayed in bed with her for a while and they talked softly to each other. It was usually the closest she felt to anyone, including her husband. She crossed her arms.

When he got out of the bathroom, he'd put his underwear back on and was smiling at her.

'You look gorgeous like that.'

She shook her head. 'Like what?'

'All angry like that. What's wrong? I thought you finished?'

'I did. Don't you know how to tell by now?'

'Yeah, your chest gets red and your face gets flushed.'

She smiled and tried to hide it. He did pay attention. 'It's not that.'

'Well, then, what's wrong?'

She looked at him. She sighed. It was hard to be angry at him when he smiled at her like that. His curly hair all messed up. He sat next to her and she stroked his stubble. 'Nothing. Don't worry about it.'

'Alright, then' He kissed her once on the neck then again slowly on the cheek.

Then he got up and pulled his jeans on, and started buttoning up his flannel.

She stood up and started putting her clothes on. Zipping her skirt up and buttoning up her shirt. Whatever frustrations she had been feeling, it would only lead to conflict if she brought them up with him. She just wanted to feel appreciated like before, for him to pay more attention to her. This time had been different like before, she started to feel like he was pulling away from her.

He slid in and hugged her from behind. He kissed the back of her neck and she smiled.

'I love you, gorgeous.' He whispered in her ear.

WILL

Considering the night before, the next morning wasn't too painful. He woke up feeling fresh. It was a cool morning with fresh air having had come into the apartment overnight through the open window. Sam was still asleep when he woke up. He smiled. She was cute and seemed like a nice girl.

He got up and went to the shower. Usually, he showered later in the morning, and even around midday on the weekends. This morning though he felt relaxed, the affection of last night had given him new energy. She was someone he could be friends with as well, they'd been able to have a decent conversation despite the fact they were both inebriated.

He turned the hot water on and got in the shower. He felt his confidence coming back. After everything lately, he'd been doubting himself. Suddenly things in his life made sense again. He sighed and thought of his friend that was now gone. He had been focusing on all the wrong things through the whole process, indulging in self pity and blaming himself. What he needed to focus on was how to solve this, to figure out who had done this and bring them to justice. He couldn't hide behind his guilt, even if there was more he could have done, even if it was his fault. It was about more than him. He needed to be there for his friend's partner, to support her and give her answers. Hopefully, she would talk to him this time.

He lost his train of thought when the shower curtains opened.

'Hope you don't mind if I join you?' She teased with a wicked grin.

He smiled. 'Not at all.' He embraced her and she kissed him. 'How are you feeling?'

‘Not too bad, all things considering. But someone kept me up last night.’ She teased.

He chuckled. ‘My bad. Thanks for making me drink that water when we got back. I feel much better.’

‘Well, someone has to look after you. Judging from your apartment it doesn’t look like you take good care of yourself.’

He realised she was right. Over the past few weeks he had been eating take away more and more. He had been so focused on his work and everything else that he hadn’t cleaned the apartment. There were still dirty plates on his coffee table, used glasses on his desk and couch.

He frowned, he must look like a slob. He looked at her face to see her reaction. She was smiling and washing herself, it didn’t seem to bother her.

‘I’m guessing you don’t have anything to eat around here, do you, boy?’

He laughed and shook his head.

‘Well, I’m starving, how about you take me out for breakfast?’ She asked, teasing.

‘I can’t usually eat on a hangover, I can’t stomach food.’

‘Well then, it’s a good thing you aren’t too hung over.’

‘That is true.’

‘Plus eating on a hangover is the best way to recover. You need protein to recover. And it is the least you could do after last night.’ She said, smiling at him.

It was true.

AOKI

The past few days had been a blur. There had been a lot of cases coming in over the weekend, and the office had been filled with constant calls and people yelling at each other to be heard. Her plan to quit smoking had completely backfired. In the past few days, she must have consumed her own body weight in coffee and cigarettes. It had taken a toll on her. When she had showered that morning she had noticed bags under her eyes. She had been sleeping poorly of late. She hadn't been able to sleep when she went to bed, tossing and turning after being stressed and on edge all day. She'd only had four hours sleep the past few nights.

She realised that it was the first chance she had gotten to think over everything since getting called in on Sunday. Whatever momentum she had built up in thinking through this Delpont issue had been completely lost in between the other cases. She hadn't had a moment to think about any of that.

She looked at the clock on her computer. It was just after midday. The office had only just started to quieten down. The phones weren't ringing as often and everyone seemed to have stopped talking to each other and focusing on their work. She knew everyone was in the same boat; all of them had a full workload. She sighed in frustration, it was becoming more and more apparent that they needed more people, but she knew with all the budget cuts it was never going to happen.

She put together a sheet of forensics and compiled it with her report on the case. Another case down. If she kept that up for the rest of the day she might be actually be ahead of her colleagues for once and have less open cases. She needed a break, though.

She ducked out of the office quickly, keeping her head low. She didn't want to attract too much attention. She headed to the lifts and made her way outside. When she was under the awning at the front of the building, she lit up a cigarette. As she breathed in the tobacco and watched the traffic go past, sighing deeply, which then made her yawn. She was a mess. Worse still, she hadn't seen Rick for the past few days because she had been getting home so late. In the moments that she had been able to see him, she could feel he was getting frustrated.

She took a drag of her cigarette and exhaled. As she smoked, her thoughts drifted to the image of Chris sprawled on the rocks. She shivered at the memory. It had been haunting her lately. More and more it seemed like a gang crime to her, at least elements of it. The body displayed so brazenly in a place where it would be easily found. Like someone was trying to send a message, to tell someone to back off.

'Aoki?'

She turned quickly when she heard her name called behind her. 'Morgan. What's up?'

'I'm going to go check over the Collins crime scene again. You want to come?'

'Isn't it a little busy?'

'That's their fault,' he said with a shrug. 'If they want shit done properly, they can hire more people.'

She laughed.

'I'm not going to compromise on my quality of work because of their own budget cuts. Fuck them.' He stated, irritation in his voice.

'Yeah, agreed. I don't know, though, I have a lot to get through.'

'Aren't you as hooked on this case as I am? Fuck the other stuff. Something is going on here.'

She frowned. 'I get that feeling too. I just don't want to get in shit for ducking out of work again. I'm sick of that team and the gossip.'

'Well, let them talk. Let your work speak for itself. Who cares what they think.' He replied coolly.

He was right. They were going to talk behind her back anyway, regardless of whether her stats were good or not. 'Alright. Count me in.'

He smiled and they headed to his car.

On the drive over she was silent, staring out the window. She noticed him looking over to her occasionally but ignored it. He always wanted to talk, but she was in the mood for silence. Her mind was on Chris Collins. The ligature marks on his neck. How he had either been thrown or fallen from the cliff above. She was starting to picture the events in her mind. They had found two sets of footprints on the cliff top, overlapping each other. To her it came across as a conflict. However, the ground had been disturbed shortly after. They had found tire marks, so presumably from a car driving away, kicking up the dirt. It was impossible to get a decent idea of what size shoes had been worn, let alone get an accurate shoe print. So far, all she had were ideas of what happened, and nothing to indicate either way.

Morgan passed by the same car park as the other day. They continued up the road and turned right.

'Where are you headed to? We passed the car park?'

'Heading to the cliff top. That's where he was thrown from right?' He smiled.

She smiled back. 'True enough.'

'So, no matter who this mope is who chucks this kid off the side, he must have scuffled, must have left something of his behind.'

'Wishful thinking, Morgan. They already checked it.'

He scoffed. 'That hipster kid from forensics checked it. My nephew in kindergarten picks up more detail.'

She laughed. 'You mean Wilkins?'

'Mm-hmm.'

'Seriously? How is he still with forensics?'

'You hear about that scene where he submitted his own footprints into evidence?'

'The Di Lorenzo case right? Fuck.'

They both shook their heads. She smiled.

Morgan pulled the car over at the end of the road. They walked along the short path to the dirt parking lot. She walked slowly, hands in her pockets, looking at the ground. She kept low and looked at the bushes, checking for anything out of the ordinary. There was nothing but sticks and leaves. A few scraps of rubbish and crushed cans. She sighed. She had felt hopeful in the car, expecting to find something. As soon as she got out of the car though her instincts felt off, it seemed such a plain scene in the light of day. Nothing was standing out to her.

'Doesn't feel like anything is going to be here.'

'Fuck it. So, indulge me this one crime scene and I'll help you out next time you have a hunch.'

'Alright, it's a deal.'

'Done.'

'I mean it, Morgan!' She said assertively. 'You better stick to that'.

'Yeah, yeah, I will. Don't sweat it.' He replied dismissively.

Morgan stopped in his tracks when he reached the edge of the cliff. Aoki rustled through the bushes, hoping something might fall loose.

'You see here, he would have been thrown off from here. It's a clear drop to the rocks below.'

Aoki stayed focused on the bushes, she didn't look back to him. 'Seems about right. Height would be consistent.'

She moved to the next bush. 'But there was a conflict, as well.'

He looked around. Looking at the ground. 'Probably about there. Looks like it is all kicked up.'

'See any foot prints?'

He squatted down and looked around. He shook his head. 'Nup. It's a mess. Looks like two males.'

'Give me a look.' She got up and walked over. Squatting next to him.

'Careful, don't take a knee.'

She scoffed. 'Don't you think I know that, Morgan!'

'Never hurts to say.'

'It does when you say it every crime scene.' She said, frustrated.

'I do?'

She nodded.

'Seriously?'

'Can we focus here? I'm trying to find a footprint in a haystack.'

'There's that one there I can see. I didn't do it last time we were here.'

‘Not then. So, maybe I should have said almost every scene. So that trail is from this one?’

‘Best I can tell. What about the one before?’

‘The suicide?’

He nodded.

‘Yep. You did it then. What do you make of this one here? The slim one.’

‘Looks like a woman’s shoe. Probably from something separate. Damn. I don’t remember it.’

‘It does look like a woman’s shoe. You might not but I do.’

‘What about last week? Sheeran?’

‘Maybe, I don’t think so. Did you see this firm imprint here? The deep one?’

He nodded. ‘I saw that too.’

‘Looks like the point of attack, right?’

‘Maybe. Only one set of footprints, though.’

‘Only one set of deep footprints.’

‘What do you mean?’

‘Exactly what I said. Maybe they didn’t need to plant their feet down.’

‘For strangulation?’

‘It’s an idea.’

‘Well, there is a lot of scuffle just here, right behind where he would have been standing.’

‘And some dragged heel prints.’

‘From moving the body?’

‘Maybe. I think it is from him kicking out as he was strangled. See how the ground is pushed away from the heel.’

‘As opposed to building up at the back of where the heel would be.’

‘Yeah.’

‘Seems more likely. This isn’t telling us much, though. I feel like if we had some decent forensics we would already know this.’

‘Well, that’s typical bureaucracy. Nothing but budget cutting.’ He said bitterly.

She frowned. *For someone who hates bureaucracy so much, it’s strange he became a cop.* ‘Yeah, but we’ve been doing it consistently for years.’

He shrugged. ‘That’s the mentality now, man. Directors have a lower budget. It looks like they did a better job.’

She shook her head. ‘What happened to police doing a better job meaning less crime?’

‘The only thing the directors care about is their own careers and their budget. And the only reason they care about their budget is because it is the only thing their bosses talk about.’

‘It’s bullshit.’

‘It’s the world post 2008, is what it is. A bunch of asshole traders gambled and made a shitload of money for themselves. When shit got fucked up they got bailed out and meanwhile everyone else is paying their tab.’

She scrunched her face and looked at him confused. ‘Really? You care about that stuff?’

He looked at her and shrugged. 'Yeah. What of it?'

She narrowed her gaze on him, and was silent. 'You don't care about these wealthy people dying, do you?'

He sighed and looked at her. 'Not really.' He admitted flatly.

She shook her head and frowned. 'So, you reckon that some bankers taking more than their fair share is a crime? What about this stuff? What about the murders?'

He scoffed and waved his hand dismissively. 'A murder ends one life. It affects a lot of people, but at the end of the day it only ends one life.'

'You think that something can be worth more than one life?'

'Sure can,' he shrugged. He was silent a moment, seemingly lost in thought. 'You earn what? Just over sixty thousand a year?'

'Just under sixty thousand.'

'Just under sixty thousand, right. So say you stop working, say you get six hundred thousand, you can survive at exactly the same level for like ten years, right?'

'Yeah. Assuming prices stay the same.'

'So, you put it in a bank account, you get interest on it. Now, assuming you live to be seventy.'

'Seventy?'

'Whatever. It's the average life expectancy.'

'It's more like eighty.'

'Alright, fine, assuming you live to eighty, how much would you need for your lifetime? From when you were born?'

'Fine. Roughly what? Sixty times eighty.'

'Yeah, what is that? Like what—' Morgan scrunched his face, moving his lips.

'Six times eight carry the zeros. Four million and eight hundred thousand. You can't figure that out without a calculator?'

'Whatever, I'm bad with numbers. My point is this—' He paused.

She made eye contact with him, waiting.

'Those same bankers, the ones that crashed their companies and after the companies get bailed out, each get bonuses. For their hard work.'

She shook her head. 'Alright.'

'That's not the worst part,' he said bitterly. 'Most of the bonuses were between five hundred and seven hundred million dollars.'

Her eyes widened. She looked at him to tell if he was serious. He had that bitter smile on his face that he often got when talking about rich people or the most fucked up criminals. In his rants, he usually considered them interchangeable.

'They caused a financial crisis, created the largest youth unemployment ever seen in Europe, America and most of the world, created a recession which has lasted for five years now. And for all that they get performance bonuses. By your own definition, they get payouts the equivalent of between one hundred to one hundred and fifty lifetimes.'

She hadn't thought of it in those terms. It made the idea of 'time as money' seem like a terrifying concept. She shook her head. 'Bullshit. So all that 'wealth is a crime' bullshit we saw at the Sheeran house, you buy that? You think that is justified?'

He looked out to the water, shaking his head. 'Yeah.'

'Fuck you. A murder is a murder.'

'Well, I don't care. If it's some rich asshole who dies then I don't care. They took more than their fair share. And don't give me that shit. I'm tired of chalking up homeless people that no one cares about. You think they don't matter?'

'That's my point, Morgan. A life is a life.'

He smiled at her. 'So, maybe if that rich person has a little less money, maybe that money goes to the homeless person, maybe he wouldn't be homeless, maybe that homeless person wouldn't be dead.'

She sighed deeply. It was a sad notion to think about.

'If you think about it that way, maybe the rich person isn't the victim. Maybe he is the real criminal. Except nobody gives a fuck about the crime because that homeless person was unfortunate enough to fall between the cracks of society.'

She looked at him slowly. 'Whatever Morgan,' she responded angrily. 'You think whatever you want.'

He smiled and turned away. He could tell the conversation was over for her. He stopped in his tracks and looked around. He looked puzzled.

'What's up? You alright?'

'Uh, yeah. I just don't understand this.'

'What part?'

'No, well, obviously this whole thing is confusing. But I'm asking myself something—ok, so, this spot is pretty remote, pretty quiet, and an odd spot to meet someone.'

He wasn't making any sense. He sometimes got like this when trying to solve something, he would think aloud but would only say half of what he was thinking, leaving everyone else with an incomplete picture. She nodded and shrugged her shoulders. These were all things they had talked about.

‘So, why would he need to do it? Even if he wanted to meet, why go to all this trouble to meet in this spot in the middle of the night?’

She frowned. ‘I’ve been thinking about that myself.’

‘Well, maybe it wasn’t because he was hiding something?’

‘What do you mean? You think he was doing something wrong?’

He shrugged. ‘To be honest, yeah, I do. All the secrecy makes it seem like something was going on.’

‘I guess that makes sense. That probably should have been my first instinct. Everything about it seemed like he was a victim.’

‘Well, I think you were right the first time. Maybe he knew he was being followed?’

She nodded slowly. ‘I guess—’

‘You guess? That’s it?’

‘It’s possible. You sound like a conspiracy theorist, though.’

‘Whatever. But, I mean, think about it. He ducks out of his place when he thinks they aren’t looking. Calls his friend to see him as soon as possible, before they can find them. Remember the voicemail?’

‘Yeah. What about it?’

‘He tells his friend to meet up at ‘that spot’ where they used to smoke. ‘By the rocks’. Even if someone else hears that then they won’t know where he was talking about.’

‘You think he was being cryptic on purpose?’

‘Maybe. But, I mean, considering that they found him anyway, I definitely think there is a chance he was being followed, and for them to find him so quickly I think it isn’t too crazy to think he was being followed closely.’

‘I guess.’ She said with a smile.

‘Why are you smiling?’

‘I think I know how we can catch whoever did it.’

He frowned at her.

‘Well, assume someone is following him, assume it was because he knew something about this Delpont thing ten years ago, who else would have known about it?’

He smiled and looked down. ‘I gotcha. His wife.’ He said excitedly.

‘Girlfriend.’

‘Whatever.’ He said quickly. ‘So you think they might still be following her?’

She nodded. ‘Now more than ever.’

‘There are a lot of assumptions you’re making.’

She shrugged. ‘Yeah, but it is worth checking out, anyway.’

‘Alright, then. Maybe we should speak to her first.’

‘Agreed.’

WILL

He stood with Don at the edge of the cemetery. Both wore sunglasses to cover their red eyes. When Beck's car arrived they opened the door for her and Don held a hand to help her out.

'Thank you, Don.' Her voice was soft, barely above a whisper.

He smiled sadly. She clung to his arm as they walked to the open grave. Will let them walk ahead. Don had been a much closer friend to Chris and Beck. He also suspected that Beck still couldn't talk to him yet. She still associated him with breaking the news to her. He could tell that she blamed him for the whole situation. She wasn't too far wrong.

The funeral was small and private; only family and a few friends. Considering the circumstances, no one had wanted to do anything big. The family had wanted it to be as quiet as possible. Originally it was just meant to be family and Beck, but she had convinced them to let a handful of friends attend.

They had said goodbye to their friend standing by his open grave. The priest had said a few words, talking about the big picture and God's plan. The words felt empty to Will. He didn't believe in any of that, and he didn't think the family did either. If there were a plan, he couldn't see how this was a part of it. He couldn't see how any good could come of it.

His father spoke next, about how proud he was of his son's volunteer and charity work. He spoke well but his voice started to choke up at the end. Everyone in attendance felt for him. When Beck started talking it had become too much. She talked about how happy he had made her. Will let go. He looked away and started to weep. Glad he was wearing his glasses. He smiled sadly and felt the tears fall, thinking about the happy times, the good moments they had shared. He thought of his friend smiling, and then looked back at the scene in front of him, the smiling photo of his friend beside the coffin and his family in tears. He couldn't process how wrong it was. Chris shouldn't be gone, there was so much more he could have done in life. He watched the coffin being lowered slowly into the ground while they played one of his favourite songs. All the possibility and potential of his friend was now lost, and Will was no closer to figuring out what was so important that he had died for.

One by one they thanked the priest. He looked each of them in the eyes. When Will thanked him, he could see genuine compassion in the man. This man felt something for someone that was essentially a stranger. He could show compassion to people he hadn't met before. In a moment like that, Will always realised how small the big problems seemed to be. The stresses, the fears, the hopes. The real nature of the world was life and death. At the end of it all, there were only those two realities. The life of a person could be summed up by whatever change he had made in the world by the end.

Will thought over his own life, what he had done. He realised most of it had been for himself. He thought of how his friend had been so generous, with his time and with his money. Will always said he cared about equality, he said he cared about a better world. He shook his head. It had been all talk. He wondered when was the last time he had gone out and done something for someone else. When was the last time he had donated some of his money? When was the last time he had stood up for the greater good? He looked at Chris' family consoling each other, hands on shoulders. He saw his friends talking to Beck, offering support for the loss of her lover. He looked on as an observer. He asked himself what he stood for, but couldn't think of an answer.

He noticed Beck excuse herself from her conversation with Don and their other friends. She looked at Will and made her way over to him. He greeted her with a hug. When they broke the embrace, she sniffed and wiped away a tear from under her glasses. He struggled to think of what to say.

‘I’m so sorry, Beck. I can’t imagine how you would be feeling today.’ It was all he could think of. It was honest. There weren’t words that were appropriate for her loss. There was nothing he could say which could adequately reflect how sorry he was.

She nodded and smiled sadly. ‘Thank you.’

‘But Chris would have been really touched by what you said. You spoke really well.’

She nodded looking down. He rested a hand on her shoulder in an effort to comfort her. She took off her sunglasses and looked him in the eyes. It was the first chance he’d had to see just how much of a toll this was taking on her. Her eyes were red and there were bags under them. It was evident that she hadn’t been sleeping. Her gaze was tense. She looked stressed out of her mind, and as though she had been having too much caffeine. There was a moment of silence and then she finally spoke.

‘I’m sorry I haven’t talked to you yet. I just—I haven’t been able to.’ She spoke softly in a hushed voice.

‘Beck, of course. I understand, don’t worry about it.’

She shook her head. ‘No, no. It’s not alright. I, um,’ She looked away. ‘I was busy blaming you.’

He felt a pain in the pit of his stomach. He nodded. ‘Fair enough. I have been, too.’

She shook her head and frowned. ‘No, no. It wasn’t fair of me. I was also blaming myself.’

‘Don’t do that. This wasn’t your fault.’

She shook her head again. ‘This whole thing is fucked up. There are a lot of people responsible. I need to talk to you. We can’t keep hiding from this.’

‘Whatever I can do to help, I’m there Beck.’

She narrowed her gaze at him. 'Are you sure you mean that? Look at what they did to Chris? Are you ready to risk that?'

He asked himself the same question. She was right. It was a lot to risk. He felt afraid but didn't want to let Beck see it. He cursed himself for the moment of weakness. He was scared, but considering what was going on, it needed to be done. He wished he were a stronger person, someone who could handle it without being afraid. She needed someone tougher. But for now, Beck would have to make do with him.

He nodded. 'I know the risks. I'm in this with you, Beck. I promise. I want to do this for Chris and for you.'

She nodded. 'Well, then, it's about time I finally tell you what is going on. Come back to mine and we can talk about it.'

'Sure thing.'

'Leave separately though, and catch a cab. Come in through the back way.'

He squinted and looked her in the eyes. Trying to tell if she were being serious, or if she were exaggerating. Her stare was unflinching.

'Chris was being followed.' She said bluntly. There was no doubt in her voice.

AOKI

'Hey. I've gotten held back. I'm going to be home a bit later.' She said softly.

She could hear him sigh on the other end. 'Are you working?'

'It's more serious than that. Morgan and I are looking into something. We think someone's in trouble.'

There was a moment of silence on the other side. 'Fine. Whatever.'

'Are you seriously upset with me about this?' She took a drag of her cigarette and crossed her arms. She looked over at Morgan to see if he was listening, but she had walked far enough away from him that he was out of earshot. He was leaning against the car with his arms crossed and looking up at the stars.

'It doesn't matter.'

'No. It does matter. Why are you upset with me?' She felt irritated, but tried to hide it in her voice. *I don't want to deal with this right now.*

'Because this always happens. You always get caught up in something and—fuck.'

'What?'

He sighed. 'It's the fucking weekend. You can't always be working. It's just a job.'

'This isn't just a job,' she said softly despite the irritation she felt. She shook her head. 'Sometimes I have to work late or come in on my days off. If I don't do what I do, then maybe someone dies.' She took a drag of her cigarette and exhaled slowly. 'Being police isn't just my job. It's a part of my life.'

She heard him take a deep breath. He was silent. She felt like she had made her point, but this topic always risked antagonising him. It wasn't that he was possessive. She knew he was just caring for her in his own way. But it wasn't his decision. It was her life and she was going to make her own choices.

'Ok, then.' Was his response.

'Is that it?'

'I guess so,' he said, resigned. 'You go do what you have to do.'

Fuck, she thought to herself. He was probably more upset now. She hated when he got passive aggressive.

'Alright. I'll be home a bit later. I won't be too late.'

'Ok, then. I'll see you then.'

'Bye, babe,' she paused. 'I love you.' She hated to be soft with him when they were fighting, but she hated to say goodbye to him when they were in a conflict and leave things on a bad note.

His voice softened. 'Yeah, I love you too.'

She heard the phone click and put it in her pocket. There would be no resolution that night. But at least things between them weren't left on bad words. She walked back over to Morgan, patiently waiting and leaning against the car. She flicked her cigarette to the curb and stubbed it out with her heel.

'Everything good?'

'Yeah,' she lied. 'It's fine.'

He smiled. 'Didn't sound fine.'

'Fuck. I didn't think you could hear.'

'It was kind of hard not to, sorry. Are you alright?'

'Just the same old stuff. You're lucky you're single.'

He scoffed. ‘It’s not all fun and games. I miss having someone to fight with.’

She laughed. ‘Bullshit. Whenever this stuff comes up it’s just constant tension between me and him.’

‘Why? What’s the problem?’ He asked gently as he opened his car door. ‘Do you want to drive or should I?’

‘You drive. I hate driving angry.’

‘Yeah, I’m not crazy about driving with you angry, either.’

She laughed and got in the passenger side. He started the car and pulled out.

He flicked the lights on. It was still dusk but it was already quite dark.

‘No, I don’t know. He just gets shitty with me when I stay back so late.’

‘Yeah. I remember I argued with my ex about that too. They always say they understand but they never do when it comes down to it. It’s not just a job.’

‘That’s exactly what I said! He just gets passive aggressive with me.’

‘How come? As in he wants you to be spending time with him?’

She shook her head. ‘No, it’s not like that. I think he just sees me working too hard. It’s different when you live together, you know. They know when you aren’t home and sleeping right and eating right.’

‘I guess. Thankfully, I’ve never been in that situation.’

‘You’re lucky. But I mean, if you can see that side of a persons life you can see when they aren’t looking after themselves. And it can be hard to watch someone do that to themselves.’

He nodded. 'I suppose.'

She sighed.

'Still, I mean, I understand this weekend. I understand this case, but the other times? You do this pretty often, Aoki. Following things down on weekends. Staying back late most nights.'

She glared at him. He kept his eyes focused on the road. 'Are you seriously taking his side?'

'Fuck, it's not about sides.'

'But you think he's right?'

He sighed. 'I dunno. I think he has a point.'

'Oh, come on!'

'I mean, I know you put a lot of hours in. You come in late, but I know you stay back most nights. You're always still there when I leave. How do you explain those other cases?'

She shrugged. 'They just got to me. I just couldn't get them out of my head. You know what I'm saying.'

'Yeah. I do. But you've gotta look after yourself. If you don't take it easy on yourself and take some time out, you'll burn yourself out.'

'I guess.'

'He's right though, it *is* just a job. And it's not worth it. They don't pay us enough to care.'

She laughed.

'Plus, I mean, it's their own fault. They want things done properly, they can hire more police. Put more uniforms on the streets. Give us more detectives. We have a stronger police presence and we can make the criminals afraid again'.

‘They’ll never do that.’

‘Well, it’s bullshit. Fucking bureaucracy,’ he swore, shaking his head. He banged the wheel. ‘But that’s beside the point. Don’t make their problem your problem. Do what you can at work and leave when you’re meant to. If it doesn’t get done then it doesn’t get done. That’s their own fault for not having enough people.’

‘I suppose,’ she frowned. *He got worked up pretty quickly*, she thought to herself. ‘Is something up?’ She asked.

He turned and looked at her, frowning. ‘Yeah,’ he said softly. ‘Bureaucracy. You don’t want to hear it right now, though.’

‘What do you mean?’

He shrugged and rested one elbow on the open window. ‘I was going to tell you later, once we’re done with this interview.’

‘What is it?’ She asked, getting annoyed.

He exhaled deeply and tapped on the wheel. ‘I went to Lawford, gave him an update on everything.’ He told her, absently.

‘Thanks for doing that, by the way’ She pursed her lips. Morgan usually dealt with their supervisor. He was better at diplomacy.

‘Yeah, yeah,’ he waved it away dismissively. ‘No dramas. It’s not about that.’

‘Oh, ok.’ She frowned. ‘What’s it about?’

‘Well,’ he sighed. ‘I took him the Delpont stuff, how we think it might be linked, all of that.’

She groaned, already knowing what he would say next.

‘Yeah, they’re telling us to stay away from it. Not to investigate or talk about the Delpont angle.’

She shook her head, irritated. ‘Why? That’s bullshit?’

‘Hey, you don’t need to tell me that.’ He shrugged. ‘I agree. But they’re telling us to stay away from Delpont.’

‘This whole thing is about Delpont, though?’ She exclaimed, perplexed. ‘How can we figure it out, if we can’t investigate Delpont?’ She shook her head again and rubbed her face.

‘Yeah, I know,’ he said, defeated. ‘I know. But like I said, fucking bureaucracy.’ He swore, teeth clenched.

She dropped the issue. *He’s clearly already irritated.*

He pulled the car over to the side of the curb. The road ran parallel to the beachfront. There was only a strip of bushland separating the beach from the street. Aoki got out of the car and could smell the salt air from where she was, she could feel the cool breeze coming off from the beach. Night had fallen while they were driving and the temperature had dropped.

‘It’s just up here, yeah?’

Morgan checked his phone. ‘Yeah, three doors up. Apartment 504.’

‘Reckon she’ll be home?’

He shrugged. ‘Worth a try. I didn’t have a number for her, so this is the only way I could think to get in touch with her.’

They entered the lobby and started the climb up the stairway. It was a quiet apartment block, there didn’t seem to be anyone else around. She wasn’t able to overhear any of the conversations from other apartments like in her block. She wished she lived there. She huffed and breathed heavily as she went up the incline.

‘Doing alright there?’ He teased.

‘Fuck. I hate stairs.’ She said in between breaths. In moments like this, she wished she didn’t smoke.

They reached the apartment and Morgan knocked on the door. Aoki hung back for a moment to catch her breath.

‘Fuck. I really need to go back to the gym.’

‘And quit smoking, maybe? How long has it been since you went?’

She shook her head. ‘Probably more than six months.’

She heard talking inside. There were two people. The peephole went dark for a minute.

‘It’s the detectives.’ She heard a muffled voice from inside say to the other.

The door opened and Rebecca stood in the doorway. Behind her, Aoki recognised Will from the crime scene.

WILL

He frowned. *What are the detectives doing here?*

'Rebecca. I'm Morgan. We met earlier?'

She nodded, 'I remember.'

'Sorry to come by so late but we needed to see you as soon as possible. We think you might be in trouble.'

Beck flashed Will a nervous look and Will glanced at both detectives. Morgan had a concerned look on his face. He was being gentle with Beck. At the crime scene he had been blunt towards Will, irritated with his responses. To be fair though, he hadn't told the detective much. Aoki, on the other hand, had a blank look on her face. She was studying their faces with her arms folded and kept looking at him suspiciously. Maybe she was wondering what he was doing here, as well.

Will took it upon himself to break the silence. 'Maybe you should come in. There's something you should hear.'

The two detectives looked at each other and then walked inside.

Beck glared at him. 'Can you excuse us for a moment first?' She asked the detectives.

They nodded and she pulled him into the kitchen and out of earshot.

'Are you crazy? You want me to tell them? I only started explaining the beginning of it to you. There's a lot more to it.'

He shrugged. 'This whole thing is getting out of control. It's too dangerous to do this alone, Beck.'

'If they see us talking to the police what do you think they will do?'

‘Maybe we need their help. They could put you under protection.’

She squinted, thinking. She shook her head. ‘They might have contacts in the police.’

He scoffed.

‘Is it really that ridiculous?’

‘If it goes that deep, then we are fucked anyway.’

She paused. ‘I suppose so.’

‘I can talk to them if you want?’

She shook her head. ‘It’s ok. I’ll do it.’

He rested a hand on her shoulder and they walked back to the detectives. They sat on the opposite side of the coffee table to them.

‘I’m going to make coffee, did you want me to get some for you too?’ He asked them. ‘You might need it for this story.’

Aoki rubbed her face and sighed. She looked exhausted. ‘Yeah. I could use one.’

‘I’ll be fine.’ Morgan declined.

‘Alright. How many sugars?’

‘Two, thanks.’

‘You like your coffee black or white?’

‘White. Thank you.’

‘Alright. I’ll be back in a moment.’

He went to the coffee percolator in the kitchen and put a full scoop of ground beans in the filter, making sure it wasn’t pressed too close. He filled the water to the line on the inside of the bottom part and put it on the stove. While he waited for it to boil he leaned against the kitchen counter and listened to the conversation.

'So you were already telling this to Will, can you fill us in?' Aoki asked.

'Alright, well, this whole thing goes back to my days as a journalist.'

'The last time you wrote about Delpont?' Morgan asked.

'Yeah. The part everyone knows is that I was writing an investment article on them. My editor said to have a look, but he suspected I would end up writing a glowing review of the company, recommending them as an investment.' She paused, taking a deep breath.

She was talking quickly and excitedly. 'I had a look at the books when I got there, they were very open. But when I went through the accounts, things didn't make sense, the numbers were all wrong. When I really looked into how they made money that was when I got worried. There were large amounts of investment coming in from companies I hadn't heard of. Massive amounts, hundreds of millions of dollars. Well, massive at the time.'

Will noticed the detectives were frowning. Aoki was taking notes.

Behind him, the percolator started to bubble. He turned off the stove and poured the coffee into two cups, adding two sugars to each. He brought in the coffee from the kitchen and set down a cup in front of Aoki. She acknowledged it absent minded while he sat down next to Beck and sipped his own coffee.

'Anyway, I won't bore you with the details but it seemed to me that it was too risky, and that there was something dodgy going on with their accounts. I wrote my article and did not recommend them as an investment. My original article was critical and implied that there were issues with the accounts.' She paused, shaking her head. 'I submitted it to my editor. I got a phone call a day later from the company asking me to come and meet them. When I get there, a few of the 'big shots' from Delpont sat me down and put the fear of God into me. Apparently, my editor ran it past them first because he was worried about his name. They told me I was completely wrong, and that I didn't understand the accounts and so on. They yelled at me, stood over me.'

'I remember reading about that. That's horrible.' Morgan said, gently.

She nodded. 'That's the part everyone knows. I eventually managed to get the article published but it was toned down. Regardless, I was the first one to ask questions.' She paused and took a deep breath, gazing out the window at the night sky. 'I told Will there was more to it. I only told people about the Delpont part of the meeting. The truth is that when I looked at the accounts I found that Delpont was only one company. They had set up smaller companies to filter losses and provide new capital. That was what I originally picked up on. When I saw that, I followed the companies, looked into some of them. They were all owned and run by a guy named Taylor Sheeran.'

Will saw Aoki's eyes widen.

'The Sheeran case, the guy that was stabbed in his own home.' Aoki said, distantly.

Beck nodded.

'So, he was part of Delpont?' Morgan asked.

'Not officially. But, yeah. He was in league with all of them. He was their right hand man.'

Aoki frowned. She opened her mouth to talk, but hesitated. Exhaling, she spoke up. 'Will, you might be involved in this more than you realise.'

Will's eyes widened. 'What do you mean?'

‘We found the words; *Wealth is a crime* scrawled across one of the crime scenes.’

‘Fuck.’ He muttered, sighing deeply.

‘It’s from one of your articles, isn’t it?’ Morgan asked, flatly.

He nodded.

‘What?’ Rebecca scrunched her face, turning to Will.

There was a moment of silence.

It was Morgan who broke it. ‘What is a reference to your articles doing at one of the crime scenes?’

‘I don’t know,’ He stammered. ‘I’ve got no idea.’ He felt his cheeks turning red, as he scratched his neck.

‘What does *wealth is a crime* mean, anyway?’ Aoki asked.

He shook his head, eyes narrowed. ‘I mean, the article was just about a theory.’

‘Which was?’ Morgan prompted.

Will took a deep breath. ‘It was just a dramatic title. My editor wanted to do it, to get more attention. All it talked about was rethinking the idea of wealth as a good thing.’

Aoki and Morgan glanced at each other, frowning. ‘What did it discuss?’ Aoki asked.

‘I dunno, I didn’t really state what should be done.’ He cleared his throat. ‘I was talking about how inequality was a bad thing. I also discussed how deregulation from the eighties led to reckless pursuits of wealth. How that encouraged risky lending and investments. Mainly, how that caused the sub-prime mortgage crisis of 2008.’ He exhaled deeply, scratching his neck.

‘Alright. But what does that have to do with Delpont?’ Aoki asked, pursing her lips.

Will frowned, shaking his head. ‘I have no idea. I never talked about Delpont.’

‘Anyway, Why wasn’t Sheeran’s name in any of the Delpont papers? How come he didn’t go to jail?’ Morgan asked, crossing his arms.

Beck frowned. ‘Very few people from Delpont actually went to jail, of the senior management that is. Most of them cooperated and pinned it on Lew Noble and his traders, but regardless, this whole thing with Sheeran was covered up.’ She smiled bitterly. ‘This is where it gets scary. After I found the first company, it led me to other linked companies. I did some more research into these smaller companies, they were managing insanely large amounts of money but only had three or four people listed as employees. Most of them were the same three or four people.’

‘Sheeran?’ Morgan asked.

She nodded. ‘And a few others. But the deeper I looked, I realised all the accounts kept ending up with one company. Azure.’

Aoki frowned and scribbled.

‘I couldn’t find much on that company, so I went back. I followed the money, looked at who was investing in them, who was recommending them.’ She sighed. ‘What I found was crazier than I could have thought.’

She shook her head. ‘The companies investing in these offshoot companies, the ones which, if anyone took a glance at their books, were blatantly making fraudulent profits with falsified accounts; they were all being invested in by the major financial firms. The ones with their names all over the front pages of papers, having their share price talked about in the evening market wrap up. The ones that control the street.’ She said, talking faster now, her face was stern and there was anger in her voice. 'The ones recommending them, it was the big four accounting firms.'

Morgan breathed out, slowly and deeply. 'That can't be right.'

Aoki looked puzzled. 'Who do you mean?'

'The main accountancy firms. There are four main corporations. Performing all the auditing of companies.' Morgan replied. 'You know those companies that pick up all the best graduates from the best colleges and universities?'

'The ones with the pictures of Beemers and Mercs on their fliers?' She asked.

'Yeah, and the ads with attractive young people talking about how they jet set the world making tons of money.' Morgan scoffed.

Will tried to hide a smile. Some of his friends had gone down that path, which looked so promising at the time. Most of them burnt out and now weren't much further along in their careers than when they had graduated.

'It couldn't be them?' Morgan said, softly.

Will couldn't tell whether he was talking to them or to himself.

Beck shrugged. 'It was.'

'But I mean.' Morgan looked up, frowning. 'If it were, then they would have been held accountable? They would have had to answer for investing in something like that. I mean, all the board of directors of Delpont had to, everyone at Delpont had to.'

'This is where it got complicated.' Beck sighed. 'Maybe I should explain what happened next.'

'I need a cigarette first.' Aoki said, shaking her head. She got up and picked out her pack of smokes and her lighter. She made a move to the balcony.

‘No. It’s fine. Smoke in here.’

‘Are you sure?’

Beck nodded. ‘It’s fine. I’ve been smoking a fair bit since Chris died. I covered up the smoke detector with duct tape. Can I have one?’

They all looked at her. She didn’t seem like the type to smoke. As long as Will had known her she had never had a cigarette.

Aoki paused, looking at Will.

‘What?’ Beck laughed.

Aoki chuckled. ‘Sure thing.’ She passed her a cigarette and the lighter.

‘Thanks.’

The two boys looked at each other.

‘Actually, can I grab one too? I could use a smoke right now?’ Will shook his head.

The three of them laughed.

Morgan frowned, then sighed. ‘Fuck it. I’ll have one too.’

Aoki passed Will the pack and a lighter. He lit the smoke and took a drag, breathing out slowly.

‘Fuck, that feels good.’ He passed the lighter and the pack to Morgan.

Morgan shook his head. ‘I haven’t had one of these in months.’ He smoked slowly, looking at the floor.

There was a moment of silence. Beck smiled and laughed, most likely at something she was thinking about. Will didn’t want to ask. Aoki and Morgan didn’t notice the moment. They were looking at the floor. Both lost in their own thoughts. Aoki sipped at her coffee slowly. Will squinted. It looked like her hands were shaking slightly.

Beck cleared her throat. Considering what she had already said, he wondered whether any of them wanted her to continue. Given the option, he wondered if he still wanted to find out how deep this went. He looked at Beck. She looked scared, but he felt like she was going to go through with it, anyway.

'Before the article came out, I was called in for another meeting. They threatened to sue me if I didn't come.' She shook her head. 'I wasn't going to go, but they sent a car for me. When I got there it was a round table and I was surrounded. There were heads of the biggest trading firms there, directors of the big four accounting firms. They started telling me how wrong I was, how I didn't understand.' She paused, taking a deep breath. 'The guys from the accounting firms, they kept telling me that my career was finished. That no one would trust me. They told me it was also a risk to my boyfriend, as well.'

Aoki let out a gasp. She covered her mouth, noticing herself.

'They threatened you?' Morgan asked.

'Yeah.' She said softly. 'They told me that if I published this, if I wrote about their involvement, then we would both have a bad name with all of the accounting firms, with all of the trading firms, with the big banks. They said that Delpont was going down, and there was nothing anyone could do about it. They talked to me like, like they were explaining everything. I was so young. At first I felt like they were threatening me, but as they kept talking, all of them looking at me, I felt like they were including me in their inner circle, like they were trying to help me. They talked to me about how their involvement with Delpont was complicated, how there was nothing wrong and it happened all the time. There was a young woman from one of the accounting firms, she did most of the talking.' Beck sighed deeply. She ran her hands through her hair. 'This girl said that if this were managed properly by me, if the article was written properly and put forward the most accurate representation of the situation, they would be grateful. If I did that for them, they would help me and Chris.'

The three of them looked at her. Will was frowning.

'So, they told you to just to talk about Delpont?' Morgan asked, frowning.

Beck nodded slowly, looking at the floor.

'Help you how?' Aoki asked with a quiet voice.

Beck looked at her, her eyes were glazed over at the memory. She sighed. 'Well, they said that we would have a place on their side, as part of their organisations. We could get jobs in our field, be well paid, be well connected. I mean, we were graduates, any one of us would have killed for a job vaguely related to what we studied for decent pay. I asked them what would happen if it were too late for me to stop it from being published.' She paused. She shook her head and laughed bitterly. 'They already knew the final draft didn't need to be submitted for two days. I was shocked at the time, but I guess my editor must have talked to them about it. Regardless, they said if that story got out, and if it came from me, then we wouldn't have any friends at their companies. They talked about how big their influence was. I mean, these are massive multinational companies, some of them have more capital and are more influential than religions. The money at their disposal, the stakes they hold in media outlets.' She shook her head and sighed. 'It was terrifying. To be honest, it still is. They're so massive, how do you go against something like that? At the time, I backed down, I played along. They talked to me and got Chris set up with a great grad position in one of the big banks. I, uh, I could never tell him how he got it, I asked them not to tell him, either.'

'That's understandable.' Will said, softly.

'I just couldn't.' She rubbed her face with her palm. She sighed. 'Anyway, he got the job a year or so later. I never told him about it. I told him everything else, though. In as much depth as I could, without, you know,' Her words trailed off, her voice faint.

They were quite for a moment. They all looked at her but she kept her eyes on the floor. Will thought it over. She'd told him this much before the detectives arrived. He still didn't understand the connection between events with Delpont and what was happening now. He hadn't had a chance to ask her. He had been about to ask her before they arrived.

'I don't understand how people get that way.' He muttered, half to himself.

'What way?' Morgan asked.

He shrugged. 'When protecting their own wealth and interests, overrides any concern for others. How could someone justify killing another simply to protect what they already had. Especially when what they had obtained was not earned, when they had broken so many rules to get it.' He sighed.

Morgan grinned. 'I figure criminality like that is similar to playing poker with a losing hand; once you have bought in you become committed. Your only option to escalate your bluffs hoping your opposition doesn't call you on them.'

There was silence in the room. Beck shook her head. 'Alright, I need to make some tea. Does anyone want some?'

Will shook his head.

Morgan rubbed his face. 'I'll give you a hand in the kitchen.'

Beck and Morgan walked into the kitchen, leaving Will in the room with Aoki. 'Morgan's your partner?' He asked, in an attempt to break the silence.

'Yeah. We work together a fair bit. It sounds like he's as against wealth as much as you are. He talks about it all the time.'

'Really?'

'Yeah, he says they take what isn't theirs and they don't give enough back.'

He nodded. 'Fair enough. I wouldn't have pegged him for the type.'

'How so?'

'Well, he kind of seems like a private school boy.'

She laughed. 'He actually did go to a private school.'

'Really?'

'The way he talks, his clothes, his taste in women, it's all typical private school boy.'

Will laughed. 'Well, I can't really talk. I went to a private school, too.'

She grinned. 'So, you're a closet snob?'

He laughed and shook his head. 'Very funny. Nah, I'm actually a pretty simple guy. I never really bought into the lifestyle. I just like simple things. I don't like expensive cars or designer furniture. I could never justify spending that kind of money on things like that?'

She shook her head. 'Yeah, me neither. I don't understand how people get that kind of money.'

He frowned. 'Usually they either inherited it, or they work too hard and have no life.'

'See that I don't get either, working that much. I barely get enough free time as it is, I couldn't justify working anymore.' She squinted at him. ‘So, how did all this start for you? How did you end up with this vendetta against rich people?’

He raised an eyebrow at her and laughed. ‘A vendetta?’ He laughed again. ‘I guess it could be described like that. I don’t know where it started, it happened gradually.’ He shook his head. ‘I mean, I guess I started thinking this way when I was at school, I can think of one thing that really stuck with me.’

He looked at her. She was listening to him, smoking her cigarette.

‘There were these two cousins I went to school with. Their family was worth a couple billion. Anyway, they spent the whole time skipping classes, wasting that opportunity for education so few people would get, wasting the money their parents spent to get them a better future. They just used to sit there during lunch, both of them, just looking through catalogues for luxury yachts, and these things cost like a couple million, and these seventeen year old kids were just flicking through, trying to decide which one to get their parents to buy. They were so oblivious. I couldn’t believe they were so out of touch. I couldn’t believe people would consider wasting money on something that expensive. I mean, most people in the world would go their entire life and not earn that much.’

She nodded, smiling sadly.

‘It just didn’t seem fair. Plus, these guys were total brats.’

She laughed. ‘I know the type. Spoilt rich kids.’

‘Yeah, and I don’t know. I guess, I always just felt things should be more equal. That’s probably why I decided to study human resources after.’

‘You did HR?’

‘At first.’ He nodded. ‘Yeah, that’s what I started studying. I didn’t stay with it, though. I ended up going down the economics path.’

‘Oh ok. My boyfriend works in HR now.’

‘Oh really?’

‘Yeah. In engagement, or something like that.’

He smiled. ‘It all kind of sounds the same, doesn’t it?’

She burst out laughing. ‘Oh, sorry.’ She giggled, trying to stop herself from laughing. ‘I had thought about the same thing earlier. No offence but it can get pretty wanky.’

He grinned. It sounded strange when she used colloquial terms like *wanky*, especially since her voice was gentle and she was soft spoken. ‘Nah, it’s fine. I feel the same. That was why I moved out of it. I loved the theoretical side of it, but working in it is very different.’

‘How so?’

‘Well, basically,’ He cleared his throat. ‘Most HR theories talk about achieving this mutually beneficial outcome. The argument is that with information workers, in knowledge type work, the final product is essentially the result of the ability of the employee.’

‘Right.’ She said slowly. ‘You mean, like, as in business workers and things like that? Lawyers, traders, teachers?’

‘Yeah, exactly. They’re all information sector workers. The product of the work is the service or skill they provide. Based on that assumption, the way to deliver the best final product is to invest in the skills and education of employees. The company gets the best possible workers and is able to provide the best possible service to clients. The employees are able to further their skills and education, and as a result, further their careers. So, the goals of workers and organisations are not necessarily in conflict with each other.’ He said, exhaling deeply.

'That makes sense. Sounds like you talked about this stuff a lot?' She said with a laugh.

He nodded sadly. *It's almost a practiced speech.* All this talk was bringing back bad memories.

'So, how come you didn't go down that path? It sounds like you believed in it?'

He paused and looked at her. Her eyes were gentle. It seemed like she actually wanted to know, so he decided to tell her the truth.

'Well, after I finished it was hard to find a job. I was trapped in that pattern of being overqualified. Not having enough experience for the graduate jobs I wanted. Having too much education for entry level jobs. I couldn't get the graduate jobs without the entry level job first. They didn't want to give me the entry level jobs because they thought with my education I would leave after a few months and get a better job. I was stuck in the middle.'

He saw her wince. He sensed it struck a nerve, her boyfriend might have been through something similar.

He shrugged. 'Anyway, that was when I realised that the theory argued one thing, but the reality was very different. The more I was exposed to it, the more I realised these companies didn't want someone who would engage their workers, get their commitment and deliver a mutually beneficial outcome. They wanted a bean counter. They wanted someone who would watch the budget. They wanted someone who would fire people quickly, but hire people slowly. Someone who would leave hiring a new worker until absolutely necessary, until the existing team was so flat out they were at breaking point. Only then, would they hire a new worker.'

She frowned. 'The budget? Yeah, I've seen it myself. Cutting short on cops, trimming the head count as much as possible.'

'It always comes down to the budget with these guys.' He said with a sigh. 'That's all they care about. They don't care about the quality of what they provide to their clients, they don't care about what sort of lives their employees lead. They don't care about their impact on the community.' It was only then he noticed the bitterness in his voice. The resentment he felt about the system was hard to disguise. It always got him agitated. 'Anyway, I'm sorry to talk so much.' He shook his head, sighing. 'How did you become a detective? Did you study forensics?'

She shook her head. 'I studied psychology.'

'Really?' He asked, trying to smile to brighten the mood. 'Why the change?'

'I don't think it's a big change.'

'How do you mean?' He asked, curious.

She shrugged. 'My motivation has never changed. I wanted to understand people.'

AOKI

Aoki heard movement from the kitchen as Morgan and Rebecca returned with tea.

She had enjoyed talking to Will, and was surprised by how much she shared in common with him. He was obviously passionate, but they were not passionate about the same things. Plus, she really wanted to talk to Rebecca. Her curiosity about the case had only grown the more she had heard the woman talk. Everyone else had seemed nervous the more she described how deep the corruption went. But Aoki felt a buzzing energy. For once, she finally had something difficult to deal with, a real issue, something that she would need to think about. She was tired of the ordinary cases. She'd dealt with so many dunkers lately that she felt like her mind was beginning to go mush. She was worried her skills and detective intuition were going soft.

She walked over to the coffee table and sat back down. This woman had dealt with so much, lived with fear for so long and had lost the man she loved. And yet, she kept moving forward. Aoki admired her strength. Under similar circumstances, she wondered if she would be display the same grace under fire. She wondered if she would be able to stand alone against such overwhelming odds and keep fighting. Rebecca clearly believed in this fight. Aoki reflected on herself, and on what she believed in, but right now she was coming up short. She shook her head. At that point she couldn't think of what she believed in, what she was willing to fight for. She looked at this calm and collected woman, standing alone amidst people doubting themselves. She seemed so brave and strong, but Aoki realised that her inner reality might be quite different.

She looked at herself in the reflection of the coffee table glass, shy and soft spoken. Then looked at Morgan, before turning to look Rebecca up and down, studying her features but not hearing her words. She watched Will as he walked inside, wrestling with his own inner conflict and insecurities. She sighed. Aoki felt sorry for this woman, that she was taking on such an overwhelming opponent with such underwhelming allies.

Rebecca looked up and made eye contact with her. She smiled. It seemed as if this woman had no doubt in her eyes, no hesitation in her actions. No matter what, Aoki wanted to help this woman find justice for her partner and for all those others who had been sacrificed for the well being of this monolithic organisation.

Morgan and Will settled back into their spots on the couch. Rebecca looked at them, sizing them up. Aoki guessed she was trying to figure out if they were committed to the task at hand.

'So, anyway,' Rebecca started talking again. 'I was up to the part where they had bribed us with cushy jobs, right?' Rebecca grinned sarcastically and looked at her watch. 'It's one thirty now, do you want to stay to hear this out?'

They all nodded, silently.

'Aoki,' Morgan said softly, looking at her. 'Maybe these guys can help us investigate Delpont?'

Aoki glared at him.

'What do you mean?' Rebecca asked.

'Well,' Running his hand through his hair, Morgan sighed deeply. 'We can't look into the Delpont angle too closely.'

She shot him a dirty look.

'What?' He shrugged. 'The cards are on the table, Aoki. They've shown theirs, it's time we show ours.'

'What do you mean?' Will asked, his face scrunched up.

‘Typical bureaucracy.’ Morgan muttered, shaking his head. ‘It’s a sensitive issue. We can investigate the murders, but only as separate crimes. We can’t look into the Delpont side of it.’

Aoki rolled her eyes. ‘We shouldn’t be talking about this, Morgan.’ She was unable to hide the frustration in her voice.

‘Why not?’ He asked with a frown. ‘Will is a journalist and researcher. As is Rebecca. She’s also a trained accountant who knows the company.’

‘Because they’re civilians. And they’ve both been through a lot. Plus, you should have checked with them first.’

Rebecca narrowed her gaze on Aoki. ‘Actually, Morgan and I talked about it in kitchen. He wanted to check I was comfortable with it first. And I am.’

‘I guess he didn’t feel like checking with his *partner* first.’ She muttered.

‘Look, all I’m saying is that they can look into the Delpont side of things. Give us some background on the people and the company. Just to give our investigation some direction.’ Morgan justified it gently. He sighed. ‘That way we can work around the bureaucratic bullshit. Obviously they can’t research at the station. But considering all the regulations around Delpont, our resources probably wouldn’t be helpful anyway.’

Fuck, Aoki thought. *We do need that information.*

‘What do you think, Will?’ Rebecca asked with a frown. ‘Are you in?’

Aoki turned to him. She could see a trace of doubt in his eyes. He nodded silently.

If Rebecca noticed his indecision, she didn’t reveal it. She smiled, cleared her throat and continued talking.

'Okay then. Well, I feel like I was the first one to clock onto what's going on now. That is, when the Delpont people started dying. I mentioned it to Chris when I heard about the first few. I didn't think much of it at first, it just seemed creepy to me. When I heard about Sheeran though, that was when I knew. If someone was targeting Delpont, they would have had to know the full story.'

'What do you mean?' Morgan asked.

She exhaled deeply. 'If someone was targeting Delpont, why was one of their targets was Taylor Sheeran?' She shook her head. 'He was Azure, not Delpont. From what I can tell, all those key people were a part of Azure. Only a few people knew about that link; a handful of Delpont staff and me.'

'So, you think it was someone inside?' Aoki asked, scribbling notes.

She nodded. 'Someone close to it. They would have had to be. Or close to someone who was.'

Morgan frowned. 'Who can you think of?'

She grinned. 'You're asking me who the murderer is?'

'I'm asking about Azure, who had knowledge about Sheeran.'

'We'll go from there, start looking through them.' Aoki added.

Rebecca squinted. 'From what I found, pretty much everyone at Delpont was in on it, they all knew about the laws they were breaking. But I mean, at the time everyone was doing it. As far as knowing about Azure, I only know of Taylor Sheeran, whom I met. Paul McDermott pretty much ran Delpont and dealt with the satellite companies. He wasn't the most senior but he handled a lot of the backdoor dealings.'

'Amber's father?' Will asked. Aoki glanced over at him, he seemed confused.

'Amber McDermott? Yeah, her father.'

He frowned and looked at the ground.

Rebecca didn't seem too fussed. 'Other than that, the only other guy I know was David Orr. You guys heard of him yet?'

Aoki glanced at Morgan. He looked as lost as she did. 'We haven't come across him yet.'

Rebecca nodded. 'He's a real bastard. Works behind the scenes. He's really arrogant, talks down to everyone below him, always berating people. You'd recognise him if you saw him. He's middle aged, has this crooked nose and these big teeth that stick out of his mouth. Typical trader. I heard a story once about a guy he interviewed back when he was just a trader. Brought him in for a job the guy wasn't qualified for. He proceeded to criticise everything about the guy, this graduate kid. Tells him he's not good enough, his marks are not good enough. That he didn't do the right subjects. I mean, he really grilled this kid. The kid just sat there and took it quietly. The guy I heard it from, he was the other person interviewing. He told me he apparently only brought the kid in to grill him. He was bored and wanted to make someone feel terrible so that he felt a little better.'

'That's not right.' Morgan said.

Aoki leaned forward, 'Who else was there?'

'Other than Taylor, Paul and David?'

'Yeah.'

'There was also Ronald Oakly. He was tall and wiry. He was the eldest, I think. He would have been in his sixties at the time.'

'That name rings a bell.' Morgan frowned.

'It should. They're one of the richest families in Australia. Worth a few billion dollars.' She said slowly.

‘They’re tied up in this?’ Morgan asked.

‘Yeah.’ Rebecca sighed. ‘He didn’t say much in the meetings but I recognised him straight away.’

‘Fuck.’

Aoki wrote the name down, as well. She hadn’t heard of him or his family before. To be fair she hadn’t heard of any of the names Rebecca had told them about. ‘Is there any one else you can think of?’

‘That’s pretty much it. But there was this other man I saw in all the meetings.’

‘Did you get his name?’

Rebecca shrugged. ‘He never said a word. I saw him again when I got in contact with them to get Chris his job. Every time I met this group he was there, but he never spoke.’

‘Maybe he’s not important then?’ Morgan suggested.

Rebecca laughed. ‘Quite the opposite. He would always stand away from the main group and watch in the corner. He would linger in the shadows. But every so often he would gesture at someone to prompt them. They kept looking at him when I spoke, as if looking for approval.’ She breathed out deeply. ‘I got the feeling he was in control.’

Aoki squinted at her. ‘What did he look like?’

Rebecca cleared her throat. ‘He was tall, he would have been sixty. His hair was greying, and he had these small narrow glasses. He had this daggy haircut, like something out of the fifties.’

Will chuckled.

‘He always wore black suits. I couldn’t see his face much because he was always in the shadows, never at the table. But there was softness to his face, like from a sedentary lifestyle. I'll never forget his eyes, though.'

'How come?'

'They were this clear blue colour. Almost transparent. They were so soft. He looked like a grandfather.' Rebecca shook her head. 'But whenever I made eye contact with him, it made my skin crawl. I could feel there was so much malice behind his eyes. His stare was so cold and calculating.'

Will looked at her suspiciously, an eyebrow raised.

'Is that why you remember him so well?'

'Exactly. But you would know him if you saw him.' Rebecca said calmly.

'Why?'

She sighed. 'No matter what, no matter when or where I saw him, he always took that goddamn book with him.'

They all looked at her, everyone appeared confused.

'Wherever he goes, he always takes that book with him. He'll stand in the corner reading it, leaning against a wall. Lean back in his chair, seeming not to listen to the conversation, reading and scribbling in that book. If you meet him, you'll know him. He'll be in the corner, with that same old copy of that bright orange book.'

ANDREA

She rubbed cold water over her face. It was too early to be up. She needed four more hours of sleep. Her husband was still snoring in the bedroom. Andrea would rather face the day with less sleep than get back into bed with him. She looked at her gaze in the mirror. Her ice blue eyes were the only part of her that still looked strong. She looked tired and weak. The shower helped her wake up, though.

As she let the hot water fall over her, she thought about her new job. She had been thinking so much about Hank lately, she hadn't noticed how routine the job had become. The days seemed to be going past so quickly. Before she knew it was late night again and she needed to go to bed for work the next day. In such a way, her days were passing by faster and faster, and only the moments with her lover to distinguish them. But she wondered what drew her to this job. For the first time, she found herself questioning why she had decided to come to the other side of the fence and work for the government. She frowned, unable to figure out her motivations. Maybe it was for the change of pace, something not as demanding as the corporate world. Though perhaps it was only because she couldn't get a job anywhere else.

She dressed quickly and ducked out of the house, writing her husband a quick note as they often did when one was awake and out of the house before the other. Small gestures like that kept them kind to each other. She spent the drive to work daydreaming, her thoughts mostly about Hank, the image of his smile in her mind. She'd been thinking lately about the idea of marrying him. She almost rear ended another car lost in those thoughts. The sudden jolt when she hit the breaks made her realise how stupid she was being. She was already married for a start. But she wanted nothing more than to get married to the man she loved, to stand with that handsome man in public and have people know he was hers. Recently though, she got the feeling he was pulling away. She pulled her car into the street she usually parked in, got out and started the walk to work. Maybe it was time to end her marriage and pursue the relationship without any restrictions.

Her morning passed in a blur. She sat at her desk and read over hundreds of pages worth of proposed legislation changes. Her previous experience with those kind of legal forms and matters was limited so it was taking her longer than it should. She sighed.

Looking out the window at the cold grey day outside, she was reminded of her days studying. She thought about how long had passed since her days as a student, how unrecognisable she was now from the girl back then. She had been full of self doubt, her head wrapped up in selfish dreams and grand ambitions. She had wanted to make an impact on the world and change the system. At the time, she'd believed she would be able to do all of it through her job. So, in her state of arrogance she had joined the financial world, fully determined that it wouldn't change her. She reflected that after the first year she no longer held those same beliefs anymore. At that stage in her life, her motivations had been purely financial and material. She had wanted a bigger apartment, a new car. After a few years, her title and her career had become primary motivating factors for her. It was at that point she came across Delpont. In the early days of the company, things had been risky and the company had been even more ambitious than her. Within a few years, they were both fundamentally altered and had undergone radical transformations.

She took a deep breath and exhaled, bringing her back to the present. She looked over to her left. One of her colleagues was glancing at her. Andrea realised and quickly turned her attention back to her screen, and began reading through the documents again.

WILL

Despite going to bed at four am, when he awoke five hours later it felt like he had a full night's sleep. He propped a pillow up against the wall and pulled himself up. Rubbing his face, he tried to wake up. Memories of everything that had happened last night came back to him. It didn't seem real in the light of day.

They had left with a plan, breaking up the tasks and agreeing to work in pairs. Morgan had told both Will and Rebecca to look into Delpont and Azure, and research all the relevant parties, to see where the financial trail led. It was a good idea for two reasons. For one, it utilised Rebecca's accounting and bookkeeping skills. For another, it allowed Morgan and Aoki to learn more about Delpont and Azure, since they weren't allowed to formally investigate it.

Will wondered about Aoki, though. She didn't seem to say too much, she was soft spoken, as well. He struggled to imagine her interviewing suspects. He chuckled at the thought.

He got up, showered and got dressed quickly. Then he sent an email to his editor telling him he wasn't coming in today, giving him some vague excuse about being ill. He could feel the chill even from within his apartment. He decided to wear his leather jacket as he headed out the door. On his way out of the building, he stopped at the base of the building for a take away cappuccino.

While he was waiting for his coffee, his phone started buzzing in his pocket. He pulled it out quickly. It was a private number. He frowned and answered the call.

'Hello, Will speaking.'

'Mr Martec.' The voice on the other end was male, the tone was warm. 'It has recently been brought to my attention that you have developed an interesting research project in your free time.'

He shivered. He felt his heart beat faster. There was a clinging feeling in his chest. He cleared his throat. 'Who is this?'

'You shouldn't dig too deeply into the past. There are things which are best left uncovered.' The voice said calmly. There was a weakness or gentleness to it, like that of someone older.

'You're trying to threaten me?' Will said in a hushed voice, so that no one in the café could hear. He held the phone back a bit from his ear. He exited the call menu and scrolled to the app to record the phone call.

'On the contrary. Consider yourself warned of the risks.' By the time he pressed the record button the voice had gone. There was a click and the call ended.

Will felt panic run through his blood. His heart was pounding in his chest and he realised they could have been watching him. He quickly scanned the café to see if anyone were looking at him, if anyone was leaving. Everyone there was either serving coffee or talking in groups. He couldn't see anyone looking at him. There were no older men around, either. He took a deep breath. Maybe someone was just trying to mess with him. Taking another breath, he tried to slow his breathing down.

'Cappuccino. Two sugars.' The barista called out.

Will nodded and collected the cup. 'Thanks.' He muttered.

He walked out, knowing that the coffee in his hand was useless now. He was wired and fully awake. Adrenaline was flowing through his blood. He took a final deep breath when he got outside and felt the cold morning air hit him. As he exhaled, he felt his heart rate return to a normal level.

He didn't know the voice; there was nothing familiar about it. Whether it was a threat or a warning he couldn't tell. The man's voice had been friendly. His tone had been warm. No matter what, nothing could be gained by telling the others. It wouldn't accomplish much more than make them more panicked, which is exactly what they didn't need at that point. They needed clear heads. As far as he was concerned, it never happened. But he realised they needed to change tact. They needed somewhere to work out of, with more privacy, somewhere they could talk and meet unnoticed.

ANDREA

She left the office on the stroke of five pm. Sometimes she missed working for a trading firm. At least there had never been dull days at Delpont. On her way out of the office she felt her phone buzzing. It was Hank calling. She smiled.

'Hey, handsome.'

'Hey, gorgeous. You finished work?'

'Yeah, I just left.'

'Glad to hear. You have anything planned for tonight?'

'Nothing yet. How come?'

'I was thinking of maybe taking you to dinner and making a decent woman out of you.'

She smiled. 'Yeah, I'd like that. Where should I meet you?'

'How about just down the road from mine? We can go to one of those restaurants along there?'

'Sounds perfect. I'll just go home and shower. I'll meet you in an hour.'

'Sounds good, darlin'. I'll see you then.'

She hung up and smiled. The prospect of seeing her lover after such an uneventful day had her excited. The fact he had asked her out eased her concerns, as well. Perhaps the loss of the passion in their relationship had all been in her mind. Perhaps she'd imagined him pulling away.

When she got home she noticed her husband's car was in the driveway. *Fuck,* she swore to herself. She didn't want to lie to his face. She was in far too much of a good mood to do that. She walked in the front door but couldn't see his keys anywhere. His work shoes were in the rack, but his running shoes were gone. She smiled. With any luck she could be gone before he got home.

After a shower she felt renewed. She put on a knee high red dress and looked in the mirror once she had zipped it up. She felt and looked like a different person to the subdued civil servant she had been earlier in the day. Calling a cab, she headed downstairs. Her husband still wasn't home. She wrote him a quick note, saying she was going out to dinner with girlfriends, feeling a pang of guilt. She hadn't been paying much attention to her husband lately. She wrote another line on the note, telling her husband she loved him and finished with; xoxo.

Her cab dropped her outside the row of restaurants. Hank was standing there waiting across the road.

He smiled and whistled. 'Loving the red dress, darling. You look like a total knockout.'

She smiled, hugged him and they kissed. 'Stop it. You look very handsome, too.'

'Cheers.' After kissing her he whispered in her ear. 'I can't wait to peel you out of that dress.'

She felt herself getting wet. She looked him in his grey green eyes. When he smiled his eyes wrinkled. She ran the palm of her hand over his stubble. She straightened the collar of his blue and red flannel shirt. She felt so lucky to be with someone she found so attractive and handsome. 'I cannot wait either, lover.'

They walked together, though he was careful not to be seen arm in arm with him, lest someone she knew saw them.

'What did you feel like eating?' She asked.

'I'm not too fussed. Somewhere with quick service. I don't know about you but I'm starving.'

She smiled. 'Sounds fine.'

'As long as we go somewhere that serves alcohol.' He leaned in and kissed her on the neck. 'I love getting you drunk, miss.'

'I know you do.' She laughed. 'I'm agreeable to that.' She smiled.

They chose a place on the corner. There were tables outdoors by the quiet street. The only noise was from the dinner and date crowd walking past. Groups of friends catching up, talking about old memories, in the process of creating new ones. Strangers getting to know each other over a date, hoping optimistically but thinking realistically that this might be the first and only time they see each other. Couples just getting settled, relationships firmly in routine trying to put some effort back in. Andrea and her lover fitted somewhere in the middle of all these dynamics.

They sat down at one of the tables outside. When the waitress came up, he ordered the chicken fajitas and she got the prawn dish, they ordered a bottle of sauvignon blanc to share. When the wine arrived he poured the two of them a glass. They said cheers and smiled. She drank a mouthful, sighing. She was so relaxed. The combination of the background music, candlelight and white wine was perfect. But the most important part of this moment for her was the man across from her. She was glad she could share a moment like this with the man she loved. She smiled. In that moment, she was happy. She looked across the table at Hank. He was lost, looking at the harbour views. He noticed her looking at him and turned his attention back to her. He smiled.

'What is it?'

'Nothing.' She said smiling. 'Just thinking.'

He smiled and nodded. 'I haven't had a chance to ask you yet, but are you happier in this new job?' He asked.

'Yeah, much happier. It's a little dull, though.'

He laughed. 'Compared to what?'

'I don't know how to articulate it. But there are moments where I miss all the excitement of those corporate jobs.'

He laughed. 'I thought you hated the hours and the culture?'

She smiled, he was more attentive than her husband. 'I did. As I said, it's a difficult notion to express. I just miss the excitement and drama.'

'You do love your drama.' He teased.

She frowned at him. 'Very funny. You'll pay for that.'

He laughed.

'How about yourself? How is that collection going?'

'Yeah, going better. Really happy with what I'm doing at the moment.'

'Well, that's good.'

'Yeah. Plus I got accepted for an exhibition.'

Her eyes widened. 'That's fantastic, darling. That's excellent.'

'Thanks.' He said bashfully. 'Yeah, I'm really happy about it. It's a pretty good venue as well.'

'That's great. When is it?'

'Next week, it's on a weeknight, though.'

'They didn't give you much notice about it.'

'Nah nah, they did. It's all good.'

She frowned. 'When did you find out about it?'

He shrugged. 'I dunno. About a week ago.'

She felt confused. 'How come you only told me now? This is huge for you.'

He smiled. 'I dunno. I just hadn't seen you. It hadn't come up in between all the fucking.' He teased.

'Why wouldn't you tell me when you found out? I want to be there to share in your successes, darling.'

He frowned. 'Sure thing.'

She rolled her eyes. He seemed to have withdrawn again. She sighed. What was a nice night only a moment ago had swiftly changed. She didn't understand why they had to come into conflict over things like that. *Why can't he just think like I do?* Thankfully, the awkwardness was broken when the waitress delivered their food.

'I'm pretty jealous, those prawns look amazing.' He said, smiling at her.

'Likewise. How are the fajitas? They look good.'

'Perfect. Exactly what I needed. Chicken and white wine go so well together.'

She smiled, glad they'd been able to move on.

'Hey, I wanted to ask you something.' He said, tentatively.

She frowned, unsure of what would come next.

'Did you always want to go into accounting and finance?'

'You mean as a child?'

He laughed. 'Fuck. I hope not. You would have been a dull child.'

She laughed.

'No, I mean in uni. When you were studying?'

She frowned. 'I guess not. I kind of fell into it. I really wanted to do law at uni.'

'Really?'

'Yeah. I wanted to be an environmental lawyer, actually.'

He laughed. 'Are you serious?'

'What's so funny about that?'

He shook his head smiling. 'You're so refined and graceful. I just, I can't imagine you as a greeny.'

She smiled, flattered. 'You're sweet. Yeah, as a matter of fact I considered joining Greenpeace for a while and going overseas.'

'That's great. That's so adventurous of you. So, what happened?'

She sighed. 'Well, I guess I didn't make the cut, my marks were just short of law. So, I ended up enrolling in a commerce degree. I planned to stay for a year and then use my grades to transfer over.'

'Why didn't you?'

She shrugged. 'I tried. I applied for the transfer after my first year but I didn't make it. I guess my marks weren't good enough.' She frowned. Uncomfortable by the memory of having not done well enough.

'I always thought you were top of your class?'

'Yeah. After my first year I was. I got good grades in all the accounting and finance subjects. So eventually, I just ended up doing a major in it.'

He shook his head. 'That's funny.'

'What's funny?'

'Just the way life works out sometimes.' He said smiling, looking away.

She didn't fully understand what he was implying.

'So how come you don't get involved in any environmental charities or organisations anymore? When did you stop volunteering and donating?'

She frowned. Despite the fact he asked gently and was smiling, his question had her feeling defensive. Truth be told, she hadn't thought much of it until this moment. She tried to think of the last time she had gotten involved with anything to do with the cause, but couldn't think of anything for many years. 'I don't know.' She said absently.

He seemed to sense this and dropped the point. He affectionately ran his fingers over her hand on the table and smiled into her eyes. They changed the conversation to lighter topics and proceeded to finish off the bottle of wine. With the bottle finished they left the restaurant arm in arm, teasing each other. He kissed behind her ear while she playfully disciplined him to behave in public. When they reached his apartment he started kissing her neck and proceeded to peel her out of the dress as he had promised her.

THE MAN BY THE HARBOUR

It was a beautiful night. He leaned against the railing by the water underneath the bridge. He could feel the cool breeze coming off the waves, smell the salt and seaweed underneath the stone boardwalk. There were tourists taking photos, talking excitedly and laughing. An elderly couple were walking arm in arm smiling. On the street running by the harbour, a limo drove past, chauffeuring a group on a night out. The city lights glimmered across the water, reflected off the rise and fall of the tide. Sandstone tiles paved the waterfront. Palm trees dotted the grass park. From the north side of the harbour, he had a spectacular view of the city.

For a moment, he forgot that he was here for a target, and just enjoyed the night. He had a clear view of the exit point his target would make; there was no rush.

He decided to go for a walk along the harbour side to pass time until his window of opportunity arose. As he walked alongside the water, he gazed at the city skyline. Despite being the collaborative result of multinational corporations, there was a beauty to the way the buildings came together to form a city. The real beauty of cities is that people spend their whole lives working towards these collaborations. Either directly or indirectly, every job is a part contributing to the larger society. Without knowing it, people add to this work in progress. And over time these skylines become more beautiful, and take on their own personality. He looked over the city lights reflected in the water as black as the night. The real beauty of these cities wasn't the architecture or the style, it was the work that went in to them. It was the sum total of the lives dedicated to these grand designs. He exhaled and watched the city from afar.

He kept walking, trying to think about his target to get him focused on the task at hand. Despite not being as wealthy as his other targets, they were a perfect example of everything that he was trying to change. Selfish, deceitful, immoral; someone who never faced justice for their part in the crimes of Delpont. Though, while all those factors were important, it was more that an opportunity such as this was hard to pass up.

He walked up the hill, thinking about where his target would be walking out of, and which direction they would be heading in. With any luck, they would have to cross a few of these streets to get to the taxi stand. He would have a few opportunities to make his move in the darkness then.

He needed to approach his target from behind. Loitering on the street was sure to get him caught in camera view. He could make his way to one of the back alleys from the main street, but he decided to take a detour through the amusement park. There was something about walking through there at night after it was closed, all the lights off and no one around. The quietness of the place was eerie. It was uncharacteristic considering how noisy and alive it were normally. What seemed fun and childish by day took on a dark and haunting tone at night. He walked past the ghost train, the ferris wheel, the small rollercoaster. He could go no further though; someone had closed off the rest of the park, so much for that plan. At least he could backtrack and make his way to the alley via one of the other entrances. He turned around and walked back, noticing two women walking his way; a young mother and teenage daughter. The mother was slim, dressed in a tracksuit with her brown hair pulled back. As they got closer he saw the mother smile at him. He ducked his head low to avoid eye contact, but he knew she would remember him. The two women kept chatting amongst themselves. They seemed friendly. He didn't know why, but he wanted to save them the fruitless venture.

'You won't be able to get through that way.' He spoke up.

The two women turned. 'Oh really? There's no way?' The mother asked.

He shook his head. 'It's closed off.'

The women giggled. 'So this isn't the way to get through to the restaurant?'

'Which one?'

'The one on the water.'

He smiled. 'I believe it's closed at this hour. But yes, you would usually get through here.'

The mother laughed. 'Fuck. Know any other restaurants around here, handsome?' She smiled at him.

He grinned. 'There's a café back by the bridge. They do good food.'

'We were there earlier.'

'Mum got kicked out.' The daughter teased.

'Oh, shut up.' The mother laughed.

He grinned. 'Well, I think you should still be able to get through.' He pointed towards the steps to their right. 'Those stairs go up to the street. If you head up there and turn left you should be able to make your way around.'

'You sure?'

He shrugged. 'Not really, honestly.' He laughed. 'I don't know my way around here too well.'

The two women giggled. It seemed as though the mother and daughter had almost a friendship dynamic. 'Are you having a good night?' The mother asked.

He nodded and smiled. 'Just out for a walk. It's a nice night out.'

'It's a perfect night. We were just enjoying some drinks over dinner.'

‘Mum was enjoying a few too many drinks.’

‘Oh, shut up.’

The two laughed.

‘That sounds like a fun night.’ He smiled.

‘So it’s up here and around?’ The mother asked him, smiling.

‘Hopefully. Hopefully, I don’t send you off in the wrong direction.’

‘Well, we’ll know where to find you if you do.’ She teased.

‘I wouldn’t expect any less.’ He laughed.

‘Have a good night, handsome.’ The mother said with a smile.

‘You too. Hope you both have a good night.’ He smiled and raised his hand.

They started walking and giggling again. He went on his way in the other direction.

As he walked away he smiled, thinking of a moment of connection between people who were otherwise strangers.

He needed to make his way to his target.

He started walking up the hill. He passed a young Asian couple smoking, arm in arm. He walked past an elderly man, who was walking along not paying attention to anyone, admiring the view. He smiled sadly. Something about the people he saw out tonight reminded him of people that he loved, people that were now lost in his life. He felt a pulling feeling in his chest. Swallowing, he put those thoughts out of his head.

He patted the right pocket of his jacket, feeling the small blade concealed within. He was within a hundred meters of the front door. A short young woman was walking towards him, he ducked his head as she passed, hiding under his black cap. Maintaining anonymity was something of a non-issue now though, either of those two women from before could identify him easily. He felt uneasy about it. The timing didn't seem right. He frowned, sighed and tried to focus. He wouldn't have another opportunity like this with his target, she was rarely alone.

From his vantage point across the road he saw movement inside, he could see her get dressed through the window. A glance in the mirror, checking her hair as she got ready to walk out the door. He could see her beauty from here, but all with her was vanity. If she had paid more attention to her actions and less to her appearances, placed less emphasis on the luxuries in her life, maybe she wouldn't be his target on this night. He took a deep breath, rested against a wall across the street and waited for Andrea Beaufort to leave her lover's apartment.

ANDREA

She looked at herself in the mirror. Her hair look neat and tidy, she felt clean and fresh after her tryst with her lover. She'd showered, applied her make up again and gotten dressed. It was as though it had never happened. Already though, she felt as though his mind was elsewhere. She looked at his reflection on the mirror, lying on the bed in his underwear. He was on his phone texting someone. She frowned. It was as though she'd already left the apartment.

'I'm almost ready. I should probably get going now.' She said expectantly.

He looked up and smiled. 'Sure thing, darlin'.'

She crossed the room to him to kiss him goodbye. 'Will you be busy this weekend?'

He frowned. 'I don't know yet. I think I've got a friend's opening on.'

She frowned.

'I'll let you know, though.' He said smiling.

She smiled back. She had a feeling she wouldn't be back here again. She leant down and kissed him, feeling his stubble against her cheek. She looked him in his eyes as he smiled at her but it was like his passion for her was gone. She'd been worried she was imagining it, but when they made love that night he was distant. He'd been passive, like he was going through the motions. For the first time the possibility of losing him felt real to her. She tried to dismiss the idea, she was being paranoid, but she felt defeated. Maybe it was like her other relationships; every time someone pulled away from her slightly she had a tendency to assume the worst, to assume the relationship was over. She took a deep breath. Sometimes she was her own worst enemy.

‘I love you, darling.’ She said, smiling.

His eyes wrinkled as he smiled. He ran his hand through his curly hair. ‘Love you, too, gorgeous.’

She turned and walked out the door feeling reassured. Maybe everything was fine.

THE MAN ACROSS THE STREET

The door opened and she walked outside, wrapped up in her own thoughts, oblivious to the man watching her. From the way she was walking it seemed like she had a few drinks, as she fumbled through her handbag looking for her wallet, dropping her keys. He reflected on the decision to choose Andrea as his next victim.

He kept thinking about how she wasn't as wealthy as the other targets. It didn't feel as satisfying for some reason. But he knew that she had lived the high life thanks to her husband's largesse. Since her days at Delpont, she had lived the life of sprawling mansions, apartments in the city for her affair and gifts of cars and expensive trips overseas. She stood for everything that had made the world what it was today. Andrea continued to take and take, and refused to give back. While her husband was a generous and charitable person, often giving away up to thirty percent of his annual income, she was selfish and obeyed only her own desires. That she was complicit in the crimes of Delpont, he was certain.

The sound of her heels on the pavement echoed across the other side of the road. He kept to the shadows and followed her. The streets had cleared in the last few minutes so there was a clear opportunity available. One block further was a small street just off the main strip where there were no cameras. A blind spot. He could make his move there and not be captured on any footage. But he would have to move quickly. He crossed the road further up and ahead of her. She was about fifty meters away and didn't notice him.

When she walked past the alley he would have to make his move quickly from behind. He felt uncomfortable, maybe it was sexist, but he'd never killed a woman before.

He ducked into one of the alcoves, immersed in darkness, lying in wait. Her footsteps got closer; she was walking quickly. It seemed indicative of her stressed personality. From what he had seen of her, he couldn't understand how such a confident, fortunate and attractive woman could be so riddled with insecurity. How an otherwise intelligent woman could make such stupid decisions and remain so oblivious about her own life. There was something tragic about this woman, she was a talent wasted.

If things had gone differently she could have been a proponent for good, she could have been an agent for change. The person she had become, the woman he was about to kill, was nothing but a complicit agent in the continued and reckless profiteering of the world by a handful of individuals. Regardless of her relatively modest wealth, her lack of appreciation for how fortunate she was displayed the same brazen attitude held by his other targets. She held the same negligence of her responsibilities towards society.

Her footsteps got closer and he saw her emerge from behind the corner. He could only see her profile as she walked past, it was dark and only half of her was visible by the streetlight. Even then, he realised she was and still remained a beautiful woman. The way she held herself, the way she walked, she seemed so confident to him. But so many other facets of what he had seen of her revealed such insecurity. He sensed it was because she placed so much emphasis on how she looked, and took all her value from that, her sense of self worth. It was sad, in a way. From this distance he could see her sad blue eyes looking down, watching her step.

He walked behind her silently, to assume his position and make his move. He had only a few moments to strike.

He felt a light sea breeze, he could smell the salt in the air, feel the coolness of the breeze from the night and the harbour. He looked out over the city lights, while absent-mindedly he heard her footsteps. For some reason, in that moment before he made his move, he thought of the two women he had seen earlier. The mother and daughter. He thought of these moments in life where two people who were strangers could connect, if only for a moment, never to see each other again. He reflected on what a beautiful part of the human condition it was.

He slowed his pace, letting her get further away from him until the sound of her footsteps faded. He watched her duck into a cab. The door closed and it sped away. Whatever his earlier justifications, they had all seemed to fade. He took a deep breath, smiled and looked out over the view of the city lights. It was too nice a night to kill someone.

AOKI

Her walk into the office was not pleasant. She'd only had a few hours sleep the night before and it was close to midday. Not only was she not rested, but it also meant she was walking in to the office half asleep while everyone else had been awake for half a day. She look down, her eyes bleary. It was always off-putting to walk into that environment.

After everything that had happened the other night at Rebecca's apartment, her mind had been working overtime. She kept wondering how the deaths were linked to Delpont. In her own mind there were two explanations; the first that it was some form of revenge, maybe someone who lost a lot of money in Delpont or a former employee who was cheated. It seemed to fit with the crime scenes. The other explanation, which had gotten more appealing over the past few days, was that they were being killed as part of a cover up. It seemed like a frightening idea already, but something she had been thinking about made it more worrying. She realised it might not be a cover up for what happened ten years ago, but might actually be an attempt to conceal something happening currently. She shuddered at the thought. She hadn't been sleeping well. Most likely, she was imagining things. No matter the truth, they faced an overwhelming opponent that they knew nothing about.

She kept her head low as she entered the security door but the beeping always attracted the turning of a few heads. That late in the day, people were always curious who was only just coming in to the office. She saw Hannah Moray glaring at her and starting up a conversation with one of her little minions. They were speaking in hushed voices and glancing at her. Even from distance, she knew the two were gossiping about her. She groaned. Moray held so much influence over the team. It was likely Aoki would get a disciplinary meeting later that day from her supervisor for coming in late.

She was planning her usual tactic for coping with days like that; making sure she stayed unnoticed. She would keep her attention focused on her screen until it was late enough for her to leave. She needed to get downstairs as soon as she could for a cappuccino.

As she walked to her desk she noticed Morgan get up.

'Aoki! You're *not* going to believe this.' He said animatedly.

'What is it?' She replied with a tired voice, sensing she would not get an opportunity for a quiet day.

'I got a call about twenty minutes ago, but he says he has information about Chris Collins' death.'

'Information? Who was he?'

'He didn't give his name. He asked to meet with me in person.'

'He didn't give his name? How credible can this guy be?'

'I don't know yet.'

'So why are we going to the effort of meeting with him on no information?'

'He did give me one piece of information.'

'What was that?'

He smiled. 'Well, he told me he had the orange drive.'

She frowned. 'What's that?'

He shrugged. 'I dunno. I want to find out, though.'

'That's it?'

'Not exactly.' He smiled wickedly. 'He also said he was the one who killed Chris Collins.'

WILL

Under the guise of a book that didn't exist, he had managed to gain a face-to-face conversation with Lew Noble. He'd called him prior and told him about his desire to tell the man's story, his rise to success and fall from grace. He'd played to the man's vanity. It seemed to work.

The man waiting for him as he entered the room looked nothing like he expected. He was a gaunt man, brow furrowed with worry lines etched in. There were dark rings under his eyes, which were further exacerbated by the paleness of his skin. Will squinted. He assumed the paleness wasn't just from lack of sunlight. His skin had a yellowish tinge to it and he looked malnourished. Lew Noble turned and looked him in the eyes. There was madness in the stare. It was off-putting. His eyes spoke to what he had been through more than his appearance. The intensity of his stare was that of a paranoid man. Will had interviewed people with that same look. But in Lew's dark eyes he could see so much bitterness.

'You're the reporter? You look like a kid.' He barked, irritated.

Will ducked his head in embarrassment. 'People always say I look younger. But yes, I'm the journalist. My name is Will Martec.'

'You're not here for my story.' He replied with a scowl. 'I'm not an idiot.'

'What?'

'You think I bought what you said about publishing my story?'

'I'm, uh, researching at the moment, trying to tell the Delpont story.'

'I don't doubt your interest in Delpont. But you're not trying to tell the story. You want to know for your own purposes.'

Will felt a chill as if Lew Noble was looking right through him.

'Anyway, what did you come all this way to ask me?' The man leaned back nonchalantly.

'Fair enough. I'm looking into the recent killings of former Delpont employees.'

The man squinted. He seemed interested now. 'I've heard. If you're a cop you're going to way too much effort to get information.'

'I'm not a cop. I'm a journalist.'

He groaned. 'Then fuck off.'

'What?'

'You heard me. We're done talking. Get the fuck out of here.'

'I'm, uh, I'm not here for an article. It's not like that, please just let me explain.'

'No. I'm done talking to you.' He waved him off dismissively. He pulled himself up, exaggerating the veins in his thin, wiry arms. The man grimaced as he got up. It was obvious that he wasn't well. He started crossing the room to leave.

'Would you just talk to me? There is a lot going on here. We need your help.'

He smirked. 'Go ask your journalist colleagues, the ones who demonised me, who made my family ashamed of me.' There was deep bitterness in his voice when he made the last point. Will almost pitied the man.

'Look, I know about the Azure accounts!' Will exclaimed, desperately. 'I know it went a lot deeper.'

'Good work. You know more than most.' He said sarcastically, knocking on the door.

Will felt the anger rising in him. This man still had all the arrogance and selfishness that defined his former life as a trader. From what he had seen so far, the man deserved his time in this place. 'I know what this leads to. One of my friends has already died because of this.'

The man paused and turned back. He exhaled, rolling his eyes. 'Fine. You've got five minutes.' He sneered, walking back. A guard came to the door to check on this knocking. Lew waved him away and sat down again. 'But you're clutching at straws if you're talking to me.' Lew stated flatly.

'What do you mean?'

Lew raised his arms. 'Look at me. If I knew something I wouldn't be in here.'

Will shook his head. 'I don't think that's true. I think you know and I think someone *made* you take the fall.'

He rolled his eyes.

'Someone is targeting those individuals. So far we found evidence that Delpont was just a front for a much larger crime.'

'Azure.' Lew stated, eyes narrowed on him.

'Yes.'

'How *did* you come across Azure?' He asked coldly.

Will felt uneasy. 'Someone came across it a long time ago.'

Lew was silent for a moment, eyes narrowed. 'This someone a reporter, maybe?' He asked, as the side of his mouth twitched.

Will looked down, realising his error. He shook his head quickly. 'I didn't know them.' *Fuck, what would he believe?* 'He was a trader with the company.' Will lied. He looked up again and stared Lew in the eyes. Lew's brow relaxed, it appeared he was convinced. Will breathed a sigh of relief on the inside, but kept his face expressionless, glad for his poker face. He was grateful for the Thursday nights he had spent in university playing Texas hold'em poker.

Lew squinted at him, the slight trace of a smile on his face.

Will exhaled deeply. 'I need your help. I'm trying to track down this group of people, the ones that orchestrated the cover up of Delpont.'

'If you think I'm going to give these people up after everything, then you're delusional.' Lew scoffed, looking bored.

'No. It's not like that.' He said, feeling frustrated. 'Right now I could care less what these people did. But it looks like someone is targeting them. I think it's someone close to them, maybe one of them, or someone they know.'

He paused, his brow furrowed. 'Someone from the inside? I don't think so.'

'Why not?' Will asked confused. 'Maybe they're trying to cover up something else?'

'Even if it was, it wouldn't be Delpont.'

'Maybe they're removing them now when all the attention is away from Delpont? When people have forgotten about it?'

Lew rolled his eyes. 'Think about it: What would anyone at Delpont have to gain?'

Will frowned, shaking his head. 'Look, it doesn't matter. I just need to know about these people, so I can figure out who's targeting them. In terms of the group of people behind it, so far we've identified Ronald Oakly and Taylor Sheeran as part of a small group of people who were linked to these accounts.'

Noble raised an eyebrow. ‘Why would I tell you anything anyway?’ He asked with a sneer.

‘You’re in prison? They profited and you took the fall. What could you have possibly have to hide?’

‘I may be in here, but I’m safe and my family is protected.’

‘Why not say something?’ Will asked with a frown.

The man shook his head. ‘I’d suffer the same fate as Andy Ling.’

‘Andy Ling? The COO? *They* killed him?’

‘I dunno.’ He shook his head. ‘He was facing a lot of jail time and he could offer them up on a silver platter.’

Will scrunched his face.

‘That surprises you? His death was so suspicious, everyone suspected something.’

‘Yeah, I know, it’s just—I always thought he had faked his own death.’ He shook his head. ‘Most people thought he was still out there somewhere.’

Lew shrugged. ‘That was the rumour.’

He didn’t know why, but he felt disappointed by the idea. It was such a let down after the years of rumours and conspiracy theories.

He shook his head and stood up. ‘Anyway, I got nothing more to say. But if you keep looking, you need to know that you’ll be putting people in danger.’

‘Because of the person targeting these individuals?’

‘No.’ Lew sneered. He stepped forward as the guard opened the door. ‘That’s the least of your problems.’

Will slumped back in his chair, frustrated. His encounter with Lew Noble had only left him with more questions. It only served to give him further doubts about pursuing these killings. Should I continue finding out the truth behind Delpont?

LEW

As he left the room he looked back at the journalist sitting inside. He grinned, thinking of the man's naiveté. He was like so many others before him, desperate to find out answers, to find out the truth, but completely unwilling and unable to handle the consequences of their actions. Unaware of the cost they would have to pay. Still, the kid had paid a heavy price already. Lew had lost friends because of the company as well. He had paid a high price for a few years of wealth.

As the guard led him back to his cell he turned. 'I need to make a phone call.'

'What?'

'I need to make a phone call.'

The guard frowned. 'How many years have you been in here now, Lew? Ten?'

'About that.'

'Not once have you asked for a phone call.'

'Well, I need to make one today.'

AOKI

Aoki wished she had driven on the way over. Morgan was too distracted to talk, he'd been thinking over something while he was driving. This left Aoki stuck on a long drive with nothing to do and no one to talk to. She sighed. It reminded her of family holidays as a kid. Of being crammed into a car with lots of luggage and food and going on drives for ten hours. They were terrible memories. As a kid, she'd hated holidays. It was only after turning eighteen that she realised they could actually be fun.

She stared off out the window, lost in thought herself. For whatever reason, she didn't think too much of the phone call from an anonymous party. It seemed like someone messing with them. Given the high profile nature of the case and police efforts, whoever it was would know exactly the consequences they would face. From the police or others. It was unlikely someone in that position would turn themselves in. Not without a very good reason.

Some way along the ride they passed a familiar bar.

'Wasn't that where we went for my birthday last year?' She asked, breaking the silence.

'Nah, we went there for Adrian's remember. Last year, we went to the bar by Circular Quay for yours. Remember?'

'That's right! And you were talking to that French girl!' She remembered.

He chuckled. 'Yeah, she was weird. Remember how she walked back with us to the city?'

She laughed. 'Yeah, I remember that. And she kept insisting she would take the bus back home.'

He shook his head. 'What an idiot. We were both telling her that a train took her right to her house.'

'And it would take an hour longer, as well. We both tried telling her that.'

'She was a weird girl.'

She looked out the window. They drove north along the road that ran parallel to Manly beach. Even on a weekday there were a lot of people down here. Wealthy couples who had retired early, out for coffee and a meal, European tourists walking up and down the beachfront, taking it all in. 'Did you ever hear from her again?'

He shook his head. 'Nah. I gave her my number but she never rang.' He shrugged and smiled. 'Her loss, I guess. I wasn't that keen, anyway.'

'Bullshit!' She pointed her finger, laughing. 'You were loving that French accent.'

He grinned. 'Maybe. But apart from that there was no interest.' They reached the house the caller had directed them to. It was a small single story house, one street away from the main beachfront. Considering the location, it was relatively quiet.

'I wish I owned a place around here. I love this area.' He said as he got out of the car, looking out at the water.

'Yeah, it's pretty.' She said tentatively. She tended to agree. It was a perfect day. The air was cold but the sun was shining. This was her favourite time of year; it got too warm for her in summer. Autumn and spring were more suited to her. She shook her head. 'I'd never want to live here, though.'

'What? You're kidding?'

'No, it's far too crowded. It's too difficult to park.'

'No way!' He pointed at the car he had just parked, on the empty street. As he pointed the shirt tightened, showing his subtle belly. 'Look at how easy that was!'

'Yeah, but it's the middle of the day right now *and* it's a weekday. No one's around.'

'Yeah.' He said unconvincingly, scratching the stubble on his chin. His small brown eyes narrowed as he considered it. 'That's true I guess.'

They walked to the front door. She reached it first, checking the house. He looked around, everything was quiet.

'Hey, whatever happened after your birthday that night?' He asked.

'What do you mean?' She said absently, realising the door was open and ajar. She gave it a slight push.

'Well, I remember you were all talking about going out after. Did you ever make it to—' His sentence trailed off as the door swung open to reveal a pool of blood and a body with several slices to the neck. 'Karaoke?'

ANDREA

The past day she had been wrapped up in the past. For some reason, after she had left Hank's place the other night she had started thinking about Delpont. She'd been walking to the cabstand when she thought about Lew Noble, about the people he had been protecting, about the people she had been protecting. But for all her knowledge about what had happened, she knew precious little about the people behind it. That led her to where she was sitting, waiting to meet with Paul McDermott.

She sat in the far corner of a café. A narrow hole in the wall style place, it was primarily a dessert café, offering only cakes and baked treats. However it strangely also sold stationary and decorations. The walls were adorned in an assortment of stationary and notebooks stylised in artistic designs and patterns. At the far end, inside where Andrea was sitting, there was also a display of vintage cameras and photography equipment for sale. Not one to appreciate items of that nature, she could still admire their beauty, intricate designs and the condition they were in. Andrea sipped at her cappuccino and savoured the taste. *At least they made good coffee.*

As she waited she reflected on the last time she had seen Paul McDermott over ten years ago. Despite all the cretins that had passed through the doors of Delpont, he was a refined man. She felt nervous waiting for him as he was always a bit intimidating. The anticipation wasn't helping either. She had been waiting for a while.

She heard his familiar voice place his order with the café staff and she turned to the entrance to see him.

She frowned, surprised. The man she saw was visibly different to what she remembered. For a start, he was wearing casual clothes; khaki chinos with a charcoal zip up wool jumper with dark brown hiking shoes. His hair was thin and greying, and he was noticeably thinner than she remembered. Despite that though, he had an energy about him that she had never seen before. He looked fit and healthy. He had a warm smile as he talked to the café staff, talking openly and laughing, being friendly and polite. He gesticulated as he spoke, though his actions now were open and confident. She had always remembered him as a bitter man who spoke directly and economically, only talking when necessary. Despite that though, he had always been polite. The man entering the café now was radically different to the one who had been at the helm of Delpont during the darkest of days. He finished placing his order and paid, leaving the counter and walking towards her. She made eye contact with him and he smiled. There was a sparkle in the old man's sky blue eyes. In all the years they had worked together she'd never seen that sparkle, in all the meetings and teleconferences they had sat through together.

'Andrea!' He said animatedly. His voice was warm and friendly. 'You look incredible! You haven't aged a day.'

She felt herself instantly charmed. She resisted the physical urge to blush.

'Paul you old charmer.' She laughed. 'It's so good to see you.'

When she said it, she spoke truly. She felt like she was catching up with a lifelong friend, not a stranger she had worked with for so long and so long ago. 'Thanks for meeting with me.'

'Oh, don't mention it. When I heard what happened. It's just terrible.' He said, his voice sincere. 'But how have you been, anyway? What have you been up to since?'

She furrowed her brow. 'I've been working at a few different places. I'm working in government now.'

'Really? Wow, that is a big change. Who with?' He said smiling.

'I just started with ASIC. I'm working on some legislation at the moment.'

‘Gee, that’s great.’ Paul said, smiling. He spoke enthusiastically. It was disarming. ‘I’m glad things are going so well for you.’ He spoke softer. ‘You must be glad for the opportunity to work for ASIC as well?’

‘How do you mean?’

He frowned and sighed. ‘Ah, well. You know, the opportunity to accomplish some good, to make some changes. To try and make up for all the damage that Delpont caused.’

She looked at him, surprised. This was the first she had ever had a conversation with him where he had let his guard down and said what he actually thought. ‘I’m surprised. I didn’t know you felt that way.’

‘Yeah, well.’ He said slowly, scratching at his scalp and thinning hair. ‘I’ve had a long time alone with my thoughts to think about everything that we did.’

‘We weren’t that bad Paul.’ She said lightly, smiling. ‘It was part of that time and place. Everyone was doing it.’

He looked her in the eyes, his face calm. Paul’s eyes seemed to sparkle as he looked at her, thinking. He shook his head. ‘That’s one way of looking at it.’

She cleared her throat. ‘How about yourself? What have you been to over the years?’

He smiled. ‘It’s been fantastic. Honestly, Delpont falling apart was the best thing that ever happened to me.’

‘Really?’

‘Oh absolutely.’ He said passionately ‘I mean, I had put so much of myself into that company, so much time. It got to the point that I,’ he squinted, looking for the word ‘I guess you could say that I defined myself by that company. Everything of who I am was tied up in it.’

He used his hands as he spoke for emphasis, shaking his head. 'Obviously when it all fell apart I felt like I had lost everything. I just remember this feeling like, the ground had come out from under me.'

She felt pained. Everything he said brought back the memories. 'I know the feeling.'

'Oh, yeah. It was awful, wasn't it? I mean, they were dragging our names through the mud. At least you and me were lucky. We left before it all came out. We were able to move on.'

'We were fortunate to not get dragged into it.' She nodded. 'But you must be kidding when you say it was the best thing to ever happen to you?'

'Oh no. Not at all. I mean it was awful, terrible when it all fell apart. And I spent the longest time in anger, in self defence. I mean, I had lost my entire identity. Everything I had worked so hard for and sacrificed for had fallen through. I defined myself as a man by how successful I was in my job, by how much money I made. And I mean, my every fear, my every insecurity had all come true. The worst possible things I could imagine had happened. I put everything of myself into something and I failed, and by my own definition I had failed as a man.' He shook his head. 'But then I remember thinking afterwards; Wait a minute. I'm still here. I just realised that despite the fact I had lost everything, I was still here. I had faced my every fear and insecurity and come out the other side.' He shook his head, smiling. 'It was the most incredibly liberating feeling.'

She smiled. 'That's incredible. I admire your spirit.'

'Oh, but it's true! And after that I just took some time off and thought about it all. About what I believed in. And what was important to me.'

'And what happened then?' She said, completely caught up in his story.

‘Well, I realised that obviously my family was the most important thing to me. My wife, Jean, and my young daughter, Amber. And, I mean, I always wanted to make the world a better place, I wanted to save the environment and make a difference for the homeless. I wanted to travel and see the world. And I realised I had spent twenty years of my life neglecting those things. I mean, I hadn’t volunteered in however many years, I barely travelled outside of work, and when I did I always went somewhere comfortable. And worst of all I barely saw my daughter. I had missed so much of her childhood by the time things at Delpont fell apart. For twenty years I had just been going through the motions. I had forgotten what I believed in.’

She sighed. ‘That sounds so painful.’

‘It wasn’t at all.’ He said shaking his head. ‘I just realised I had to start living my life. So I started taking my wife out on dates again, we started travelling together, going to new places we had never seen. I took time off my new job to spend with my daughter. I stopped working late, I stopped buying into the company line of what they needed. I learnt how to say no to what they wanted.’

She nodded. ‘It’s important to draw the line.’

‘That’s exactly it.’ He said smiling. ‘You have to be able to draw the line. You have to be able to say no, otherwise it will never stop.’ He sighed. ‘And then after that I started being proactive, I started going out and doing things and facing whatever other fears and insecurities I had left. If there was something I wanted to do, I would go out and do it. I started donating to charities for environmental causes and homeless people, helping out with a community group cleaning up a national park every fortnight, volunteering for charities.’ He smiled. ‘Just basically being more proactive and actually doing something about what I believed in instead of just talking about it.’

She smiled. ‘That’s incredible, Paul! I’m so glad to hear. You seem so much more confident now.’ She stated genuinely. There was conviction and emotion in his voice, he spoke passionately. 'You seem so different.'

He smiled, nodding. 'Thank you. Oh, I feel so different. I have real meaning in my life now. I believe in what I'm doing. And I mean my wife and daughter are so happy as well. I was absent before. I'm really happy to be able to help with them. My daughter Amber is just incredible, I'm so proud of her. She used to be so quiet and shy when she was young, but I've been able to talk her through the same issues I was having and she has really come out of her shell.'

'She's lucky to have such a positive role model like yourself.' Andrea could feel herself being drawn in by his personality, there was an inherent magnetism in Paul. She felt inspired just talking to him.

He smiled. 'I'm lucky to have her too. She's not just my daughter, she's my friend. Someone I can talk to.' He lowered his head and cleared his throat. 'Anyway, sorry to go on about myself. How are you? How is everything going with your husband?'

'Things are great. I love him.' She smiled. It felt true. 'We've been married a while now. It's been going well.'

'I'm glad to hear. Any kids?'

'No,' she cleared her throat. 'No, not yet.'

'Oh, that's a shame. You've got to. Honestly, it's the most incredible thing.'

She smiled, saying nothing. She hoped to cut that line of conversation off at that point. It was a question she was asked often and one she was used to fielding.

'Enough about all that, though. We should talk about what we're both thinking.'

She nodded, smiling sadly. 'I know.'

‘When did you first start worrying about it? When did you notice they were all Delpont people dying?’

She shook her head and sighed. ‘I don’t know. I ran into our old receptionist at the supermarket, she told me that she’d been to Kelvin’s funeral.’

Paul nodded slowly. He exhaled. ‘Yeah, that was probably the most upsetting one I heard about. He, uh, he really came around after Delpont. In the first few years we talked to each other a lot, even did some charity things together.’

She nodded. ‘Sounds like something you could both share. When was the last time you saw him?’

‘God, I would say almost five years ago.’

‘Really? Why so long?’

‘Well, I would say that it was because people come and go in each other’s lives and people grow apart, but it wouldn’t be true in this case. I honestly think, after a while, after we both moved on, we couldn’t see each other anymore because it just reminded us of Delpont. It brought back all those memories.’ He shook his head sadly. ‘It kept us trapped in the past.’

She nodded. Saying nothing, but understanding what he meant. Maybe it was why she had made no effort to keep in touch with anyone from those days. She found it easy to move on with her life when she had cut all ties with those days. ‘It’s easier to forget about it and move on than it is to try and justify it to ourselves, to come to terms with it.’

‘Ah, come on. Don’t talk like that, don’t talk like them.’

She frowned. Unsure what he meant. ‘How about you? When did you figure it out?’

He sighed. 'Not all at once. It was a gradual realisation, but I mean, even now I wonder whether I'm imagining things, whether I'm getting paranoid, connecting things that are unrelated.'

'I know the feeling. And you're not.'

He sighed. 'I mean, even when I heard about the first death I was suspicious. As soon as I thought about it, I just felt it was linked.' His brow was furrowed, he was staring down at the table. His thoughts seemed far away.

She focused her gaze on him. 'What do you think they want? Why us? Why now?'

He glanced at her, frowning. 'I keep thinking it's one of us.'

'What?' She said perplexed. 'That doesn't make any sense.'

'They know so much about what happened. They knew about Sheeran.'

She sighed. That was a valid point. 'That could mean any number of things. Maybe someone researched us and figured it out.'

'Then why wouldn't they go to the police? Why not just go public?'

She took a deep breath and felt a knot in her stomach. What he was saying was making her uncomfortable. She sipped her coffee, wishing they were at a bar. Contrary to her usual taste for wine, right now she felt like a beer.

'Honestly, I think someone is trying to make an example of us. I think they're trying to make a statement.'

She wished he hadn't said it. Andrea felt her skin crawl.

WILL

Will sat at one of the tables outside, under an awning. He looked to his right, at the perfect spring day and the beach, at the ocean beyond. The water looked a darker and cleaner blue that he could remember. It seemed like a long time since he had last been to the beach. There were no clouds in the sky and as he looked out into the sea that went on forever, he felt a breeze come past. He pulled his leather jacket tighter. Regardless of how perfect the day seemed, there was a deceptive coldness in the air. No matter how beautiful something could look, the reality could be quite different.

From around the corner he saw Aoki walking to the café. He waved at her to get her attention, clearing his bag off the table so there was room for her. She had called him that morning and told him what had happened the night before. When he thought about how the man had died just a block from where he was sitting, he came out of his calm thoughts. He was brought back to reality, the sound of cars passing by, the sound of so many conversations around him, a baby crying. He exhaled deeply.

'Thanks for coming to meet me.' She said softly, stubbing out her cigarette. She smiled slightly, an effort at being friendly. He could see the tired expression on her face. She looked worn down.

'Don't worry about it.' He squinted as she sat down. 'What time did you end up leaving the crime scene last night?'

She rubbed her face, it was only then he noticed the red in her eyes. 'Just before midnight. I went home and went straight to sleep. I couldn't stay there all night, I needed some rest.'

He nodded. 'Is Morgan here with you?'

She shook her head. 'No. He stayed at the scene until late this morning. He only left a few hours ago.'

‘Fair enough.’ He paused. He felt sorry for what these detectives were going through. ‘So who was the guy?’

She cleared her throat. ‘We checked the rent, his mail, license. We’re certain his name is Victor Malceski. Born in Australia but his passport showed a lot of travel, like several trips a year.’

He frowned. ‘For work?’

She shrugged. ‘Not sure. Apparently, he worked as a security contractor.’

‘As a guard?’

‘No, as an advisor on security systems. We checked his bank account though and we found large, regular deposits.’

‘How did you get access?’ He asked.

She shrugged. ‘For someone who worked as a security contractor he was awfully lax about his own security. He left the password on his phone, in a note titled “bank details”.’

Will chuckled and shook his head. ‘Nice. Is that legal, though?’

‘Meh.’ She shrugged it off. ‘It’s not like we’ll use it in making the case. It was there and we needed background.’

He frowned, concerned by her attitude. He wondered how many other detectives took the same approach.

‘Anyway,’ she continued, rubbing her temple in irritation, ‘He was getting regular payments of tens of thousands a month. But from what we can tell he didn’t work many hours.’

He nodded. ‘Yeah, that does seem strange. So who were the payments from?’

She shook her head. ‘I got Morgan to chase it down so we’re still figuring it out.’

The waitress arrived and delivered a cappuccino to Aoki. She thanked her. The waitress smiled and went to serve another table.

'I didn't order a cappuccino, though?' Aoki asked, a confused look on her face.

'Yeah, I ordered one for you when I got here. I figured you would need one.'

She smiled, taken aback. 'Oh, thank you. That's so thoughtful.'

'That's fine. I got it take away. I figure we can walk and talk.'

She nodded. He picked up his leather jacket and slipped it on, straightening it up.

AOKI

She walked ahead and lit up a cigarette. As she did she heard a disapproving scoff from behind her. She turned to see a passing mother staring. Not like the woman could claim the moral high ground though, she was keeping her toddler on a leash. She wore the typical spoilt mother uniform; tracksuit, cap and the designer sunglasses that she hadn't earned. She knew the type and hated her instantly. Even if Aoki forced the kid to smoke an entire pack it would still be better than how demeaning the leash was. Regardless, she stubbed out the cigarette. It was one of those councils that had banned smoking in public places. The petty woman took that as a victory and instantly brightened.

'Thank you.' The woman pronounced, faking a smile. She turned, stuck her nose up and walked away.

'No problems.' Aoki said glaring at her back. 'I hope your husband cheats on you with a whore and gives you herpes.' She muttered under her breath.

Will finished paying his tab and came to join her.

The two crossed the road towards the beach. It was only marginally closer than they were before but the ocean breeze was stronger. Aoki looked out to the blue horizon, squinting from the brightness. The water was a dark radiant blue. She wished she had one of her cameras with her. The ocean looked perfect on a day like that. She knew from experience though that it was always difficult to capture a scene like that, she had never been able to capture the overwhelming feeling of looking out at the endless sea. Nowadays she mostly focused on photos of the city at night. Photos of skyscrapers lit up against the blackness, people passing each other on the street. Not only were her cameras better suited to it, but it was also a better fit with her hours.

The sound of a loud crash of waves brought her back to Will and the present moment. She realised she'd drifted off for a few minutes. She turned to Will to see if he noticed the silence. He was staring off into the distance, frowning. She followed his line of vision. His gaze was focused on the cliff at the far side of the beach, the dark red sandstone jutting up from the ocean. Aoki looked at the apartment blocks atop the cliff, thinking about how precarious their position was there with the sea crashing against the rock, wind beating down on the cliff. The lofty position was wearing away, eroding, with each passing day. It would become increasingly tenuous until inevitably the buildings would collapse into the water. Thoughts like that made her think about how insignificant an individual life was in terms of the big picture. She could see Will staring at the base of the cliff though. The waves crashed again on the rocks and she saw a pained look on his face, he flinched slightly at the sound. She realised the memory of his lost friend was still such a fresh wound. The place his body had been found was only two beaches up from here. He shivered. She couldn't tell whether it was because of the wind or not.

'You know, I didn't realise it when we met,' she spoke up, changing the topic. 'But I have actually come across some of your work before.' She said, trying to get him to open up and talk.

'Oh, really?' He turned towards her and raised an eyebrow. 'Which one?'

'The economic argument about criminality. I can't remember what it was called.' She said, shaking her head.

'The spiral bankruptcy theory of criminality?' He asked.

'Yeah, that's it. I studied it during a course. I only realised the other day when I came across it again.'

'They teach that in courses?' He laughed. 'I didn't think many people knew about it'

‘Really?’ She smiled, glad her attempt to make conversation had brought him out of a bad place.

‘Yeah, it never did that well.’ He said with a frown, his voice trailing off.

‘Something about the theory stuck with me.’

‘How so?’

She shrugged. ‘I don’t know, just the idea that harsher sentencing on lower level criminals could make it harder for those organisations to find people.’

He nodded. ‘Yeah, I mean, it wasn’t just harsher sentencing, it was also about an overall crackdown on low level offences, and making those kinds of jobs seem less desirable so less people look for work in that area. So, as a result, criminal organisations need to pay more to get people for those positions.’

Aoki tried to interject but couldn’t get a word in. She rolled her eyes and smiled.

‘So in terms of the supply and demand labour model,’ he continued, ‘The overall effect is that it leads to both a lower labour supply with less people to hire, and also a higher wage price that the criminal organisations need to pay to these workers due to the lower supply.’ He said, speaking slowly and calmly. She noticed that he spoke differently when talking about this topic. He spoke with a calm sense of assurance. She assumed it was because he was so comfortable in these areas.

‘Yeah, exactly.’ She exclaimed, frustrated. She found it refreshing to see the calm and confident side of him but she was irritated at getting a lecture. ‘Anyway, that idea that it would drive up wages stuck with me.’

He nodded and smiled. ‘That was really all I wanted to accomplish.’

‘What do you mean?’

He shrugged. ‘I don’t know, just to get people to think about the idea. I didn’t know what I was arguing for, but I was just hoping it would generate discussion.’

She nodded.

‘But, I mean, it went even beyond wages. The whole theory about increasing wages in criminal organisations is that it reduces profitability. If it then starts to eat too much into their profit then all of a sudden the people who run those organisations start to look for other industries to invest their money in. Industries that are not as aggressive, and which are more profitable.’

She shook her head. ‘I forgot about that part. Yeah, that is a really interesting idea.’

‘Yeah, in theory you could all of a sudden start to shut down major criminal organisations.’

‘Did you believe it would work?’

He frowned. ‘I was never advocating the use of it. Like I said, I just wanted to generate discussion.’

She nodded.

When they reached the house there was no crowd outside, save for the two officers patrolling the premises. She pulled out her badge and the officers moved aside to let them through. Will hesitated.

Aoki turned back. ‘Is everything alright?’

‘Am I allowed to even be here?’ He looked sheepishly, adding quietly, ‘I’ve never been at a crime scene before. Other than when we met.’

She smiled. ‘It’s fine. If anyone asks you were here to verify a few details.’

He nodded.

The two walked in and she showed him the scene. He stepped carefully and kept his hands in his pockets. He was a natural at making his way around a crime scene.

‘It isn’t much of a place.’ He noted.

It was true. Despite being a freestanding house, there were only two regular sized bedrooms. It was one storey, and the living room was connected directly to the kitchen. The back of the living room was all glass and it allowed a lot of natural light in. It was sparsely furnished, save for a few items.

‘I know. This isn’t what I would expect from someone earning hundreds of thousands a year.’

‘Maybe he couldn’t declare his income?’ Will suggested.

‘Maybe.’

She walked back to where the body was found. The floor was still covered in blood. Will didn’t seem affected by it. Despite his earlier insecurities, he didn’t seem troubled by a crime scene.

‘This is where we found him. He had a gunshot wound to the neck. There didn’t seem to be any signs of a fight or confrontation when we arrived though. The only disturbances around the area seem to be where he fell. No damage done to the door or lock, either. The windows and other entrances were locked and also undamaged. Me and Morgan,’

‘Morgan and I.’ He said softly, pursing his lips.

She exhaled. ‘Morgan and I. Whatever. We think he knew whoever came to meet him. I’m guessing they were probably let in. The entry point was to the front of the neck, near his throat, so it seems to back that up. He would have been looking directly at them when he was shot. He most likely wasn’t jumped by a stranger but was killed by someone he knew.’

Will nodded. 'Ok.'

She continued. 'The shot seemed pretty straight, went in one side and came out at around about the same height. We found the bullet embedded in that wall over there.' Aoki said, pointing to her right. 'Which means the shooter would have been standing about,' She took a step forward and turned 'here, when he shot.'

'They.'

She frowned. 'What do you mean?'

'You said he. You don't know it's a guy.'

She waved him off. 'Whatever.'

'You should stop being so sexist.' He teased, grinning.

'Fuck off! Whatever!' She laughed and shook her head, clearing her throat. 'Anyway, based off the height of the entry and exit wounds it was almost a level shot. So the shooter would have been about 5'9' or 5'10'. It seems pretty consistent with the bullet embedded in the wall.'

'Ok.' He said, contemplating. 'So what did you want to show me? What makes you think this is connected?'

She smiled. 'Check this out.' She lead him over and tapped her finger on one of the photos pinned on the fridge with a magnet. It was of two men on a boat, holding up two large fish. 'Have a look at that. This guy, Victor, is on the left. Have a look at who is on the right.'

Will squinted and looked closer. 'Paul McDermott.'

THE MAN IN THE MOTEL

He sighed. The deeper he got the more he felt there was a weight on his shoulders. The room he had been living in for the past few months was decrepit. The motel was a fraction of the cost of hotels, and cheaper than long term rents. Though the real advantage was the lax state of record keeping. There was a limited paper trail that, even if followed, would only lead to various fake credit cards he had set up under others names. The environment was unpleasant though. He could always overhear couples having arguments, married people cheating on their spouses in privacy, the occasional pornography being filmed in one of the other rooms.

The most worrying to him was coming home to find police around the building, reporting to the scene of another murder or kidnapping or assault. In moments like those half of him worried that he'd been discovered. He would accept his fate, walk towards the police only to be let past and into his apartment. They were always someone else.

He turned to look at one of walls of room, the one that was plastered with paper. All the meticulously taken notes and research, with photos was pinned to it. The path he'd chosen, the one he was on now, ended only one way. *It wouldn't always be someone else.* He exhaled. *One day the police will be waiting for me. But today is not that day. I'll be damned if it were going to be today. I'm so close*. He looked at the photos of Lew Noble. Of Paul McDermott. Of Ronald Oakly and Darren Orr. They were scared. He knew it. Right now he had them on the back foot and they were starting to take notice. But it wasn't them he was trying to get through to. It wasn't them he wanted to be afraid. *I'm so close*.

He turned to the photo of Andrea Beaufort. He'd been thinking about her lately. How he'd let her go. For some reason he didn't feel he could try again. He ran his hand through his hair, thinking about how he had been so close. It just didn't feel right. He would like to believe it was because he doubted her guilt and complicity, but he suspected otherwise. If he were honest with himself, it was because she was a woman. He wondered how sexist that made him.

He looked at the maze of plans and ideas in front of him and none of it made sense. It was all a mess and he didn't know where to go from there. He needed to get out of the dump of a hotel room and get some fresh air.

He put on a jacket and left the lights off, ducking out the door and into the night air. As he walked up the hill to the restaurants and bars he could hear the screeching of the train against the tracks from a block away. In the distance there was the sound of police sirens. He exhaled as he walked. The train screeched because the lines were old and in disrepair, because the government was short of funds and because the system was corrupt. The police sirens were sounding because the approach to solving crime in the western world was focused on statistics and applying a band-aid solution. It existed because no one had the fortitude to make real changes, to fix the underlying issues. It was the product of a system that cared only about profit and not about the human cost. He took a deep breath listening to the sounds of the city, to the realities of the status quo.

After walking for twenty minutes he reached the main road and the main strip of shops. It was a weeknight but there was still hustle and bustle. Couples walking arm in arm, groups of friends laughing after dinner and drinks. The neon signs and street lights illuminated the sidewalk. Over the sound of the traffic, he heard conversations and laughter from the restaurants he passed. He rubbed his trimmed beard, looking at the faces of couples and families. People who love each other. He felt weighed down by sadness in that moment. The path that he could have followed was in front of him, a simple life, an ordinary life. He exhaled deeply. It was a life of complicity. The people he loved were gone or far away. This city felt empty nowadays, he walked the streets alone. Walking the same places he had walked before. His old life had been here, a life of happiness, sharing in that same conversation and laughter. This city seemed haunted now, every corner he turned brought back an old memory.

He walked into the same bar that had been his regular when he'd worked in the area. It was an old fire station that had been turned into a multi level bar. It was usually only busy on weekdays from the after work crowd. The tables were crowded, the music loud and the bartenders busy. Still, it wasn't the sort of bar one would ever struggle to walk through.

He wasn't sure what had possessed him to walk in there, he just wanted to be around people in that moment. Despite facing his demons, and all the belief he had in what he was doing, he still doubted himself sometimes. He was only human. The only people who never doubted themselves were either madmen or fools.

He ordered a gin and tonic with the bartender. He hadn't had one since his last job. The bartender smiled at him as she mixed the drink, something in her expression revealed youth and naïveté. He smiled politely back. He was almost old enough to be her father. Still it had been a long time since he had felt any warmth in his life, he thought of the one he loved so far away. Part of him was tempted, but he knew that for the rest of his life he heart would belong to another. Any intimacy with someone else would be a lie. She handed him the drink and he paid, tipping the rest of the note. She smiled and thanked him. He nodded in acknowledgement. He always felt the need to tip customer service staff regardless. If he didn't, then it would be hypocritical, it would be inconsistent with what he wanted to achieve.

As he crossed the room, retreating to a quiet corner where he could observe from, he recognised a face. He frowned. They looked so familiar but he couldn't tell who they were because of the poor lighting and the distance. He stopped in his tracks and turned slowly. He checked that none of them had noticed him or recognised him. Walking back past the group slowly, he tilted his head subtly to get a closer look. He smiled when he saw his face. That crooked nose, the cruel eyes. He recognised Darren Orr as the one talking to the group. He was bragging about how he had humiliated a graduate employee, laughing at his own story. It wasn't an accident that he had run into him that night. He took a deep breath, feeling calm and collected. It felt like divine intervention running into him like this, being presented with something so unexpected and fortuitous. He had felt confused, but he knew then what his next move would be.

He made his way across to the entrance of the bar and found a seat. Somewhere he could observe the comings and goings of this bastard of a man.

AOKI

She smoked outside the building. It was midday and there were various corporate types swooping around; businesses trying to hustle another client. She knew little of the corporate world, but whenever she made it downtown all she saw were people trying to get more business. The wine and dine lunches seemed to be all that the senior people did, always trying to sweet talk their way into another account only to neglect them once the money started to roll in.

She called Andrea Beaufort early in the morning to meet with her. She had no idea whether this woman knew anything, but they had tried every lead they could think of. Right now, Aoki was desperate.

She and Morgan had been excited after discovering the link to Paul McDermott at the previous crime scene, however, it had quickly run into a roadblock. Despite whatever evidence there was suggesting McDermott was involved, they had been unable to bring him in for questioning. Or really their senior was unwilling to bring him in, as the evidence was thin and McDermott was strongly protected by a team of lawyers.

There was something going on that she didn't understand, and as much as her seniors tried to isolate the incidents to avoid messing up the statistics; something more serious was happening. Will had told of his conversation with Lew Noble, who he described as a 'wreck of a man'. According to Will, he hadn't said much. Lew Noble wasn't talking, whether it was to Will as a journalist or herself as a detective. The man had lost his family and his former life, and yet he was still hiding something. Her only hope right now was this woman Andrea, this woman who, she hoped, had something to lose and everything to protect.

The glass doors swung open as Aoki finished her cigarette. The woman walked out, made eye contact with her and smiled. Her movements were graceful and confident.

'You must be Aoki Sun.' She pronounced calmly.

'Yeah, that's right. You're Andrea Beaufort?' She tried to sound confident amidst stubbing her cigarette. She wasn't sure it worked.

'Correct.' She smiled 'You don't need to worry about smoking around me. I'm not fussed. Did you want to walk and talk?'

Aoki smiled. 'Sure. Thanks. Yeah, sorry, I just lit one up.' She didn't know why she was making excuses. From the moment they made eye contact this woman had taken control of their interactions. Her every movement was precise and deliberate. Her diction and tone were perfect. Aoki felt instantly intimidated.

'It's fine.' The woman said, beaming. She lowered her voice as they wandered up the street. 'Let me guess; you're here to ask about Delpont.'

The question was off-putting. The bluntness of this woman surprised her. Whenever she asked people about Delpont they always tried to answer the question vaguely. 'Yeah, I'm investigating a series of murders at the moment.'

'I heard. All former Delpont staff.' She said in a sombre tone, sighing deeply. 'I can't help you. I'm sorry.'

'Because you're afraid?' Aoki suggested tentatively.

The woman laughed. 'No. Because I don't know what is going on. Honestly, I've spoken to some other Delpont people about this and they don't understand what's happening either.'

'Oh.' Aoki was lost for words. All her plans had suddenly gone out the window. She'd planned to press her for information.

She rubbed her face to wake up. It was too early for this. 'I was hoping you would be able to give me some answers.'

Andrea smiled sadly. Aoki looked at her gaze as they walked down the street, the woman was staring off into the distance. She was visibly saddened by the thoughts of Delpont but her every action was so calculated that she couldn't help but feel that Andrea had her own agenda.

'Did you want to stop for coffee here? We could sit down and have a proper conversation?'

'That would be good.' Aoki felt lost. In her head, the conversation was going to run very differently. She felt like this woman would be defensive and on the back foot, instead she had been helpful and prepared. *She's hiding something.* Aoki frowned. *Her diction's too perfect.*

It was only when they were inside that Aoki realised they were in a bar which just happened to be opened during the day. She scrunched her face, unsure of whether she wanted to try the food there. Andrea ordered a garden salad and a cappuccino. Aoki was content with just a coffee. They ordered and then the two sat inside, picking a spot by the corner.

Save for the two of them, the bar was empty; a good place to talk. It was only then Aoki noticed lounge music playing. She reflected how it was such an ongoing daily occurrence, but she rarely noticed when music entered her life. It was usually so subtle, perhaps part of that marketing culture, or perhaps the music was specifically chosen to be as discreet as possible while at the same time encouraging her to be a consumer.

Aoki narrowed her gaze. 'When did you start thinking something was going on?'

Andrea cleared her throat. 'I don't know exactly. Maybe the second time it happened? I felt like there was more to it. Especially, when Anderson died.'

'Anderson?'

'Yeah, Kelvin Anderson. I know that upset me. That was when I started thinking there was something happening. It couldn't just be random.'

Aoki's eyes widened. *Fuck, another one?* She sighed. *How can I find out more about that death, without letting her know I am clueless*?

'What was it about Anderson's death that made you suspicious.'

Andrea's mouth twitched. She ran a finger across her eyebrow. 'I couldn't say exactly. He was killed earlier, stabbed when his car was stolen. But considering everything that has happened since, it must be connected.' She squinted.

Aoki scribbled a note down, hoping Andrea didn't notice.

The bartender arrived with their coffees. It was mostly foam but Andrea thanked her regardless.

Aoki sipped at hers and could instantly tell that the beans had been burnt, and that the milk had been frothed at a high temperature. The taste was bitter and not in the soothing bitterness that she'd come to depend on. When the bartender was out of earshot Aoki sighed. 'So far we've encountered nothing but dead ends.' Aoki glanced at Andrea.

Her cold blue eyes were focused on her. She was analysing every word, perhaps hoping to get information she could use to help herself. Aoki had to be careful not to reveal too much. 'What is the view of the police department? Are they considering that this is the work of a serial killer?'

Aoki shook her head. 'I'm sorry, I can't discuss that.'

Andrea frowned. 'I can understand. It must be frustrating to work in that sort of environment. One that is so bureaucratic.' Andrea laughed. 'I'm starting to understand that now, working for the government. It's novel to me.'

'Oh, you're not working for banks anymore?'

'No, not anymore.' She shook her head. 'I'm working for ASIC now. I'm on the other side of the fence.'

'Oh, ok.' Aoki said, genuinely surprised. 'Good for you.'

Andrea looked at her quizzically. Aoki didn't want to explain what she meant, she felt defensive enough around this woman as it was.

'I know you must be hoping that I have answers for you.' Andrea said calmly, her diction perfect. 'But I don't know what is going on any more than you do. The truth is that I've asked around to try and understand what is happening, and like you I assumed that someone would know. But no one does.' Andrea's mouth twitched, and her eyes narrowed.

Aoki sighed. It felt like a kick in the gut. She ran her hand through her hair in frustration. 'I can understand.'

'I apologise. I should have explained this over the phone but I wanted to set the record straight in person.'

Aoki narrowed her gaze, studying Andrea. She was calm and collected with her hands in her lap, but she could see her fists were clenched tight. She was afraid for herself. 'Thanks for the honesty. I appreciate it.'

'It's fine, Detective Sun. I appreciate that you put yourself out for the good of the public. I would help you if I could.' She smiled, still maintaining her ever-professional composure. 'I should get back to work.' She said calmly, preparing to get up.

Aoki narrowed her gaze, lowering her voice. 'You're scared.'

Andrea's mouth twitch, then she laughed. 'What?'

‘I can see it.’ She said calmly.

Andrea shook her head. ‘I’m afraid you’re mistaken.’

‘No,’ Aoki said slowly. ‘I’m not.’

Her brow was furrowed, her manner had noticeably changed. There was uncertainty in her voice.

Andrea scanned the room and shot a glance behind her. ‘Assume there’s something else going on. These people avoided jail for crimes they committed on record. They’re a small select group of individuals who have operatives who work in the public eye, but they themselves stay out of sight. Their operatives were on the covers of magazines for almost ten years, the face of a company that made millions illegally.’ She spoke slowly and smiled, but her eyes betrayed nervousness.

Her hand trembled slightly as she continued. ‘They themselves profited while others fronted their ventures. When those operatives took the fall, this group of individuals escaped unscathed and moved their investments elsewhere. To this day, no one knows their names or where to find them. They continue to profit and prosper unchallenged. The depth of their influence exceeds even that of the government. They are, in a sense, above the law.’

Aoki felt her heart beat faster. She felt a rising sense of fear merely by what this woman was saying. It sounded crazy, but she could see real fear behind those blue eyes. Based on everything she had seen so far, it still seemed like a stretch. She knew this company was connected, but she doubted that these murders were some kind of cover up, and no matter what she had seen she refused to believe it was part of an elaborate corporate conspiracy. Still, this woman had seen the world from the inside, she must know more about it.

Andrea locked eyed contact. Her voice was calm and collected, in her eyes Aoki could see that she was pleading and warning her.

‘Firstly, how exactly do you hope to find them? And secondly, how can you possibly think that they’ll face justice?’

There was a moment of silence as Andrea kept eye contact with her. Aoki went to shake her hand but the woman began to gather her things in a hurry. She stood up uncertainly, and smiled as she darted past Aoki.

When she turned and walked back into the city streets, her head was high and her stride was confident. She was a different woman. Aoki was left feeling like her feet were stuck to the floor, her mouth was dry. She rubbed her face and scratched her head, taking a deep breath. From out of nowhere this woman had opened up. She wondered how much of what was said was an exaggeration.

She walked out of the café slowly and back into the street. She was immediately greeted by the sounds of traffic rushing past mixed in with heels clicking the pavement. She walked through the crowd, everyone heading in different directions, and negotiated her way past people who were almost colliding with her. Her mind was somewhere else.

She thought of the look in Andrea’s eyes and the idea of a faceless group who could commit crimes for so long and go unnoticed. Maybe Andrea had meant to warn her, to scare her off, but it had the opposite effect on her. Aoki started to understand what Morgan felt like, the sense of injustice that some crimes would be vilified while others would be forgiven simply because they were in power. What she had first felt as fear was now becoming a desire to expose the truth.

WILL

He had gone to the café with every intention of doing some proper research, of getting up to date with the article he was supposed to hand in by the end of the week. However, he'd been easily distracted as his thoughts wandered to Paul McDermott. He kept finding himself looking the man up, trying to find information about his career, about the trials, about what he had been up to since. Anything that could reveal what his involvement in all this was.

It was almost eleven at night. The café was down the road from his apartment, and became a bar at night. It had a Cuban theme, low light and candles with salsa type music. It had a relaxed atmosphere, which was good for Will. It was a weeknight but there were still a lot of people getting dinner and drinks. Will had opted to stay away from alcohol for a while. He got a slice of berry cheesecake and a hot chocolate, checking out the blonde bartender as she brought his food. She smiled at him. She was the type of girl that teenager boys dreamed about being with; blonde hair, a cute face with a button nose. He couldn't help but imagine what she looked like underneath the jeans and button up work shirt.

But for all that, he thanked her and watched her walk away. He didn't feel like flirting tonight, maybe it was because of Samantha. Though he also thought that what seemed like a dream was never that simple. When he tasted the hot chocolate, though, he immediately felt tempted to reconsider; the waitress had made it with melted chocolate and it was amazing.

His phone buzzed with a message from Sam. He smiled. She'd been texting him more and more lately, despite the fact they'd only seen each other a few times. They spent their time together hanging out at either of their places, over a few drinks and sessions of being intimate. He thought about her curves and pale skin, her dark hair and her dark eyes. The way she looked when she was on top.

In her texts, she told him about her day painting, asked him what he was up to and they made plans for when they could see each other next. It was everything he'd wanted after being single for so long, but his mind still kept wandering to Amber and her big blue eyes and perfect smile. It was a stupid notion; he knew she was a pipedream.

He tried working for another half an hour on the article but it became apparent he would get nowhere. He sipped at his hot chocolate that was now cold before packing up his laptop. He picked at the remains of his cake and the garnish of strawberry slices. After a few minutes, he slipped on his leather jacket and picked up his things. He smiled at the bartender and said goodnight as he walked out into the street.

As he walked he thought about everything with Sam and Amber, feeling desire for both women. One accepted him the way he was, there was mutual attraction and she was a girl he could trust. She was a good person. The other he knew so little about, but he felt drawn to her. She had such an effect on him, representing everything he had wanted and the man he had always wanted to be. He exhaled. Whenever he was in situations like this he usually screwed it up or made the wrong choice, and ended up being with neither girl. He didn't want that to happen this time, he wanted to have a real relationship.

His train of thought was interrupted by a man in the street ahead. He was sitting on his parked motorbike, and appeared to be talking to himself. Will looked around. He was on the highway and there was no one else walking around, just the traffic on the road. As he got closer he saw the man look around, his helmet on, visor open. He was definitely talking. As Will got closer he looked at the man strangely, he wasn't insane he was just having a conversation on the phone, he must have hooked it up through his bike helmet. Will hated people who talked on their phones through headsets in public places, they always looked like douchebags. His bike was bright orange and his bike gear was an equally bright fluoro camouflage pattern in several colours. As he was closer now, Will could hear him.

'Yeah, I've lost her. She's too far ahead. What's the call!' He shouted to the person on the other end.

As Will was looking at the man, his head turned and the two made eye contact.

A confused look formed on his face. 'I've gotta go, I just saw the other guy. He just passed me.'

Will quickly turned his head away, feeling instantly nervous. The man couldn't have been talking about him. He walked quicker as he heard the bike start.

'Fuck!' He heard the man say loudly. Will shot a quick glance behind him and realised why, there was too much traffic so he couldn't turn around. Will was walking in the opposite direction to traffic. He kept walking and turned the corner.

He heard the bike speed up and down the street, into the distance. As he kept walking, he heard the bike charge down and get closer again. He waited at the next set of lights, his heart beating faster. *This guy's gotta be part of this Delpont conspiracy. Am I going insane?* He breathed quickly. *Am I just being paranoid?* He heard the bike get closer as he anxiously waited for the lights to change. He thought about all the traffic around him. *This man couldn't shoot me here.*

The light changed and he crossed the road quickly, noticing himself walking quicker. He was breathing quickly now. He turned and looked behind at the bike approaching.

The bike was in the wrong line and had to turn right along the road, with the rest of the traffic. The engine roared. Will was puffing and breathing faster, moving as fast as he could. He stuck to the side of the road and walked on. The bike had turned right so it wouldn't be able to follow him.

He walked down the street, keeping himself to the shadows out of fear, and as he took another step, he heard the bike approach again. *A third time: There's no way this could be a coincidence.*

Will was far down the street now, it was quiet and into the suburbs. There were no other people on the street and no cars on the road. Usually he found it so comforting to be alone on the streets at night, alone with his thoughts but as he heard the bike tear up the street, getting closer and closer, he wished he wasn't alone.

He crossed the street, he was almost home but he could hear the rider getting closer, coming from the other direction. He couldn't see the bike yet, but they had to be heading straight for each other. He was in plain sight. There was an alley ahead that ran straight to his apartment. Will quickened his steps. He heard the engine revving as the bike tore towards him. He only had a few seconds before the bike could see him and he was still in the open. His heart was beating fast. He made a move for the shadows, unsure what this man would do if he caught him, almost sprinting to hide himself in the darkness as the headlights of the bike illuminated the the footpath Will had been standing on only a moment earlier. Not wanting to tempt fate, Will didn't turn around and kept walking down the alley, concealed in the shadows.

The man on the bike had already turned the next corner, and as Will walked to his apartment, he heard the rider circling the streets around him, looping around the alley. At any moment, the man could ride into the alley. He felt like an animal trying to make its way to safety with a bird of prey circling above, screeching.

He reached his apartment, the sounds of the bike becoming further and further away. It was only when he closed and locked the door that he realised how quickly he was breathing, and that his hands were shaking.

AOKI

The call answered on the third ring. 'Hello?'

'Hey, Rebecca. It's Aoki.'

'I was just about to call you! Can you give me a moment?'

'Sure thing.'

'Sorry, just one tic.' There was the sound of rustling on the other end. 'I've parked at the petrol station now.'

'Oh, sorry,' Aoki exclaimed. 'I didn't realise you were driving.'

She laughed. 'That's fine. I needed petrol anyway.'

'How did you go today?'

'Fantastic! You know how I told you I was following the account transactions?'

'Yeah.'

'Well, I had no luck with Azure. It's pretty tightly set up and I couldn't get any information on where the account was set up or whose name was on it.'

Aoki sighed.

'I mean, whoever set it up did their due diligence. Despite the fact all the accounts ended with a link, the only direct link we could find was with Delpont. The other transactions were linked to smaller company accounts, none to any personal accounts.'

'Ok.'

'But when I looked into the smaller accounts.' There was silence on the other end for a moment. 'They weren't set up anywhere near either. Some of them even had deposits from personal accounts.'

Aoki gasped slightly.

Rebecca laughed. 'I know. We have names.'

'Who do you have?'

'Oakley, Orr and Sheeran. On a platter.'

'Yes!' Aoki said excitedly. 'That's awesome! Good work!'

'Thank you.' Rebecca said tentatively. 'Yeah, I'm looking forward to a drink now.' She laughed.

'Did you want to come over and we could open up some white wine?'

'I'd love to. Can you text me your address?'

'Yeah, sure thing.' Aoki exhaled. 'I can't get over that. That's incredible work. We're finally getting somewhere with this.'

'I know.' She sighed. 'My eyes are killing me, though. I spent almost the entire day looking at accounts and researching things on my laptop.'

'Yeah? That sounds rough.'

She laughed. 'It was.'

'I'll clean up a bit but feel free to come over whenever. We can talk it all out then.'

'Sounds good. I'll head over now.'

'Have you told Will about this yet?'

She frowned. 'No. Not yet. I tried calling him but he wasn't picking up. He sent me a message saying he wasn't feeling well and we could talk later.'

‘Oh, ok. No problems. We can talk, just the two of us.’

‘That would be nice. Do you want me to pick a bottle of Sav Blanc?’

‘Ahh, maybe.’ Aoki laughed. ‘Sorry, I don’t have anything at home.’

‘No problems, I’ll swing by the bottle shop on the way over. Are you fine with a white?’

‘Yeah, that’s perfect!’ Aoki said cheerily. ‘That’s what I drink.’

‘We’ll get on famously then.’ Rebecca said, laughing. ‘I’ll give you a call if I have any issues finding your place.’

‘Sure thing. I’ll see you soon!’

Aoki disconnected and she put down the phone. She messaged her address to Rebecca straight away, otherwise she knew she’d forget.

As she waited for Rebecca on the couch, she looked out the window, staring off into space. It was a beautiful and quiet night out. The windows were down and the cool air was coming in. She felt at peace. At the same time, however, there was a nagging feeling, like déjà vu.

Aoki felt a chill run up her spine, and took a deep breath. She glanced around the apartment. *There’s no one there.* Shaking her head, putting those thoughts out of mind. She busied herself with dishes while she waited, scouring the pan.

When that was done she sat on the couch and read. Eventually, she lost track of time.

A breeze coming through the window brought her back to the present. She glanced at it. *It’s dark out.* She thought with a frown, glancing at her watch. It’d been an hour since Rebecca called. *She should have been here ages ago.*

She called Rebecca. It rang out. She breathed deeply.

She tried again. No answer. She ran her hands through her hair, and rubbed her face. Her heart started to beat faster.

She tried calling again. No answer. Her palms were getting sweaty.

She kept trying the number.

On the seventh call it answered.

'Hey,' Aoki said frantically. 'Is everything OK?'

There was crackle on the other end, it was almost deafening.

'Hello? Can you hear me?' Aoki asked, biting her lip.

There was silence. 'Um, hi. Sorry, it's my first week, I don't know what to do.' It was a man's voice. He was young and sounded nervous.

'What? Who are you?' Aoki asked, her heart pounding through her chest.

'Um, I'm sorry. I'm just a paramedic. I don't know what to tell you. This phone was smashed into a thousand pieces. I didn't think it worked.' The voice stammered, talking quickly. She could hear him take a deep breath. 'There's been an accident. Sorry, I mean. Ms Fulton, uh, Rebecca. She was in a car accident.'

THE MAN IN THE LEATHER JACKET

He sipped at his gin and tonic, watching Orr from across the room. He'd been following him for almost a week, watching the movements of this bastard.

He was cheating on his wife with various escorts. He wondered whether this man with the crooked nose would even use protection. He pitied the man's wife, but he supposed that she earned her fate when she married a man for nothing but money. Orr was rarely home, working long hours at the office, yelling at his subordinates and berating them in front of others. As near as he could tell, Darren Orr would abuse others to feel powerful, to feel in control. In his own mind, the man believed he was invincible. He operated under a false assumption.

Even now, sitting and talking with friends, Darren talked down to them and also the bar staff. He had seen his house and the way he lived. This man took everything from the world and gave little back to it. He lived in an expensive house and drove an expensive car; he stood for everything that had destroyed this world. If men like this had their way they would continue to rape the world until there were no resources left. He had never paid for the crimes he committed so many years ago. But this man deserved a fate worse than death.

As the two men left the bar, he got up and threw on his leather jacket. It was a cold night out so no one thought twice that he wore a baseball cap to warm his head. As he walked in and out of the bar he had taken care to avoid the cameras. He felt the knife in his pocket, making sure it was still there. Orr had dragged a younger co-worker with him, presumably so the two of them could snort some cocaine before going back to work in the morning.

It was a sad notion, this man had so much wealth but there was no depth to him. He had no loyalty and believed in nothing.

Whatever friends he once had were gone now, or living the same selfish lifestyle. He pitied the man but like his wife, this man had made his own decisions and had sealed his fate.

He hung back as the two walked and talked shit. They talked about themselves and their approach to investing, they talked about their talents and coups in booking large profits. He suspected the two were already high, but it was possible they just possessed the typical trader arrogance.

'Timmy, you should've seen this fuckin' trade I did the other day, hey. I absolutely smashed it. I fuckin' saw in the ticker feed that this mining company was about to make a press release.' Darren said, slurring. 'So like, I'd been checkin' 'em out for a while and checked with a mate of mine who was a project engineer on the company, and yeah, he told me they had found a massive shale oil deposit.'

'No shit.' Timmy said. He was stumbling and hiccupping. He was a skinny kid in his early twenties. He wore an expensive suit that was hanging off him. The kid didn't understand yet that style was about the fit more than the brand. 'That's amazing. Good work.'

'Yeah, I know, kid.' Orr said dismissively, it seemed he was insulted that someone so many levels below him would compliment him. 'So, anyway, an hour of work and I booked a two hundred million dollar profit.' As he said the word profit Orr's mouth started to froth.

'Wow! That's so good. I wish I had those big accounts. I can't wait.' Timmy said, excitedly. 'My exposure is so small at the moment.'

'Mate,' Orr said, sneering and puffing on a cigarette. 'I'm tellin' ya, you stick at it, you'll have those accounts in no time. You just gotta do those first five years earnin' no money and workin' those twelve hour days then you can take it easy.'

'You think so?'

‘Yeah, mate. Oi, I know, I may say you’re shit at work and embarrass you, but you gotta go through that, it’s part of the ritual.’

‘Nah, nah! Don’t even worry about that! I understand fully.’ Timmy said, proudly.

‘Good on you, mate. You understand you have to eat shit for a while until you get to be like me. Mate, the first couple years are rough but hey, if you stick in there then you’ll kill it, hey.’

‘I’m gonna fight and get in on those accounts. Don’t you worry. I know that if you pick on us it just means you think we can do it.’

‘Exactly, mate.’ Darren said sneering. ‘I’m glad you understand it. We only pick on you because we think you can do it.’

He wondered how people like this managed to still fool the younger workers to do their bidding. Every year, they would hire young staff and make them go above and beyond. They would make promises of luxury cars, big paycheques for little work and jet setting lifestyles. Except they always told them they had to ‘do their time’ at the bottom, and soon they would earn it.

As someone who had made it to the top, he knew how bullshit this promise was.

These companies promise every one the top but they rarely deliver. Most of the graduates ended up burning out early and dropping out due to stress. Some of them even committed suicide or got laid off. He remembered hearing once that only something like one in ten of the graduates survived longer than five years. Yet the rest of the company continued to maintain the status quo of the financial industry. The executives were only coming into the office once a week for teleconferences, delegating work down the hierarchy or usually just telling everyone they were ‘working from home’. People like Orr would get paid well over two hundred thousand a year with a month of annual leave, plus because he was so senior he could take as many days off as he wanted and wouldn't need to log it. He had been a part of this world before, he knew how it worked; the more senior the person, the less they had earned it.

Still, he understood where Timmy was now. He knew this guy would not make the cut, from what Orr was saying, he was a workhorse; someone who worked hard, worked so hard that they were more valuable not being promoted. They would burn out within two years and be replaced with someone else, after that they would be forgotten. In the financial world, everything was replaceable.

He stuck to the shadows as the two walked through a quiet alley. There were no apartments or cameras here, only commercial buildings. He approached on the balls of his feet making no noise.

He seized Orr and pulled him back, pulling the knife out of his pocked and holding it to his throat. Orr gasped, his eyes wide with real fear. It wasn't the fake corporate intimidation he tried to install in everyone else. When Timmy turned and saw, his body started to tremble.

'Please don't hurt me.' Orr stammered. Terror in his eyes as his body went limp. 'I have money.'

'Please, please.' Timmy whimpered. 'I'm sorry. I'm sorry.'

'What do you want?!' Orr suddenly shouted, defensively, trying to sound tough. 'If you want money you can fuck off. I earned it, you fuckin' bum. It's mine, not yours. So why don't you just go die in an alley somewhere and be forgotten just like you should.'

'The act is pretty transparent, Orr. It's nothing more than the loud barking of a scared and cornered animal.' He mocked. 'The false coked up bravado is duly noted though, very smart decision.'

'No, please, I'll give you money.' Timmy begged.

He held the knife closer to Orr's throat. All at once the fight left the man, his eyes were begging.

‘No, please, wait! Don’t! Don’t!’ He pleaded. Typical. The corporate world encouraged people to pretend to be confident but never made them face their fears. It continued to exist solely because of the illusion of confidence by weak selfish men like Darren Orr. ‘I’ll do anything!’ He started crying, holding his hands up in supplication.

‘I want you to listen to me.’ He said in a low voice. ‘You took too much and profited too recklessly. You didn’t give back to the world and you lived a selfish and superficial life. You made no difference to the world.’

‘Oh god! No, please, I’m begging you!’ He could see Orr trembling, his contorted face was weak and rubbery. His twisted mouth, that had screamed and belittled so many people below him, now had a blade an inch away from it. This man had spent his life maintaining an illusion, projecting an act of confidence and control. He had treated people poorly, and had tried to make people below him feel afraid, to make himself feel better. Now that he was faced with real fear for the first time in his life, he showed his true character.

‘You’re a weak man.’ He said slowly. ‘And that is why you’re going to die.’

With that Orr broke down, trembling and crying. Darren Orr seemed to collapse but the knife slit his throat before he could hit the ground. He cried and blubbered in a heap on the ground as he bled out.

He turned to Timmy, pointing the bloody knife.

‘No, wait, I’m sorry! I don’t understand! Please, don’t! I won’t do it again! I don’t know what’s going on! Please don’t!’ He stammered and begged, scrambling to back away.

‘As for you,’ he made sure to say each word deliberately and slowly. He needed him to remember. ‘You make sure you tell them exactly what happened. Do you understand?’

Timmy was a nervous wreck, but he nodded frantically. He had spent years practicing how to fake confidence and to come across as bold in the face of fear. But just like every other aspect of the corporate world, the focus was on appearances. The focus was on the superficial. There was no emphasis on changing the person at the core. There was no intention for these corporations to change the world, only to make sure a select few individuals continued to profit of the work of others.

'You tell them, that if things don't change then more people will die.' He took a deep breath. 'The world is going to change. The financial world has committed crimes and controlled everything for so long. They continued to profit while others took the fall for them. When they ask you what happened tonight, tell them that Darren Orr was a selfish man intent on making profit with no desire to give back to the community or make the world a better place.'

Timmy nodded. 'I will! I will! I promise.'

'Make sure they know that wealth is a crime.' With that he punched Timmy in the face and watched as the young man collapsed. He checked his clothes for any traces of blood, turned and exited the alley, making his way back home.

WILL

He had gotten dressed quickly and driven in a hurry. He had only spoken briefly with Aoki but she'd been frantic. As he parked at the hospital, he saw Aoki smoking not too far from the entrance. She stared at the ground.

'Have you seen her yet?' He said as he approached.

She glanced up at him then stared down again, shaking her head. 'I checked on her with her doctor, though.'

'How is she? Is she alright?'

Aoki shook her head. 'He said it's pretty serious.'

Will was worried. He knew that she had been in a car accident but Aoki hadn't told him much more than that. 'What happened?'

She looked at him blankly. 'She was coming over to talk about everything but she didn't show. I got worried. I called her again and again. Eventually, it was picked up by the paramedics.'

'Jesus.'

'They said she'd been in accident. A truck had driven straight through the lights and into the side of her car.'

Will felt sick. He hadn't thought it would be that bad. 'Fuck.' He exhaled, scratching his head.

'She's, uh, she's pretty cut up. Her car was flipped several times. She's pretty badly injured.'

He shuddered. *My friend being injured like that*. He thought, feeling bitterness and anger. *Especially, after everything that she had been through*.

‘I was lucky her phone wasn’t too broken. Otherwise we wouldn’t have known.’

He nodded. ‘Chris would have still been her emergency contact.’

She nodded back. ‘Where did you go last night? Rebecca tried calling but she couldn’t get a hold of you.’

It was only then that the implication of last night set in. ‘Holy fuck.’

‘What?’

‘Last night, someone was following me.’

‘What the fuck?!’ She said with a raised voice, shooting him a look.

‘Yeah, I was walking home and I heard this guy on a bike, he was talking about missing someone else. But then he saw me and,’ He ran his hands through his hair. ‘He chased after me but I was able to hide. I think they targeted Rebecca as well.’

He saw Aoki shudder. ‘Oh my god.’ She shook her head and then said in an angry tone, ‘Why the fuck didn’t you tell us?! Why would you just tell her you weren’t feeling well?!’

‘I know, I know.’ He looked down, he felt bad enough as it was.

‘Maybe you could have warned her.’ There was a tinge of disgust in her tone.

‘I wasn’t going to say anything. I just thought I was being paranoid. But with what happened to Rebecca—’

Aoki exhaled, her tone softening suddenly. ‘Yeah, I know. Fuck. I’m sorry, I shouldn’t have said that.’

He shook his head bitterly. ‘No, you’re right. I was scared and I didn’t know what to do.’

Aoki looked at him gently. 'I can understand. I've been in the police for a while and I've never seen anything like this.'

'It's insane.' He sighed. 'Who do you think did this? Do you think whoever is targeting Delpont is targeting us as well?'

'I don't think so.'

At that moment they heard Morgan call out. He ran up to them from the parking lot. 'Hey, is she alright?'

'She's not doing well.' Aoki said. 'I've just told Will what happened.'

Morgan sighed. 'I'm so sorry, Will. We'll find whoever did this.' He said confidently. There was intensity in his voice. 'She's going to be fine.'

Will saw Aoki glare at Morgan. 'Thank you.' He said to Morgan.

'From now on we're not going to take any chances, though. Me and Aoki are going to make sure you and Rebecca are protected.' He locked eye contact with Will. 'We're going to make sure that nothing else happens. We'll make sure these guys at Delpont get brought to justice.'

He nodded, looking down. He heard Aoki scoff.

'I'm, uh,' He cleared his throat. 'I'm going to go inside now. Are you coming in?'

'In a moment. We'll meet you in there.' Aoki said.

He nodded and headed inside silently.

AOKI

'What the fuck are you saying that to him for?!' She said as she hit Morgan's arm.

'What?'

'Getting his head filled up with this Delpont bullshit.' She shook her head, taking a drag on her cigarette. 'That's the last thing they need right now. Just give them some time to deal with this.'

'Whatever.' He scoffed dismissively. 'I don't know about you but I'm sick of these rich kids killing off whoever they want.'

'What do you mean?'

'This isn't one group. There are two things going on here. Someone is killing the Delpont people, whatever, who gives a fuck. They have it coming. But this group of people who ran Delpont; they killed Chris and now they've tried to kill Rebecca. They're covering something up.'

She squinted at him. His theory made more sense. 'What about the Malceski murder? How does that fit in?'

He shrugged and sighed. 'Yeah, I don't know about that.'

'Fine. But even if you're right they don't need to get angry right now.'

'You're damn right! They need to get even.' He said coldly.

'What are you talking about?'

'The killings of these banker wankers.'

'What of them?'

He sighed, rubbing his stubble. 'I'm done with that investigation. You can keep looking if you want but I think these bankers are getting what they deserve.'

She couldn't believe what she was hearing. 'Are you seriously saying what I think you're saying?' She didn't feel like dealing with Morgan running his mouth off again right now. 'You swore to protect and to serve. And now, what, you're openly saying you don't want to catch a killer?'

'Not this killer.'

She sighed. *There's no getting through to him.*

WILL

After being directed to the room, he found the doctor by her bedside, checking her bandages.

Rebecca was in worse shape than he thought. She had a neck brace and her right arm was in a sling. Her right eye was bruised quite badly. He stood at the door and stared, he felt his throat tighten at the sight of his friend in that condition.

The doctor turned and raised an eyebrow. 'You must be Will.' He looked in his mid sixties, with short white hair and dark brown eyes. He was thin but he had a slight belly. He wore thin glasses that had a strap around them.

Will turned and looked at the doctor, slightly dazed. 'Yeah.'

'The detective mentioned you would be coming. I'm Doctor Carroway. You can come in if you like.' He had a gentle voice and a friendly smile.

'Are you sure?'

'Your friend is in a coma. She suffered quite a nasty knock to her head. She won't be waking up for a while.' He said with a sad sigh.

Will walked up and stood by her side. He looked at her lying there, she looked so thin. He wanted to hold her hand but didn't want to hurt her.

'Your friend is pretty tough. She's lucky she didn't die.'

He smiled. 'Beck is quite strong willed.'

The doctor looked at him and smiled sadly. 'She, uh, I don't want to get your hopes up. She suffered quite a bad concussion. She's in a coma at the moment, she's suffered quite a serious injury.'

‘Ok.’ Will said slowly.

‘She, uh, it could even be years before she wakes up.’

The words hit Will like a kick to the gut.

‘But I’m more worried about her back right now.’ He said softly.

‘Oh, Jesus, fuck.’ Will exhaled in anger, he felt his eyes tear up and covered his mouth.

The doctor cleared his throat. ‘She’s suffered some spinal damage.’ The doctor put a sympathetic hand on his shoulder. ‘I don’t want to alarm you, I just want you to be prepared for this, but she may not walk again.’

Will was about to swear. Rebecca groaned and opened her mouth.

Both men took a step back. The doctor’s mouth dropped.

Rebecca groaned again and whispered something. She tried to open her eyes.

The doctor leaned in closer to listen. ‘Rebecca, can you hear me?’ He asked gently.

She groaned again. ‘Go fuck yourself, doctor.’ She said in a broken voice. She cleared her throat and spoke faintly. ‘I’m going to walk again.’

Will laughed impulsively and felt his eyes well up.

The doctor hung his head and then laughed.

AOKI

When Will walked out of the room both he and the doctor were laughing. Despite being horrified at first, she laughed when they told her what Beck said.

‘Is she still awake?’

Will shook his head. ‘No. She went to sleep shortly afterwards but she’s looking good.’ He frowned and cleared his throat. ‘They’re not sure about her back though.’

Aoki nodded. She tried to think of something to say.

‘Oh, fuck off.’ Morgan shouted. He flipped one of the chairs in the waiting room over. ‘You’ve got to be fucking kidding me.’

Everyone turned. A few of the nurses looked nervous. Aoki walked over to see what it was. He was staring at the television in the waiting room. She looked at it and felt a sinking feeling when she saw the news.

‘Fuck.’ She said softly.

‘He came out, running and screaming.’ An elderly woman on the news said to the camera. ‘He was crying. Then I saw him on the ground, bleeding all over the place.’

The report then switched to the Detective Superintendent speaking at a press conference.

‘There was another man who witnessed this, thankfully he wasn’t hurt, but he’s quite traumatised by the event.’

‘Fuck, fuck, fuck.’ Aoki swore, rubbing her face in frustration.

There were shots from the crime scene and photos of Darren Orr. The reporter did a voiceover over the top of them. ‘The killing took place last night around ten pm, as people were making their way home from dinner. Orr had long been a controversial figure. His links and involvement in the Delpont scandal were often a topic of conversation. Police continue to comb the area for clues, though, they still have no official suspect. At this stage, they're downplaying any connection to the earlier deaths of former Delpont employees.'

'Oh, this cannot be fucking happening?!' Will said incredulously. She turned, he was watching from behind her. He shook his head.

She turned back to the news article.

'However, not all people believe it isn't connected.' The reporter said.

It then cut back to footage of the press conference. A journalist asked a question from off screen; 'How do you respond to claims that this is linked to the earlier unsolved killings of Kelvin Anderson and Marcus Docker? Is there a serial killer targeting Delpont employees?'

The superintendent paused and squinted. 'No, at this stage, and I would like to emphasise this, there is no evidence suggesting that this is the work of a serial killer.'

'Anderson?' Will asked with a frown.

'He was killed ages before.' Aoki replied sullenly.

'Why did it take so long for us to link it?' Morgan asked, raising his voice.

Aoki shook her head, defeated. 'It was a completely different district. I only started looking into it when Beaufort mentioned it.'

Morgan huffed and shook his head. 'Didn't take long for the media, though.' He muttered.

The report then cut to a clip of a woman, a more senior reporter from the network. She spoke directly to the camera. 'It seems that there is evidence to suggest that someone is targeting Delpont employees, perhaps some kind of vigilante. Right now, the police are not investigating this angle and in doing so are endangering further lives.'

'Oh bullshit!' Aoki yelled. 'Go fuck yourself!' She reacted in anger and frustration, her only way to vent was to throw a magazine at the TV. The magazine flew open and fluttered to the ground.

Will tried to cover up a smirk.

Aoki turned and shot him a look that was enough to make him keep quiet.

Morgan walked over to her. 'Alright.' He exhaled deeply, cooling down. 'This may not be the worst thing for us.' He said calmly.

'What are you talking about?'

'Come on, we've been trying to get some serious effort into investigating the serial killer aspect.' He pointed to the TV screen. 'And now there is some serious pressure out there that this is the case. Maybe, they'll finally put some more resources behind this.'

'Like what?' She shouted.

He shrugged effortlessly. 'I dunno. Maybe some extra people? Look deeper into Delpont, go back over these old cases in greater detail? I mean, maybe even a psychologist to create a profile of this guy?'

She exhaled, frustrated. 'But there's no evidence, Morgan!' She raised her voice, speaking slowly. 'We've been looking and we've found nothing. And what is the psychologist tell us that we don't already know?! That he's anti social? Probably highly intelligent? Probably worked at Delpont?'

'For fucks sake.' He swore. 'I'm just trying to look at the bright side of this. No need to freak out at me.'

Both Aoki and Morgan huffed and crossed their arms. Fighting like that was getting them nowhere. They were frustrated. At that moment, she noticed Will walk out of the hospital. Morgan went to get him.

‘Nah, it’s alright. Let him go.’ She said gently, touching Morgan’s arm.

ANDREA

She couldn't explain why she was out the front of his house. He told her he was busy but she wouldn't take that for an answer. She had initially decided to surprise him by coming over, but for some reason she hadn't gotten out of the car. So, she had stayed like that for an hour, watching his front door. It had become dark out. *It's crazy*, she thought, *I knew he loves me, he told me*. She shook her head. She needed to keep her cool about this, otherwise, she would lose him.

She wrapped her hands on the wheel, feeling like there was a knot in her stomach. Every time someone walked past she thought it was him. There were no windows on the street side of his building, so she couldn't even tell whether the lights were on. She looked at herself in the rear view mirror; she looked tired. Her eyes were red and she noticed lines under them. She hadn't been sleeping lately. After her conversation with Paul, she'd been left feeling nervous all the time, and without seeing Hank she had no way of relieving that anxiety. Especially today. When she had found out about Darren she had taken the rest of the day off work. She'd intended on going home to sleep it off and try and do some research on Delpont, but she couldn't fight her desire to see Hank. It was all she could think about, it was all she wanted to do.

She saw a man down the street and got excited when she realised it was Hank walking home. She realised she didn't know what to do. She wondered whether she should surprise him, but then thought what she should do. She picked up her phone and sent him a message, asking him if he were still busy and that she wanted to see him.

From across the street she saw him get his phone from out of his pocket and check it. He looked at the screen for a while, and then put it back in his pocket.

As she watched him walk into his apartment, she felt deflated. It was a mix of her frustration at coming so close to him but not being able to see him, and a sinking feeling that he did not love her like she loved him. She tried to fight those thoughts and stay positive.

WILL

He was grateful for the opportunity to go out for his friend's birthday. He needed a distraction after such a long day. He should be talking to people but all he wanted was to sit down after drinking so much already. It was almost midnight and he'd been drinking quite quickly.

For some reason, he had messaged Amber earlier, trying to see if she were free tonight. Sam had wanted to see him, but there was someone else on his mind, and he couldn't stop thinking of her. Amber replied she would be out in the city. He replied that he was seeing friends on the north side of the bridge, and they probably wouldn't be going in. He'd joked that he couldn't be bothered to go in. In his own mind though, he knew he would have cancelled plans if she wanted to see him, but he didn't get that feeling. She'd left the conversation saying they should do something soon, but she always said that. He realised she often made promises like that which turned out to be empty. He gave up, and felt foolish for trying, especially when someone already liked him.

Still, when his group of friends decided to go into the city, he had sent her a message joking about the fact he had ended up in the city despite his earlier decisions.

As he sat on his own, reflecting quietly on everything that was happening, he was surprised to find his phone buzz with a message from her. It was blunt; it asked where he was.

He replied, and told her the name of the club. He felt embarrassed at telling her he was in a place like this. He wasn't much a fan of clubbing.

His phone buzzed again. It was from her. She told him he was at the same place, and asked where he was. A sense of anticipation came over him. He replied back that he was outside.

A few moments later he watched as she walked outside. Every time he thought he wouldn't be affected by the sight of her, and every time he was wrong. Her golden blonde hair went past her shoulders, she wore a black top and a knee high skirt which had a raw umber colour. He saw her look left and right and then look at her phone. He got up and walked over to her.

'Hey, how are you?' He called.

It was only when he greeted her that she saw him for the first time, he looked into her eyes like blue crystals. He felt his heart beat faster. She smiled sadly at him.

'What's wrong?' He asked.

She giggled. 'Nothing. I'm just drunk.'

'Me too.' He said, laughing.

'I need to sit down. It's too crowded in there.' She ran her hand through her hair and walked over to the seats outside. He was walking behind her when she reached her hand back to hold his. He felt the warmth of her touch. Her slender fingers wrapped around his and he felt the touch of her thin arm against his skin.

When they sat down she continued to hold his hand, and leant up against him. Her friends came out and joined her.

'You two look cute together.' One of her friends cooed.

Amber smiled and said nothing. Leaning closer to Will.

He couldn't understand what was happening. He should have felt conflicted, he was seeing Sam and she was a kind person. *But it's not serious between us, we're not really dating.* He knew that he wanted Amber. His heart had been hers since they'd met. *I'm just following my heart, that's all.*

The two talked for a while and caught up, talking about her interior design business and she asked him about articles he was working on. They didn't talk about Delpont, moreover he didn't want to bring it up, especially considering her father's involvement. In that moment, all he wanted was her. He felt an excited anticipation that something might happen.

He kept looking at her and admiring the small details of her; her smooth skin, her bright smile, but mostly he kept feeling a rush of excitement every time they locked eye contact and he looked into her beautiful blue eyes. When she smiled and looked at him like that he felt that she looked through him, that she understood him.

When she told her friends she was leaving she asked Will if he wanted to come. He left without saying goodbye to his friends. As they walked to a cab, they kept talking and he held her close to keep her warm. They stood on a corner and waited for a cab, and she turned to look at him.

There was a moment of silence. She looked incredible. He could see men turning their heads as they walked past. From somewhere within him, he felt courage. He moved a little closer to her and placed his hands gently around her waist. There was a gentle look in her eyes and a slight smile. She leaned in to kiss him. He felt her caress his cheek with her palm and with the other she grabbed his hair. He wrapped his arms around her waist and pulled her close. His heart was beating fast and he felt himself get hard.

A cab pulled up and they both got in. She gave him her address and she asked if he minded dropping her home first. He said he didn't mind, but felt a sinking feeling that nothing would happen that night. She became quiet demure in the cab, she continued to hold his hand but spent the ride looking out the window, and the trip passed in silence. He reflected that it would probably be a while before he would see her again. It had taken so long to see her; their meeting tonight was only a random occurrence.

When the cab stopped outside Amber's place, she went to pay. There was silence as she frowned and opened her clutch. He couldn't explain why, but he pulled out his wallet and offered to pay. He said he would get out there and make his own way home. They got out and she looked at him confused.

'Why did you do that? You're so far from where you live.' She smiled.

He squinted, unable to come up with another response other than the truth. 'I just wanted to have more time with you tonight.'

She smiled and laughed. She moved to him, wrapping her arms around him and they kissed. He felt the warmth of her body against his, and started to breathe faster. He started gently kissing down the side of her neck, and heard her exhale as she grabbed his hair and held tightly. As he started kissing further down, along the edge of her black top, he lightly licked her collarbone with the tip of his tongue, and kissed along her chest. She held him tighter and with his head against her chest he realised she was breathing faster too. He pulled back and could see the look in her eyes as she smiled.

'Oh my god.' She said laughing, she ran her fingers back through her hair. She took a deep breath. 'We can't do this here.'

He looked around. It was a quiet street just outside her house, but if anyone came past they would be easily seen. 'Can't we?' He suggested with a grin.

She glared at him playfully and slapped his arm. 'Very funny, Will!' She looked around and then back at him. He couldn't stop thinking about this perfect woman. He loved her big blue eyes, her high cheekbones and her bright smile. Even now, after a long night, she always looked graceful with her svelte frame and sense of style.

'I've wanted you for so long.' He said softly, shaking his head. 'You have no idea how gorgeous I think you are.'

She took a deep breath and smiled. They made out again. He wanted her so badly. He ran his hands down her back and grabbed her behind. She ran her hands over his body and moaned. He was still drunk and felt quite brave, and slowly lifted her skirt. He looked at her as she bit her lip. He gently slid a finger down her panties and inside her.

She gasped and held him tight as he touched her, feeling how wet and warm she was. He teased her by sliding his finger inside her slowly and then out again, playing with her clit with his thumb.

'Oh god.' She whispered softly. 'Fuck, not here.'

'Should we go inside?' He asked hopefully.

She nodded in silence, biting her lip, and led him inside. They made their way quietly to her bedroom, he wasn't fully focused on his surroundings but he noticed it was an immense and open home. She must live with her parents.

When they reached her room she closed the door behind him, as he kissed her and slid her top off. She laughed quietly and took his jacket and t-shirt off. She unhooked her bra and it fell to the floor, and he looked at her small perky breasts. He started licking her nipples as she dropped his jeans and pulled his underwear down. He moved her back towards the bed and she lay down, giving him a sly grin. He leant down and kissed her clit and licked as she moaned. He continued to play with her until her legs tightened and her face went red. She pulled him further up and helped him inside her.

He looked down at this perfect girl, sliding himself in and out of her. She moved her hips backwards and forwards and moaned quietly. She closed her eyes and gripped his arms. He kept kissing down her neck and licking her breasts. He wished he hadn't had anything to drink tonight so he could be his best for her; for the girl who had only been a dream, this girl he never thought he would be with.

She pulled him close and wrapped her arms around his neck. 'Come inside me.' She whispered in his ear.

He moaned and felt a wave come over his body. He did as she asked.

AOKI

It was an overcast day and there was a chill in the air. She wore her three quarter length black jacket over the top of her button up shirt and grey pants, but the chill still came through. As she approached from around the corner she could see and hear the crowd of people waiting outside. She took a deep breath. She felt nervous. She was relieved that Rick had given her a lift in today, she felt glad for his support.

As she turned the corner she saw her chief, Detective Peter Wisniowski, talking to the media. He spoke calmly as always, he never let on whether he was fazed or not. She wished she had that ability. She tried to keep her head low and not get noticed. She wasn't sure whether they knew her name.

'Aoki! Aoki!' A young female journalist piped up, raising a hand to get her attention as she ran over.

'Fuck.' She muttered softly. She kept walking.

Noticing that something had sparked her interest, the rest of the pack of reporters turned and seemed to swarm in on her.

She felt a moment of fear and wanted to run. She kept looking down and hurried her pace inside.

'Miss Sun! Should the Australian public be worried about this serial killer that is on the loose?' The first journalist asked.

'Should people be worried that there is a vigilante out there?' A second piped up.

'Why isn't the police department taking any action on this?' Another asked rather rudely. Aoki glared at her as she kept up her quick pace. In a moment, she would be blocked from entering the building by the crowd.

'Alright, alright!' Peter came over and tried to break up the crowd. 'I've already issued a statement so we have no further comment at this stage.'

'You can't keep saying this isn't the work of a serial killer.' A young male reporter exclaimed. 'Someone is clearly targeting Delpont.'

'As I said before,' Peter said slowly 'There is no evidence to suggest this at present.' His voice was calm, but from his look she knew he was seething.

He led her inside and away from all the reporters who were shouting at her. When safely inside she exhaled deeply.

'Wow.' She said, shaking her head. 'That was crazy.'

He shook his head. 'It's always like that, you'll get used to it.' His tone was flat and he spoke with a deep voice that was the result of a lifetime of smoking. She had only met him a few times but she knew that he was a humourless man. He was never rude to anyone but he wasn't encouraging or sympathetic either. The two started walking down the corridor.

'Thanks for distracting them and helping me out of there.'

'Not a problem.' He said absently. 'We've set up the briefing room in the back with all the material, and we're working on background reports at the moment.'

'Ok. Sure thing.'

He suddenly slowed his pace and turned to look at her for the first time. 'Is it true that you and Morgan have been following this Delpont link?'

She paused, unsure how to answer. She didn't know enough about this man to understand his approach. She decided that her only option was the truth.

‘Yeah, that’s right. We’ve been tracking down some former employees and doing some research into the back story.’

He squinted at her. ‘That’s good news. We’ll have somewhere to start with. We won’t need to play catch up.’ He kept walking and led the way through one of the security doors.

‘Well, actually, we haven’t found much yet.’ She interjected softly. ‘We understand a lot more about Delpont but we haven’t figured out what these killings are about.’

‘That’s not an issue.’ He cut her off. ‘One way or another this whole situation is linked to Delpont and we will need all the information under control.’

She frowned. ‘I thought the Department wasn’t pursuing the serial killer angle?’

He scoffed. ‘This isn’t the work of a serial killer. There is no common method or murder weapon and it doesn’t display the typical anti-social behaviour found in the crime patterns of a sociopath.’ He said dismissively. ‘But whatever is happening, it’s linked to Delpont.’

She was taken aback. Firstly, by the fact that he could dismiss the serial killer aspect so quickly, and secondly, that he was willing to accept it could be linked to Delpont. Other than Morgan, he was the only person in the department that had been willing to consider it. She kept quiet as they walked past the rows of desks, considering whether he could be right. She wondered whether they been so eager to solve this that they had simplified their way of thinking. She thought about what Peter had said, and wondered whether there was something more going on, something more complicated. It would certainly explain all the discrepancies. She frowned, lost in her train of thought.

WILL

When he woke he wasn't sure where he was. It took a few minutes for him to figure out what day of the week it was. He turned and saw her walk out of the bathroom. She smiled at him.

Then he remembered what happened last night. He must have been drunker than he thought.

She'd showered and was washing her face and brushing her hair. She wore a white and cream silk nightgown. She sat down at her dressing table and styled her hair.

'I was hoping I could put my face on before you woke up.' She joked.

He moaned. 'It's the best thing I've woken up to in a long time. And you shouldn't worry about putting on your make up, you're gorgeous without it.'

'You're sweet.' She smiled, then took a breath and resumed her attention on her reflection in the mirror. 'But you don't know me very well.'

'I know you well enough.' He said to the reflection in the mirror. Everything was reversed.

She squinted, catching the eye of his reflection. 'I'm not perfect.'

He smiled. She seemed so down to earth. He still felt intimidated by her; she was a gorgeous, confident and creative woman. But she was right, at the end of the day, she was only human.

'Do you have anything planned for today?' She looked at him as she got ready.

He frowned. 'No, I didn't have anything planned. You? Are you getting ready for anything?'

She smiled. 'Yes. I've got brunch with my girlfriends. I don't know if I can stomach food, but hopefully I can at least look up to the occasion.'

He was saddened by the idea of leaving her. He had hoping to spend the day with her, having waited for so long to see her.

He pulled himself out of bed as he watched her pick out clothes from her wardrobe. She picked out tights and a skirt as she dropped her robe. She was still in her underwear. He still wanted her.

He pulled himself out of bed and rubbed his face. He felt light headed. He caught a look at the time and sighed. He'd only slept for four hours. He frowned, looking at the woman who seemed unperturbed. He doubted her earlier statement that she was only human. She showed no sign of the night before.

He wanted to feel her touch again. He walked up behind her and gently kissed along her neck, putting his hands on her hips as she prepared herself. He saw her smile in the mirror.

'Careful.' She said, teasing. 'You'll get me all messed up again.'

He smiled. 'What if you want to get messed up then? What am I to do?' He taunted her.

She laughed. 'True. But not right now.' She squinted and focused on her gaze in the mirror. She dismissed him.

He felt defeated and wondered whether last night was a mistake for her. Observing her reflection in the mirror as she got herself ready, he sighed at the thought. That he had held this woman briefly but who now seemed unavailable to him. He watched the way she put on her foundation, the minor and minute fractures it made upon her skin. It was only up close that he saw the cracks in the mask.

THE MAN ON THE BOARDWALK

It was a bright sunny day and there wasn't a cloud in the sky. The sun was a welcome change, though, he was glad there was still a chill in the air. By his own definition, the weather was perfect. He wore his hiking boots, jeans, and a wool, charcoal coloured zip up jumper. He couldn't help but smile thinking how well everything was going, and not just that day.

He passed a café as he headed to the beachfront. Inside there was a TV on mute, playing the round of news and sports. He squinted, he felt like a coffee, anyway.

He ducked inside and joined the queue, looking around the place. It had a nautical theme to it; there were ropes, vintage lanterns, anchors and paintings of the ocean adorning the walls. The furniture and counters were all wood. The theme seemed fitting considering the location with a sweeping view of the beach across the road. It had an earthy feel to the place, he felt comfortable there.

He ordered coffee and sat down to watch the news cycle. It was the same footage he had seen several times; the detective chief talking to the media and denying everything, the senior columnist making some rash assumptions that were nonetheless accurate, and footage of the scene where Darren Orr had died.

He felt uncomfortable looking at the crime scene in the light of day. There was something about the blood on the sidewalk and the forensic techs reviewing the scene that made it feel so clinical. He took a deep breath, trying to ease an anxious feeling gnawing at him. He wasn't used to that feeling anymore, he hadn't felt it for years, but he had learnt how to handle those emotions. He took a deep breath and looked at the images that caused him discomfort, which he wanted to ignore. He needed to confront them and accept them. He needed to see the reality of his actions and not just the ideal that he held onto. He watched for a few minutes until he could settle his nerves, until he stopped fighting it and accepted it. It was an ongoing process. He would never be able to ignore the human cost of what he was doing, but his belief in this cause mandated that there would need to be sacrifices. Both of himself and of others.

He didn't want to ruin such a nice day with those thoughts though. He was glad that everything was going well and that this was finally starting to draw attention. There was no discussion occurring yet, but he knew it would take time. He frowned, realising that there had been no discussion in the news about Taylor Sheeran. It was likely that no one in the media had connected those dots yet, but there could be a chance it was being concealed. The people who owned those media organisations were all friends with the players from Delpont, or at least had the same agenda.

The waitress brought out his mocha and smiled at him. He thanked her and looked up. Tanned skin and dark eyes with straight jet-black hair in a ponytail. She wore a flannel and jeans. She was the type of girl he was attracted to. He sighed, thinking of how his heart would always belong to another.

He stared out at the ocean, thinking over everything while he looked out into the dark blue endless sea. He wondered whether he had presumed too much, that the discussion would naturally follow after being shocked by these killings. He sipped at his mocha. Maybe they needed a push. Maybe he needed to be more direct.

He finished his coffee and thanked the waitress as he left. She said goodbye with a sly smile. He pondered what things would have been like in a different life, with different beliefs. He walked up along the beach to get on with his background research and canvassing of his next target.

WILL

When he got home the reality started to sink in. He had avoided Sam's messages last night. He had justified everything to himself, and it hadn't bothered him at the time. When he got home and was alone it was a different story. He looked at her messages and felt the guilt he had tried not to feel last night. She had sent him a few nice messages. He read over them and shook his head, regretting what he had done. In the heat of the moment he had told himself that he was just following his heart, and had told himself that things with Sam weren't serious, they hadn't talked about being in a relationship. Reading over them, he realised he knew that wasn't true. He had felt something for her, and he knew she felt something for him. She was a sweet person and didn't deserve to be treated like that. But he knew how he felt about Amber. He knew he had to tell Sam the truth.

He wrote back to her and told her that something happened last night, and that he was really sorry.

She swore and said she was really worried, and asked what happened.

He told her the truth. That he had gone home with someone.

She swore again and said she was really upset. He felt a rising sense of guilt. She asked him what that meant for the two of them.

He winced. He had to tell her the truth. He told her that he felt something for this woman, and that he wanted to see what would happen. He told her he was sorry and he hadn't wanted to hurt her. He had made a mistake.

Her message back showed more pain than he realised he would cause. He didn't think it meant that much to Sam. She was angry and hurt. She told him how unfair it was, how she had felt something for him and now she couldn't find out where that would lead. She swore and cursed at him.

He shook his head and rubbed his eyes. He felt worse and worse. He hadn't realised how guilty he would feel, how much pain he would cause. Last night, it had seemed so simple. In the light of day everything was so different. He tried to fight the regret he was feeling. He had done what he believed was right; he wanted to be with Amber. He tried to explain but he couldn't.

His phone kept buzzing with angry messages from her. After a while, he couldn't read or reply to them anymore. He was starting to feel sick with guilt. He lay down, closed his eyes and tried to ignore the feeling of hating himself. He tried to think of Amber, but even the beautiful memories seemed rotten by the pain he had caused.

ANDREA

She checked her phone again. There were no messages. Her heart sunk. She felt frustrated and was torturing herself but she could think of nothing else. Everything was a mess.

She ran her hands through her hair, opened her eyes wide and stared at her screen, trying to focus. There was one project that was taking up a lot of her time lately. One of the other people in her team had been drafting up legislation on the derivatives market, however, while they had experience in the legislative side of it, they were essentially useless when it came to any knowledge of what derivatives were and how they worked. When she had talked about it with them, the guy had gotten confused between puts and calls. She had tried to explain that a derivative was a contract with the option to buy or sell equities at a specific price by a specific date; however, it was clear she'd lost him after she mentioned the word 'contract'. How someone like that was working for ASIC had left her at a loss. It was typical of the efficiency of a bureaucracy.

The work had been good, though, and she was grateful that everything that happened at Delpont could be put to some use. Although, it was bringing back uncomfortable memories and was making her think again about the people who had lost their savings as a result. She tried to ignore those thoughts as much as possible; no good could come from dwelling on that.

She checked her phone again. There were no messages. She took a deep breath and went back to her work.

She was startled when her desk phone rang and almost jumped. It had rang less than ten times since she had been here, a far change from her life in the corporate world where it had rang every minute. Even then, she still felt physical pain when her phone rang. She looked at her phone and picked up the handset, it was a call from reception. She sighed.

‘Hello, Andrea speaking.’

‘Oh, hi.’ The girl spoke timidly, she had frustrated Andrea to no end. ‘It’s Gwen from reception.’

‘Hi Gwen. What can I do for you?’ She had to keep it short and to the point or the girl would ramble. She was timid and scared of everything, but very intelligent and talented. Andrea could not stand her weakness. Perhaps because it reminded her of her own meekness when she started working.

‘Oh, it’s just, umm, I have someone here to see you. They asked for you, should I send them through?’

Andrea frowned. ‘Oh, who is it?’ She wondered if it was Hank. But realised he wouldn’t ever see her at work. It could be her husband, but he hadn’t been spontaneous like that for years.

‘Umm.’ She paused. Andrea realised that Gwen hadn’t asked these sorts of questions yet again. ‘I’m not sure. Let me check.’

‘It’s fine.’ Andrea sighed. ‘Don’t worry about it. I’ll come out.’ She couldn’t stand to waste time.

Gwen started to say sorry but Andrea had already hung up on her and started walking out of the workspace to reception, half because she didn’t have the patience to deal with Gwen and half because she was curious to find out who was coming to see her.

As she exited the second set of security doors she was greeted with a surprising sight. The gentle old man turned and smiled at her sweetly. His hands rested in his lap clutching an orange book.

‘Miss Beaufort.’ He said while walking over to her. ‘It is a pleasure to meet you.’ He held his hand out, she offered hers and he gently shook her hand while his clear blue eyes looked into her eyes.

‘Who are you?’ She said in the most confident tone she could manage. She wasn’t sure why this man put her off.

‘We share common interests. We both shared involvement in the life and times of Delpont. Or should I say the life and crimes.’ He smiled.

As soon as he mentioned the name she felt anxious.

He glanced at Gwen to make sure she wasn’t listening. ‘Similarly, we both maintain an equal share in the culpability.’

‘I think it best you leave before I call security.’ She said coldly and calmly, effectively hiding the growing sense of fear she felt when she spoke to this man.

‘I would advise you that it is in your best interests to remain calm.’ He smiled kindly. She saw a cold malice in his clear blue eyes for the first time. ‘Considering the knowledge I currently possess about your extra marital affairs.’

She felt the wind get taken out of her. The more she spoke to this icy man the more she felt trapped.

‘A woman with so much largesse has similarly so much at stake.’ He frowned. ‘So much she could lose.’

She glared at him.

He smiled. ‘I’m glad you comprehend the gravity of the situation.’ He looked around the ceiling of the room. ‘I must say, it is rather fortunate that this building is so lax in their security. Otherwise, this meeting would not have been possible.’

She swore under her breath.

‘Now then.’ He cleared his throat and narrowed his gaze. ‘It was recently brought to my attention that you were looking into things best left in the past. I trust my implication is understood?’ He looked at her inquiringly.

She glared, but she nodded.

‘I’m glad. You’re a bright woman with a resilient spirit.’ He smiled again. His eyes wrinkled as he did so and showed a gentle harmlessness. ‘You show an excellent survival trait.’

She wanted him gone. She wanted to speak to him but there were no words.

‘Regardless, the purpose of my visit is simple. I am trying to locate an item that has become misplaced.’

Her heart was beating fast. She was barely listening. She knew he was involved in Delpont, but she had never seen this man before.

‘I am trying to track down this item. However, I am at an impasse as I do not want to reveal excessive details about the aforementioned item, lest I put this item at further risk.’ He cleared his throat. ‘Nod if I am understood.’

She took a breath and nodded.

‘Excellent, by this same token you may have come across this item and not realised the potential significance. As such, I need to provide you with enough information that you could identify it.’ He smiled. ‘I trust you understand the difficult position in which this places me?’

She nodded again, holding eye contact.

‘I am grateful that you do.’ He bowed slightly. ‘Now then, so as to keep this as simple as possible, I will ask only this,’ He exhaled and squinted at her. ‘The item I seek is information, azure like the bluest sky.’ He spoke, slowly and deliberately.

And so he stood there, studying her. Perhaps her confusion was evident on her face. He smiled gently.

‘I don’t know what you’re looking for.’ She said softly, shaking her head.

‘Very well then.’ He cleared his throat. ‘It was to be expected. I merely came to you in an act of desperation and I feel I have overstepped my bounds.’ He took a deep breath and ruffled the pages of his orange book. ‘I offer you my sincere apologies.’

‘I’d like for you to leave now.’ She said calmly.

‘Naturally.’ He said with a warm smile. ‘But bear in mind what I said, if your interests don’t lie in the past, then we have no interest in your present or your future.’ He nodded and turned out of the office, his back hunched over slightly as he walked. She felt his frailty was deceptive, or the man might be using it as a mask.

When he was gone she walked back to her desk. She sat down and tried to steady her shaking hands. She wanted to scream but she had no privacy. She tried to slow her breathing and she put her hand to her chest, feeling how fast her heart was beating. Her palms were sweaty and she wanted fresh air, but she didn’t want to risk going outside. The thought terrified her, at least she felt slightly safe at her desk. But it wasn’t the old man who scared her. For the first time, she realised that losing her husband might become a reality. As much as she had wanted the passionate love with Hank, her husband had been her life and her identity for almost half her life. The thought of losing that safety was truly terrifying.

AOKI

'You're seeing who?' She scrunched her face.

'Amber.' He grinned. 'I know. I can't believe it either.'

She shook her head. 'No, I wasn't being cute. I actually have no idea who that is.'

'Oh, Amber McDermott.'

'The daughter of Paul?'

He sighed. 'Yeah, but she isn't like him. She's creative and really intelligent and really gorgeous.' He spoke with the reckless romanticism of someone who was head over heels in love. It never lasted.

'Oh really?! Her?!' She said with feigned excitement. She had a feeling he would come crashing down to earth soon enough. But considering everything he had been through lately, she decided to humour him. 'Wow. That's really good. Good for you.'

'Yeah I know!' He said with a childish grin. 'I really like her.'

'That's good.' She said smiling. She suddenly thought of something. She frowned. 'Do you think she might know anything about her father's involvement? Maybe anything that might shed light on whether he's still involved today?'

He pursed his lip, his expression becoming serious. 'I don't know.'

'I don't want to cause any problems for you.' She tried to backtrack, realising that it may not have been an appropriate thing to ask. 'Maybe she doesn't know anything. But it could help.'

He nodded. 'Ok.' He said slowly. 'Maybe, I might ask her.'

‘If it comes up though.’ She said gently. ‘There’s no need to bring it up directly. Just be subtle about it.’

‘I will.’ He said pensive, the idea seemed to make him uncomfortable.

‘I’m sorry.’ She said shaking her head. She felt guilty for bringing down his mood. ‘I feel bad now. I shouldn’t have brought it up.’

‘No, it’s ok.’ He said looking out the window.

‘I’m really happy for you though. It seems like you really like her. She’s a gorgeous girl. Nice work!’ She added encouragingly.

That seemed to make him smile. ‘Thanks. Yeah, she is. I can’t wait to see her again.’

‘Aw.’ She cooed. ‘I’m happy for you.’ She said beaming. She was glad to have cheered him up again. She cleared her throat, and tried to focus her attention back on the case files in front of them. She had a feeling he would go too far off topic if she kept talking to him about this woman.

Aoki hoped that coming to this library might focus them again, but right now it felt about as productive as a group study session at university. Despite this, she felt calm and focused. It was a good environment for her. They sat in the basement of the library, with the bright blue lighting that made her most comfortable. There were big glass windows in their room looking out onto the bright green garden outside. They were alone, the only sound was their own voices and the hum of the air conditioning system. She wondered if she would have been able to get more done if she were alone.

She checked her phone. There were no messages back from Andrea. She frowned. She’d invited her to come along, hoping she’d be able to help, but hadn’t heard a reply.

She put the thought out of her mind and tried to get Will back on topic. ‘See, I keep on looking through these photos. These were taken so soon after the crimes but there's no evidence of footprints or anything like that.'

'Huh?' He said absentmindedly. 'You mean in the photos or at the scene?'

'Both. I even went back to one of the first crime scenes, the one where Marcus Docker was stabbed. He had systematically planned his route to and from the crime scene to avoid any cameras.'

'Are you sure?'

She nodded. 'I went through and walked the scene. There were a few cameras, and the only way to avoid them all would be to cross the road several times. It wouldn't have happened by accident.'

'Hmm,' he frowned and rubbed his stubble. 'Good point.'

At that moment Morgan walked in with their coffees. 'How's everything going here? Made any progress yet?' He said cheerfully.

'Not really.' She said quietly, studying the photos. 'Just looking over the photos of the old crimes scenes. Hitting the same walls.'

'Aoki was just telling me about how he avoided the cameras in the Docker case.' Will added.

'Yeah and how he knew where they were. Have you told him about the Kelvin Anderson case?'

'What about it?' Asked Will, squinting.

Aoki sighed. 'There were some distinctive lines in the ground by the road.' She rustled through the photos and pulled one out. She pushed it forward to Will and indicated on the photo. 'Around here, these were taken pretty soon after the officers arrived onsite.

They took photos trying to collect evidence without being able to see any. We were lucky they took these ones.'

'What am I looking at?' Will peered closer.

'The thin lines running along the dirt there. Like really thin scratches.'

'Oh, yeah.' He looked confused.

'Well, we think he may have used a tree branch to cover his tracks. You can faintly see some tracks further away from the road. It was a quick and rushed job, but it was a pretty effective way to cover his tracks in a hurry.'

'It may have been crude.' Morgan said. 'But for the first officers who arrived onsite it took them time to get their bearings and track him. It may have only bought another twenty minutes, but by the time they figured out where he went, it was far too late.'

She nodded slowly. 'We think he crossed the national park here. He could have come out anywhere. We lost his tracks.'

'Fuck.' Will said and shook his head. 'This guy is smart.'

'Exactly.' Aoki said.

'Did you tell him about the profile yet?' Morgan asked smiling. He seemed happy with himself.

'No, not yet.' She said shaking her head. 'We only just got here.'

'What about the profile?' Will asked.

'Well,' She tried not to smile, but she was glad to be able to use her education in psychology. 'In terms of a psychological profile, most serial killers will tend to have similar traits. The most important of which comes from the socialization theory.'

'What is that?'

‘Well, basically, that in childhood the person was evident to some sort of violent or traumatic act. Early childhood experiences like these often have a lasting impression on the behaviour of an individual.’

‘So you think he maybe came from a violent household?’

She frowned. ‘It’s not as simple as that. It could be anything. Maybe he witnessed a robbery, a murder, a rape.’

‘I don’t think so.’ Morgan added. ‘I don’t think there is any sexual motive to the crimes.’

Aoki sighed at having being cut off. ‘Morgan doesn’t agree with parts of it. But we both hold the same opinion. In any event, these childhood events are impossible to trace, most of them wouldn’t be reported. Plus, I mean, this person may not have been witness to a horrific act, they may have been victimised, bullied. It sometimes isn’t so simple.’

‘Alright then.’ Will replied sceptically. ‘What do you think about the motive?’

‘I think it’s pretty straightforward,’ answered Morgan. ‘I think the only thing these victims have in common is a background in the financial industry and, as simple as it may be, they’re all quite wealthy.’

Aoki rubbed her face in frustration. Everyone had been talking about it. In every news report they had referred to this person as ‘the vigilante’. It seemed to be simplifying matters to her. ‘But why this particular company? Everyone that has been killed so far has been involved with Delpont in some way or another.’

‘You both agree it has something to do with wealth and the financial industry?’ Will asked, looking at the two of them.

‘Pretty much,’ said Morgan casually. ‘A common motive for serial killers is some kind of grand plan, and what we’ve seen is pretty consistent with that.’

‘There is a classification of “mission-based” serial killers.’ Aoki said softly. ‘They’re motivated essentially by a belief that they’re acting for the greater good, by fighting the evil of the world.’

‘Usually, though, for these types of killers there is still some underlying sexual element, the victims are usually female.’

‘But these cases don’t have any resemblance to that?’ Will frowned.

‘Yeah. From this, we have an idea of the profile for this shadow in the dark. Someone highly intelligent, possibly with some trauma in his childhood, likely to be late twenties to early forties, and motivated by a belief in the righteousness of his cause.’ Aoki explained slowly.

Will sighed, considering it. There was a moment of silence before he spoke again. ‘I think all of this is somehow tied into Delpont. I think there is a connection whether he worked for them, was involved in the case or maybe lost money from the collapse.’

‘You think maybe there is a revenge aspect for financial reasons?’ Morgan replied, an eyebrow raised. ‘Wouldn’t that undermine the whole idea of wealth as an evil, if this person had been trying to profit themselves?’

Will shrugged. ‘I don’t know, but it’s possible. I think the key thing to all of this is Delpont.’

There was a moment of silence. Morgan scratched his chin frowning, considering everything.

Aoki took a deep breath. ‘I think we should look into former Delpont employees. There must be a record of resumes or profiles of staff hired. They must have collected all that information for the trial.’

‘What would we be looking for?’ Morgan asked.

‘Maybe something in terms of interests and activities? Maybe look for anyone with any background in military, the police or even martial arts?’

Morgan looked at her quizzically.

‘Because of the way these people were killed. This person was prepared and knew how to kill. More importantly, they knew how to not leave a trace. That doesn’t happen overnight.’

‘True.’ Morgan nodded.

Morgan and Will fell silent as they considered this.

‘There might be something in Delpont that could be useful.’ Will spoke up. He cleared his throat. ‘In most of these big corporations they need to keep reports of staff, especially if there are any incidents.’

‘What do you mean?’ Asked Morgan.

‘Well, it’s mostly if staff act inappropriately. It’s usually for instances of things like sexual harassment, any conflict between staff, or any other inappropriate behaviour that breaches the company code of conduct. They keep it as a record so that even if they don’t dismiss the staff the first time, if another incident occurs in the future they can refer back to this.’

‘Ok. But how would those sorts of things help us find this person?’ Aoki asked him. She could see how this could be a useful reference for most things but didn’t see how it would help them find someone like this.

Will frowned. ‘I don’t know whether it would be true of this company, but a lot of big companies want to make sure that their staff believe in what they’re doing. So if there are instances where someone does something to suggest they’re against big business or the financial world, then the company would want to keep a record of that too. It could be classed under insubordination or something like that.’

‘Fuck.’ Morgan said slowly. ‘Yeah, that would be useful.’

‘Yeah, that’s what I was thinking. I mean, this person knows the full story of Delpont pretty well, which makes me think they worked there. But they seem to be a very strong believer in the immorality of the financial world and of wealth in general. If anyone spoke out about this it would have been noticed, and probably would have caused some worry in a community like that.’

Aoki narrowed her gaze and thought about what Will was saying. ‘It’s a long shot. I mean, even if they worked at Delpont, what if they developed those beliefs after the company failed?’

‘Yeah, and I mean, fuck,’ Morgan swore, scratching his head. ‘After the Delpont crash, the 2008 recession, practically everyone got screwed over, who wouldn’t have cause to hate these guys?’ He laughed, shaking his head.

‘I know. But we don’t have too much else to go on. And especially considering everything that happened during the final days, about the people losing all their retirement money and things like that, it’s pretty likely that they would have said or done something. Even if they didn’t fully believe in it as they do now.’

Aoki picked up her bag. ‘It’s worth a try. I’m going to try and track it down now.’

‘Right now?’ Morgan laughed.

She nodded. ‘We keep on hitting brick walls. We really need to get an idea of who this vigilante is. I’m tired of having no idea what to do. This is the first time we’ve had an idea of who they might be.’

‘Where will you go?’ Will asked.

She scratched her head thinking. She only had half an idea of what she could do. ‘I know that all of the emails on their server were saved and stored for use in the trials. Records of them still exist, but nothing from the executive management was found.'

'Right, but you think they might have kept these incident reports? The people trying to clean up after Delpont might have not destroyed them.'

She nodded. 'Maybe they didn't think anything of them at the time.'

WILL

Aoki left in a hurry. After that he and Morgan talked for a while longer but hadn't been able to get anywhere further. Her knowledge of psychology had really helped them. From what he could gather, Morgan's skills as a detective were best suited to looking at evidence and problem solving. Aoki also said he had a gift for reading people and getting them to open up. In a case like this, those talents were wasted. Morgan had gone off to take a break and get his mind off Delpont. He'd invited him, but Will had plans and headed home instead.

As he showered and got ready to go out, he kept checking his phone. He told himself he was waiting to hear from Iz, but in truth he was hoping to hear from Amber. The longer it had been since he saw her, the more he felt a growing sense of excitement and nervousness. He had been so calm and relaxed after spending the night with her, he felt confident. But the longer it had been, the more he waited to hear from her next. Sometimes they would message each other and have a long conversation. Other times she would take hours to reply. He got the sense that she was flighty and he'd always struggled in relationships like that in the past, but he wanted to get used to it so that things with her would work out. He checked his phone again and was let down when he saw there was nothing there.

He wore a black t-shirt, dark denim jeans and a black leather jacket. He messaged Iz and checked where to meet her. After he put on cologne and his blue Vans, he got a message back from her telling him the name of the bar. He caught his reflection in the mirror and had to look away. When he looked at his reflection lately all he could see was the pain he had caused Sam. He felt an uncomfortable feeling in the pit of his stomach whenever he thought about it. He hadn't heard from her for a while. He had tried to make her feel better, but nothing he could say would do that.

He put the thought out of his mind.

Arriving at the bar before Iz, he ordered a bottle for the two of them. He sat down at a wooden table while he waited. Sipping at his wine, he took a deep breath.

'Hey.' He heard her voice from behind, and a gentle hand on his shoulder. 'I heard. I'm really sorry.' She said soothingly as she hugged him.

He scratched at his hair. 'Yeah, thanks.' He said silently, his voice suddenly thick.

'How are you doing?' She asked as she sat down, her bright green eyes narrowed on him. She poured herself a glass of wine and as she took a sip, she rubbed her tanned arms.

He sighed and narrowed his eyes. 'It's so complicated.'

'It's ok.' She said gently. 'Don't want to talk about it?'

He smiled, nodding. 'Yeah, you know me too well. I've been working with these two detectives on these murders.'

'That's crazy.'

'Yeah.' He sipped at his wine. He wanted to explain and give her an idea of what was going on. But he didn't want to make her worry by telling her the whole story.

'Well, look on the bright side.' She put her glass down and clapped. 'When this is all over, we can finally start up our detective agency!' She joked, trying to cheer him up.

He wasn't sure what, but something she said reminded him of the reality. He cleared his throat. 'They haven't given me a gun yet, so no.'

She laughed. 'Matter of time, darling. If you need anyone sorted out I can rough 'em up.' She joked.

He couldn't help but laugh. 'I'll keep it in mind.' She was a slight and short woman. He thought of her throwing punches at someone and tried to stifle a laugh. 'With you as my muscle we could maybe shake down some primary school kids.'

She glared at him, grinned, and jabbed at his arm. 'Let that be a lesson to you.'

He laughed, rubbing his arm. 'Yeah, that stings. Maybe we might have a shot then.'

'Are you sure you don't want to talk about it all though?' She asked him with sincerity.

'Yeah, it's complicated.' He smiled. 'It'll work out.'

'Alright then. Are you still talking to Amber?' She frowned as she asked him.

'Yeah.' He chuckled. 'We actually hooked up.'

'Really?!' She asked loudly. A group nearby turned and looked at her quizzically.

He nodded and laughed. 'Yeah. You're not upset with me? After what you told me.'

'Fuck, no. She's hot.' She slapped his arm. 'Good for you.'

He laughed. 'Thanks. Yeah, I really like her. I want to see what happens with her.'

'Hmm,' she said with a narrowed gaze. 'I don't know about that. I mean, there's a difference between fun and, you know. You should be careful.'

'Why?'

She took a deep breath. 'I know how you get hurt like this. You get too serious too soon and then find out they don't want the same things as you.'

‘Yeah.’ He took a deep breath. She was right. ‘Fair enough. We have such similar interests, though. I feel like we really hit it off.’

She nodded. ‘I just don’t want you to get hurt.’

‘I won’t.’ He said the words but he knew he didn’t need to worry about that. He knew Amber wasn’t like that, even if his friend couldn’t see it. He wanted to defend Amber, but didn’t want to upset Iz. He took a gulp of wine and swallowed hard. He thought about Amber and checked his phone. There was no message.

AOKI

She had spent the afternoon trying to track down the files from the trials of Delpont. Little paper evidence had been kept, most of that had been shredded by people trying to protect themselves in the last few hours of the falling empire.

However, a lot of the files on the network could be recovered. She was hoping to track down a copy of them. She'd no luck with the police records, mainly because of an overwhelmingly bureaucratic approach in terms of access to information. So she had left frustrated, starting to consider leaving the police force. However, she had remembered someone who could help her.

As she walked into the hospital again and made her way to Rebecca's room, she wondered if it was a good idea. She was not sure whether she'd be able to talk, but right now she was desperate. At the very least, she wanted to see her and how she was doing.

She walked into the room and almost took a step back.

Not only was Rebecca awake, but was also pulling herself up from the bed. She was pulling at the straps above her bed and had almost lifted herself fully upright.

'That's really good! Keep at it! Hold it!' A physio cheered loudly. He held his hands underneath in case he needed to catch her.

There was a strained look on her face and she was breathing quickly, but Aoki could see a fierce determination in her eyes.

Beck held herself up, her arms shaking. The physio said nothing and didn't hold her. It looked as though he had stopped doing the work for her some time ago. Finally, she could hold herself no longer. As she fell back the physio caught her and eased her down.

'That's incredible work!' The man said, encouragingly. He beamed at her 'You're absolutely flying!'

When she laid her head on the pillow, she closed her eyes and tried to catch her breath. It was only then Aoki could see the strain it had taken on her.

'Thanks.' Beck said in between breaths. 'If I'm doing so well how about you bring me some wine as a reward.'

The physio grinned and laughed. 'You would have earned it.'

'Well, then, what's the problem?'

He shook his head smiling. 'You know you can't have it.'

'I know. You're terrible at rewarding good work.' Beck teased. She opened her eyes, still catching her breath, and noticed Aoki in the room. 'Aoki! Hey.'

'Hey.' She said softly. 'Wow. You're doing amazing.'

Beck waved the suggestion off dismissively and with a smile. 'I'm doing alright. I was thinking of doing a marathon tomorrow but I've been told I can't.'

The physio chuckled.

Aoki shook her head. She wondered if she would have the same attitude under the same circumstances.

'I'll leave you two to it.' The man said. 'Give me a yell if you need anything.'

'Will do.' Beck said.

He left the room and smiled at Aoki.

'I'm so impressed, Beck. You're doing so well.'

‘Thanks!’ She said, beaming. ‘I’ve been working pretty hard. I’m doing well at the moment, but I know it may be harder further down the road.’

‘True.’

‘I’ll just keep fighting, though, keep working.’ Beck shook her head. She had regained her breath ‘I refuse to let this be my fate. I’m not going to let this dictate my life.’ There was a calm certainty in her voice. She was angry but determined at the same time.

‘When did you start moving again?’ Aoki said narrowing her gaze. She was perplexed by this rapid change. ‘The other day they told me you might not ever move again?’

‘The day after you saw me, I don’t know. I couldn’t sleep. I had to move. I tried small, just my fingers. Within an hour, they were moving fine again. After another hour, I got my hands to move properly.’ She sighed. ‘I just kept going. I had this itch all over. I had to get up.’

‘That’s amazing.’ Aoki bowed her head. ‘I can’t believe it. You should take it slowly, though.’ She added with concern.

‘You sound like my physio!’ Beck smiled and laughed. ‘I’ll be fine.’ She cleared her throat. ‘What brings you down here though? Just checking up on me?’

‘Yeah. I wanted to see how you were doing.’ Aoki squinted.

Beck grinned. ‘For a detective you’re a pretty crappy liar, you know?’

‘Fuck.’ Aoki swore under her breath.

‘What else is it?’

Aoki exhaled. ‘I also might need your help.’ She said gently.

Beck smiled. ‘Sure thing.’

'I'm sorry!' Aoki said, apologetically. 'I feel terrible coming to you right now.'

'It's fine.' Beck chuckled. 'Honestly it's a little nice. I'm a bit sick of Will looking at me and feeling pity. It's nice to be needed.'

'I know. I should let you rest though.'

'I'll be alright.' She groaned as she propped up a pillow behind her and sat upright. 'What's up?'

'Well,' Aoki said slowly. 'I've been thinking lately how this vigilante is targeting Delpont people, and seems to know,' She paused, noticing Beck frown. 'What's wrong?'

'Nothing.' She said sighing. 'I just hate that label.'

Aoki smiled. 'I know, me too. Sorry. I just gave in because it was easier.'

Beck smiled. 'Yeah, I know. So what are you thinking? Are you back on the idea we talked about? That this person worked at Delpont?'

'I think it's likely.' Aoki nodded. 'It's worth looking into.'

'But how?'

'I was telling Will and Morgan.' Aoki sighed. 'I think there might be records of incidents kept somewhere. And there might be something to find in there.'

Beck smiled. 'That's true. That's a good idea. What are you looking for though?'

'I'm not sure.' Aoki shrugged. 'But I'll know it when I see it. I tried looking through the department and trial records but it was too long and complicated, and I don't think they took the incident files. Do you know where I could track these records down? I thought you might have come across them before.'

‘I think so.’ Rebecca frowned. ‘A few years after Delpont fell apart, a website popped up. It basically leaked all of the emails and files they secured from the server.’

‘Really?’

Beck nodded. ‘Yeah. Apparently someone in the legal team leaked it. It was shut down after a few weeks but I saved all the information they leaked.’

‘That sounds pretty promising.’

‘It should still be on my computer at home. I’ll write out the password for you and the folder it’s in.’

‘Sure thing.’ Aoki ducked into her handbag and rummaged through to find a pen and paper and handed them to her. As Beck started to write out the details, Aoki smiled to herself. She felt like this might give them some real information.

ANDREA

She watched the billowy clouds pass by overhead. The sky was bright blue but obscured by cloud patches. There was no breeze in the air. The whole day everything had felt so silent to her. Like there was nothing happening.

Within her was a different story, however. She felt constant anxiety. Every day at work had been wasted, torturing herself thinking about him. She had sat through quiet dinners with her husband unable to think of anything else. She should have been worried about the threats made by the strange man, but she was not. Any desire to look into the situation at Delpont had gone that day. Even from the beginning, she had little desire to dig into that section of her past, and there was nothing she could do now that would change it. Or, more importantly, what people thought of her.

She stared at the clock. It wasn't even midday yet. She sighed, thinking about how she had started this job. She had seen it as a way to accomplish some change, so that situations like Delpont wouldn't occur again. However, she'd been overwhelmed by all the interlocking webs of regulation. The more she learnt, the more she realised how complicated it was. It was a task so big that she had no idea where to start. It had seemed impossible to accomplish any real change and because of this she had stopped trying.

Her phone buzzed in her bag. She glanced to make sure no one was watching before getting it. Her colleagues would check their phones in visible sight, so she knew there was no stigma attached to it. Despite this, she never wanted to compromise her image of professionalism at work.

She felt her heart tighten as she read the screen. It was a message from Hank. She quickly opened it, feeling both excited that he might want to see her but also nervous that he might not want to see her anymore. He had been elusive lately.

She smiled. He said he wanted to see her today, but only during the day. She swore under her breath, she would be stuck at work for at least another five hours. She didn't want to message him back though. She would try to see him that night. She ducked out of the office as inconspicuously as she could. She made for an unoccupied meeting room and dialled him.

'Hello?' She heard his voice on the other side. It sounded rough and low. She smiled. He had probably been drinking last night. She loved his voice after a night out.

'Hey, darling. I just got your message.'

'Oh yeah?' She heard him laugh on the other end. 'You're quick, I just sent that.' He teased.

'I know.' She felt self conscious that he had noticed. 'I had to call. It was too difficult to sort out by SMS.'

'Fair enough. Come over. I want to see you.'

'I can't. I'm at work right now.' She sighed, exasperated. She wanted to see him so badly, and felt so frustrated that was trapped at work. 'How about tonight? I was meant to have dinner with friends but I can skip it?'

'Nah, I can't do tonight. I'm going to life painting.'

'You're doing what?' She asked, feeling a flush of jealousy.

He laughed. 'Yeah, life painting. Me and a few friends signed up for it a few weeks ago, something together during the week.'

'Oh ok, I didn't know that.' She felt uncomfortable by the thought of him in front of a naked woman. She started to imagine him in a room looking and admiring nudes. She assumed there would be a gorgeous woman there. She felt bitter with jealousy. She had to see him today. She thought maybe she could get him to skip the class. 'Fuck, I really want to see you.'

'Just skip work.' He teased. 'It's not that big a deal.'

'I shouldn't.' She replied tentatively. She frowned thinking about it. She never would have done that. She used to put everything into her job and how she was seen at work. She never revealed weakness.

'Come on. I know you want to.'

She bit her lip. It was true. 'Ok.' She replied meekly. 'I'll get out of here and come over.'

'Sure thing.' He laughed. 'Give me a buzz when you're out front, gorgeous.'

He hung up.

She got out of the meeting room and ran her fingers through her long hair. She tried to think of something to say, but decided it best to keep it as short as possible. She walked over to her boss's desk. He sat there gazing at his screen with a smile on his face. He seemed to spend a lot of his time like that, always trying to come up with an idea.

'Charlie, hey.' She said meekly. 'Are you busy?'

'No, not right now.' He said smiling. 'What's up?'

She frowned and looked down. She tried to look as unsure of herself as possible. 'I'm not feeling too well, I think something might be wrong.'

'Oh really?' He said with a look of genuine concern on his face. He stood up and checked her out. 'Yeah, you look in pain. Are you alright?'

'I'm ok.' She winced. 'I feel pretty sick though. I'm sorry to be a pain, but is there any way I could go home? I'm sorry to do this to you.' She made sure to speak apologetically and to try and sound uncomfortable about asking.

'Of course! Don't worry about it.'

'I'm sorry to leave early.'

'No, it's fine, don't beat yourself up about it. Just go home and get some rest.' He winked at her.

'Thanks, Charlie. It means a lot.' She felt guilty now for deceiving him. She turned to head to her desk. 'I'll come back in tomorrow, though, I think I just need some rest.'

'Don't stress about it.' He waved her suggestion off dismissively. He smiled 'If you're not well, don't come in tomorrow. Just take some time off if you need it.'

'Thank you, Charlie.'

'It's alright.' He said kindly. He turned his attention back to his screen and tried to come up with another idea.

She turned and went to her desk to collect her things without drawing too much attention. She looked at Charlie sitting there focusing on his work as she walked out of the office. She would have felt guiltier had she not been so consumed with lust.

THE VIGILANTE

He liked the name they'd given him. The term implied a pursuit of justice, someone operating outside the law. He smiled. He felt proud of the name.

It was a cool, clear night. The night sky was pitch black. The city lights shone bright. The conflicting office lights and clashing neon signage created a mosaic of colour and light. Everywhere he walked there were people sitting to dinner, laughing, drinking, smoking. Music from the various bars and restaurants drifted down. These people were out living real life. On the other side of Darling Harbour the skyscrapers stood tall and proud. They stood at different angles and were different shapes, but from this distance they all looked like one monolithic structure. He pulled his hood back up to cover his face and he zipped his jacket up further to try and keep warm.

Something about that night reminded him of the night that started this. He remembered the torment he had felt drinking away his pain. Sitting alone in a bar ordering glass after glass of scotch. He had been truly alone that night. But more than anything, he thought of the anger and injustice he used to feel, preoccupied with the idea that the system had failed him. The next morning after losing everyone he had awoken reborn. He had lost all hope that night, but woken up the next morning and life had gone on.

He had woken to news of companies sending jobs overseas while making record profits. There had been articles about the deteriorating economy and rising crime, and at the same time that the wealthiest percentage had increased their wealth several fold over the past year. He had spent the day intently watching the news networks, heartbroken by the rising unemployment and crime through all the cities in the country. He had realised that the system had not failed him. The system had failed the majority.

He took a deep breath to steady his nerves. Everything he had done since then had been in accordance with his beliefs. He had a clear purpose. He had a reason to live and he wanted to change the world, no matter the cost.

He looked out across at the city skyline across Darling Harbour. The city wasn't always seen from this angle. It was usually seen from the Circular Quay harbour. From this angle, he noticed how far the city went on for. He could see all the different blocks of the city and how the atmosphere deteriorated moving away from the waterfront.

He took a deep breath when he reached his waiting spot. McDermott would be his hardest target yet. The man was a creature of habit, but he was extremely careful. He had a sense the man had been living in a world of paranoia since the downfall of Delpont. He was rarely alone and never vulnerable. The only time that he had been able to see so far was in a short window.

He suddenly saw McDermott approaching from across the bay. He made the same trip each time he came to the city. The old man walked quickly and with purpose. He had a smile on his smile, a look of great contentment. He wore a daggy hat with jeans and a fleece top. He didn't look like a man who was once one of the most powerful and influential in the world. Though even from here, he could see his sparkling blue eyes and knew the strength of will that resided beneath.

He pulled up his hooded jumper and started following McDermott at a distance, so as not to draw his attention. Despite his meek appearance now, the man represented much of the evil of Delpont. This man had been at the heart for so long, he knew that his hands were not clean. He had only a small knife on him tonight, in case an opportunity presented itself.

Up ahead, he watched as the man passed a homeless man on the ground. He had at least the courtesy of looking at this homeless man before walking past him. The homeless man lay slumped on the ground with a crudely drawn sign.

He shook his head, this man had all the arrogance of wealth. People like this believed themselves superior to those that could not make it in their game. In their eyes there were only winners and losers.

He pulled back a bit as he noticed McDermott pull into a convenience store. He hung back in the shadows and looked like he was waiting for someone. He put his earphones in and pretended to listen to music.

McDermott walked back the same way with a bag from the grocery store. He was going the wrong way. He clung close to the wall to be less noticeable, and stayed in the same spot until his target would go back the same way. From a distance he frowned as he watched McDermott approach the homeless man.

'Hey, mate.' Paul said softly. He knelt down and handed him the bag. 'I got you some things here. There's beef jerky, bread, juice, clean water, some lollies, as well. To keep you going.'

The homeless man looked up confused and smiled. He took the bag and rummaged through it. 'Thank you.' He said sincerely.

'No worries.' Paul said kindly. He turned to walk away. 'You take care of yourself, mate.'

The homeless man opened the bag up and rummaged through it. He opened up some of the food and started to eat, while packing away the others into his rucksack.

McDermott kept walking towards the car park with a smile on his face. His eyes twinkled as he walked passed.

He did not follow the man. He stayed in the shadows as he watched his target walk further away into the night. He smiled. He couldn't remember the last time he had been so wrong about someone. Maybe this man deserved a second chance. He couldn't tell yet, he would need to look into the man further.

ANDREA

She lay there content. Her skin felt warm and there were still beads of sweat on her chest. She looked over at her lover getting dressed, at his broad shoulders and the muscles in his back that flexed as he moved. She slowly caught her breath, feeling happy again. But more than that, for the first time in a long while, she felt like herself again.

She couldn't feel the anxiety anymore and she was no longer uncertain of herself. This man loved her. She could tell by the way he made loved to her. He turned and smiled at her then crawled up the bed, slowly kissing up her legs.

'You look gorgeous like that.' He said softly.

She sighed and smiled. 'You don't look too bad on your knees.'

He broke his kissing and laughed.

'You're wearing far too much clothing though.' She teased as she leant up and tugged at his underwear. She kissed him on the mouth as she did so. 'Come back to bed.'

'Darlin',' He smiled. His grey green eyes wrinkled as he did so. 'Would that I could, but I told you I'm seeing friends tonight.'

'Come on, just skip it.' She wrapped her arms around him and started kissing again.

'You know I can't.' He said with a smile. He pulled himself back up and off the bed and continued getting dressed. 'I promised I would see them.'

She slid back down on the bed realising he didn't want her at that moment. She watched him getting dressed as a knot formed in her stomach, and the doubts and anxiety came back.

She took a deep breath as she felt increasingly anxious. She started thinking about him in his life drawing class, looking at another woman naked. She imagined him smiling as he did so. *She might seduce him if he were feeling weak that night.* She felt a rising sense of anger and frustration. *I need to make sure that doesn't happen.*

'Hank.' She said hesitantly, biting her finger. *I have to keep control of him.*

'Yeah?' He replied absently, dressing himself. 'What's up?'

She paused and tried to calm her nerves. 'I don't like the idea of you seeing someone else naked.'

He looked quizzically at her. He looked as if he was about to laugh, but instead he started to look annoyed. 'Why? What do you mean?'

She sighed. 'This life drawing class. I don't think it's appropriate for you to see someone other than me naked.' She tried to speak gently but it came out sounding confrontational.

'What? Are you seriously telling me what to do?'

She tried to hide how much it pained her. *I'm not expressing myself how I wanted to.* 'If need be, then yes.' She said firmly, feigning confidence. She tried to sound gentler now. She leant forward to him and almost pleaded with him. 'I love you, Hank.'

He looked at her strangely and then took a step back. 'Andrea,' He shook his head. 'I don't think you understand what you're asking.'

'Of course I do.'

He shook his head again. 'You don't, I love you too. But how can you ask something like that of me when you're still married to someone else?' He spoke calmly, looking down as he spoke.

There was faint emotion in his voice, but she couldn't tell what he was feeling.

'I know, I'm sorry.' She put her face in her hands. She tried to hold back from sobbing 'I think about you all the time.'

He looked at her with sad eyes but said nothing.

'I don't love him anymore. I want to be with you.' She pleaded with him to understand. 'And I don't want you to be with anyone else.'

He shook his head. 'Andrea.'

'Have you been with anyone else?' She blurted out. *Fuck,* she thought, *I couldn't stop myself from asking.*

'You can't ask me that.' He said softly, turning away from her.

She grabbed his arm and pulled him back. She glared at him. 'Answer me!' She couldn't hide the anger in her voice. She felt so defensive and didn't know why she was attacking him. *I just want to control him,* she thought desperately. 'Have you been with anyone else?!' She demanded.

'I'm not going to answer that. You don't have any right to ask me, Andrea. You're still married to someone else. I never ask whether you're intimate with him.' He replied tersely.

'But I'm not!' She replied quickly, moving closer to him. 'I haven't been with him since I've been with you.'

He sighed, shaking his head. 'I don't want to talk about this right now.' He said dismissively. He kept on getting dressed.

She felt infuriated at the way he dismissed her so casually. She felt a passionate rage, which she attributed to wine and jealousy. She clenched her fists, not knowing what to do with all the anger. 'Fine!' She shouted out, quickly crossing the room and putting her clothes on. 'If you want to be like that then I'll leave! You've clearly been fucking someone else.' She felt the fury run through her blood.

He recoiled at the accusation. 'Calm down.' He said softly.

'No! No! I won't!' She shouted, her clothes clenched in her fist as she pointed at him. She kept raising her voice at him. Her body was shaking with anger. 'If you don't want to give me a straight answer then you must be fucking someone else!'

'Fuck, Andrea.' He muttered, wide eyed. 'You're acting crazy.'

'Crazy?!' She whipped around at him quickly. She pulled her pants and shirt on quickly. She felt a button rip off her blouse but made no move to pick it up lest she lose face. 'Don't you fucking dare!' She shouted. 'You're the one who isn't being honest with me!'

'Fuck, just calm down.'

'Don't tell me what to do! I'm leaving, and don't you dare try and stop me.' She demanded loudly. *Please try and stop me*, she hoped silently.

He looked down at the ground as she packed up her things. His head hung low at he scratched at his scalp. He looked defeated.

The entire time she was packing she wanted him to say sorry. *Please try and stop me, I'll give in and make love to you.* He could get her pregnant and they would run away together. She took as long as possible to get her things together in the hopes he would stop her. She wanted to cry. She wanted to say sorry. *I can't give in*, she thought, *I have to stay strong.*

The entire time he stood there and said nothing. He solemnly watched her pack her things. There was none of the joy that was always on his face, there was only pain.

She walked to the door and was about to open it. She turned to him and spoke as confidently as she could. 'I'm leaving now then.' She said it as a statement, hoping he would stop her.

He looked at her and frowned. He shook his head sadly. 'Fine then.'

It felt like a slap in the face to her. She felt angry again, but mostly hurt. 'Ok then, I'll just leave.' She tried to say, but he had already turned and had left the room.

She turned and left. Each step to her car she kept hoping he would run to her. Her lip trembled as she tried to stop herself from crying. She got in her car.

As soon as she closed the door she broke down. She wept while she gripped the steering wheel. She couldn't understand her actions or why she had exploded at Hank. She shouldn't have brought it up in the first place. Regardless, she couldn't understand his ambivalence to answer her questions.

After a few minutes, she composed herself and started driving home. She looked like a mess and if her husband saw her it would have been obvious that something had happened. At that moment though, she didn't care. Her life was already bad enough, she didn't mind if it got worse. She kept checking her phone the entire way home, hoping he had texted her.

When she arrived home she was glad to find that her husband was out. She walked upstairs and took her clothes off. She checked her phone as she got ready for bed, but there were no messages.

She had to fix the situation. She sent him a long message saying how sorry she was and that she was wrong. She told him she'd made a huge mistake and she hoped he forgave her. She waited for a reply but there was nothing for ten minutes. She sent another long message hoping to get a response from him, but again she received no reply. She wanted to keep trying. She thought that if she sent a few more messages she could get him to talk to her.

Deep down though, she knew he wouldn't talk to her right now. She lay down and fell asleep as soon as her head hit the pillow.

AOKI

When she walked into Rebecca's apartment she could tell straight away that no one had been there for a while. There was a musky smell and all the blinds were closed. It was dark and the air felt stale. It was a far cry from the clean, well presented home that Aoki had seen the first time she had been there. The apartment now felt haunted. She could imagine how difficult it would be for Beck when she came home. She would need help.

She found Beck's laptop without difficulty and opened it up. She had no issues with the password and was able to find the files quickly. However, once she found the files the difficulty started. She was overwhelmed by the sheer amount of information. There were copies of every email ever sent within the company, all the salary information, and every resume that had been received. The depth of the record keeping was staggering. She knew that some people had been able to have their emails deleted, and she had assumed that there wouldn't be much left. However, what she found was a colossal amount of information.

She looked through it for half an hour but found that most of it was not of much use. A quarter of what she looked at were office in-jokes, most of it sexist, racist or just crude. There were a lot of corporate newsletters and invitations to company functions, which were useless for what Aoki needed. The rest of what she found was cryptic account and trade information. This would have been useful for the trials several years ago, but did not shed any light on the identity of this vigilante.

By using a few search filters, she found ways of blocking out this unnecessary information. After another half an hour she managed to find several incident reports. She used the information in those to narrow her search parameters and pull up only those types of documents. She smiled, having successfully pulled up all the information she needed. But even after narrowing it down to just the relevant information, there were still over a thousand entries.

She heard someone's footsteps in the hallway. They were heavy footsteps, like boots. She started to worry, feeling frightened. She went to quickly put a USB in Rebecca's laptop, but fumbled and dropped it. She swore softly and picked it up in a hurry. Fright took over as the footsteps appeared outside the door, but they slowly moved past.

For a moment she felt confused, and then realised that they had walked to the end of the hallway. She sighed and shook her head, and gradually calming down. She had been so on edge lately; she was not surprised she had overreacted like that. Regardless, she decided it would be best to look over the information at home. She picked up the USB, put it in Rebecca's laptop, and began copying the information. Despite the small file size, it still took several minutes due to the sheer overall volume.

She disconnected it after it was done and shut down Beck's computer. As she started walking to the front door, she heard the heavy footsteps walk back down the hallway. She slowed her steps, feeling increasingly afraid. She hoped the person would keep walking. *Fuck,* she swore to herself, *why didn't I bring my gun?* She hoped it was just another overreaction. *I'm just being paranoid.*

Slowly the footsteps got closer until they stopped just outside the apartment, with the heavy boots visible through the gap underneath the door.

WILL

It had been a pretty boring night. He had spent it in his apartment with Iz, watching eighties movies. Normally something like that would have been fun, but she had fallen asleep at the start of the second movie. So she had curled up on the opposite couch and had caught up on sleep. She needed a good night sleep, and he knew she hadn't had one since getting back a little while ago. The two had gone out almost every night lately, as well.

He had gotten caught up in the movie and didn't want to turn it off. *If I turn the movie off there would just be silence*, he thought. *Even though my friend is there, I'd feel profoundly alone*. The thought terrified him.

As the film got to the big song and dance number towards the end, he felt his phone buzz. It was a private number. He frowned, but decided to take the call anyway.

'Hello.'

'Will, hey.' A gentle voice said. 'It's Amber.'

'Amber.' He felt confused. 'Hey, how are you?'

'Good.' She said briefly. 'I'm in your neighbourhood at the moment.'

'Really?'

'Yeah, I'm just at the café up the road from you, if you were free?'

'Uhhh,' he said slowly, looking over at his sleeping friend. *She'll be asleep for a while*. 'Sure thing. I'll just get changed and head up, is that alright?'

‘That’s fine.’ She said in a kind voice. ‘I’ll be here for a little longer.’

‘Ok.’ He wondered what he was getting himself into qne unsure of how he would fare with her friends. He needed to ask her. ‘Who are you there with?’

‘No one.’ She replied in a coy voice. ‘I’m on my own.’

‘That sounds good.’ He smiled, and started to feel excited. Thinking about how much he wanted to see the beautiful woman. ‘I’ll be there soon.’

‘See you soon, then.’ She replied, and hung up.

He put the phone down, confused. It was an unexpected development. He didn’t want to complain though. The beginning of things with Amber had happened quite unpredictably. He tucked a blanket over his friend and wrote her a quick note. He quickly changed shirts and put on fresh deodorant, then sprayed himself with his favourite cologne.

He could walk up the street, but he didn’t feel like making her wait. He picked up his car keys on his way out of the house.

AOKI

'Fuck!' She swore silently. It sounded more like hissing. She spun around, looking around the apartment for something. She looked left and right, frantically searching the apartment for a way out. She screamed again in a voiceless whisper. 'Fuck! Fuck! Fuck!'

From outside she heard the person rummage through a bag, and heard a clattering of metal. It sounded like tools.

In her mind she swore again. She quickly turned around and in a panic sprinted nervously and noiselessly to the balcony doors. Out of instinct she moved like a cat, on the balls of her feet, leaping from step to step. Her breathing was quick and it felt like her heart would tear out of her chest.

She felt a full-blown sense of panic as she heard a device pushed into the lock. There was an electrical grinding noise.

She turned and quickly put Beck's key in the balcony door, fortunately picking the right key the first time. She quickly slid the doors open and slipped out. As she closed them and pulled the blinds over behind her, she heard the lock fall out and hit the floor.

She waited nervously to see whether she had been noticed. Anything could tip the assailant off to her presence; if they had heard her open the doors, if the blinds were still swinging. Her heart was pumping and she was breathing heavily, but she forced herself not to make any noise.

From inside, she heard footsteps as the person slowly made their way around the apartment. They scanned the room with their torch, a spotlight moved across the blinds. They moved slowly and deliberately, it appeared they were looking for something. She took a deep breath, relieved that they had not noticed her.

For the moment, she was stuck on the balcony. She walked on her toes to the edge and looked over. From the fifth floor, it was a straight drop to the parking outside. There were trees and shrubs to break her fall, but it didn't overlook any rooftops she could get to, and as such was not an option.

She turned as she heard items being shuffled and moved back. She edged slightly closer to get a glimpse. Through a small gap in the blinds she could see someone rummaging through the desk. She could tell they were wearing heavy clothes, but couldn't see properly, however, as it was dark inside. Beck's laptop was open and the person appeared to be looking for the password. Aoki smirked as the person inside swore and became increasingly frustrated. She couldn't see their face but they had short hair and looked relatively brawny, although that could have been due to the heavy gear.

There was a faint buzzing noise. Her eyes widened as she went to check her own phone. However, the person inside remained natural and put a hand to their head.

'I'm here now.' They said. It appeared they were using a hands-free device. 'I've found the computer but there's no password.'

Aoki frowned. *Were they looking for the same thing I was?*

'No, I can't just copy everything, it'll take too long. We don't know what she came here for.' He said to someone on the other end.

She felt a wave of panic wash over her. She had a feeling he was talking about her. There was no way, however, that anyone could have known she was coming. She had come directly after seeing Beck. The only other people who had known might have been Morgan and Will. She scrunched her face up. It was not possible that either have them could have told anyone. She did not know Will as well as Morgan, but neither would have helped these people out.

'No, there's no sign she's been here yet. I think I beat her here.'

She shook her head and swore under her breath. *He's definitely referring to me*.

'No! I can't just do that!' The man sounded bothered. He kept flicking through pieces of paper and checking around her desk, hoping she had left it written as a note. 'Because if I take the laptop it will be obvious someone was here! It doesn't work like that.'

He turned and walked to the other side of the apartment. She could no longer hear him. She knelt down and walked closer to the glass, hoping to listen in on what was being said again. She gently approached and lightly rested her hands on the glass as she leaned over.

She heard a loud clattering sound. Her heart stopped. She looked down and saw the apartment keys lying on the balcony, having fallen out of her handbag.

'Fuck. I heard something. I think she's here. I've gotta go!' He said loudly. She heard footsteps move quickly inside.

Panic took over her. There was no time. She turned and saw the balcony ledge. It was her only option.

'Oi! You!' He barked from inside. His shouts were loud and violent. 'Stop!'

Her hands shook as she quickly ran to the edge and climbed over, resting on the railing.

The doors swung open quickly and the man ran out onto the balcony. He stopped in his tracks when he saw her teetering over the edge.

It was a dark night, even from a few meters away his face was still obscured. His voice seemed to calm and he shook his head and chuckled. 'You're too high up. You'll die.'

She looked down tentatively. Seeing the drop beneath made her legs go weak. Her arms almost lost their grip on the railing from the sweat on her palms. She couldn't feel her heart beating in her chest anymore. There was a rush of blood to her head and, despite the cold night, she felt like she was overheating.

As he started to slowly approach her, pulling a gun out of his pocket, she thought to herself, *what would my cat do?*

With that she quickly lowered herself, her knuckles white as she gripped as hard as she could. A meter below her was another balcony. The doors closed. Her legs shook as they dangled in mid air.

She felt her foot touch the railing below. The man walked closer, he appeared unsure of what was happening. She quickly stretched down, lowered herself from the concrete balcony. She moved quickly, leaving her off balance, and she lost her footing. There was a moment of panic as she felt herself fall through the air, and then land on the balcony of the apartment below.

She looked up to check that the intruder had not followed her. She could not see him come over the railing. But at the same time she couldn't tell what he was doing on the balcony above. She got up quickly, and started banging on the glass doors to the apartment.

'Hey! Hey! Open up!' She cried out frantically, trying to get attention. She hoped someone was home.

The blinds moved and a face peeked out from behind the blinds. He looked at her with a confused look.

'Please! Let me in!' She pleaded, unsure of whether he could hear her.

'What the hell?' She saw him mouth the words but she could not hear him. He laughed, perplexed.

She rummaged through her purse quickly, glancing above to check whether there was anyone there. She pulled out her police identification and pressed it to the glass.

Suddenly his eyes widened and he looked serious. He quickly pulled the keys out of his pocket, fumbling with them for the right key. It seemed as though he understood there was some danger now.

As soon as the door opened she burst inside and slammed them shut behind her, she yanked the keys off him and locked the door.

'Get away from the windows.' She ordered. 'Make sure the front door and all the balcony doors are locked.'

He nodded and walked in a hurry to the front door. His face seemed white.

'Do you have any weapons here?' She asked hopefully.

He turned as he locked and bolted the front door. He shook his head, looking at the floor.

'Fuck.' She swore softly. She regretted not bringing her gun. She rarely carried it with her. She felt bad for bringing this stranger into it, but she had no other options.

She took a deep breath as her thumping heart started to beat slower. Her lips felt numb. She looked down and realised her hands were shaking. She reached into her bag and pulled out her phone. She took another deep breath to steady her voice, and then called the station for backup. She knew he would be gone by the time they arrived, but she was taking no chances. She patted her pocket to make sure the flash drive was still there. She wondered what was on it that these people were so desperate to cover up.

A few minutes later, she heard the sound of a motor starting. She looked out the window to the parking lot, and watched as a guy on a motorbike rode away in a hurry. She could hear the police sirens approaching.

WILL

He saw her sitting outside the café. She calmly read a book, a content smile on her face. She was dressed in a white singlet, silver bracelets on her wrists, with denim jeans and black heels. Her wavy blonde hair fell to one side, occasionally running her hand through it as she read.

He breathed deeply, feeling nervous at the sight of her. He wanted to hold her again and kiss her. She looked perfect. Her light blue eyes looked up and she smiled as he approached. She folded a page in the book and put it down as she stood up to greet him.

'Hi, Will.' She hugged him lightly. 'Good to see you.'

'Yeah, you too, Amber.' He returned the hug. He felt a tingle as her skin touched his.

She pulled back and smiled. 'Did you want a coffee?'

'No, I'm fine. If I have coffee this late I can't sleep.'

'Really?' She asked with a laugh.

'Yeah, of course. Can you really drink that and go to sleep?'

She nodded. 'I can have a coffee and go straight to sleep. But I won't sleep until later tonight, anyway.' She said with a sly smile.

He felt a flush at the implication of what she said, wondering whether she meant what he assumed. 'You're staying up late?'

'Maybe.' She said slowly, pulling back and sitting down. 'I usually sleep quite late anyway, at like two am.'

'That's quite late. What about when you have work?' He sat down opposite her.

'I'll still go to bed at that time.' She said elusively.

‘What time do you get up?’ He couldn’t understand how she could function like that.

‘Like six am or so? Usually about then.’

‘Fuck.’ He grinned, shaking his head. ‘I wouldn’t be able to function like that.’

She laughed. ‘It doesn’t bother me. Most nights I only sleep for four hours.’ She said with a shrug. ‘I’ve always been a bit like that.’

He shook his head. ‘I couldn’t do that.’

‘Well, maybe you should toughen up then.’ She teased with a smile.

He frowned. He knew she was kidding but he was sensitive about not being tough. ‘So what have you been up to?’ He asked, changing the topic.

‘I’ve been quite busy.’ She squinted, sipping tentatively at her coffee. ‘You know how it is; there is always something on.’

‘Yeah, sure thing.’ He said nodding, though he found it quite the opposite. For him there never seemed to be much on. She seemed quite gregarious. When around people like her it made him feel like a loner in comparison. *I wonder whether I could keep up with the lifestyle of this beautiful woman.*

‘How have things been for you?’

‘Yeah. Going well.’ He paused, considering what Aoki had said to him in the library. ‘Actually, I’ve been caught up in some murder cases. I’ve been helping out the police.’

‘Really?’ She asked animatedly, a sceptical smile on her face. ‘Wow, that’s so interesting!’

‘Yeah, it’s been pretty crazy.’ He beamed. He cleared his throat, thinking of the best way to bring up the topic gently. ‘Actually,

I've been looking into the deaths of the former Delpont workers.' He spoke softly and avoided eye contact, making sure to have a serious look on his face.

'Oh.' Her smile sunk. She frowned and looked away.

'I'm sorry. I know you may not want to talk about it. I can understand, it's a sensitive issue.' He added.

She shook her head and cleared her throat. 'No, it's fine. I had been concerned about those incidents myself lately.' She maintained her calm tone as she spoke. He admired her ability to remain graceful even when discussing a difficult topic like that. Despite her delicate appearance, he felt she was a strong individual.

'I can understand. Worried about your father?' He asked gently.

'Yes.' She replied reluctantly, looking down. He sensed a trace of bitterness in her answer. Perhaps it was a question with an obvious answer.

'I'm sorry, I'm sure he will be fine.'

'Thank you, that's kind of you.'

He could sense she had pulled away. She seemed slightly distant and defensive after he'd brought it up. He felt foolish. 'I've been working with the detectives lately. They're getting closer to figuring out who this guy is. One of them is chasing down a lead at the moment. It looks pretty promising. I'm sure they'll catch him soon.' He said reassuringly.

'Really?' She turned back to him and smiled again. There was a sparkle in her ocean eyes. That seemed to brighten her mood. 'That is really good news. Who do they think it might be?'

'Well, they have been looking into whether it might be someone who was within Delpont. Especially considering how much this person seems to know about the company.'

‘Hmm. That does make sense.’ She narrowed her gaze, considering what he had said. A smile crept on to her face. ‘So did you just meet up with me to see what my father knows? Whether he suspects anyone?’

He laughed. ‘No, no, not at all.’

‘Did you come to see me with an ulterior motive, Mr Martec?’ She teased him, smiling.

He laughed and shook his head. ‘No, nothing like that.’ He cleared his throat and made eye contact with her. ‘I’ve just been wanting to see you.’

She looked up and held his gaze. ‘You’re sweet.’ She said, smiling. He had come to expect responses like this from her. It neither discouraged nor encouraged his advances. As always she didn’t reveal her own feelings. She was constantly elusive.

‘But, regardless, your father might have an insight into what is going on. He may suspect someone on the inside.’

Her eyes narrowed as she stared into eyes. Then she relaxed and smiled. ‘That sounds like a good idea. I don’t know how much my father knows, but I will try. Maybe you should meet him?’ She asked with a smile.

He flushed. It was an encouraging sign that she wanted him to meet her father. Immediately, however, he considered that he was reading too much into the idea. ‘I would like that.’ He smiled back.

Her response was warm, however, she quickly changed the topic. The discussion then moved onto other matters like mutual friends and work. On topics like that she seemed to close off, as though she was going through the motions. Considering the amount of people she knew and the social life she led, he could not find it surprising that it came so natural to her.

They talked for a while longer before she cleared her throat and checked her phone.

'It's getting quite late.' She said softly. 'I'm sorry, I should probably go. There are a few things I need to get done at home before tomorrow.'

'So tonight will be another late night for you then?' He teased. He felt upset she was leaving, he had hoped to spend the night with her.

'Naturally.' She replied with a sly smile. She collected her bag and rose. 'I do my best work in the night time.'

He stood to say goodbye. He hoped to spend more time with her, and considered inviting her back to his apartment. 'I have my car nearby. Did you want a lift home?'

She looked up and made eye contact, then smiled. She reached out and held his hand. 'That's sweet of you.' She said as she reached out to hold his hand. Her touch felt warm, however she quickly released her hold and pulled her hand back. 'But it's fine. I drove here and my car is parked down the road.'

'Ok then.' He said reassuringly, despite feeling deflated. 'Did you want me to walk you to your car?'

'No, it's not necessary.' She smiled and waved away the suggestion dismissively. 'You're very kind, though. I'm parked in the other direction to where you are.'

He frowned. 'How do you know where I am?'

She laughed, and pointed up the road. 'I saw you cross the road up there. I'm in the other direction.'

'Ok then.' He nodded. 'It was nice to see you and catch up again.'

'And you too.' She turned and grinned as she packed her bag. 'We should catch up again soon, Will.' She said warmly.

He smiled. ‘Yeah, I would like that.’

‘I’ll let you know when my father is free. You’ll like him. He’s a very outgoing and engaging man. We will have to set something up soon.’

‘Yeah, that would be nice. I’m free whenever. Just let me know.’

‘I will.’ She smiled warmly. Her bright blue eyes sparkled as they caught the streetlights overhead. ‘I’ll see you soon.’

With that she turned and Will watched as she walked away. He wanted to see every last moment of her. Each time he saw he wondered whether it would be the last.

THE VIGILANTE

He sat in the bar and worked on his expensive laptop, one of the last relics of his old life. The more he read about Paul McDermott, the more he realised how wrong he had been. During his Delpont, McDermott had been a cheerleader for all the deception and fraud. He had been guilty of the worst crimes that others in Delpont had been charged with, however, he had escaped at the time and spent the years since in freedom and comfort. Ideologically, this man had represented everything he wanted to fight.

Though, since the fall of Delpont, his life had taken a different turn. It seemed he had found peace, or meaning to his life. He had dedicated his time to charity and helping others. Despite shying away from a media presence in the years since his role as CEO, from the rare interviews it was apparent that his personality had changed as well. There was an openness and kindness that would have seemed out of character before.

He took a deep breath and sipped at his drink. He thought of just how wrong he had been, and how close he had been to taking out someone who no longer deserved it. Whatever the man's crimes, he was accomplishing change now.

He ran his hands through his hair. He felt something he had not experienced since his darkest days; for the first time in years he doubted himself.

He looked around the bar and saw traders with content smiles on their faces. They sat with friends and talked and joked about their days. They had community. One of them made a joke about the million dollars he had made from an hours worth of work. The same man then went to the bar and ordered a drink, discretely putting a hundred dollars in the tips jar as the bar staff looked away. They did not see his act of anonymous generosity. They would discover it later. As he watched the trader walk away, he wondered what the reason was for the generosity. It could have been because he understood how difficult customer service was, or because he merely wanted to be generous. The group of bankers seemed kind to each other and the staff.

He put his head in his hands and rubbed his eyes. In a moment such as this, he could no longer see the evil he had once seen in that world. It was not defined as one amorphous structure. It was composed of individuals making their own choices. He sighed and tried to fight a growing sense of unease. He believed that everything that had happened was for a reason. He was not a religious man, but he felt that there was a greater purpose, and that all the pain and failure he had been through in the past were so that he would emerge the other side stronger than before. He had believed that he had spent so long being lost so that he could have found this cause he could dedicate himself to, something that would make the world a better place. Sitting in the bar alone, he wondered whether he was lost again.

He knew he would not stay down long. He would recover and would find his conviction again. But he knew it was a lonely road he had chosen.

'Hey, hun. Are you alright?'

He looked up. The bar girl looked at him, she had a look of concern on her face and she looked at him gently with her soft brown eyes. He sensed it was a look of pity. He gave her a sly grin and looked back at his drink. 'Things are fine. Thanks for the concern, miss.'

She frowned. Her face was soft and gentle. She ran her hands through her straight blonde hair. 'I always see you in here, drinking alone.'

His smile faded. He felt uneasy to have been noticed. He cleared his throat.

'Why do you come here?' She looked around to see if anyone at the bar was watching, then sat down next to him.

He frowned and sipped at his drink. 'I don't mean to be rude but I prefer being alone.'

She smiled and looked at him. 'No, you don't.'

He felt confused by her tone.

'I know you don't. I see the way you look at groups of people. You want to talk.'

He shook his head. 'No, I think you have me mistaken.'

She narrowed her gaze. 'Where is your accent from? I like it.' She gave him a wry smile.

'Don't try and change the subject. I appreciate the concern but I'm fine.'

'Maybe. Maybe being "fine" means drinking alone in a bar, I guess.' She teased.

He gulped the last of his drink down. As he stood up he realised he was starting to feel drunk. 'I can accept that.' He grinned. 'But let me tell you something I've learnt.'

She looked at him and crossed her arms.

He picked up his jacket from underneath the table. 'If you truly want to stand up for what you believe in then sometimes it means standing alone. The path to change is a lonely one.'

She frowned, a confused look on her face.

He picked up his jacket and walked out of the bar. It was a cold night out. He looked forward to the walk to clear his mind.

As he left the bar though he realised he no longer felt the same doubts he had minutes before. Something about saying it out loud seemed to reaffirm it to himself. He smiled and started the walk home.

He realised he could never go back to the bar, she had recognised him.

AOKI

As she smoked her cigarette she realised just how tired she was. Usually a cigarette would wake her up but she could feel herself falling asleep while sitting up in the police van. Despite that, however, she felt calm and in control. A patrol had walked around the apartment block looking for her assailant, but they had found nothing. She sat at the back of the police van while officers quietly looked around the scene. She was fortunate that they hadn't drawn a crowd.

A car pulled up and braked quickly. She saw Morgan get out and walk over to her in a hurry. He was almost running to her.

'Hey, are you ok?' He asked. He pulled up the blanket next to her and draped it over her shoulders. 'Here, keep this on. You need to stay warm.'

She nodded, but took the blanket off her straight away. 'I'm fine, I don't need it. Anyway, I got lucky.'

'What happened?' He was speaking quickly. She rarely saw him upset like this.

She shrugged. 'Someone else was headed there as well. They knew I was coming.'

'But how?' He shook his head. 'Only you and Bec knew you were going there. Here, put the blanket back on.'

'I don't need it.' She said softly, shaking her head. 'I have no idea, they must have heard us.'

He sighed. 'Maybe. Anyway, did you find what you needed?'

'I think so. I haven't had a chance to look at it yet.'

'Really?' He smiled excitedly. 'Can I have a look at it?'

'I want to check it out first. I don't know if anything will be on there.'

'Fair enough.' He frowned. 'Come on, you need to put the blanket over you, you've gotta be in shock.'

She felt a rush of blood. 'Jesus. Fuck, Morgan! I'm fine!' She shouted.

He frowned and looked down. A few officers passing by turned their heads briefly before continuing on.

She sighed. 'I'm warm enough as it is. I'm overheating at the moment with this fucking blanket.' Her voice was raised in frustration.

'Sure thing.'

'Everyone keeps telling me I'm in shock and I need to wear it, but I'm fine. I'm sick of sitting in this fucking van.' She blurted out. She felt herself getting more irritated.

'Ok then.' Morgan said softly. He looked away and exhaled deeply.

He stood there in silence and said nothing while she looked around the scene. The sun was beginning to come up and she was exhausted. She rubbed her eyes. She'd need coffee soon to make it home. The cigarettes would not keep her awake for much longer.

'Are you ok?' Morgan asked gently.

Aoki sighed and nodded. 'Yeah, I'm alright. I'm sorry. I'm just tired and sick of everyone making a fuss. I feel fine.'

'It's alright, I understand.' He frowned. 'But your hand is shaking.'

She looked down as she took a drag on her cigarette. It was true. She dropped the cigarette and stubbed it out, then rubbed her palms together and rubbed her face. 'Yeah, I don't know why. I think I'm just tired.'

He nodded. He always became so passive whenever she got angry. For whatever reason it usually made her more frustrated. This time it didn't.

ANDREA

Since her fight with Hank she'd spent every day with a twisting feeling inside her. She realised now how obsessed with him she'd become. She felt sick with embarrassment. She'd spent the day slumped over her desk, tortured constantly with a desire to message him. When she managed to fight the temptation, she felt better for a while, however, the thoughts would quickly come back, louder and stronger. She would feel weaker each time until she gave in, and then she would spend hours in a worse state of agony, checking her phone for a message from him.

Her heart was broken. Her every thought was a longing to have that love again, to have someone to talk to. Now that the love was gone, she longed again for the companionship she had with her husband. Yet it was only when she needed him that she realised how absent he was in her life. She realised how much his life was dominated by his work commitments and his time spent networking. She was completely alone and totally lost. She wanted to scream but had no energy. She wanted to cry but was not able to.

'Hey, Andrea do you have a moment?'

She turned to see Charlie looking at her with gentle eyes. *He must want to talk about the change in my demeanour at work.* 'Sure thing.'

'Maybe we could talk in one of the meeting rooms?'

She nodded and stood up, following Charlie as he walked to one of the far meeting rooms. She should have felt worried, she should have felt panicked that she was being disciplined. She had always been the hardest and most tenacious worker in the office. Instead she did not care. She felt dead inside.

When he entered the room he closed the door gently behind her. She sat down and looked at the floor. He sat down and cleared his throat.

'Look, I don't want you to feel like you're in trouble. You're not at all.' He said smiling. 'I just wanted to talk.'

She nodded, staring at the ground. 'Sure thing.'

He stretched and exhaled, trying to make himself comfortable. 'I just wanted to ask you if anything is wrong. It may be none of my business, but I'm just concerned.' He added gently.

She tried to smile but could not hide the sadness.

He nodded, encouraging her to talk.

'I'm sorry.' She said softly, running her hand through her hair. She wanted to hide the emotion from her face, but she felt like her mask of calm and confidence was cracking. 'I never wanted anything personal to impact on my work.'

'Hey, it's not like that.' He said slowly. 'To be honest, I had noticed a change.'

She felt a sinking feeling in her gut.

'And I was starting to get worried.' He spoke gently. 'You haven't seemed like yourself. I just wanted to talk.'

'Thank you, Charlie.' She exhaled deeply. She wondered how much to tell him. Thinking about it now she realised how much of a mess she was in. 'It's such a long story.'

'It's ok. I'm here to listen.' He smiled kindly. 'I don't know what is going on, but you can tell me. If you want to.'

'Where to start?' She shook her head, she laughed bitterly. 'I have just been feeling so,' she paused, searching for a word to cover all that she'd been feeling lately. 'Lost.'

He frowned. ‘In what way?’

She ran her fingers back through her hair slowly and cleared her throat. ‘I’m alone, Charlie.’ The words escaped from her.

He took a deep breath and narrowed his gaze.

She averted her gaze downwards. She would normally give that kind of honesty to someone she did not know well.

‘Are you talking about relationship issues? Or is this something else?’

‘I don’t know. It’s complicated.’ She said, sighing.

‘It’s ok, I can understand this is difficult for you.’ He said reassuringly.

She scratched behind her ears, avoiding his gaze. She could feel that he was looking directly at her, and felt uncomfortable. She felt put on the spot. However she couldn’t help but talk. It was the first time in a long time that she felt she could be honest with someone without worrying about losing something.

‘It’s ok, Andrea, you can be honest with me.’ He said gently.

She thought of the pain at how things had changed so much with Hank, how she had lost him. She thought of the way he used to feel about her, and about how that part of him was now closed off to him. He had once felt something so strong for her and now that was gone. All of a sudden the words came flooding out. ‘There have just been a lot of things happening lately, things at home.’

‘I can understand.’

‘I have just been needing something in my life, a connection with someone, some compassion.’

‘Of course.’

‘And, I mean, I felt like there were people in my life I could count on, who would always be there. It was only when I needed them that I realised they weren’t.’

‘That must have been so difficult.’ He said, a look of concern on his face.

‘I suppose it was, I hadn’t really considered it like that until just now.’

‘It’s ok, Andrea, you’re still figuring this out.’

‘I mean, I just feel betrayed.’

‘Betrayed?’

‘It takes so long to finally open yourself up to someone. They try so hard and for so long to tell you that you can trust them, how much they care about you.’

‘I know what you mean.’

‘And then, in one moment the way that they felt about you is gone. They just take it all away like it was nothing and. I don’t know, I feel like the ground is coming out from under me.’ As she said the words she felt as though a weight was taken off her and it was only when she *said* the words that she realised it was the truth. At the same moment, she suddenly realised how vulnerable she had made herself. She shook her head and straightened her sleeves. ‘I shouldn’t be talking about this with you. It’s not appropriate.’

‘Andrea,’ he smiled warmly. ‘Something is clearly on your mind, and we are going to be working closely together for a long time, I want you to feel comfortable here, like you can be honest about these things, when you’re having issues and so on.’

‘Thank you.’ She looked and smiled at him. She felt like her voice was catching her in her throat. ‘I greatly appreciate your support.’

'Don't worry about it. It's fine, but I don't think your issue is this other person.'

She looked up at him. 'No? What?' She was confused. 'What do you mean?'

'Look, maybe it isn't my place.' He sighed. 'But I can only be honest. You cannot control what other people will do, but you can control how much it affects you.'

She nodded. 'That's true. So you're saying I should be more careful?'

He smiled. 'Of course not, that's the nature of love. There's always a risk.'

She shook her head confused. 'So what are you saying?'

'Well, I think it all comes down to identity, how you define yourself. And I think that part of that is finding something you truly believe in, finding a cause you can dedicate yourself to.'

'Ok. How do you mean, though?' She couldn't understand what he was implying.

'I mean, if you find something you believe in and you work at that, you find real meaning in your life.' He said with a smile. 'And if you find that, then you might still get hurt, but it won't be as bad.'

She smiled. 'I hadn't considered it like that.'

'It's true, as well.'

'So you think you've found that in your life?'

'Yeah, definitely.' He said smiling. 'I work quite a fair bit with a Leukaemia group. Raising money, I donate every month, and I also volunteer for them on weekends.'

She squinted. 'Really, Charlie? I had no idea.'

‘Yeah, I’ve been involved with them for five years now. And also earlier as well, I suppose, since my diagnosis.’ He said with a frown.

‘Diagnosis?’

He nodded slowly. ‘I was diagnosed with Leukaemia a long time ago. I recovered, though I wasn’t expected to. Since then I have been extremely grateful for every moment that I get.’

‘That is so amazing, Charlie. I had no idea.’ She said with awe. It seemed like such a shock to her.

‘Well, I didn’t escape unscathed.’ He laughed, running his hand over his shiny bald head. ‘I’ve been bald ever since.’

She laughed. ‘Oh, Charlie, I admire your spirit.’

‘That’s just who I am.’ He said smiling.

She sighed. ‘That is such a crazy story, Charlie. You’ve been through so much. I can’t believe we have been talking about my problems in comparison.’ She shook her head bitterly, angry at herself.

‘Don’t be silly.’ He waved away the suggestion dismissively. ‘It was a long time ago, and I learnt a long time ago that you cannot compare your life to others. You never know what their journey is.’

‘You’re so right, Charlie.’ She said, forcing a smile. ‘I should think about that more often.’ She spoke emphatically, trying to sound genuine. She didn’t understand what he meant though.

‘We all get a little lost sometimes. Don’t be so hard on yourself.’

‘No, no, it’s true.’ She said shaking her head. She cleared her throat. ‘I really appreciate you talking to me, Charlie, it means a lot. I feel a lot better.’ She said, sincerely.

‘Of course, and to be honest.’ He leaned in closer. ‘I believe you’re incredibly capable.’

She took a deep breath. His words were affecting her more than she thought. ‘It has been a long time since anyone said that about me.’ She said quietly, rubbing her eyes and forehead. She shook her head ‘Not since Delpont?’

‘Come on, that can’t be true? You have such a strong career and you have achieved so much.’

She shook her head and smiled. ‘Don’t worry about it, it’s beside the point.’ She hoped he would drop the point. She did not want to talk to him about it.

‘No, I’m serious.’ He said encouragingly. ‘You’re an incredibly capable worker. I’ve seen some of your work on other projects and I know what you can do.’

She looked at him and smiled. ‘You’re kind, Charlie.’ She said softly.

‘Well, I mean it. Just don’t sell yourself short. I think you’re a superstar.’

She smiled and felt a wave of emotion wash over her. It was an unfamiliar feeling. ‘Thank you, Charlie.’

‘Sure thing, anytime.’ He said with a smile and laughed. ‘But I mean it doesn’t matter anyway.’

She frowned at him, confused. ‘What do you mean?’

He shrugged. ‘It doesn’t matter. Doesn’t matter what I think. It doesn’t matter what any of them out there think.’ He said with a calm voice.

‘How so?’ She asked, her gaze narrowed.

He looked at her, confused. ‘I can’t be the first person to tell you this?’

‘Tell me what?’

He shrugged again. When he opened his mouth to speak he spoke in a calm an easy-going manner. ‘What others think of you doesn’t matter. There is only one opinion that matters, and that is your own. How you see yourself. How you define yourself.’

‘Thank you, Charlie. That is true.’ She said with a forced smile, dismissively. She didn’t want to talk about that, and it didn’t feel true to her. She rose to her feet. ‘I really appreciate you taking the time to talk this through with me. It means a lot. You have been a great help.’

His eyes wrinkled as he smiled. ‘No problems, Andrea. You can talk to me any time.’

WILL

'I don't know why you wanted to come along today.' He wondered aloud.

Iz shrugged. 'I'm bored of looking for a place, it's such a hassle.'

He laughed. 'And you think this will be so exciting?'

'Oh, come on! Investigating some murder intrigue? Ooh la la, Mr Martec!' She joked. 'This whole thing sounds very sexy.'

He shook his head smiling. 'It'll be dull.' He said flatly.

'So who are we looking for, anyway?'

'I,' he corrected her. 'Am trying to find out who the person was the other day who followed Aoki.'

Iz scrunched her face. 'Doesn't she have a partner? Why isn't he doing this?'

Will sighed. *It's true*. 'He's got his work cut out at the moment. He's working a lot of those cases at the moment. I just offered to do this for him as a favour.'

'Fair enough. Next time I get a job maybe you could do some favours for me too' She suggested sarcastically.

He rolled his eyes.

'So, now you've moved from journalism into detective work?' She teased.

'Something like that.'

'Why don't you cut me in on that? We could open up that detective agency we talked about!'

He laughed. 'Sure thing. We would just end up investigating cheating spouses and infidelity.'

'Growl. You sure know how to talk dirty, Mr Martec.'

'What are you going to bring to the table?'

'I'm on surveillance, obviously! I'll be the tail. You know, follow the targets, get some evidence.' She said lifting her camera up.

'You're the photography expert, after all.'

'Fuck yeah! I mean check out how far this zooms.' She leant over to him as they walked down the street. She focused on a person in the distance and zoomed in. The person showed up as clear as if they were right in front of them.

'Are you serious? That is crazy.' He frowned.

'Yeah, I know. I definitely paid for it, though. Maybe you should be my first client.' She suggested teasingly.

'What do you mean?' He frowned.

'Following Amber around.'

He sighed.

'I'm sorry, but I don't trust her.' She said defensively. 'I don't want to see you get hurt.'

'It's ok, she isn't like that.'

'You don't know her, though. She could be seeing someone else.'

He shook his head. 'Don't say that.'

'Fine, but just be relaxed about everything with her, don't rush in, you know.'

He smiled. 'Sure thing, mum.'

She slapped his arm and laughed. ‘Shut up. What number is the building?’

‘62.’ He said pointing. ‘This one here.’

It was only as they were walking in realised he had been thinking of this place as a crime scene. He had forgotten it had once been Rebecca and Chris’ place. He had once come here to see friends. Now there was police tape everywhere. He thought of when Beck and him had met Aoki and Morgan here, and how much had happened since then. The door to the apartment was broken but the keys still worked. Inside it was evident the apartment had been searched by both the intruder and later the police. Neither had found anything. Aoki had gotten all the records first, and the intruder had been forced to flee before getting anything.

‘So what are we looking for?’

He leaned over the balcony and looked out to the parking lot. ‘Aoki said she saw someone leave here in a hurry the other night. They were riding a bike.’

‘She thinks there may have been footage of them?’

‘Yeah, she thinks there might be. It’s worth a try. She thinks she saw them around there, next to that pole with the sign on it.’ He said pointing. He opened the door and stepped out to the balcony, looking down the building like Aoki had told him to do.

‘Are we even allowed to be here?’ Isabelle said as she took a picture of the pole with the sign. .’

He nodded. ‘They searched already and found nothing. So they opened it back up. This is Rebecca’s place, anyway, and she gave me her keys.’

‘Alright, but why isn’t Aoki doing this?’

Will frowned. He felt the same, and didn’t know what he was doing. *I just want to help her out,* he thought, *she’s been through a lot lately.* He didn't want to tell Iz that though, but he felt obliged to defend Aoki. 'She's going through what she found on Bec's computer. She says she found something.'

'Cool. That is pretty promising.' She said flatly. He suspected that checking out the apartment bored her, but appreciated that she wanted to keep him company.

He squinted. 'I think I see something down by the entrance.'

The two descended the stairs in silence. Iz flicked through the photos on her camera and systematically deleted the photos she no longer wanted. Despite her creative and expressive side, he had noticed she became almost clinical and surgical when culling the photos she took.

At the base of the building they found the security office. The building superintendent had seemed intimidated of Isabelle, her looks and her tattoos. So she had decided to take the lead. She told how her bike had been stolen the other night, and that she had just noticed a camera outside. He had only been too happy to help.

The search through the footage was productive. Not only was the superintendent able to give them a shot of the rider fleeing the scene, but they also had the license number of his bike.

AOKI

Despite not leaving the house all day, she was exhausted. She debated whether to make herself another coffee. It was the only thing keeping her energy levels up. She was glad for the opportunity to be at home, after all the running around lately she only just realised how drained she was. After the run in at Rebecca's apartment the department had let her take a few days off. The official reason they had given was to take some time off following a stressful situation in the line of duty. However, she knew that she was in trouble. She had been following down a lead in her own time, without support and without informing anyone of where she was going. In truth she had been following a hunch that Rebecca might have something. She had not truly expected to find something. For any other detective something like this would not have been an issue, however it was not the first occurrence for Aoki. They had warned her that there were issues with taking work into personal time, and also visa versa.

Regardless, it had given her some time to go through all the information she had found on Rebecca's computer.

'Good to see you making the most of your time off.' Rick joked as he sat down on the other couch. He set his cup of tea down on the coffee table.

She smiled. 'I know. I just wanted to have a look through it again.'

'Because you can't stop thinking about it?'

She nodded.

He shook his head. 'If you keep that up, you'll send yourself insane. You can't keep working like that.'

She ran her hands through her hair. 'Yeah, I know.'

‘Why don’t you get out of the house today?’

‘And do what?’

He sighed. ‘I don’t know. You used to love going up to the Blue Mountains, why don’t you take a trip up there? Maybe I could come too, we could stay overnight?’

It was true. She used to love going up there. Her and Rick used to go up all the time on weekends, spending their days in cafes and second hand book shops. She could still remember the smell of the faded pages mixed with the aroma of the coffee. She frowned. ‘I can’t. I need to work on this.’ The idea of going was not possible while so much was happening with the case.

He shook his head and exhaled. ‘Fine, then.’

‘Are you mad?’

‘Do what you want Aoki.’ He sighed. He turned and started walking out of the room.

‘Where are you going?’

‘I’m going to read for a while.’ He said, not turning his head to look at her. He walked out and went into the bedroom.

She shook her head. He always read in the living room with her. She did not feel like fighting however, it would not change anything.

She went back to her computer and the incident reports. She had been scanning through them but it had been a much longer process than she thought.

There were reports of each instance that something had occurred which could lead to problems later on. They were worse than she had suspected. Traders had been reported for sabotaging each other’s personal lives to gain a promotion or get their bonus. Some of the damage included causing divorces, people to get arrested or in some cases people losing custody of their children. While the reports had been made, it did not seem like it was considered serious. Some notes even openly encouraged such cutthroat behaviour, that the company appreciated those who wanted to get themselves ahead no matter the cost. No disciplinary action had been taken against any of the individuals, and one had even received a hundred thousand dollar bonus the same week. The subjects became more lurid as she progressed; traders hiring prostitutes and charging it to the company, female interns being encouraged to sleep with clients or their superiors to get ahead, reckless use of cocaine and other drugs at workstations in full view of everyone, fistfights between employees during trading hours. Intern traders were encouraged to work until 6am and then come back to work at 8am, giving them enough time to go home and shower while the taxi waited outside. They had nicknamed it the *magic roundabout* routine.

As she went through one particularly large report caught her eye. It was one of the latest reports, from the last few weeks before the company was shut down. She opened it and started to read. It detailed how a trader named Anders had an outburst, after getting into an argument with another employee, Mikkel. He had lost his temper and had spoken out against the corruption and reckless profiteering of the company. The two had started yelling at each other as Mikkel dismissed what he was saying as media propaganda, people trying to throw stones at the company out of jealousy. It had stopped anyone on the floor from being able to work and had caused a scene. When confronted by his supervisor and told to keep quiet, Anders and then yelled out to the whole office that they were all complicit in the crimes of the company, he had yelled that there was a revolution coming and soon companies would have to pay for their crimes. Immediate action had been taken and he had been dragged out of the office by security, while he resisted and shouted about the crimes of Delpont. The report mentioned that his actions were not in line with the values of the firm and posed a risk to the long-term objectives of the organisation, and that drastic action needed to be taken given the *current challenges* faced by the company. The employee had been fired the next day without severance pay.

Aoki frowned and looked away from the screen. It struck her as bizarre that someone could be dismissed so quickly for something like that, considering that others had received only warnings for other things she considered much worse. She assumed that it had perhaps been used an excuse to fire someone who had been a problem for a while, but after searching his name through the reports she realised it was his first and only incident report. She rubbed her face and exhaled, she suspected there might be clues in his personnel file. The incident may have been used as an excuse to dismiss a poor performing employee. His full name was on the top of the report; Anders Sorensen.

It took her a while to find his employee profile. When the files had been transferred there were formatting changes, and all the file names had been messed up as a result. Spaces had been turned into underscores at times, and had been deleted entirely at other times. Eventually she found it in an unnamed folder.

She found his personal details inside; Danish born and raised, and studied Finance and Economics in Denmark. He had high results and received a scholarship for his study. He moved to the country when he began the graduate intake program with Delpont. He worked as a trader, and had excellent performance reviews. Despite being one of the youngest of the team he was highly intelligent and a high performer, and was identified as a top trader, although not in the same league as the *big three* traders. She did not know what the term referred to. There were notes in his profile that he had leadership potential and demonstrated attributes of becoming a key resource for the business. There was a photo of him in the report, although it was from around a decade ago. He was wearing a suit and seemed tall, and had short dark blonde hair slicked back and dark green eyes. She squinted, reflecting that he was quite handsome. It appeared to be a photo taken by the company; he was smiling and there was the city skyline visible through the large glass window behind him.

She exhaled. There was nothing written about him other than that. It seemed like almost overnight he had gone from being one of the best to a pariah. On the basis of that incident it seemed like an overreaction. It did not tell her much about who this person was, but she felt a sense of excitement while reading over the report. She had a gut feeling that she was on the right track.

She reached for her phone, but was unsure who to call. She wanted to talk to Andrea, to see if she knew who this person was. She wanted to speak to Will, to ask his opinion on the case. But there was one person she wanted to speak to first before she got her hopes up; her partner Morgan.

WILL

'Are you sure you want to come along?' He asked her as they drove along.

'Yeah, definitely!' Isabelle said, stretching in her seat. 'The only other thing I have to do at the moment is look for work. I need a break from it.'

'You should be doing that, though.' He said frowning.

'I know! I'm just so sick of handing out resumes and getting nothing but rejection.'

He sighed, remembering when he had done the same. 'I can understand that. What places have you been applying at?'

She shrugged. 'Anything that I can get; cafes, bars, supermarkets, clothes shops.'

'And you haven't heard anything yet?'

She shook her head. 'No one is looking for people at the moment.'

'I'm sorry, that *is* really difficult.' He said sympathetically. He felt sorry for his friend. She was a talented artist, and yet could not find even the most basic job.

They pulled up the car outside the station. Morgan was waiting out the front. He waved and smiled as they approached.

'This is the cop?'

'Yeah. This is Morgan.'

'I can see his receding hairline from here.' She frowned, disappointed.

Will laughed. It was true.

When she got out of the car though she was friendly as always. 'Hello! You must be Morgan!'

'I must be.' He teased, eyes twinkling.

Will tried to hide a smile. He could tell already that Iz was Morgan's type.

'You're Iz? Love the tattoo.' Morgan said as he gently touched the art on her shoulder with his fingertip.

She laughed. 'Thank you. Will told me a lot about you. He didn't mention that you were such a charmer.'

Morgan looked at her with a devilish grin. 'Well, maybe that is because I've never tried to hit on Will.'

Isabelle laughed and slapped his arm.

'Kids, kids.' Will grinned and shook his head. 'We have work to do.'

'Oh, speaking of,' Morgan said, his smile dropping. 'I just got a call from Aoki, did she reach you yet?'

'No, not yet. What is it?'

'She thinks she might have figured out who this killer is.'

'What?!' He exclaimed, cutting him off. 'Who is it?'

He shrugged. 'I don't know how sure she is yet. We haven't checked it out. But his name is Anders, he was a trader at Delpont.'

Will frowned, perplexed. 'A trader?'

'Yeah, he was apparently one of the best.'

'Really? That doesn't make sense.'

‘How so?’

Will shook his head. He couldn’t explain it properly.

‘I know what you mean.’ Iz said, her eyes narrowed. ‘Someone from that world, living the life, guys like that who are living that lifestyle of excess. What would make some guy like that turn on his own kind?’

‘Yeah, that’s what I was thinking.’ Will studied his friend. He was glad to have someone so close, sometimes she could articulate things that he was thinking.

‘That’s true.’ Morgan said scratching his stubble. A cheeky smile formed on his face. ‘Sexy and smart? I can see why Will was keeping you away from me.’

‘You charmer.’ Iz said with a laugh.

‘Anyway, I will talk with Aoki about it later. She sounded pretty sure on the phone, so I’m sure there is a good reason for it. Oh, sorry, I forgot about the footage.’

‘Yeah, right.’ Will said, remembering. He pulled the disc the security office had burned him from his bag. ‘I can’t believe they still put these on CD.’

Morgan shrugged. ‘Yeah, I know. Most of the systems are still outdated. They work off DVD players, connected to computer systems from ten years ago. Having said that though, burning to CD is still a secure option. Did you get a printout, as well?’

‘Nah, their office didn’t have a printer. Even if they did I don’t think their security would have known how to use it.’ Will said, shaking his head.

Morgan chuckled loudly. ‘They never do, most of the times guys like that at security offices and banks have no clues how to use their own CCTV equipment.’

'Seriously? Yeah they had to get a technician in to download the footage for us.'

'That is what usually happens.' Morgan exhaled deeply, smiling.

'That's insane, but I wrote down the license details here.' He said, passing the number to Morgan.

Morgan squinted as he looked at the number. 'Hmm, ok then. I'll have to get the CD analysed by our tech team before I can see if there is anything else in the footage. But I will get the plate run through our system today.'

'Sure thing.' Will zipped up his jacket to leave. 'If you get anything let me know.'

'Hey, before you leave.' He said, stopping him. 'Can you help me with something?'

'Yeah, what is it?'

'I was thinking we should draw up a list of likely targets. Maybe we can get some kind of idea of who he's going after next. Given what you know about the company I figured you could help.'

'Sure thing.' Will nodded. He turned to Iz. 'You ok with hanging around here for a bit?'

'Fine with me! I need to get a coffee, though.' She said, looking up and down the street for a place to go to.

'Just send us a message when you get back and we'll let you inside.' Morgan said.

Iz laughed. 'No offence, but I've got no desire to voluntarily go into a police station.'

'Fair enough.' He said smiling. 'We will try not to be too long.'

The two men turned and walked inside as Iz walked off to a café. Morgan casually showed his identification at the desk to let them in. The way he did it seemed so natural. Will wondered if he would ever have the same easy confidence if he had been a detective.

‘She’s a personality.’ Morgan said, a wry smile on his face.

‘Iz? Yeah she’s a character. She’s been a friend for a long time.’

‘You’re a funny pair.’

‘How so?’

He shrugged. ‘I don’t mean this in a bad way but she seems pretty cool, she seems like a rebel and an artist.’

Will smirked. ‘And I’m straight edged?’

‘A little.’ He said gently.

Will shook his head. ‘I guess it’s true. I studied business subjects, I almost ended up working in that world.’

‘Oh, yeah?’

He nodded. ‘I went in a pretty different direction to what I thought I would.’

‘Do you regret it?’

‘No, not at all, that world wasn’t what I thought it would be. And eventually I found people who thought the same as me. Like Iz.’

‘So you’re more similar than it seems?’

‘We feel the same way about issues like that. We actually have pretty similar personalities as well.’

‘Huh. Wouldn’t have pictured that. It’s this door here.’ He gestured. He held open the door as Will walked inside. The room was pitch black. Morgan turned on the lights but they just flickered. ‘Fuck! This always happens.’

Will walked over to a whiteboard that was set up across the room. There were pages pinned on it. As he walked over the lights suddenly flicked on.

‘Finally. Make yourself comfortable.’ Morgan said, hanging up his jacket.

Will took a seat just in front of the whiteboard. There were a few random articles on there about the case. Morgan proceeded to clear them off and pull out a folder full of paper.

‘How did you want to do this?’ Will asked.

‘Just hang on to this for the moment.’ He replied, handing him a printout. ‘It’s the organisational chart we worked on together. I’ll write it up on the board.’

‘Ok.’

‘The black marker is for the positions in the company, the blue marker is for who had that job, and the red,’ He said, holding up the red marker. ‘Red is for the people the vigilante has killed.’

‘Sure thing. Alright, well it starts off with the CEO. It was Paul McDermott, but it passed to Marcus Docker shortly before the end. How do you want to do this? There were a lot of moves just before the end.’

‘Right.’ He said, as he drew it up. ‘Maybe I’ll put both down under each title, and an arrow showing who moved from which position’. He wrote the names in a box with blue marker.

‘Alright. The next level down is Chief Operating Officer. This was held by Marcus Docker, and went to Andy Ling, but he died while on bail.’

‘Alright, I’ll put that in too.’

‘And underneath that, all these five positions report to the COO.’

‘The what?’ Morgan turned around and asked.

‘The COO, chief operating officer.’

‘Oh ok.’

‘The first one is Chief Financial Officer; Lew Noble. Then there is the Chief Accounting Officer; this was Andrea Beaufort, but it went to Kristen Worthington. Then there is the Head of Investor Relations; Kelvin Anderson. Head of Human Resources; Murray White. Lastly the CEO of Delpont Property,’

‘There already is a CEO?’ Morgan cut him off.

‘That’s the CEO of the whole company. This guy is the CEO of the property division.’

Morgan sighed and slumped against the whiteboard. ‘These fucking titles.’ He said softly. ‘It’s so overly confusing. It’s like they just give themselves these fancy titles that don’t have any meaning.’

Will laughed. ‘Anyway, CEO of Delpont Property; Michael Blake.’

‘Fine.’ He said irritated. ‘Done. Now the first person killed was Kelvin Anderson.’ He said as he used to red marker to cross out his name. Next to the cross he wrote a small number one. ‘Then Marcus Docker.’ He said as he did the same for the second name.

‘Yeah, but then the third person to die was Taylor Sheeran. He doesn’t fit within that structure.’

‘Fuck, yeah, true. How will we do this?’

‘Maybe group all of those people together under Delpont. Then the people from Azure just above that.’

‘I guess, it makes sense.’ He said as he drew up the next level. ‘Who were the people from Azure again?’

‘Firstly, Taylor Sheeran. There was also Ronald Oakly, Darren Orr, and ah, I don’t know how you want to write in the last guy?’

‘The guy without a name?’

‘Yeah, the one who carries around the book.’

‘The grandfather type yeah?’

‘Yeah, and the book is orange.’

‘Fine.’ He said as he scribbled on the board. ‘The man with the orange book’. At least until we figure out a name.’

‘Alright then, the next person to be killed was Darren Orr.’

‘Fuck, he’s going for the heads of this snake.’ Morgan swore as he crossed out the name. ‘Seems like he changed strategy right?’

‘I guess so,’ Will replied tentatively, not wanting to commit on an answer. He knew nothing about criminal strategy and didn’t want to suggest something that could be wrong. He wondered how Morgan could be so lax about it. ‘Maybe don’t write anything down about that yet. We can look at that later.’

‘Yeah, fine. Now in terms of which of these guys is behind bars, I know Noble is still serving maybe a decade at least.’ Morgan wrote down *jailed* next to Noble’s name with a blue marker.

‘There were two primary traders who received jail sentences as well.’

‘I remember that “Shark” guy escaped jail time, what was his real name.’ He muttered to himself.

‘Yeah, you’re right. His name was Andrew Hunter.’ He answered, exhaling. The trial had been a big story at the time.

‘Right. I know about him. I can look up the other two if you don’t have it written down?’

‘No, it’s fine. They’re Warren Francis and Steve Socek.’ He remembered the names from his research, when he had found the message from the serial killer. He thought back on the realisation that his theory was being used as a justification for murder. There was a madman out there who could be killing people because of something he had written. He should feel guilty about his role. Instead he could only think of the crimes of these men that went unpunished, or at least under-punished. 'Both traders are in jail now. They got a few decades behind bars. I don't think anyone is going to be targeting them.'

'Alright so, would it be the same thing with Lew Noble then?'

Will shrugged. 'As far as I know, he's going to be behind bars for at least a few decades.'

'I will forget about him, then. I doubt our guy wants to target him. So Shark is still a free man?'

'As far as I know. There was a news story a few years ago about how he was working as a trader on Wall Street.'

'Wall Street?' Morgan laughed. 'That's hilarious. They must be loving him.'

'I don't know what he's doing now.'

'Alright, then. I will write these guys in the chart.'

'They were reporting to Lew Noble.' Will said, scanning the notes. 'So it might be best to put them in underneath him.'

Morgan wrote their names in and put *jailed* next to Francis and Sosek. 'Done, anyone else?'

'Give me a second.' He frowned as he flipped through the pages of notes. It was messy. Morgan had taken detailed notes and his research was good, but he had not organised any of it. The pages had been put in randomly, and there was no order to it. It was hard for him to find what he was looking for. 'It says here that Kristen Worthington was arrested.'

'The HR person?'

He nodded. 'Not sure why, but she didn't go to jail. She was fined and did community service.'

'Alright then.' He scoffed, shaking his head. 'Any others?'

'Looks like it's the same deal with Michael Blake; he was arrested but never jailed.'

Morgan shook his head. 'Really? Doesn't seem the way I remember it. I remember there were lots of arrests.'

'Yeah arrests, they were found not guilty though and not sent to jail.'

'What the hell? How does that work?' He asked incredulously. There was bitterness in his voice.

'This company was huge, a lot of people worked there. Most of them only knew a little bit.'

'These crimes are such a mess.' Morgan sighed, rubbing his temple. 'In the murder cases I work it's either you find the person who did it or you don't. People either are guilty and they committed the crime or they're innocent and they had no involvement.' Morgan was quiet for a moment, staring at the board. 'It seems like there are a few people this guy is likely to target. I mean Paul McDermott is the most likely target. I have no idea how he isn't in jail already.'

'True. Assuming this guy is targeting rich criminals, it's likely he's angry at Paul as well. And I mean any of those other guys behind the scenes would be likely targets too.'

'Oakly, Orr, the grandfather guy?'

'Maybe.' Will shrugged. 'He may even know who that guy is.'

'Who else?'

Will frowned. 'I think Andrea Beaufort is a likely target, she seems to have gotten out of it unscathed. Andrew Hunter, definitely. Assuming this guy can get to New York. And then Kristen Worthington and Murray White are also possible targets.'

'I guess so. You don't think he would target anyone less senior?'

'He hasn't yet.'

'Alright, well maybe it's best we limit it to those people then?'

'True.' Will felt uncomfortable that Morgan was asking him these questions. He didn't know how to think like a criminal.

Morgan shook his head. 'These people in the company. I mean how do they get to the point where they're committing these crimes. Do you think they just don't think about it?'

Will sighed. 'I think they just believe that everyone else is doing it. I think they believe all the other companies are doing the same thing, and that everyone knows about it. They may think it's illegal, they may think what they're doing is wrong. But I don't think it makes a difference. Everywhere they look it's encouraged. They create false profits and their company looks better. The share price goes up. Everyone wants them. The more they cheat and lie the better the company does. And if they believe that, then it's all, ok.'

Morgan frowned. He exhaled. 'Maybe. I think everyone makes an individual choice though.'

Will crossed his arms. 'I don't think the issue is the people.'

'That's a cop out.' Morgan scoffed. 'You can't just say the people aren't to blame.'

'I think it goes beyond that. I don't think you can blame most of these individuals. Personally, I think that the idea of the corporation is inherently amoral.'

'Companies are evil?'

'Not evil. But not good either.'

‘So, you mean, amoral in the sense of like, being impartial.’

‘I guess. You have a situation where you cannot blame individuals. One way or another they’re amoral. They exist only to profit.’

‘I don’t know.’ Morgan shrugged. ‘If that isn’t evil then what is?’

‘Well, a company isn’t a person, so it can’t be either good or evil.’

‘In my line of work there is nothing that isn’t good or evil. Maybe it’s a cultural issue or something. But saying things like that are an excuse.’

‘For what?’ Will frowned.

‘Any crime is the same, Will. Imagine these big companies were a gang, a mafia or something. Would you say that any member of that gang is guilty?’

‘I suppose, but they knew about it.’

‘Pfft,’ Morgan scoffed dismissively. ‘Fuck that. It’s naïve to think these guys don’t know what they’re doing. Just because a crime is organised doesn’t mean those at the bottom are powerless. A bottom level thug is just as guilty as the mob boss. Every person makes a decision whether they want to work for the gang or not. They make their own individual decision. Everyone that goes along with that decision is an enabler. They’re just as guilty.’

Will looked back at the board and the list of names. He considered what Morgan had said, and the decisions each of those people had made. He did not know which idea worried him more; that each knew the crimes they were committing but were powerless to stop it, or that they were not bothered by the cost because the reward was so substantial.

ANDREA

She exhaled slowly, feeling relaxed. She had made real headway with her work. After a rough period she finally felt like she was back in control of her life. She saved and closed what she had been working on. Another thing she could tick off her *to-do* list. It had only been when she focused her attention on her workload that she realised how far she had let it slide. It was at breaking point. It had been a moment of panic for her, and usually it would have never happened. She was always in control, always the high achiever. It was so out of character for her. After a few frenetic twelve-hour workdays she had managed to get through weeks of neglected work. It had been stressful though. Taking a deep breath, it was only then she realised just how stressed she had been. Surviving on a few hours sleep a night, she had needed coffee to get through the neglected workload. While it allowed her to work faster than usual, it had taken a toll. She felt like her heart had been pumping in double time. The time had passed in a frantic blur. She felt like the armpits of her blouse had been sweaty whenever she was at work. Her hair had been messed up because she had been running her fingers through it nervously as she got through her work. She had felt gross and the pressure had left her numb. It reminded her of the days at Delpont, and at university before that.

Still, she had gotten through the work, and could start to relax because there was nothing to do. She was not going to let that happen again.

She got up to take a break. Stretching and taking a deep breath, her heartbeat started to slow down. Already she felt more relaxed, satisfied in the knowledge she had gotten through her entire workload. There was something about getting through everything that always reminded her of the moment she had handed in her final assignment at uni. Everything before that had been chaotic and stressful, at that moment she had been so relieved at first.

Afterwards though she had struggled without anything to do, she had not known what to do with herself if not work. It had been who she was.

She walked to the coffee room. She needed to have a meal, and drink something other than coffee. It was almost 4pm, most people were on their way out of the office, especially since it was a Friday. The coffee room was empty, and was quiet save for the sound of news on the TV. They were running an article that one of the major Wall Street banks had been fined just over ten billion for fraud charges related to mortgage backed securities leading to the financial crisis. Andrea sighed. The reporter was heralding it as a win, but she knew it was almost nothing for those companies. Due to those fraudulent deals the company would have made at least double the fine, and that was in the years after the crisis, let alone what they had made during the heyday of the fraud before being caught in 2008.

As she pulled out ingredients for a sandwich from the fridge, Charlie strutted into the room. His collar was unbuttoned and he wasn't wearing a tie. There was a sparkle in his dark brown eyes, he was very charming when he was in a good mood.

'Hey, Charlie.' She said smiling.

'How are you doing superstar?' He asked with a big smile. He was always cheery on a Friday. It was infectious. 'Hey, I saw you smashed through that workload! Good work!'

She chuckled. 'Many thanks.'

'Maybe you might even be able to inspire some of these typical government drones to finally do some work, hey?' He joked.

She laughed. 'Very funny.'

'Nah, I'm half serious, though.' He said sighing. 'You're a breath of fresh air around here. Most people are just content to come in and kill time, waiting for payday. It's nice to see someone so driven.'

‘Thank you.’ She smiled, genuinely touched. ‘You’re too kind.’

‘Ah, don’t mention it. But I hope you’re getting ready to leave the office now! I don’t want you working late!’ He teased.

‘Yeah, I only just realised how late it is. Today went past quickly.’

‘Well it’s almost five, I won’t tell anyone if you want to skip out before then.’

‘That’s nice of you, I might just check a few things before I do. Are you on your way out now?’

‘Absolutely.’ He straightened his collar and his sleeves. ‘I have a date tonight.’

‘Ooh nice! Who is the lucky lady?’ She said with a smile.

‘Ah, a friend set us up. I’m taking her salsa dancing.’

‘You can dance?’ She asked, eyebrow raised.

‘Oh, absolutely! I’ve been dancing for years!’

‘Really?’

‘Hey, don’t sound so surprised. I have some serious dance moves.’ He said with a straight face, imitating some of his moves through the staff room.

She laughed. ‘Very good moves, Charlie. I’m sure the lady will be swept off her feet then.’

‘Oh!’ He exclaimed, feigning offense. ‘I’m not entirely sure I like your tone!’

She threw back her head and laughed.

‘Anyway, I should probably head down to the bar! I wouldn’t want to be late.’

‘Sure thing. I hope it’s a fun night!’

‘Thanks.’ He said with a big smile, starting to walk out of the office. He turned back quickly. ‘Oh! There was something I wanted to talk to you about!’

‘Oh!’ She said surprised. ‘Anything wrong?’

‘No, no, nothing like that.’ He said, waving his hands dismissively. ‘Just needed to talk about something.’

She frowned.

‘It’s nothing bad!’ He laughed, still backing out of the room. ‘I promise. I’m in a bit of a rush now, is it alright if I call you later though?’

‘Yeah, sure thing.’ She replied, confused. She couldn’t imagine what he could need to talk to her about. But she believed his word that it wasn’t anything serious. ‘That’s fine with me. I’ll have my cell on me.’

‘Alright, then.’ He said, almost out of the room. It seemed like he was in a hurry. ‘Sorry for not being able to talk about it now, I’m in a bit of a hurry! I’ll call you later though!’

‘Sure thing, Charlie! Talk later, and have fun!’ She called out, as he had already left the office.

‘See you!’ She heard back from the lift lobby.

She laughed. He was kind, but an odd man sometimes.

It was a relief to be able to leave early. It had been a productive day. Stressful, but productive. Having gotten through it she was completely relaxed. She sighed, already feeling quite relaxed by the prospect of the weekend. She felt confident again for the first time in a long while. She felt like her normal self.

She felt the impulse to get in touch with Hank. She knew she probably shouldn't, but felt like things would be fine now, she felt like herself again. She sent him a message.

A moment after she sent it, she could see that he had read it. She smiled, waiting for him to reply.

As she waited longer and longer, she became increasingly anxious. As she left the office, she checked again to see whether there was a reply. Nothing.

When she walked out of the building, she felt like a nervous wreck. All of the confidence she had felt shortly before was gone.

AOKI

'Have you moved since I left?' Morgan said as he walked back into the office. He was wearing a t-shirt and jeans, his gym bag slung around his shoulder. The t-shirt was half a size too small for him, and was tight around his waist. 'It's the weekend Aoki! They don't pay us to be here now.'

'I guess I haven't. How come you came in then?'

'That's different. The gym here is better than the one in my neighbourhood.'

She laughed. 'How long were you at the gym?'

He shrugged. 'About an hour. Here! Check this out!' He said, flinging a newspaper at her desk.

It took her by surprise. She lifted her arms to shield herself and squealed.

He laughed. 'It's a newspaper, Aoki.' He laughed, teasing her. 'How will those cat like reflexes be when it's bullets flying at you and not newspapers?'

'Very funny.' She glared at him, fuming. 'What am I looking at?'

'Underneath the top article, there's a big story about Delpont.'

'Really?' She asked, surprised. 'People are talking about it again?'

'Yeah, pretty much. It's basically all about the company, and how people are targeting the company.'

She frowned, flicking through it. It was a pretty comprehensive history of the company. Some of the details were wrong though. She smirked. 'Did you see this? It says that Paul McDermott was CEO when the company went under.'

He laughed. 'There are a few other errors. The journalist basically argues that McDermott was beyond the whole thing, and that he should have gone to jail'.

She laughed.

He shrugged. 'Other than that it's a good article. Anyway, this is what I wanted you to check out.' He said pointing. 'Look at this.'

She squinted, reading. Then she gasped. 'Are you serious? *The case is being investigated by detectives Aoki Sun and Moncan Kerr*. Holy fuck!' She gasped, covering her mouth.

He laughed. 'I reckon, right? We're famous.' He laughed. 'Even though the bastards spelt my name wrong.'

'That's pretty good.' She said hesitantly, reading. The idea was more intimidating than exciting. 'Moncan is almost an improvement, though.' She teased.

'Shut it.' He grimaced. 'Still haven't found anything on that Norwegian guy?'

She sighed. 'Anders, and he's Danish. No, nothing on the system.' She said absently, staring at the screen. She was scrolling with one hand, and resting her chin on the other hand. 'Come have a look.'

He sighed.

'Come on, Morgan! I need your help.' She pleaded.

'No, you don't. This can wait until Monday.' He said flatly.

'Please? Just a favour.'

He groaned and started walking over. 'Fine.'

'Thank you.'

‘Whatever.’ He said exasperated. He dropped his bag on the ground and got comfortable at her desk. He peered over her shoulder at the screen. ‘What am I looking at?’

She smiled. Sometimes he acted like such a child when people asked him for things. ‘Have a look at this. Up until about ten years ago I can find everything; home address, credit card details, bank account details. Then he gets fired from Delpont, and look at this.’

He looked closer to read. ‘What is this?’

‘I got in touch with his bank, they sent this back to me yesterday. Apparently he closed his bank account five years ago and withdrew all his money’.

‘It happens.’

‘But look,’ She pointed. ‘I did a search and haven’t been able to find anything set up in his name since.’

He frowned. ‘Maybe you’re right. That’s very suspicious. Sure he’s not dead?’

She shook her head. ‘I searched births, deaths and marriages. Absolutely nothing.’

‘Maybe he left the country?’

‘I checked immigration. He hasn’t left the country in six years. He has an electronic passport as well.’

‘So it would register whenever goes out through customs and immigrations?’ He asked.

‘Yeah, exactly.’

He leaned back and crossed his arms. ‘Alright, I’m interested.’

‘I know right?!’ She said excitedly, turning briefly to look at him. ‘I knew there was something to it.’

‘What happened with his apartment?’

‘He was out of there like a month after being fired from Delpont. It was a pretty expensive place so it’s natural I guess. It had harbour views, security in the lobby, a pool and a gym.’

He scoffed. ‘Hard life.’

‘Anyway, it has changed hands a few times since as well, so that is a dead end.’

‘Right.’ He paused, scratching his stubble. ‘Hmm what else then?’

‘He had a personal email address when he was at Delpont, but it hasn’t been used in five years. I can’t find any current numbers for him either, he last had a mobile contract which lapsed five years ago’.

‘He stopped paying?’

‘Yeah. It was closed pretty quickly. The number has been disconnected for years.’

‘Fuck.’ Morgan said softly. He leaned back, putting his hands on his head. There was a moment of silence. ‘Fuck. Fuck. Fuck. Alright, I think there is something here. Five years ago he went completely off the grid.’ He shook his head, his eyes narrowed. ‘He’s either dead or hiding’.

‘I think he’s involved. Somehow. I have a feeling.’

‘I think you’re right. It’s pretty exciting stuff. But,’ He slumped his bag around his shoulder and sighed. ‘It can wait until Monday!’

‘Are you serious? You don’t want to do this now?’

‘Fuck, Aoki! Of course not! It’s the weekend.’ He exclaimed in disbelief.

'Aren't you interested in this, though?'

'Of course. But I need to get away from work on the weekend. You can't keep staying late and working weekends. It'll do your head in!'

'This is different though, Morgan. This is a huge case'.

'Yeah I know, and I remember you didn't even want to get involved in it at the beginning.' He teased.

She frowned. It was true. 'I guess I hadn't thought about that for a while. But yeah, I was. I was scared at how much attention there was.'

'And now?'

She shook her head. 'I don't know. I'm beyond caring about that now.'

He nodded. 'It doesn't bother you anymore?'

'It does. It always will I guess. I'm still scared of screwing it up.'

'Then why do it?'

She turned to look at him. She squinted, trying to read his face. 'Because I have to know who this person is. I have to find out why he's doing this.'

He grinned. 'That's cool. I like that.'

'So you'll stay and help me?'

'Hell no.' He laughed. 'But I can understand why you're doing it.'

She sighed. 'Fine. Can you at least give me what you found on the license plate?'

'I didn't get the identification sent back to me yet.'

‘When did you last check?’

‘Yesterday.’ He said, scratching his head.

She looked at him expectantly, waiting.

‘I’m not going to check again!’ He said, adjusting his bag. He looked eager to leave.

‘Oh! Come on! It will be so quick.’

He groaned and rolled his head back. ‘Jesus, Aoki! Can’t it wait?!’

‘Morgan.’ She locked eyes with him. ‘What if we can find out something because of it? And what if someone dies in the meantime?’

He groaned again, louder. He sighed and rubbed his face. ‘Fine!’

She smiled. ‘I really appreciate it.’

‘Yeah, yeah, yeah. Sure thing.’ He was talking quickly. ‘Really quickly, though!’

‘Of course.’

‘I mean it!’ He said, walking briskly to his desk. He was clearly irritated. He stood over it while he logged onto his computer. ‘I’m not staying. I’m not even taking my bag off.’

‘Fine with me.’ She said, trying to hide a smile.

He was quiet for a minute as he went through his emails and messages. ‘Yeah, ok I found it. Happy?’

‘Yes.’ She said with a laugh. ‘Thank you, Morgan!’

‘Don’t mention, huh.’ He exclaimed. There was a moment of silence while he read his screen.

‘What is it?’ She asked, concerned.

‘The guy on the bike, his name is Luke Wade’.

‘Ok, sure thing.’ She felt her stomach tighten. *Something’s wrong*. She got up and walked over to have a look at his screen. There was a photo of Luke on the screen: Short dark blonde hair and his dark green eyes. His skin was tanned.

‘Aoki.’ He turned to her slowly. There was a worried look in his eyes. He spoke in a defeated voice. ‘Aoki, this guy is a cop.’

Her eyes widened. She opened her mouth to speak, but could not think of anything to say.

He shook his head, looking out the window. His brow was furrowed. He looked worried. ‘I guess I’m going to be here for a while.’

LUKE

He stopped his bike just outside the old building. He had no idea why they wanted to meet here. It used to be an office or a factory, now it was just a run down dump. It was so far from any of the other meeting points.

He left his helmet with the bike and headed inside. There was no one around to steal it. He walked into the dark building, stepping over a door that had fallen down, stepping past to avoid a light that was hanging down. The building was falling apart. There was graffiti everywhere. There were signs that homeless people had been living in it. It was definitely a dump.

He turned the corner and opened the door. The three old white men were waiting inside. They all wore expensive suits, hair cropped tightly.

'Wade.' The oldest guy said, with a deceptively kind smile. Always acting like a gentleman, though Luke knew that his gentle grandfather appearance was deceptive. 'Thank you for meeting us on such short notice.'

'I'm just following orders.' He said, dismissively. 'What do you want?'

'We've got a problem.'

'No. *He* has got a problem!' Oakly said nervously, pointing an accusatory finger at him. His hair was thin and grey, and he was so thin he looked like a bag of bones. This one could never handle stress.

'What is he talking about?' He asked flatly. He didn't have time for these old men right now.

Paul sighed. 'Wade, the police have put out an arrest notice for you.'

He squinted. He was in trouble. ‘Ok.’

‘Ok?! Is that all you have to say?! You’ve been caught, you fucking moron!’ Oakly tittered. His hands were shaking. He was probably on drugs again.

‘I haven’t been caught yet.’ He replied coolly. ‘I need you to calm down right now, Oakly.’

‘He’s using my name!’ The old man looked around at the different faces. He seem panicked. ‘Why is he using our names?! He’s wearing a wire!’

Luke smirked.

‘Ronald, calm down.’ Paul said slowly. ‘He’s not wearing a wire. If they want to arrest him then he’s not going to be able to make a deal. He’s too far complicit’. Luke liked working with Paul. He always had a cool head. ‘Isn’t that right, Luke?’

‘Exactly. And they would never have let me go. How did you hear about it?’

‘Detective Sun called Mr Martec some time earlier, informing him of the development.’ The old man stated clamly.

He nodded. ‘How did they find out?’

‘The crime scene at Ms Fulton’s apartment. The camera got footage of you arriving and leaving, and also a clip of your face.’ Paul said. ‘They got the license plate of your bike.’

‘You fucking idiot!!’ Oakly squealed. He always threw tantrums like this. Rumour had it that his two spoilt grandchildren were even worse. ‘Why weren’t you using the bike we gave you?!’

The old man with the orange book smiled. ‘While I disagree with his outburst, Mr Oakly has a valid point. We provided you with a motorbike with an unregistered plate.’

‘That one is on you guys. I just follow your orders. You called me when I was out; I didn’t have time to change bikes, you said it was an urgent matter so I went as soon as possible.’ He shrugged. ‘I did what you wanted.’

The old man smiled, his eyes wrinkled. ‘It would appear Mr Wade has the right of it.’

‘I gotta ask you something. You’re tapping a police officer’s phone?’ Luke asked. ‘Even for you that seems beyond possible.’

‘Not Ms Sun’s phone, no.’ The old man said with a smile. ‘But Mr Martec was quite easy. He has a smart phone. Several of the apps on it are from companies we have deals with. We’ve been monitoring his calls for some time.’

‘That’s how you got the heads up about Collins?’

Paul nodded, a frown on his face. ‘Not that I thought it was a good idea.’

Luke smirked. ‘I don’t even know why you told me that we didn’t need to kill him, if you were going to do it yourself.’

Paul shot him a look. There was malice in his eyes. It seemed out of character for him.

‘Yes, Paul.’ The old man said with a curious smile. ‘I am interested in that, as well. Why tell young master Wade the kill was not required, and then proceed to handle the matter yourself?’

‘Something else arose. Time was a factor.’ Paul said flatly, looking down.

‘But you personally argued that we didn’t need to kill Collins?’ The old man queried curiously.

Luke frowned. He hadn’t known that.

‘I didn’t agree with it.’ Paul ran his hands through his thin greying hair. He looked older than his years. There was a sad look in his eyes. 'I may not have agreed with it. But if it needed to be done, then we needed to act fast.'

Something about it didn't seem right to Luke. But he was not going to force the matter in front of the others.

'And as for the blue disc?' The old man asked. 'Mr Wade recovered it when carrying out the kill on your rogue man Malceski. I trust there are no issues with the security on the disc?'

'That is the only copy besides the original.' Paul replied coldly. 'How Collins was able to get a copy of it is beyond me'.

'I am, however, hearing conflicting stories; some refer to the disc as blue, others refer to it as orange. Do you know anything about this, Mr McDermott?'

Paul shook his head sadly. 'I have no idea.'

'What I am interested in, is why you ordered Malceski to kill Collins, only to have your loyal security man go straight to the police? He had been with you for how long?'

'Almost two decades.'

'And he just freaks out and tries to cooperate with the cops after one tiny kill?' Oakly said, panicking. His voice was shrill. 'It doesn't make sense.'

Luke squinted. It didn't.

Paul shot an angry look at the old man. 'It doesn't matter. It's done. Collins is dead.'

There was a tense moment of silence. The two men who once made so many decisions together were now stuck in a standoff.

'Oi, I have to ask. Does Will know is phone is being tapped yet?' Luke asked, trying to change the subject so they could get through this as quick as possible.

‘Not yet. Though, I’m sure once you disappear they might.’ Paul replied.

‘Thanks for the heads up.’ Luke replied.

The three old men exchanged a look between each other. ‘You aren’t concerned about us?’

He shrugged. ‘I guess you probably want to kill me. It would keep me from talking.’

Oakly nearly fainted. Luke liked him the least.

‘It had crossed our minds.’ Paul stated.

‘But you guys know as well as I do that I’m more valuable to you alive than dead, even if I’m not a cop anymore.’

‘How do you know that?’ The old man asked.

‘As soon as they found out I was involved, my life as a cop ended. My life as Luke Wade is no longer relevant. Now I’ve ended up in this mess with the police. Like you said, I’m too complicit to turn informant.’ He scratched his nose. ‘Still, you need agents to gather intel, and I know the situation. My skills and knowledge are still an asset to you.’

‘I assure you, Mr Wade, an associate of ours will ensure the media aspect is maintained.’ The old man stated calmly. ‘He is an influential stakeholder, and will do his utmost to minimise exposure of your identity. Rest assured, the situation will be contained. The police aspect however; we hold less control over.’

‘I’d expect as much.’ He replied, disinterested.

‘Wade, you know as well as we do that a new identity will be provided to you.’ Paul said.

‘Yeah, I know. You got it ready for me now?’

‘We require one more thing of you before you leave with a new identity.’ The old man smiled. ‘We require that you clean up this mess.’

Luke frowned. He was quiet for a moment considering. ‘Fine.’

They all looked at each other.

‘That’s all you have to say?’ Paul asked. He sounded a little surprised.

Luke shrugged. ‘Whatever. I don’t really care, mate. As long as the money is good then I’ll follow the order.’

‘I told you gentlemen, he is a good soldier.’ The old man said.

‘Don’t you have issues killing a police officer?’ Paul asked, looking him in the eyes.

‘Do you have issues giving me the order?’

‘I’m not the one doing the killing.’

‘But you’re the one giving me the order? Don’t you have issues?’

‘Of course.’

‘But it doesn’t make a difference does it? It has to be done.’

‘I suppose.’

‘Then you have your answer.’ Luke replied.

‘Excellent, gentlemen.’ The old man joined in. ‘Now all we need to do is wrap up this matter of the serial killer and we can resume profitable operations.’

‘Not me.’ Paul said, shaking his head. ‘I told you years ago I was done with this. I have a family. I’m coming back now to survive this, and then once the killer is gone I’m done.’

‘Your choices are your own, Paul. But with Sheeran and Orr gone, well, there are considerable opportunities arising. Some of their business ventures need someone to maintain ongoing concerns. It would present a substantial financial opportunity for yourself.’

‘I’m done.’ Paul said coldly. ‘I told you. I don’t want to work anymore.’

The old man smiled. ‘Paul, the four of us here, Mr Wade included, we all share something in common. We are men of business. We all share the same fundamental motivation to profit, to make money. You may be able to take a break from the work, but you will return to it. Because you know the truth of men like ourselves; we only ever feel alive in that moment when we generate profit.’

Paul looked at the floor, arms crossed. ‘You keep telling yourself that.’

The old man laughed. ‘It would seem that Mr McDermott is unwilling to hear this message at the moment. No matter. Mr Wade, when last you checked was there any update on the identity of our killer?’

Luke shook his head. ‘Last time I checked they were looking into Delpont, they didn’t have any suspects. I can’t check again anymore, my access codes would have been revoked.’

‘This is true. Mr Wade, before you go, do you know where we are standing? Do you know this building?’

‘This dump? No idea.’

He smiled. ‘Very well then, I suppose it’s irrelevant.’

‘Are we done here?’ Paul asked flatly. ‘I have things to do.’

‘Definitely. Gentlemen, I believe our business here is concluded. Mr Wade, I trust we will hear from you soon?’

‘Yep. I’ll get it done. Don’t worry.’ Luke was short with him. He was sick of talking with these corporate snakes. Their money was good, but they loved the sound of their own voice.

As he walked outside, he kept thinking about Malceski. It had bothered him to kill someone he once worked with, especially not understanding why. It didn’t make sense that Victor would suddenly try and hand over that information to the police. It didn’t make sense that Paul would order Victor to kill Collins. Paul had been against the idea. No one wanted to kill Collins.

He thought back on the angry look Paul had given the old man when asked about it. Nothing could upset this man. There was more to it.

Luke frowned, suddenly troubled. The look in Paul’s eyes filled in the missing information. He knew why Victor had died. He needed to handle the situation with the police, but there was someone he needed to talk to first.

WILL

‘So that’s the guy?’ Iz asked, confused. ‘How can a cop be involved in this?’

Will shook his head. ‘I don’t know. Aoki and Morgan think that he was being paid for information. They know he was there at Beck’s place. When they showed her a photo of him, she recognised that he was at the petrol station before someone tried to kill her. They think he’s involved in that.’

‘And you recognised him too?’

Will nodded. He felt a chill run down his spine. He looked at the black and white photo of Wade. He remembered those eyes looking into his that night, before he had been chased down.

‘Are you ok? Do you still think about it?’ She asked.

He nodded slowly. ‘If I hadn’t been lucky that night, this guy could have killed me.’

‘They’ll catch him though, babe. I’m sure someone will see him.’ She said reassuringly.

Will sighed. She was right. A corrupt police officer like this wasn’t likely to escape. Every police officer was looking for him. Still, Will considered that his face should have been all over the news by now. The media would have loved the story. It appealed to their sensationalist headline culture. Despite that, the story hadn’t made the news.

‘Are you sure you want to do this now though?’ She asked. ‘I know you like Amber but is now a good time to see her?’

‘It’s not about that anymore.’ He lied. ‘I have to see her now. I have to talk to her father. He’s tied up in this, and he can lead us to Azure’. It was only half a lie. They needed to talk to

McDermott, he was the only lead at this point. But he still wanted Amber. With everything that had happened, he just wanted to hold her, to see her smile at him.

Iz shook her head. 'I don't trust her Will. I just want you to be prepared that she might be seeing someone else?'

He scoffed. His friend was trying to look after him but he was sick of hearing it. 'It's fine. She isn't like that. And even if she is, we aren't dating.' It was true, but the mental image still hurt him.

She shrugged. 'As long as you're sure.'

'You don't have to come along.'

'It's fine. I'll wait outside.'

He nodded. They stopped outside the McDermott house. He hoped Amber was home. He hoped her father was home.

'This street is ridiculous.' She shook her head. 'These houses are colossal!'

'Yeah, well, they don't call it "Millionaire Avenue" for nothing'.

'What do you mean?'

'This street,' He gestured up and down the street. 'Is Boardwalk Place. It has more millionaires on it that any other street in this hemisphere. Most of them are with the banks, or the oil companies, or the big multinationals. It's referred to as "Millionaire Avenue".'

She shivered, zipping her leather jacket up tighter. 'Any criminals?'

'Plenty.' He smiled.

'What sort of criminals?' She asked. 'Drugs? Guns?'

'The worst kind.' He laughed. 'White collar.'

‘Very funny, Will.’ She said, frowning at him. ‘How can it be called Boardwalk Place? Isn’t a street either a Boardwalk or a Place?’

‘I don’t know.’ He shrugged. ‘I think it’s named after someone or something.’

The two walked up the steps to the front gate. There was an extensive security system at the door. As soon as they got close to the gate the lights turned on automatically. There was a small security building by the front gate. Two guards were in side. They were from a professional security company. It would have been expensive to hire them to constantly patrol the premises. Will frowned, he didn’t remember seeing them when he came back with Amber that night.

‘A completely different world.’ Iz whispered to him.

One of the guards approached the gate. He had a ruddy face and a beer belly. ‘Who are you here to see?’ He said bluntly. There was no edge of friendliness to his voice.

‘Amber. My name is Will and this is Iz. I need to talk to her’.

‘It’s late.’ The other guard said. He was tall and angry. He looked like the military type.

‘The sun is literally still setting.’ Iz said, scrunching up her face.

The guard glared at her. Will tried to hide a smile. It was true; it was only just past six pm.

‘It’s important.’ Will added gently.

The guard grunted. The fat guard waddled inside.

A few moments later Amber walked out. She was dressed in jeans, a white top and a brown leather jacket. She hugged her jacket close to her. It was obvious she had not been sleeping.

‘Will.’ She smiled. ‘I’m glad to see you, but you have to call next time.’

He tried to hide a smile. It was nice to hear that she was glad to see him. ‘I know. I’m sorry. It’s really important. I should have come here a long time ago.’

‘What is it?’ She frowned.

‘I need to talk to your dad. It’s about Delpont.’

She looked at him strangely.

‘I know, it’s really strange. You probably think it’s crazy, but I’m worried something might happen. Please?’

She narrowed her gaze. It seemed she was considering what he was asking.

‘Alright, Will. I trust you.’ She replied slowly.

He smiled.

The guards grudgingly let Will and Iz through. They walked to the front door in silence. Amber walked with her arms crossed, not looking at Will.

‘This is really icy.’ Iz said quietly to him, so Amber wouldn’t overhear.

‘What?’ He whispered. ‘What do you mean?’

She shrugged. ‘Amber. She’s acting strange. She’s being really cold.’

He shook his head. ‘She’s probably just confused as to what is going on. We probably made her uncomfortable.’

‘I guess.’ She replied, her tone unconvincing.

He couldn’t tell whether he had made Amber uncomfortable. But he had no option.

Amber walked them through the front door into the entry hall of the house. It was huge. Will and Iz both looked around, taking it all in. The floor was dark polished marble. The walls were a light cream or white, Will couldn't tell because there were only dim mood lights on. As they walked past a hidden control panel Amber pressed a button. The room was flooded with light that made the marble sparkle. There was a wide spiral staircase at the other end of the room, leading to the walkway on the floor above and several other rooms. Below the staircase was a small garden, and a rock pool with plants growing in it. There was a soothing sound of water running over the rocks as they walked past. There was also a glass elevator in the middle of the hallway, which seemed unnecessary given that there were only three floors.

'Different world entirely.' Iz commented in a whisper. She took the cover off her lens and snapped a few photos impulsively. Amber turned at the sound of the shutter, frowning.

'Sorry.' Iz said, covering her mouth and laughing nervously. 'I didn't mean, it's just really pretty.'

Will shot her an angry look.

Iz shrugged and rolled her eyes at Will, implying he was overreacting.

'It's fine.' Amber said flatly. 'My dad is upstairs, Will.' She stopped and pointed towards the wide staircase.

'I should probably talk to him alone.' Will said quietly to Iz.

She nodded. 'Sure thing.'

He walked up the stairs slowly, worried he would slip on the polished marble. It was such an elaborate house. Amber stayed waiting in the hallway with Iz. He felt in that moment that she was out of his league. Her place was like a castle.

Paul McDermott was waiting, leaning against the door to his study. He stood up when he saw Will, and greeted him with a smile.

'Hey Will. It's really good to see you. Amber has told me so much about you.'

He felt nervous at first, meeting the father of the woman he liked. Paul greeted him with a soft handshake and a smile. His eyes sparkled a bright blue, there was a lot of life in his eyes. The rest of him seemed tired. His hair was grey and thin. He was thin and moved slowly. He was only around fifty, but he seemed older. Despite that, there was real warmth to his voice. He made Will feel instantly comfortable.

'Thanks, Mr McDermott.'

'Call me Paul.' He laughed. 'Mr McDermott was my father.'

Will smiled. 'Sure thing.'

'Come in, come in.' Paul said, leading Will into his study. 'Get comfortable, please. Did you want something to drink?'

'Ahh, whatever you're having?'

He laughed. 'A red wine then?'

Will nodded. He didn't usually drink red.

'Good man, good man.' The old man said cheerily.

Will found him so warm and welcoming. It was hard to imagine him as the CEO of a company like Delpont. He sighed. This man must have made some of the key decisions at the company. He would have been a key component of the corruption and fraud.

'So what brings you here, Will?' He asked, offering him the glass of wine. 'It's about Delpont?'

'Delpont, and also Azure.' Will said as he accepted the glass, looking Paul in the eyes. He took a sip of wine, it was rich.

Paul's eyes flickered slightly. 'I thought it might be.'

'You don't deny it?'

'I know what you know.' He said with a sad smile. 'I was involved.'

Will took a deep breath. It felt surreal to hear. 'Are you still involved?'

'No.' He said, sipping the wine and looking at the floor. 'But they know about you and Aoki. I'm glad you came to meet with me. You're all in danger.'

'What?' He said softly. He felt dizzy. 'What do you mean?'

'You're a real danger to them.' He said sadly. He sighed. 'I shouldn't be talking to you.'

Will frowned, looking at Paul leaning against his desk. 'So why do it then?'

The old man looked up. His eyes were sad. 'You know the damage that Delpont did?'

He nodded.

'I tried for the longest time to reconcile that.' He shook his head. 'It took me to an angry place. I was defensive. It was a dark time. And then I had to deal with these reports coming out; our workers lost their whole life savings, grandparents lost their retirement that was invested in our stock, our graduates never found work again, and all the suicides.'

Will sipped at the wine silently. 'You blamed yourself?'

'Of course. But we were all to blame. We defined ourselves by the company, by how much profit we made, by the share price that kept going up. We were winning. We sacrificed every value we had, all in the pursuit of profit. Eventually I learned to accept what I had done.' He sighed, and smiled. 'And after time passed I came to find meaning in my life, I found identity. Do you know who you are, Will?' He asked with an eyebrow raised.

Will frowned, unsure of the question. 'I guess, I mean, I think I know myself. What I'm like, what I'm good at.'

He laughed. 'If that is your answer then I don't think you do. Will, I want you to remember this; you strike me as a man who hasn't figured himself out yet.'

He felt angry at the comment. He felt insulted. But mostly he didn't understand what he meant; *a man who hasn't figured himself out yet*.

'Don't be upset.' He said gently. 'It's a journey we all go on. Maybe it's the journey of life. I think what happened in my life happened for a reason. Because I know I now have a choice, we all have a choice. What we choose to do, what we accept in this world. We all have a decision to make, the only decision we can make; what we do in this moment right now.' He stated calmly. He took a deep breath and exhaled slowly 'They have put out a kill order on Aoki and Morgan.' He said softly. 'You need to warn them.'

He suddenly felt afraid. He opened his mouth but couldn't think of what to say.

'I read a few of your articles, by the way. You argue that being rich is a crime. I think you may have been wrong. I don't think wealth is the crime; I think business is the crime. When the only goal is the pursuit of profit, every other value or moral is ignored.'

Will shook his head. 'I think my argument got taken out of context.'

‘Maybe, from what I learnt it might have been what started this serial killer.’ He looked Will in the eyes. ‘The message left when they killed Sheeran?’

‘You know about that?’

‘They knew about everything, Will.’ He sighed. ‘I don’t think you realise how far this thing goes. But whether it inspired this killer or not, I’m sure you’re considering whether you’re responsible for it or not?’

Will nodded. ‘I think about it.’ He said softly.

‘Let me ask you something; do you agree with what he’s doing?’

He frowned. He was put in an uncomfortable position, unsure of the correct response.

‘I think I have my answer.’ The old man smiled sadly. He shook his head. ‘I personally don’t know what this killer is trying to accomplish. I mean think about it; is it revenge he wants? Is he trying to make some kind of statement? Is he trying to change the world, by getting rid of what he thinks are the bad guys?’

‘Do you think it would work?’ Will asked impulsively.

Paul looked up with a faint look or surprise. ‘Changing the world? Maybe. It’s inevitable though. The era of the financial banks has ended regardless.’ He laughed. ‘They just haven’t gotten the memo yet.’

‘Do you truly believe that?’

He nodded slowly. ‘2008 wasn’t the problem though, the problem was what happened after. I mean it was sickening. The bailouts being used for bonuses. Did you know that the elites are now richer than they were before the crash?’ He shook his head bitterly. ‘I do what I can to fix the problems, I can help out some of those who have been affected the worst, but we all have a decision to make. We all have a battle we must fight. You have yours now, Will.'

'What do you mean?' He asked. He felt uncomfortable.

'You need to make sure Aoki and Morgan survive. Then they can uncover what happened at Delpont. Maybe if you tell the story of Delpont then you can reveal Azure. Maybe that will stop them.'

'Stop?' Will's eyes widened. 'They're still around?'

'They never stopped.' The old man shook his head. 'I don't know much about Azure, but from what I can tell they're running other things now, I don't know what though. I know that Azure goes further. As far as I'm aware, Delpont was just an experiment.

'I uh.' Will stammered. 'I don't understand.'

'What don't you understand?'

'Everything.' Will was bewildered. He had so many questions but he was lost for words. There was one pressing question though. 'How does the vigilante fit in with this?'

The old man sighed. 'To be honest, I don't know. Neither does Azure. Maybe that's what they brought me in.'

'You weren't originally part of Azure?'

He shook his head. 'I was only given orders when I was CEO. I was protected after it fell, that's when I found out about them. It's much larger than me. I was only brought in towards the end. I think that they believe this killer is someone from Azure. I'm lucky you came here, I had no way of getting in touch with Aoki and Morgan without them finding out. The relationship between you and my daughter was a piece of luck.'

Will smiled. 'What can Aoki and Morgan do?'

'Your friend Rebecca is important too. She's extremely capable. She was the beginning of the end of Delpont. This all comes down to accounting; there is a trail of records from Delpont that leads to Azure, I don't know why he hasn't started a new company yet.'

'Who?'

The old man looked suddenly pale. 'Oh, never mind. Look, this place is safe to talk long. But they can hear you pretty much everywhere else. I don't know about Aoki and Morgan, but I know your phone has been tapped.'

Will felt sick. 'What?'

'You have to be careful though, keep using your phone as normal. Just don't talk about the case work over the phone. And make sure that Aoki and Morgan are warned. Then they can catch this serial killer.'

'The vigilante?' Will asked, confused. 'With everything that Azure has done, how can you want to catch the vigilante?'

'Everyone is going to think differently about this, Will.' He said slowly. 'But the man is a murderer. And this is not how to solve this situation, this isn't how to prevent it from happening again.'

Will frowned. Based on everything that Paul had told him, he disagreed. 'Alright then.'

'Once he's caught then you will be able to focus on stopping Azure, and I will help if I'm still alive.'

'What do you mean?'

He laughed. 'I'm taking a risk by talking to you, I don't know whether they will suspect me. But regardless,' He sighed. 'There isn't much more I can tell you about Azure anyway. I know everything about Delpont, but it doesn't seem like there are many people alive anymore that need to go to jail for that, so I'm not much help. But there is a copy of all the records, copies of all the documents from Azure that they destroyed.'

‘Where is it?’

‘I don’t know.’ He shook his head, looking at the floor. ‘They recovered it off your friend Chris, but the truth is I don’t know where it is now.’

Will thought back, Chris had found a flash drive. He thought about everything that Paul had said. He wondered if he could trust him, and whether he was telling the truth. If Chris had held the flash drive, then he knew his friend must have been killed by Azure. But if Paul was telling him to find it, then perhaps he truly wasn’t with Azure.

‘What about Victor Malceski?’

‘I don’t know what happened.’ He said, shaking his head. ‘He was my security. I don’t know why,’ He stopped mid sentence. ‘I’m sorry for your friend.’

‘Victor was the one who killed him?’

He nodded. ‘Azure then killed Victor. He went rogue. They recovered the flash drive from him, but they don’t know how Chris had it in the first place. And you already know who killed Victor.’

Will frowned, thinking. ‘The cop?’

‘Luke Wade.’ He nodded.

‘But wait.’ Will shook his head, perplexed. His head was spinning. *I don’t understand any of this.* ‘You think your man killed Chris?’

‘I told you, I don’t know why.’ He said, scratching his head. ‘I found out when Azure contacted me, informing me that my security man had been killed.’

‘You expect me to believe that?!’ He demanded angrily, shaking his head.

‘Believe me if you want.’ Paul said, rubbing his face. He seemed exhausted. ‘I’m trying to help you, to save you time.’

Will thought for a moment. He studied Paul’s face. He appeared to be sincere. ‘And you still don’t know why Victor killed Chris?’

He shook his head. ‘It doesn’t make any sense. He was my friend for years. He wouldn’t have done anything unless I asked him to. And he never would have killed Chris, the guy was innocent.’

Will felt overwhelmed. He felt like Paul was telling him the truth, or at least most of it. ‘Alright then, but how are you going to convince them that you didn’t help me? If they’re following my phone they must have known I was coming here?’

Paul smiled. He held up a small black phone case. It was empty. ‘If they checked, and I don’t think they would, but they would think I was in the middle of the CBD right now. Along with my phone and everything else they could track me with. My house is clear of any recording equipment. The security guards don’t look like much, but they’re professional. When I let you out, Amber will comment that she’s sorry I’m not home, and that it was nice to share a tea with you.’

He smirked. ‘Nice.’

‘Thanks.’ He smiled. ‘I will be fine. Don’t worry about me. Worry about yourself.’ He added gently.

Paul led him out slowly. He spoke to Amber and explained what she needed to say. Will took Iz aside, and explained what Paul had told him. He told her not to use the phone. She thought at first that he was messing with her, but eventually accepted it as the truth. Everything ran as smoothly as Paul had suggested.

‘It was so nice to see you again, Will.’ She smiled, her eyes bright.

‘Likewise.’ He smiled back. He wanted to stay and chat with her, to talk about everything. He missed seeing her. He thought he would invite her to do something.

Her phone buzzed with a message. She frowned, looking upset. ‘I’m sorry I can’t talk for longer, Will. But I have to go see a friend now.’

‘That’s alright, I understand.’ He smiled. It felt like there was always something keeping them from seeing each other. Bad timing. ‘We should go then.’

She hugged him goodbye. She held him close as they hugged. He felt an unexpected warmth from her hug. She looked into his eyes as she let go and smiled.

It was well and truly night by the time they left the mansion. Will and Iz walked out into the cool night air.

‘See!’ Will teased Iz as they walked to the car. ‘I told you she likes me.’

‘Whatever you say.’ Iz said flatly. She seemed concerned, most likely because of her phone.

He sighed. He felt bad for involving his friend in this. He opened his mouth to say something, but she cut him off.

‘I don’t need a lift back. There’s something I have to do.’ She said. She seemed distant.

‘What’s wrong?’

‘Nothing.’ She turned to face him. ‘Nothing. I promise. I will just see you later.’

‘Alright then, I’m sorry for getting you involved in this.’

‘It’s fine.’ She replied shortly. ‘Don’t worry about it.’

‘But I do.’ He said. She had turned to walk away before he finished talking. ‘Ok! We’ll talk later then!’ He called after her.

He frowned. Wondering why his friend was acting strange. He shook his head, unable to understand why. On the drive home Will was quiet. He thought about everything Paul had told him, and about the death of his friend. Despite the information however, it still did not make sense.

ANDREA

‘Thank you for meeting me so late.’ Charlie said with a smile. ‘I know it’s the weekend.’

‘There is no need to apologise, Charlie.’ Andrea said, her voice clear. It masked the anxiety that she felt inside. ‘The only issue for me is that it’s rather late for a coffee.’ She added jokingly.

‘Yeah, I suppose.’ He chuckled and coughed. ‘Sorry for meeting so late, I had a big night last night.’

She smiled. ‘How was the date?’

‘It, ah, went well.’ He said with a sly smile. ‘Anyway, that’s beside the point. I know you said that you couldn’t stay long today.’

‘That is very true.’ She lied. The truth was that she had been feeling sick with anxiety the whole day. ‘Thank you for being so understanding, Charlie.’

‘Ah, don’t mention it.’ He waved his hand dismissively. ‘Truth be told, I can’t wait to get a bacon hamburger and go back to bed. I’m on Struggle Street.’

‘Fair enough.’ She laughed. ‘What did you want to talk about?’

He narrowed his gaze. ‘I wanted to talk to you outside of work.’ He sighed. ‘To let you know something, in a no pressure type circumstance.’

She frowned. ‘Ok then.’

‘What I’m asking of you right now, I want you to know.’ He held his palms up. ‘You have no obligation to say yes. You understand that right?’

‘Alright. That’s fine. I understand.’ She said.

‘Good.’ He smiled and exhaled. ‘I’m glad. You seem relaxed too, I’m glad I haven’t made you worried.’

‘I’m not worrying.’ She smiled. It was half true. She was worried about something completely different. The truth was that she didn’t care about what Charlie was going to talk about.

‘Alright then.’ He took a deep breath. ‘I have to confess; I had an ulterior motive when I hired you.’

She raised an eyebrow at him. She was not in the mood for games. ‘Explain.’

‘Ok, fair enough.’ He laughed, nervously. ‘There is a passion project of mine. It’s something I have been working on for some time.’

‘You want to go follow Delpont.’ She said flatly, eyes narrowed.

He gave her a sly grin. ‘You know me too well.’

She sighed. It was nothing she didn’t know already.

‘But it goes beyond that, you know as well as I do that the people behind Delpont never went to jail, and, well,’ He said, not finishing the end of his sentence, leaving it for her to figure out from his implication. He looked at her expectantly.

She shot him a look, feeling enraged. He had gone too far. ‘This is not something I want to talk about Charlie. You really want to go after people like that?’ She asked, getting worked up.

He looked confused. ‘But it’s true? There were people who invested in the company, who made decisions, and they never went to jail. Am I right?’

She rolled her eyes subconsciously. ‘Perhaps it happened. I never knew about that side of it.’

‘Oh, come on.’ He waved his hands dismissively. ‘I’m not going to judge. You must have known.’

She sighed and crossed her arms.

He scratched his bald head, not saying anything. ‘Look, I’m sorry.’ He added gently. ‘I don’t want to cause trouble for you. I don’t want to target these people directly. I wouldn’t ask that of you.’

‘Then what do you want, Charlie?’ Her eyes were starting to water. She tried to make sure it would not show.

‘I want to stop it from happening again.’ He said energetically, his voice full of hope. ‘That’s why I hired you!’ He said slapping his knee. ‘I want to bring in new regulation.’

‘You’re so naïve.’ She sighed. She didn’t intend to say it out loud. There was no taking it back now.

‘Hey! That’s not true.’ He said slowly. ‘Not true! I mean come on; with your knowledge of the company, with your knowledge of the industry.’ He spoke gently but calmly. It was only now she realised how confident he was; he would have made an excellent salesman. ‘I mean, if we worked together we could really accomplish something!’ He said with a smile.

She leant back in her chair, her arms crossed. She was silent for a moment. ‘You know you would be making enemies?’ She asked him, almost smirking.

‘Of course.’ He said with a smile. ‘I figure; if you’re trying to do the right thing, and you aren’t making enemies.’ He shrugged and laughed. ‘Well, then, I guess you wouldn’t really be doing the right thing, would you?’

She laughed and shook her head. He seemed certain. She considered what he was proposing; trying to regulate an industry that thrived on deregulation. ‘There is so much more to it than that.’ She said softly.

‘I can totally understand.’ He replied gently. ‘I don’t want you to feel pressured. That’s why I wanted to meet outside of work to talk about it.’

‘Thank you, Charlie. I appreciate that.’ She said sincerely.

‘Look, if you want to get more involved in this, then that’s fine. If you don’t, well, that’s fine too.’ He stood up slowly, and continued speaking in a reassuring tone. ‘I figure you should just take some time and think about it, and just let me know your decision.’

‘Sure thing.’ She replied, distantly. It was the last thing on her mind. She looked out the window of the café, lost in thought. Her mind was in turmoil. She rubbed her face. She had never felt so lost, even during the worst days after Delpont.

When she looked up to reply to Charlie he was gone. She looked around but he had left the café. She sighed, feeling guilty. Maybe she should have been gentler with him, more supportive. He did have the best of intentions.

She shook her head and left the café, trying to put those thoughts behind her.

For a reason she could not explain, she ended up outside Hank’s place while trying to drive home. The uncomfortable conversation with Charlie had left her wanting some comfort. She felt that if she could just explain everything to Hank, to see him and hold him again, that she could fix things. She felt like it would go back to normal.

There she sat in her car and waited as time passed by. She realised at some point that he was not home, but she could not make herself leave. She wanted to see him.

Hours passed before he finally arrived home. She felt sick as she saw him walking down the street, smiling, his light eyes wrinkling as he did so. All her anxiety came back. She watched as he walked along laughing and talking to the girl on his arm, and watched as he led the girl into his apartment.

It all became too much to handle. She dropped her head and started to sob. The tears came slowly but soon she was bawling.

AOKI

She'd been feeling ill all day. Too much caffeine and working at the computer had left her feeling tired and anxious. She had barely eaten. What bothered her most though was that she had not accomplished anything.

If she spent all day and all night in front of the computer and ended up resolving something, then at least she could feel some sense of accomplishment. But she had no such luck. After a day of thorough research she had only more questions.

She was sure the killer was targeting these individuals because of their involvement in Delpont. She exhaled. She was sure of it. Everything she felt led her to believe that the killer was Anders Sorensen. But she had researched everything about the man and could not find anything. There was nothing registered under his name for five years.

She had spent the day looking through every detail of the case. She had looked over the police and autopsy reports and whatever footage they had. There was nothing there. The killer had left no traces of hair or fingerprints. The only thing they could tell was that his shoe was size 10.

She rubbed her face in frustration as she read through the case files on her computer. It seemed more and more as though he was killing these people like gang shootings. There was a random pattern of attack. There was no clue to the order he was targeting people. It wasn't by wealth, date of birth, position at the company, nor any other detail that would give her a clue who he was targeting next. They seemed to her like crimes of opportunity; he had identified his targets and would strike them in whatever order was easiest.

She sighed. No criminal was perfect.

She closed all the documents she had open. There was no point reading through the reports from Delpont and police again. She had been through them so many times, there was nothing more to be gained from them. Having read so much that day as well, the words on the pages were starting to blur together. She needed the energy to push through.

She went to the kitchen to make another cup of coffee. She knew it would not help with her anxiety, but it was more important to solve the case. If she did not solve the problem in front of her then someone else would die. She filled the percolator with water and put ground beans in the filter, then secured it and put it on the stovetop.

While waiting there was a knock on her door. She frowned. Rick was not meant to be home for hours. Regardless, he wouldn't have knocked.

The person knocked again as she walked to the door. She looked through the peephole to see who it was. She frowned and opened the door.

'Will?' She asked him, confused.

'Hey. I'm really sorry, I would have called.'

'What is it?'

He sighed, and then looked her in the eyes and explained everything; from his meeting with Paul, how a kill order had been placed on her and Morgan, and how their phones had been tapped.

She sat on her couch as she contemplated what he had told her.

'I turned the percolator off, by the way.' He said as he came back to her living room.

'Fuck.' She swore in a whisper. She rubbed her face. 'I totally forgot about it.'

‘It’s alright, I’ll do it.’ He said gently. ‘I’ll have one myself, anyway.’

‘Thanks.’ She smiled weakly.

She became lost in her own thoughts when he went into the kitchen. There was so much to think about. The situation was a total mess, and only further complicated the case.

‘Are you doing ok?’ Will asked tentatively when he returned from the kitchen. He handed the cup of coffee to her, and sat down with his own cup on the opposite couch. ‘You haven’t said anything since I told you.’

‘I guess so.’ She sighed. ‘I should be afraid probably.’ She said flatly. She looked out the window, eyes narrowed in contemplation.

‘But you aren’t?’ He asked, frowning.

‘I just want to solve this.’ She shrugged. ‘I just want it to be over.’

‘Yeah, but that is something else. The vigilante is something separate to this syndicate.’

‘Will, I don’t care about the syndicate.’ She blurted out in frustration, cutting him off.

‘How can you not?’ He looked puzzled. ‘They’re the ones who put an order out to kill you?’

‘Yeah, yeah, I know.’ She shook her head, irritated. ‘But I was never interested in them. I was only ever interested in the murders. They only did that because they thought I was targeting them.’

‘And we aren’t?’

‘You are.’ She replied bluntly. ‘I never agreed with you and Morgan about chasing this company.’

'But you said it yourself?' Will replied, his tone frustrated. 'That the key to finding this guy is in Delpont.'

She glared at him. 'Don't act like that.'

'Like what?'

'Like you want the same things I do.' She noticed her voice was raised. 'This isn't about the killings for you, you want to expose this syndicate.'

He rubbed his eyes and looked away. He exhaled deeply. There was a moment of tension between the two. She did not know what to say.

'Fine.' He said softly.

'What do you mean?'

'I mean, fine. Maybe you're right. I think they should be exposed.'

She sighed. There was more to talk about, but she sensed it would end in a fight between the two of them. She sensed he did not want to deal with that confrontation, and she would most likely end up frustrated. 'Anyway.' She said, trying to change the topic. Before she could do that however, she became distracted. She frowned.

'What's wrong?' Will asked, noticing her focus was on something else.

'I think I just saw something.' She replied absently, staring at her computer. She had forgotten about the footage, and it had continued to run in the background.

'What is this?'

'It's the footage from the Docker case. From one of the cameras at the private residences.' She said, leaning in to her computer. She went into the footage and started rewinding it.

‘I thought you already checked it?’

‘Yeah, I did.’ She shook her head. ‘I thought I did. I checked everything around the period the vigilante was there.’

‘So?’

‘Well, this is footage from around midday the next day.’ She looked at him, and pointed to the screen. ‘I never checked this before.’

Will frowned. ‘I guess it wasn’t relevant.’

She narrowed her gaze, when she saw a flash on the screen. ‘There! That’s what I saw’. She pressed play and the footage continued playing at normal speed.

‘What am I looking for?’ Will sighed, leaning in closer.

‘I’m not sure.’ She mumbled. She did not know what she had seen.

The two sat in silence, staring at the screen. She started to feel nervous. Maybe she had gotten excited over nothing.

‘Holy shit!’ She gasped, pointing at the screen. ‘Here! Look!’ She exclaimed excitedly, fumbling for the pause button.

When she found it the image froze on the screen. It was not perfect quality, but she could clearly make out the face.

‘It’s Anders.’ Will replied confused. ‘It’s actually him?’

Aoki felt shocked. Seeing his face on screen felt surreal. She squinted to make sure.

‘What is he doing there?’

‘I don’t know.’ She scratched her head. She sat closer to her screen and reviewed the footage closely. He walked casually down the street. Dressed in dark blue jeans, a black leather jacket with a black hood, he looked laidback. In the way he moved there was an easygoing confidence. He was still as handsome as in the photos from Delpont years ago, but he had a trimmed beard and his hair was longer. His clothes weren't the type that defined his highflying days as a trader. If she had not known who he was, she might have mistaken him for a thief. His clothes were a little tattered, and he looked rough. Despite that, there was nothing remarkable about him. Even when she watched the footage again he blended into the rest of the scene. He did not draw attention one way or the other. He walked down the street and then off the screen. She stared at the screen, hoping to find her target again. She felt increasingly frustrated. They waited in awkward silence, Will watching her.

'Maybe that was it?' He finally spoke up, breaking the silence.

She refused to believe him. There must be more. It was her first time she had seen her target. It could not be all.

'Aoki?' Will asked gently.

She didn't want to talk. She stared at the footage more intently. There must be something. She had only just found who she was looking for, she could not lose him so soon. She refused to give up.

There was an image on the screen as a car drove past.

'There!' She jumped, grabbing his arm and pulling. 'There! Look!'

Will smiled as he looked at the footage of Anders driving away. It was an early 90s sedan, a European make. It was a dark blue, and was not in great condition. Only one side of his face was visible, but based on the footage of him just before, they could clearly tell it was him.

She exhaled and leaned back. She had him. She smiled.

'Why do you think he came back?' Will asked.

She shrugged. 'I'm not sure. It doesn't make sense.'

'Did you check the footage from the night before? To see him arrive?'

She nodded. 'Yeah, definitely. Me and Morgan—'

'Morgan and I.'

She scowled. 'Whatever. Morgan and I went over that footage a hundred times. There was nothing!'

Will sighed. 'You sure.'

'I'm sure!' She said defensively. She didn't understand why he doubted her. 'I never make mistakes.'

He grinned. 'Ok then, sure thing. I'm sorry.'

'He must have come to pick his car up?'

'Was that a question or are a statement?'

She frowned, thinking. She wasn't sure. 'A statement, he must have left his car there the night before.'

'Ok then.' Will narrowed his gaze. 'So why not drive it away the night before?'

She shook her head. 'It would have been too risky, for him. Docker's guard called the police as soon as it happened. Officers were on the scene within minutes, stopping any cars in the area.'

Will nodded. 'Ok then.'

'He must have made a mistake.' She said absently. 'None of the other crime scenes were this messy. He must have seen an opportunity and taken it.'

'And he wasn't as careful?'

'Yeah, exactly. He must have needed to park close to the scene. He was in a rush.'

Will exhaled and crossed his arms. He seemed to be lost in his own thoughts.

'I should be able to find a license plate from this footage.' She suggested, viewing the footage frame by frame. She paused when the license plate was in the shot. 'I think I can read it, it's SLQ.'

'That's not an L, it's a T. See?' Will said pointed.

'STQ, yeah you're right.'

'The numbers I can't make out though. Can't you enhance it or something? Make it clearer?'

She groaned. 'That's science fiction. It only exists in lazy cop shows. The resolution from this camera is too low. I think it's 108.'

'No, that last number looks like a 3.' He suggested.

'So, STQ103?'

'I guess so.'

'I'll check it.' She said, opening up her access to the department records. She had tortured herself many nights with this software, endlessly checking details of cases. Usually hoping in vain for some kind of breakthrough. It seemed for once it might reward her. She typed in the license plate. It ran slowly. It was not complicated technology; the capability to check a list of all registered license plates was available in every police car. Regardless, the network was slow and had not been updated in years. When the result came up she immediately checked the footage.

'Does it match?' Will asked.

‘Same car, European make. It says it’s a 1992 model, which fits the appearance. Colour is hard to tell, but it’s registered as a dark purple.’ She said slowly. ‘It matches.’

A big grin formed on Will’s face.

She started to feel excited. She had done it. She had found him. It was getting late, she knew she should sleep, but she could not wait. She pulled out her phone.

‘I just have to call in the license plate, I’ll be quick.’ She said.

‘Sure thing.’

She ducked into the other room and put out an arrest notice on the car using her police phone. She gave them the license plate and the woman at the desk placed the notice.

‘All good?’ Will asked when she returned.

‘Yeah. Fine. I should call Morgan and let him know. I don’t know how I will tell him about the kill order.’ Her thoughts were interrupted by her phone ringing.

‘Who is it?’

She ignored his question and picked up the call. She had no idea. ‘Detective Sun speaking.’

‘Detective Sun, the car you reported has just been seen.’ The voice from the desk said on the other line.

She raised an eyebrow. ‘Already?’

‘An officer spotted it in the Mosman district. It was parked down the bottom of Boardwalk Place.’

‘Where?’ She frowned.

‘You know.’ The woman replied casually. ‘They call it Millionaire Drive.’

Her eyes opened wide. It felt like a truck hit her. She started feeling panicked.

'Do you want the officer to wait with the car?' The woman asked, frustrated.

'Yes,' She said softly, her voice catching in her throat. 'Yes. I'll drive to the scene now.'

She hung up quickly. She turned around to see Will looking at her strangely.

'You alright?' He asked.

'You're never going to believe this.' She said, shaking her head. She had too much energy. She didn't have time to explain. She just wanted to call Morgan and drive there as soon as possible. If she did not act quickly then someone would die. She would not let it happen again.

THE VIGILANTE

The house was empty, save for his target. His daughter had gone. His wife was away. There would be no complications, save the small security team at the front gate.

He scaled the wall quickly. He wore black leather gloves so he did not leave any fingerprints. He wore a dark blue down jacket. When he reached the top he looked out over the complex. It was a beautiful sprawling mansion, built overlooking a cliff. From studying the building he knew it was designed in the 1930s and updated. Despite the renovations, it still held the charm of the streamline modern style; utilising curved edges, a smooth exterior surface, and a long horizontal design. It was beautiful and elaborate.

The night sky was the darkest shade of blue, and the stark light of the full moon illuminated everything. The grounds of the mansion were all visible. The moonlight washed over the building, making it glow a pale blue.

He sighed, thinking of the beauty of the scene. These people lived a beautiful surreal life. The overwhelming majority of people on the planet would never be able to glimpse this world, let alone live it for themselves. They lived in blissful ignorance of the daily struggles for everyone else in the world. They made their money by creating a system that tailored to their needs. Over time they had built up an industry around it, and then this banking sector had influenced government to bring in the policies of deregulation that would allow them to exponentially increase their profits. People like this had enjoyed thirty years of profits, and when their system fell apart they let the public cover the deficit, then continued to profit as before. These people were complicit in these crimes of fraud and corruption, and that was why they had to die.

He descended the wall. He started the cross the grounds slowly, trying not to be seen by the security office. He was frustrated at having to work so slowly, but he would not take any chances. In his days as a trader he had embraced risk, but he was now risk averse. He was careful above all else.

ANDREA

She could so vividly remember seeing him with someone else, and could so clearly recall the feeling.

She had never felt so tired before. It was almost dawn and outside of the car it was the coldest night. Her eyes were red and irritated, she had cried until she could no more. Her hands had been locked onto the steering wheel. She hadn't wanted to stay the whole night, she had tried to leave, but she hadn't known where to go.

Her whole life she had defined herself as a winner, but she could not remember the last time anything had gone right for her. Her thoughts were a mess. She had been consumed by thoughts of Hank and the heartbreak she felt. But she had also tortured herself with thoughts of Delpont, the vigilante, all her failures to get a job in the past decade. Maybe the attempts to get jobs were not failures; maybe it was her that was the failure.

She felt cold and alone.

The apartment door opened. The woman walked out, tired and smiling. Hank walked out after her. The two hugged and said goodbye. He made a joke, she laughed as he ran his hand through his hair. As she turned to leave she touched his arm. Even from a distance she could still read his lips as he said he loved her. Andrea watched the woman walked down the street as dawn started to break. Hank closed his door and went back inside.

She took a deep breath. Inside her a storm was growing. She felt fury and wrath and scorn. *It wasn't fair*. She would not accept it any longer. Her heart started to beat faster. Her vision was starting to blur. Her hands gripped the steering wheel tighter.

The door opened again and Hank walked out. She took a good look at him. His dark blonde curly hair pulled back, always in a mess. She could not make out his grey green eyes from a distance, but she could see the way his eyes wrinkled as he smiled. She could make out the flecks of grey in his stubble. As always, he was wearing a flannel shirt and jeans, she could see a stain on his shirt from his sculpting clay. She loved this man with an intense passion. He looked so happy and content. He was most likely off to get a morning coffee.

As she sat there watching him, he turned and noticed her. He looked puzzled to see her. Then he smiled warmly at her and waved.

She was overcome by a feeling of blind anger and jealousy. He was hers. She screamed in frustration. She would not let anyone else have him.

He started to walk towards her and he turned the key in the ignition, her breathing coming in faster. The car turned on. She could feel fury and adrenaline running through her. She looked at him as he paused in his steps. He looked puzzled by the angry look on her face. She put her foot on the accelerator as she screamed as loud as she could. The wheels spun and the car took off. There was a screeching sound as tears started to stream down her face. He looked panicked as he turned to run away. She screamed and shouted as the distance between them became less and less. Tears blurred her vision and she could no longer see the man she loved. She heard a shout. She could no longer see anything when she felt a collision and felt the car become weightless. There was a loud tearing sound, and then silence. She closed her eyes.

She sat in silence for several minutes before she realised that her hands were shaking. She opened her eyes and realised she was bleeding. *It was over. It was all over.* There was nothing left. Far away she heard the sound of distant sirens. She felt like she was being enveloped by blackness, and falling into a pit of darkness. She had lost everything she wanted, and in that moment she let go. When she did, the tears starting coming, and suddenly she was crying for every pain and failure and regret she had felt her whole life.

She let go of everything, and let herself fall into the black abyss.

AOKI

Her car flew through the streets. Far away she heard a call on the police radio, a car crash nearby. She should have been driving more carefully but there was no time. For the first time in a long time she felt adrenaline run through her. Her anxiety and nerves seemed to drift away as she took control of the situation.

The night was still dark and cold. The dim streetlights let her see the road but not much else as she flew across the freeway. The skyscrapers surrounding her were illuminated as always. Even at this early or late hour, she could still see people working inside. The corporate machine never stopped.

All at once the buildings gave way as she drove onto the harbour bridge. She could see the harbour below and the national parks to the north ahead of her. In her rear view mirror she could see the city in the south. As she drove further away from the city, she lost sight of the individual buildings, and could only see the city skyline as one monolithic object.

To her right she looked out towards the harbour and the ocean beyond, to nature and freedom. It would be dawn soon.

She had never driven so fast in her whole life. Still, she didn't know whether it would be fast enough. She finally had the chance to save someone, but even then she might still be too late.

WILL

'Fucking hell! How could she just go off on her own?' Morgan was fuming.

'I don't know. She just ran out and told me to get you.' He replied in a deceptively calm voice. They were driving either into a crime scene, or directly into the path of a serial killer. Either way, he had no idea what to do.

Morgan was shaking his head. 'She's so stubborn sometimes, would it really have taken that much longer to drive to mine and pick me up? Or she could have at least called me, figured out a way around the phone taps?' He shouted and banged the steering wheel.

Will shrugged. 'Yeah, I don't know. She ran out. You know as well as I do that she needed to get there as soon as possible.'

Morgan exhaled. His eyes narrowed. 'I know.'

The two sat in silence for the rest of the journey. Will could understand Morgan's frustration. The man wanted to help his partner, and believed that he should be there with her. However, even if he drove fast he still might be too late to help her.

Will did not want to be there. There was nothing he could do to help either Morgan or Aoki if the situation turned bad. He felt out of his element. He just wanted it to be over.

THE VIGILANTE

He scaled the balcony and pulled himself up. The cold night air still lingered as dawn approached. From the balcony he could see cracks of sunlight starting to break over the horizon. He looked inside the windows of the house; none of the lights were on. Inside seemed warm and inviting compared to the cold outside. He moved slowly to the door, stepping softly so as not to make any noise. He had taken his time crossing the grounds of the mansion, being careful to avoid security cameras and sensor equipment. He needed to be thorough. This was his most difficult target.

He went to check the door for security systems, but stopped his hand just as he was about to touch the handle. The door was already open. He frowned. It was strange for such a careful man as Paul McDermott to be so careless. He peered up and down the door for signs of any active security systems, for any lights or devices. He found nothing.

Slowly and deliberately he opened the door. Crouching low he made his way through the room. From his research he gathered that the room off the balcony was a library. He scanned his surroundings as he walked through; the shelves were rich, dark polished wood. In between each row of shelves were identical antique lamps. The books were mostly expensive architecture and design books, and a lot of fiction. As he walked further he saw a section that must have belonged to Paul. There were countless books about technical market analysis, Japanese candlestick charting, and other methods of analysis. He saw books about interviews with market wizards, about the psychology of investing and trading, in addition to books about the history of economics. He smiled and shook his head. A lot were the same books he had read and studied when he had learnt finance and when he had passionately pursued a life in investing. He wondered how two people could read the same texts and make such different decisions in life.

He exited the library and crossed the dark hallway. He saw a dim light coming from the study. He cautiously opened the door without making a sound.

At the far end of the room sat Paul McDermott at his desk. He was leaning back in his chair, sipping from a rocks glass with a dark liquor and ice. Paul looked up calmly when he noticed him enter.

'Hello, Anders.' He said with a sad smile.

AOKI

She parked in a hurry, almost crashing her car in the process. She sprinted up the footpath. As she was about to go into the main gate of the house, she realised she had forgotten her gun.

'Fuck!' She swore loudly, scratching her head. She turned and ran back to her car. She was unsure of whether to be frustrated or to laugh at herself. She grabbed her weapon and then fumbled with her keys to lock the car again.

With her gun in hand she ran to the front gate, looking for the security. She rang the bell several times but there was no answer. She exhaled deeply. She kept ringing the bell for security but heard no response. She looked left and right for a way in. Further up she could see where the security office was located. She ran to it, fighting the urge to call out for help. She did not want to let her target know she was here. There was no sign of activity from the building. The front gate had been left open. She should have felt anxious. However her nerves did not betray her. She knew what she had to do. She had a clear sense of purpose.

She found the security booth and opened the door, and found the two guards asleep on the desk. She frowned, puzzled. They were snoring loudly, clearly in a deep sleep. She shook her head, confused and ran out. They would be no help to her.

She ran down the main path towards the mansion, making her way past the low garden lights and perfectly trimmed box hedges. The garden was perfect and green. The house was immaculate and beautiful. The thought of something so violent happening in such a place seemed so surreal and impossible to her.

He exhaled and smiled. 'How did you know it would be me?' He replied coolly.

'I didn't.' Paul said softly, sipping at his drink. He looked older than he remembered. He seemed thin. His hair was mostly grey and thinning. Despite looking older than his years, he looked healthy. He still had the same strong blue eyes that sparkled when he talked. He had a cool composure he did not remember. He looked out the window. 'I recognised you from outside, but I expected whoever you were, you would be coming for me at some point. Forgive my manners, would you like a scotch?' He asked absently.

'No.' He replied.

The old man frowned, looking out the window.

He felt himself breathing faster. There was something strange in the demeanour of the old man. He did not let it disrupt his cool composure. 'You remembered me?'

The old man turned to face him and smiled sadly. 'From Delpont. Yes, Anders. You were one of the best. You accomplished some impressive results. You had great potential and you had a bright future at Delpont.'

He scoffed. 'Pity. I would have loved a future with Delpont or one of the many other corrupt entities like it. Would it be too late to be reconsidered for a position as a trader?'

'You certainly have the loose morality for it.' The old man smiled bitterly, sipping at his glass. 'I don't blame you.' He said, the words catching in his throat. 'I don't disagree with you. Delpont did a lot of bad things, and I was responsible for a lot of that. I was complicit.'

‘But you changed.’

The old man looked up, he squinted. ‘Yes. My life changed. Following the collapse a lot of my beliefs changed. How did you know?’

‘I saw you one night. I saw that you had changed. My original intention had been to kill you that night, I hope you understand.’

‘Thanks.’ The old man smiled. He shook his head. He narrowed his gaze and looked him in the eyes. ‘So, why come back for me then?’

‘You know very well. You became involved with Azure again.’ He smiled bitterly, feeling himself becoming angry. ‘You’re complicit in their ongoing crimes and attempts to control the markets, the media and the government.’

Paul frowned. ‘I had no choice.’

‘We all have a choice.’ He said scathingly.

‘Did you?’ Paul asked, an eyebrow raised.

‘What do you mean?’ He asked, frowning. He stroked his trimmed beard.

The old man looked out the window again and sighed. ‘Never mind.’

He shook his head. He felt conflicted. ‘Why didn’t you run?’

‘Because I wanted to stop you.’ Paul said slowly, he turned and locked his gaze.

‘You?’ He raised an eyebrow. ‘Mr McDermott you’re hardly a youth anymore, or are you hiding a weapon underneath that scotch?’

He raised his hands slowly and shook his head. ‘No weapons. Just me. I wanted to talk to you.’

He smirked. ‘Do you want to try and sweet-talk your way out of this? I don’t know if you Azure men do your research, but I’m not really the sort of person to be motivated by financial rewards.’ He said sarcastically.

‘Just words, Anders. You’re a smart man. I wanted to try and make you see reason.’

‘Oh, Mr McDermott.’ He said shaking his head. He slowly pulled the handgun from his jacket pocket and pointed it at him. ‘You disappoint me.’

‘I accept my fate, I accept myself.’ Paul said frowning, seemingly undisturbed by the threat.

‘Then why negotiate with me?’

Paul narrowed his gaze, he seemed to be looking through him. ‘I don’t think you fully realise what you’re going to set in motion.’

‘Oh? Do tell then, what will I cause?’ He said with mock sincerity.

The old man ignored it. ‘My guess has been that you’re trying to make some kind of statement. That you’re trying to deliver some kind of social justice.’

His eyes narrowed, he felt anger. ‘Social justice? That’s an understatement. People like you and Azure have profited too much and for too long. Manipulating the system so that you can get ahead at the expense of the general population.’ He waved his hand, gesturing out the window. ‘Everyone knows about the corruption of the financial world. The crimes of the banking system are a matter of public record.’

‘So what is your goal then? Revenge?’

He smiled. ‘Adjustments to supply and demand.’

The old man frowned. ‘What?’

‘Never mind, Paul.’ He said, cocking the gun. ‘It does not concern you.’

‘But it does. Anders, you,’ His thoughts trailed off, he shook his head. ‘You’re trying to force change by targeting these groups? Do you think they won’t fight back?’

‘They’re welcome to try. I’m an individual. My cause is an idea. Even if I fall then there will be others.’

He shook his head. He sipped at his scotch slowly. ‘What do you think will happen to your message? They will call you a terrorist.’

‘They can call me what they want.’

‘They will.’ Paul looked at him. ‘They will use you as an example. Even if they let you live then they will use everything you did to further their own agenda.’

He shook his head. He was confused. ‘What do you mean?’

He extended his arm, gesturing. ‘How about tighter control over information security? They will argue that you would have never been able to commit those crimes if governments had more surveillance powers over its citizens.’ He looked down into his glass. ‘They will extend the capabilities and regulation to allow for less privacy rights. They will use your attacks to garner sympathy for the big banks.’ He shook his head. ‘Your *cause* will be manipulated and adapted to suit their own needs. Everything you wanted to accomplish will be used an excuse to extend their own powers, hell.’ He raised his arms in frustration. ‘They will probably use your attacks in some way to decrease regulation over the financial industry.’

‘That is a bit pessimistic, don’t you think, Paul?’ He asked half serious. He was considering the logic of the old man’s argument.

‘You’re going to cause chaos.’ Paul stated. ‘That much I know. I believe the chaos will cause more damage and harm than you could have ever imagined.’

‘See, that is where we differ, Paul. I believe that chaos is exactly what the world needs right now.’ He said emphatically. ‘People need to have these ideas of corruption and greed of large corporations discussed in the larger media. With the current monopoly of media outlets by the major corporations, do you think any of these ideas that are dangerous to them will be discussed unless there is a dramatic statement?’ He asked bitterly, his accent coming through.

Paul looked at him curiously. He shook his head. ‘If you truly want to change inequality and stop the exploitation by the elites then you would realise the only way to accomplish real change is through regulation.’

‘Well, I disagree.’ He said, aiming the weapon at the old man. ‘And besides; why do you think this is all I’m trying to do anyway?’ He asked, feigning offense.

Paul looked quizzically.

‘Anyway, Paul.’ He smiled, putting his finger on the trigger. ‘It’s been a pleasure catching up.’

‘Freeze!’ He heard a shout from behind him. It startled him so much he almost pulled the trigger.

He turned. Standing in the doorway was a demurely dressed Asian woman with a fringe. She was pointing a gun directly at him.

AOKI

She stood in the doorway. Weapon pointed at her target. She took a deep breath and narrowed her gaze, trying to keep her focus. She had wanted to be face to face with this serial killer for a long time. Standing only a few meters away from him, she felt slightly disappointed; he looked more like an out of work model than a criminal.

His hair was longer than in the corporate photo. His short and dark blonde hair was now mid length and a light brown. It was the same colour as his beard. He did not look much older than when at Delpont, with the exception of his eyes. In those dark blue eyes she saw an intensity compared to the calm corporate gaze she had seen in the photo. He wore a black wool zip up jumper, a black cotton beanie, dark khaki pants and black runners. He had on a small dark grey hiking backpack, presumably for any equipment he needed. She squinted. On his hands were black leather gloves. She assumed this was why she had not found any fingerprints.

'Who are you?' He asked with a smile and a sense of curiosity. He had a smooth, deep voice. She could hear a faint trace of his accent.

'Ahhh,' She stammered, confused. She glanced left and right, searching for an answer. *Fuck*, she thought, *who am I*? She could see an amused smile on his face. 'Aoki!' She said defiantly. She tightened the grip on her pistol. 'I'm a detective!'

'How did you find me, Aoki?' He asked smoothly. 'I have been meticulous.'

'There was footage, a privacy camera at one of the residences.'

'No. There was none.' He shook his head bitterly. 'I researched every location. I noted all the cameras.'

‘The car.’ She said tentatively. ‘The one you drove to the Docker crime scene.’

‘No.’ He said slowly, shaking his head. ‘I made sure to avoid all the cameras on that street. I was in a rush that night but I avoided all of them on that street that night? It can’t have been.’ He shook his head, a frown on his face.

‘That night, yes, but when you came back the next morning,’ She left the sentence hanging.

‘No.’ He said softly and slowly. He looked at her dubiously. ‘Really? I made one small mistake?’

She shrugged. She was unsure of what to say.

He grinned. ‘It would seem you’re meticulous as well.’ With that he lowered his weapon off Paul McDermott. Paul continued to calmly sip at his drink.

‘Will the guards be alright?’ She asked, narrowing her gaze.

‘Guards?’ He asked. ‘What do you mean?’

‘That was me.’ Paul added. He sipped at his drink calmly. ‘I gave them sedatives. I knew this man was coming for me, I wasn’t sure of his methods, but I didn’t want them to be caught up in this.’

Anders pursed his lips. ‘Awfully noble of you, Paul?’ He asked with mock sincerity.

Paul glowered, ignoring the insult.

‘I know that you have been targeting Azure.’ Aoki said to Anders.

Paul frowned and looked into his glass.

Anders looked up at her, almost pleadingly. ‘If you know about Azure, then you must know everything that was done under that name.’

‘I do.’ She nodded.

‘I mean really know about it, the blackmail, the share price manipulation, market control, control over the government and regulation, the rampant corruption?’ He asked her, a confused look on his face.

‘Yes, I know.’ She replied calmly.

‘How much do you get paid?’ He asked flatly.

‘Just above minimum wage.’ She responded.

‘And you want to save this man’s life?’ He asked, slightly incredulously. He smirked. ‘As part of Azure he has been part of a group of individuals who use every criminal tactic and a team of expensive legal experts to do nothing other than profit for the sake of profit. These rich, old, white, bank people like him would earn, at least, one hundred million dollars a year. They would make your annual salary in three hours by committing what in any other industry would be found a crime. Yet they use their government connections to get regulation rewritten around what rules they need. They have caused inequality in society, causing a collapse in the relative wage since the 1980s. They won’t stop in their reckless pursuit of profit at the expense of everyone else. They want things to get much, much worse.’ His thoughts trailed off, he shook his head and frowned. ‘Can you really want to stop me then?’

She narrowed her gaze on him, thinking on everything she had found out. ‘Yes.’ She said flatly.

He seemed perplexed. ‘But why?’ He asked softly.

‘Because murder is a crime.’ She responded slowly and calmly. ‘It’s not your decision to make which lives to take or not.’ She responded slowly.

Anders shook his head with a smile. He stood there, placidly.

She slowly approached him, one hand holding her weapon on him, with the other she pulled out a pair of handcuffs from her pocket.

'What are you doing?' He asked curiously.

'Arresting you.' She said timidly.

He raised an eyebrow at her, then grinned. 'Now why would I let you do that?'

In the corner of her eye she saw his hand raise the gun. *Shit.* She kicked out in a wild panic, faster than she thought she could move. She caught him off guard, connecting with his wrist.

He swore, dropping the gun.

She went to raise her gun.

His open palm moved so fast, she could hardly see it.

She felt a slap, and suddenly realised it was no longer in her hands. *Fuck.*

His body weight shifted slightly back, his knee twitched briefly.

She pounced back, landing on the toes of her feet.

His leg shot at her head, quicker than she would have imagined. She narrowly avoided it. His arms rested by his side.

Shit, she thought. *I was hoping he might just give up.* She noticed his stance, and the way he kicked. *Quick leg movements, swing kicks, aiming for the head.* She thought to herself. *Was that Taekwondo?*

His stance changed. *One fist held above the other, open palm, lower fist closed.* She scurried back, narrowly avoiding a lightning sharp cut to her head. *Aiming for my temple.* She thought in between rapid breaths. *Fuck, it's been too long. Was that kung fu?*

She kept her knees bent, realising the threat in front of her. *He's had training.* She breathed quickly. *Proper martial arts training. Not the self defence classes I've done.*

His feet moved quickly, as he circled her.

She grinned. *Well, there's something he would have never learnt.*

His weight shifted to his back leg. When he swung next, she was ready. The kick launched at her chest, but she darted to the left.

She noticed the opening, and sent a quick and light kick directly to his crotch.

He yelled and coughed instantly. 'What the fuck?' He swore, a confused look on her face. He was almost doubling over.

Before he had a chance to recover, she flicked out at his eyes.

He drop to his knees, covering his eyes. 'You fight dirty.' He coughed the words out.

He was placid as she arrested him. When the cuffs were on she exhaled deeply. It felt like simultaneous waves of calm and excitement coming over her.

She had caught him.

WILL

As he and Morgan exited the car, they saw from a distance as Aoki walked out of the house. She led Anders Sorensen out of the mansion in handcuffs. The two smiled.

'Yes!' Morgan cheered, punching the air. 'You're a superstar!' He yelled out to her.

She frowned and waved at him dismissively, telling him to be quiet. It was not yet dawn. They could see her fighting a grin. As she walked towards them he could see her talking into her police radio, calling in the arrest.

'We should be quick.' Morgan said, his face turning to a frown. 'Pretty soon this street will be full of journalists. No offense, Will.' He added with a teasing smile.

'None taken.' He laughed.

'William?' Anders said slowly, with an interested smile on his face. 'You seem different to how I expected you. It's good to finally meet you.'

Will took a deep breath. He felt intimidated in the presence of the man. When he realised the man in front of him was a talented and intelligent serial killer, any thoughts of his ideology vanished in reality.

'What's the matter? Do I frighten you?' He asked in a mocking tone with a raised eyebrow. He shook his head. 'Will, Will, Will. You disappoint me. Though, I suppose they do say that about meeting your heroes.'

'The spiral bankruptcy theory?' Will asked with a worried look on his face.

'Precisely, it's an inspiration to me.' He said in a cold tone.

Will shuddered slightly. There was something chilling about the confidence in Ander's eyes.

'What is he talking about Will?' Aoki asked slowly. She looked concerned.

Morgan turned and looked at him strangely.

He looked back at them both and shook his head. He would have to explain later.

'You never talked to them about this, Will? Tsk, tsk.' Anders said with feigned disapproval.

'How?' Will asked softly. He raised his hands. 'Everything you have done, you're saying it's all in the name of one of my theories?'

'Not all, but inspired by those theories. I'm, what was the term the media is calling me? A *social vigilante*.' He said with a smirk. 'But look around you William, can you honestly say you approve of this world?' Anders asked with an accusing tone.

Will frowned.

'You're one of the main economists opposed to inequality. You know the truth.'

'What's that?'

Anders smiled bitterly. 'Behind the corporate façade lies the corrupt nightmare of reality. Lives spent trying to attain wealth, chasing the consumer dream. Under the corporate rules, morals and compassion are the first casualties. Cities continue to build on top of themselves, and all the while the faceless and immoral corporations continue in their relentless pursuit of profit no matter the cost.'

Will narrowed his gaze. 'So how were you going to change that? I don't see it?'

'We will have plenty of time to discuss everything I'm trying to accomplish later.' Anders added with a grin.

'Trying to accomplish?' Will asked. He shook his head and frowned. 'You're arrested? This is the end.'

Anders took a deep breath and shook his head. 'End?' He smiled confidently, and narrowed his gaze. 'William. This is only the beginning.'

Will frowned, concerned with the confidence of this serial killer.

'Yeah, well,' Morgan said, grabbing the handcuffs and leading Anders to the car. 'Good luck changing the world from jail.'

Anders grinned, looking down.

Aoki laughed. She sighed. 'I have to call Rick. Can you—?'

'Sure thing.' Morgan smiled. 'I've got it, you go do it.' He turned to Anders. 'Hey, off the record, I have to ask you; what do you know about Malceski killing Chris Collins?'

'Malceski?' Anders raised an eyebrow. 'Hmm, maybe that was why he was killed,' He said absently, cryptically.

'Fine. Be that way.' Morgan sighed. 'You don't have to say anything if you don't want to.'

Aoki turned and walked away to call her partner. Will smiled. She seemed so calm. He was happy for her.

He felt something. He checked his pocket and pulled out his phone. It was Iz.

'Iz!' He said excitedly as he answered. 'They caught him!'

'Will, I need, really?' She said distantly. 'Ok, that's good.' She responded, she sounded distracted. 'I need to see you! Please, as soon as possible.'

Will frowned. She sounded upset. ‘Right now? I mean it’s going to be pretty crazy here?’

‘It’s urgent.’ She pleaded sadly. ‘Please, trust me.’

‘Ah yeah, ok. Yeah sure thing, can you talk about it?’

‘Not on the phone.’ She replied softly. ‘I’ll come over now.’

‘I’m not home—’ He started to say.

‘Please, just make an excuse, get out of there and meet me now.’ She sounded desperate. ‘It’s important.’

Will started to think of an excuse as he heard the sound of police sirens in the distance. They were getting closer.

LUKE

He watched the scene unfold from a distance. The detectives, vigilante, the journalist, all in the same place. His trigger finger felt itchy. The gun metal felt cold. Over the horizon, the sun glowed red as it started to come up. The police sirens were getting closer.

Sighing deeply, he made the call through his hands-free. 'Nothing we can do now.' He said when it answered, squinting. He unloaded his gun. He gestured up the road. 'The police will be here in a few minutes, there is no time.'

'Hmm.' The voice on the other end groaned. 'This won't go down well.'

'I already said there's nothing we can do. Why are we still discussing this?' He asked, agitated that they questioning him.

'You've got visual contact?'

'And in a few minutes so will another ten police officers. There is no way to kill them and plant a scene. We'd have the vigilante to deal with as well.' He shook his head. 'Think it through; how would I even make a getaway with all the extra police cars on the road? How many minutes would I drive for before getting stopped?' He shook his head again. 'I'm not taking action when there is no viable exit strategy.'

'I say again; this won't go down well.'

'Well then, whatever.' He said, packing his equipment. 'Tough break. I've already made the decision. I got the information too late and got here later. They got lucky this time.'

'You have a plan?'

He frowned. He had nothing. ‘Next time.’ He said between clenched teeth, tightening his grip on the cold metal in his hand. He did not like to fail.

WILL

He drove home quickly, having explained to Morgan and Aoki that it was a personal emergency. They had been distracted celebrating their victory, and hardly noticed him leave. There were a lot of police at the mansion by that point. They had wanted to take over custody of Sorensen, but Aoki had refused to let him out of her sight.

He went through the door to his apartment and walked straight to the couch to lie down. He sighed deeply. It had been such a chaotic journey over the last few weeks that he couldn't believe it was over.

He rubbed his eyes. It seemed Iz wanted to talk about something important, but he would have given anything to deal with it another time.

There was a knock at the door. He sighed and went to answer it.

When he opened the door and found Amber standing there. He frowned, confused. She was wearing the same clothes as when he had seen her last night, her tan leather handbag at her side.

'Will, I'm sorry. I didn't know where else to go. I heard what happened to my father.' She said calmly, looking at the floor.

His face softened. 'Hey, hey. It's ok.' He said gently. He put a hand around her shoulder reassuringly. 'Come in.'

She looked up and narrowed her gaze at him. She then smiled sadly, walked inside and made her way to the couch. She sat down slowly and then put her head in her hands. 'I just couldn't go back to that house Will, my father was nearly killed by that madman.' She said pleadingly.

'It's ok. Don't mention it. I'm happy you came to me.' He smiled gently.

She looked up at him. She smiled and wiped her eyes. 'Thank you.'

He exhaled. He felt sorry for her. She had been caught up the middle of this situation. The crimes of Delpont, the syndicate of Azure, the serial killings of the vigilante. She was the beautiful calm in the centre of the storm.

There was a knock at the door. He frowned. He'd forgotten about Iz. 'Oh, sorry.' He said gently. 'I forgot. My friend needed to come over to talk to me.'

'It's ok.' She shook her head, smiling. 'You don't need to apologise. I came over uninvited; you go talk to your friend.'

He smiled and turned for the door. He wished that Iz had picked another time to have an emergency. He just wanted to be there for Amber.

He opened the door to see his friend. She looked scared. She wore her camera around her neck. 'I'm really sorry to come over like this, I wouldn't have done it if it wasn't urgent.' She scratched her head.

'Yeah, I know. What's wrong? Come in.' He said, gesturing inside.

She sighed, stepping in. There was a frenetic energy to her movement. 'Will you aren't going to believe this. I really need you to trust me, ok?' She asked, gently.

'Ok.' He frowned. He felt entirely confused. 'What is going on?'

Iz took a deep breath. As the two walked into the living room, she opened her mouth to start talking. It was then she noticed Amber and froze.

Amber looked up at her and smiled, but Iz turned to him, pointing at Amber. 'What is she doing here?!' Iz raised her voice. She seemed to be pleading.

'Hello, Iz.' Amber said calmly.

'Will?!' Iz repeated, worried. 'What is she doing here? I told you I wanted to talk.'

'It's ok.' He said softly. 'The vigilante tried to kill her father. They caught him. But she's shaken up. She came to see me. Be gentle.'

She shook her head angrily, and scratched her head in frustration.

'Anything you want to say to me you can say in front of her.' He said gently to Iz.

'No I can't!' She said angrily. 'Will, don't you get it?! It's about her!' She shook her head again. She seemed to be on the verge of tears.

'What are you talking about?'

'Look. I followed her last night, ok? I didn't trust her, I thought she might have been seeing someone else.' She talked fast.

'Iz.' He sighed.

'Will, I saw her with him! With the police officer!' She held her camera up to show him. 'Will, please.' Her eyes looked sad. 'You have to believe me.'

'Iz,' He said frustrated. 'I have no idea what you're talking about?'

'Please!' She shouted. 'Please! Look here.' She held the camera closer to him. 'See here, in these photos, that's Amber and the officer having a fight! Remember, the officer you showed me the picture of?'

'Luke Wade?' Will asked softly, looking at the photo. It looked like Luke talking to a blonde woman. But the photo was from a distance. He felt confused. He turned to Amber. 'What is she talking about?'

‘I have no idea, Will.’ Amber said sadly. Her eyes looked to be welling with tears.

He shook his head. ‘Iz, the photo isn’t really clear. That doesn’t really look like Amber? What are you trying to say anyway?’

Iz looked him directly in the eyes. She looked distressed. ‘I don’t know, Will! But she’s mixed up in this somehow. I don’t trust her.’

He exhaled, irritated. ‘You’ve never trusted her.’

Iz sobbed. ‘Please, Will, trust me.’ She wiped away tears. ‘Look, I mean, this Luke guy is meant to be the guy that tried to kill you, Rebecca, and that other killer.’

‘Malceski?’ He asked, shaking his head.

‘Yeah! Yeah, exactly!’ She nodded. ‘So maybe Malceski and this Luke guy had something to do with Chris?’ She pleaded.

He frowned. The mention of his friend upset him.

‘I know, it’s crazy, but please believe me Will!’ Tears fell down her face. She looked scared. ‘I think she had something to do with this, with these deaths. She’s standing here having an argument with the guy?!’

‘Yeah, I don’t understand.’ He said softly.

‘Will?’ Amber spoke up gently. She reached into her tan leather handbag. ‘I don’t know what she’s talking about?’

‘Fuck!’ Iz groaned. ‘You cannot seriously be falling for this shit?!’

‘Your friend is scaring me. How can she say those things about me?’ Amber buried her face.

He sighed. ‘Look, Iz, we can talk about this later? I mean, Amber is clearly upset right now.’

‘That’s bullshit!’ Iz screamed, tears falling down her face. ‘Will, please don’t fall for this! I’m telling you the truth.’

‘You’re just attacking her!’ Will shouted back, anger in his voice. ‘You never liked her!’

Iz shook her head with a bitter smile. ‘I don’t care. If you really don’t believe me, just ask yourself; why is she here?!’

He frowned and turned to Amber.

‘I, Will, I don’t know what she’s talking about.’ Her eyes were sad. There was a gentle fragility in her gaze as she got closer to him. Her voice was soft. ‘I came here after I heard about my father. I told you this, Will?’

‘Yeah.’ He said softly. ‘That’s true.’

‘Will?’ His friend’s voice caught in her throat. ‘She must have seen me take the photo, she must have tried to stop me.’

He rolled his eyes. ‘Iz! That’s insane!’

She sobbed and shook her head.

‘None of what you’re telling me is any proof!’ He shouted.

‘Will, please?!’ She shouted, her aqua blue eyes welling with tears. ‘I need you to believe me.’ She pleaded. Her aqua blue eyes swelling with tears. She was angry, but begged him to understand.

The bullet tore through her chest, right above her breast and left through her wing tattoo.

In shock, he heard the explosion.

Her eyes went blank as she fell.

Everything was forgotten as her ran to hold her, take her in his arms. He cried as he held her. Her arms clung to him, grip loosening with each second.

He held his friend, and looked over his shoulder at the woman. Her smile still warm and welcoming, only her ocean blue eyes betrayed how cold she truly was.

Tears fell down his face as he held his dying friend, the friend that he loved, his little sister.

He realised she was right. Her eyes look into his, the last of her life slipping away. Her hand fell as she left him. Her small body held tightly in his arms.

He cradled the body tightly, promising to never let her go.

Far away, he heard metal hit the floor, and a door closing shut.

ANDREA

She was led through the police station. Her body numb. She was in another world, far away. All of it must be happening to someone else.

She felt a hard tug as she was led to a cell. The guard told her emotionlessly to go inside, and told her he wasn't going to be patient. She kept her head focused on the floor and walked inside. Far away she heard a loud banging sound as the door slammed behind her.

Suddenly, she was aware of the silence all around her. She turned around quickly, in a panic. The room was cold and unforgiving. There was a small open window on the far wall. The bright morning light shone through. Her body was drained. She was truly defeated. It was only when locked away that she realised what had actually happened. Frantically she moved around the room, looking for a way out. Secretly she hoped she would wake up, and that it would all be a bad dream.

She spent half an hour trying to deny reality. Gradually she realised she was trapped. Slowly she moved to the steel bench and lowered herself.

She buried her face in her hands and cried. She'd made a stupid mistake.

It was just one moment of her life, but she felt as if nothing would ever be the same. Everything had happened so fast. She just wanted to go back to her own life. She realised that she had made a colossal mistake by letting Hank become so important to her. He was just a fling. It had gotten out of control.

'Stupid, stupid, stupid.' She swore aloud in between tears. She hit her head in frustration.

She just wanted to see her husband. She really did love him, he was a good man, and she needed him. She shook her head, realising he might have found out about her madness. The situation seemed so surreal. She wondered what he would make of it.

Her body started to shake, she couldn't be sure whether because she was overtired or due to stress. In the past few hours her life had fallen apart. She was breathing faster and faster as she sat there sobbing. Whatever happened next, she was out of control. There was nothing she could do. It was up to her lawyer. Maybe her husband would do something. The door was locked behind her. She was truly trapped.

Several minutes passed as she sat waiting, and then her body crashed.

The next moment she was awoken from an uncomfortable slumber on the cold steel bench. She was instantly alert, looking around the room, trying to figure out what was going on. The armpits of her silk blouse were stained with sweat. Her hair was in her face.

Her body was filled with terror as she remembered she was out of control.

The guard stood there talking to her. He didn't care. She could not tell what he was saying. She could see his mouth open and close, but could not make out the worlds. He rolled his eyes and grunted. He looked irritated. He walked out and left her alone again.

She pulled herself up, suddenly aware how tired she was. She felt weak and light headed. There was no fight left in her. She was truly lost.

She didn't give a fuck anymore.

There was a noise at the entrance to the room. She looked up to see her husband standing there.

Her stomach filled with dread at the sight of him. His stare was stern and impassive. He looked like he could care less. She hung her face in her hands. All her guilt and feelings for him were dredged to the surface. She had ignored their shared past and forgotten how she felt. As he stood there in front of her, powerful and unemotional, she remembered why she fell for him. She looked at him hesitantly, trying to judge how he felt. He was unreadable. All she saw was the face she hadn't looked at properly in so long. His beard was thick and black, with flecks of grey. His hair was balding at the peak, but greying and trimmed short everywhere else. He wore khaki trousers and a black woollen turtleneck jumper. His arms were crossed, emphasising his broad shoulders and stocky build. There was a stern scowl on his face as always.

He stood there looking at for a moment saying nothing. She wanted to break the silence, but her voice caught in her throat. She twisted in her clothes trying to get comfortable. She straightened her thigh high skirt and adjusted her tight blouse, looking up to see whether her sexuality could soothe his temper. There was no softness in his face. She struggled to recall the last time she had been intimate with him. His skin looked even darker than usual in the dim morning light.

'Nothing to say?' He asked indifferently.

She looked up at him and smiled weakly. She racked her brains thinking of a solution, something creative and credible. Several minutes passed in an awkward silence. Nothing came to mind.

'Khalifa, I'm so sorry.' She said pleadingly.

He looked her up and down. 'Is that all?' He asked flatly.

She scanned the ground, searched her mind for something. There was nothing.

'Hmm.' He muttered. 'Much as I suspected.'

She smiled again. 'I think, this whole situation is a misunderstanding.'

He sighed loudly and stepped from side to side. He looked out the narrow window. 'Unlikely.' He said indifferently.

She looked down and shook her head. That tact would not work. 'I'm truly sorry for causing you this trouble. This is just a mess. I don't know what came over me.' She stated. She put herself in the character of a remorseful wife. Her ability to maintain professionalism would be the only thing that might allow her to survive it.

He narrowed his gaze at her. 'It won't work this time, Andrea.' He said emotionlessly.

'What do you mean?' She asked with a smile, trying her best to look as though she did not understand his implication.

'I've known about this Hank for some time now.' He said shaking his head, his teeth clenched. There was bitterness to his tone.

'I'm sorry.' She said impulsively.

He looked at her with suspect curiosity.

She shook her head, realising her mistake. 'But I don't know what you're talking about, darling?' She added, correcting her error.

He looked at her with venom. He shook his head again, clenching his fists. The morning light caught the flecks of grey in his black beard. 'I think you do.'

She tried to look as confused as possible. She needed to save the marriage. Without it she was lost.

'Do not look at me like that, Andrea. I have known about your infidelities for some time.'

'Khalifa, please, I'm truly—' She pleaded.

‘Don’t!’ He spat, venom in his words. His voice was spiteful but he kept his anger in check. She realised he had calculated his every word. ‘I have tolerated your discretions for some time. After all, marriage is not perfect.’ He said with a sad smile.

‘Darling, I think—’

‘Let me finish.’ He barked the words coldly. ‘I do not want to hear you speak. Not anymore.’ He said, taking a deep breath. She had never seen him so infuriated. She realised he knew with certainty. He sighed. ‘I thought it would perhaps just be a temporary infidelity, that you would get over it and come back. I thought we could save this marriage.’ He said flatly.

‘But we still can!’ She grabbed his hand, her voice gentle.

He looked at her with disdain. ‘But we cannot. Things between us are done.’ His tone was final.

There was another silence. His words hit her hard. She broke down and started sobbing. She didn’t know what was happening. She was lost.

Nevertheless, he continued speaking. ‘Did you seriously think I was not aware of you and Hank?’ He shook his head angrily. ‘Did you seriously think you could continue lying to me and cuckolding me?’ He demanded, his voice filled with fury. ‘I shall not be humiliated like that!’ He shouted, his words echoing against the wall.

She looked down at the floor mutely, avoiding his gaze. He exhaled deeply. It seemed to soothe him slightly. ‘Darling,’ she said gently. ‘I love you, I truly do.’

He turned and looked at her. There was a deep sadness in his eyes that she had never seen before. In the past decade his time was usually spent looking into the screen of his laptop, he scarcely looked at her anymore. She had forgotten the warmth of his gaze. ‘What about Hank, then?’ He asked with a bitter smile.

She looked down and shook her head glumly. She realised how fucked she was.

‘This is what is going to happen.’ He said, taking a deep breath, calming down. He cleared his throat. ‘I have arranged for this matter with the police to be resolved. Hank decided not to press charges. He’s confused.’ He shook his head. He looked up at her and sighed. ‘He wasn’t even cheating on you Andrea.’ He said perplexed, shaking his head.

She narrowed her gaze at him, confused.

‘He told me about it, the woman leaving his house, it was his sister.’ He looked away, eyes narrowed. There was a bitter smile on his face. ‘Apparently, he had never been with anyone else. The man actually did love you.’

Andrea closed her eyes and hung her head in her hands. It was too much to handle. She felt the world was falling away from under her. She couldn’t have imagined it all.

‘Regardless, he does not want to be involved with you any further.’

Tears built up in the sides of her eyes. She sat mute, listening.

‘Be grateful he was so cooperative, you were lucky in this instance.’ He barked at her, coldly. ‘As to the matter of the car crash, I have arranged with the police for it to be put down to a temporary, non recurring issue. We have yet to determine an exact reason, but I need to discuss it with my attorneys further. Maybe a psychological issue.’ He stroked his beard pensively. ‘However, part of my deal with law enforcement requires you attend anger management therapy.’

She looked up at him in between tears, confused.

‘I asked for it specifically. You will attend, and you will go through the complete treatment. You need to figure yourself out, Andrea. I want you to do this for yourself. Do you consent?’

She nodded with a sad smile. She tried to think of something to say, but nothing came to mind. She felt as though she was being taken away with the current, with no control.

'Very well. In terms of things between us, moving forward,' He breathed deeply, he stroked his beard, his solid frame standing over her. 'Things between us are done, Andrea. I want a divorce.'

She opened her mouth to plead with him.

'This is not a matter for discussion. Not anymore. I will arrange for some funding for the transitionary period over the next few months while you find your own accommodation, but beyond I don't want anything to do with you anymore.' He said with a sad sigh. 'Things have not been working for some time. I've been angry for a long time with your actions and your betrayal. But I have accepted it.' He sighed again. 'All I want now, is to move on with my life.'

She shook her head. She wanted to react with anger and frustration and fight. She felt defensive. But more than anything else she was lost for words. She felt a sinking feeling as she realised she was losing him.

'I have discussed everything with my attorneys, and have arranged adequate representation for yourself as well. I will not be vengeful. You will be well looked after for the next few months, you will have every resource that you had when we entered this marriage, plus any money or assets you accumulated through your own career. However, and mark my words; beyond that you're cut off from any of my funding or networking resources.' He sighed as he looked at her with cold, unemotional eyes. 'You're on your own from now on, Andrea.'

She looked at the ground in shock. Trying to process everything that he had said. 'I'm sorry.' She said softly and honestly. 'I know it won't change anything now, but I am truly sorry.' She said, looking at him as she spoke.

He looked at her gently. He smiled and shook his head. 'Have a good life, Andrea.' He said gently. He lingered for a moment as he looked at her, then he turned and left the room and walked out.

The cell door closed loudly behind him.

She took a deep breath. Absorbing the information that had just been given to her. Within a few minutes her life had changed dramatically, and had changed permanently. There was no possibility of going back to her old life. It was gone now. She knew from what Khalifa had said that he would be unwavering. She was dimly aware of the guards entering the room to escort her somewhere. She did not know where.

She walked out of the cell, feeling lighter already. As though there were less pressure on her. Her mind raced as she was led through the police hallway. Faces passed in a blur. Some paid her no attention. Some looked at her with curious smiles.

She could not care anymore. When she had felt herself fall into the blackness she had lost everything. There was nothing to lose anymore. It was a strange thought. She sighed with relief. She felt free in a way she never had before.

Far away she heard a laugh.

'Did someone schedule the Delpont reunion here today?' She heard a sarcastic voice ask her. She looked up to see a handsome man with light brown long hair and rough stubble of the same colour. As he smiled she could see wrinkles by the sides of his eyes. Wearing chains around his hands and ankles, he was being escorted by a crowd of anxious police officers. They were passing by her in the corridor, heading in the opposite direction.

She frowned. Confused. She did not know what to make of the scene.

He shook his head sadly. 'You don't remember me, do you?' He smiled. 'Probably for the best. Paul McDermott is around here somewhere. If you see him, send him my regards.' He said smugly.

'Keep moving.' One of the guards said, shoving him along.

Before she could think of what to say, the man was behind her, being led down the corridor.

THE VIGILANTE

He wondered what Andrea was doing at the station. He grinned. Most likely being manipulated in an attempt to testify against him. Or purely fabricate some evidence. She was, after all, the typical Delpont criminal. She would toe the company line and do whatever was told. He scoffed. He should have killed her when he had the chance.

They pushed him into an interview room. The detective named Morgan was sitting there waiting, leaning back in his chair. He already didn't like him.

'Where's Ms Sun?' He asked. 'Her and I already have a thing going on, you see.'

Morgan rolled his eyes. *This one was quite humourless.* 'Whatever, dickhead. Shut up with your garbage and just give me a direct answer.'

He frowned. Already he liked this one less. He sat at the chair opposite Morgan and slumped back.

'Now,' The detective said casually as he fiddled with the recording device on the table. He had an easy-going way of talking. It seemed like he would fit well in the banking world. 'Would you please state your name for the tape?'

'First name, Robin. Last name, Hood.' He said each word slowly and flatly.

The detective looked up and glared at him.

He tried to stop himself from grinning. At least he could have a little fun.

Morgan sighed. 'Fine then. Would you please confirm that your name is Anders Sorensen?'

He feigned shock. 'I'm afraid there has been some terrible error, this is all just a grave misunderstanding, my name is Robin Hood. No,' He said slowly, raising his hands apologetically. 'Not that Robin Hood, but you wouldn't believe how many people make the same mistake. I'm but a simple baker.'

'Fucking, damn it.' Morgan muttered softly. He sighed loudly, shaking his head.

'Ok then,' He said gently. 'You twisted my arm. I'll admit it, I'm in actual fact a diamond thief from the underground of Paris; by day I steal hearts, by night I steal diamonds.' He said with false excitement. 'I make my way unseen through the city, carrying out elaborate heists. It's an interesting story you see—'

'Fine.' Morgan cut him off. He rubbed his forehead and exhaled deeply. 'I get it. You're hilarious.' He said flatly.

'Would you believe me if I said *Robin* is just a nickname?' He asked, one eyebrow raised.

Morgan shook his head, scribbling notes.

'Where is Aoki, anyway?' He asked sincerely.

'Why? Did you prefer her?'

'Yes, and I admire the tenacity and resourcefulness with which she used to find me.'

'That sounded almost sincere.' Morgan commented absently.

'It was sincere.'

'Alright, whatever,' He exhaled. 'Aoki went home, she was exhausted. You'll get a chance to talk to her later.'

'Fine then.'

'Will you say anything to me? Or are you just going to keep feeding me bullshit?'

He smiled. 'I'm only going to talk to Will.' He said slowly. He had been repeating it to Morgan ever since Aoki handed over custody of him.

Morgan banged his head on the table. He groaned.

'We have a lot of things to talk about you realise. Why don't you bring him in here and I will tell him whatever you need.' He said with mock enthusiasm.

'I swear,' Morgan shook his head. 'You're like a child.'

'And you would be a horrible parent. Where is Will?'

Morgan sighed. 'There was a complication, something happened.' He shook his head. 'Will won't be here for a while. You're going to have to make do with me.' He replied sarcastically.

Anders leaned back in his chair and crossed his arms. He frowned, wondering what could have happened. He exhaled deeply, watching the frustrated detective look absently through documents and scribble some notes. Hardly the person he had planned on having intelligent and ideological conversations with.

'Where is your accent from anyway? You're French or something. Right?' Morgan asked absently.

Anders sighed.

AOKI

She had slept for almost ten hours. Her sleeping patterns would be screwed up for a few days, but she didn't care. It had been worth it. When she had awoken she felt reborn.

It had been an impossible case for her. It had confronted her every fear of drawing too much attention. The anxiety she once felt was subdued. She had slept just fine.

She walked out to the living room to find Rick in the kitchen, cooking some food. She smiled at the sight of him. He grinned. They held each other tightly. She had been buried in the case for so long, it felt like she had come home. Their moment was broken abruptly when the smoke detector started going off because of the food, startling them both. They laughed, before finding a chair and resetting it.

When she eventually checked her phone, her moment of celebration had ended. Something was wrong. There were too many missed calls and messages. When she called Morgan back her broke the news to her.

They drove in silence to see Will. He had not picked up his phone. He was not at his apartment, Morgan had told her that much. What was once his home had become a crime scene. Morgan had told her that it would take a long time for them to clean up the blood once they had processed the scene. She had called around before she had found him. Rick realised that she needed quiet and respected that. She stared out the window, thinking. She had no idea what to say to Will.

'Are you sure you don't want me to come in with you?' Rick asked as they parked.

'No.' She replied softly. 'It's fine. I think I need to talk to him alone.'

He nodded. 'Alright, I can understand.'

She sighed and got out of the car. Walking up to Rebecca's apartment she thought of what to say. She had met this man after one of his friends had died, and now another had been killed.

As she knocked on his door, she felt nervous.

Beck opened the door tentatively. She supported herself with crutches. She smiled sadly at Aoki. *She's making an incredible recovery.* 'Will's in the living room.' She said as he stepped away from the door and walked back into the apartment, leaving the door open. Aoki followed in. She saw Will's worn brown leather travel bag in the living room. She recalled what Morgan had said on the phone, how he had needed to help Will pack it. Morgan said he had been in a mute state.

Will sat on the couch in the living room. His eyes were red, his hair was scruffy and a mess. There was anger in his eyes. He was wearing different clothes to when last she saw him. They were creased, it looked as though he had slept in them. He picked up his glass of tea, still steaming. He held it with both hands.

Aoki walked up and hugged Beck. 'You're doing so well, it's amazing.' She said in a quiet voice so Will could not hear. It was true.

'Thanks, it means a lot.' Beck said with a smile. 'I still have to use crutches, but they let me get out of the hospital.'

'That is incredible.' Aoki said, shaking her head. 'Considering they said you would never walk again.'

Beck smiled wickedly. 'Pfft, doctors, what do they know?' She teased.

Aoki grinned and shook her head. Beck was tough. Aoki turned and looked at Will. 'How is doing?' She asked gently.

Beck winced. 'Not well. He hasn't said much. He just showed up. I was so shocked when I opened the door.'

Aoki looked confused.

'All that blood on his shirt, he didn't seem to realise. I didn't know it was Amber who shot her until you called me.' She sighed. 'It's all so sick. Right in front of him?' She shook her head as she filled the teapot.

'I know. I hadn't thought much of Amber when he told me about her, she seemed dull.' She exhaled deeply. 'I had no idea she was so sick.' Beck paused, she looked up at Aoki with a great sadness in her eyes. 'Is it true, what Will thought? That Amber arranged to kill Chris, as well?'

Aoki exhaled. She hadn't considered the effect it would have on Beck. She felt guilty. 'We think so.'

Beck shook her head bitterly.

'I'm really sorry, for all of this.' Aoki said gently. 'This must be so difficult.'

'It's ok.' She replied, looking down. It looked as though she was about to cry, but she cleared her throat. She sighed and smiled sadly. 'We have all been through a lot. We're all in this together. I just keeping thinking,' She shook her head, furrowing her brow. 'I just don't understand, why? Why would Amber get that Malceski guy to kill Chris? It doesn't make any sense still.'

Aoki frowned. 'I had been thinking about that too. When Chris asked Will to meet him that night, Will said he had something to tell him or show him. Something about Delpont.'

Beck ran her hands through her hair. She sighed. 'Maybe, but why Amber?'

Aoki shook her head. 'I don't know. It doesn't make sense. She's involved with Azure somehow, but I can't figure out how. I can't understand why McDermott would involve his daughter in it.' Her words trailed off as she thought about it. She sighed.

'And I mean, why did Amber kill Malceski afterwards?'

Aoki exhaled, frowning. 'That I have no idea. There is so much more to Delpont and Azure. So much more I'd wanted to investigate.'

'Wanted?' Beck asked, puzzled.

Aoki smiled sadly. She wanted to explain it to Will first. She walked out of the kitchen and into the living room. She put a reassuring hand on Will's shoulder. It seemed to make him flinch. He looked up her. She could see he was on edge.

'Will,' She spoke softly, her voice catching in her throat. 'I'm so sorry. I came as soon as I heard.'

The grief became fresh on his face, as she spoke she brought it all back to the surface again. He looked at her and then nodded silently.

'I'm so sorry about Iz.' Aoki said as gently as possible. 'She was really amazing.'

He nodded sadly, visibly upset at the mention of her name. He said nothing in response.

'Morgan told me that people are searching everywhere for Amber. She hasn't been found yet.'

His eyes narrowed, she saw a flash of rage. Again, he said nothing.

She sighed. She felt guilty at what she needed to tell him. 'Will, I didn't just come here to see if you were ok. Morgan told me something on the phone.' She shook her head. She had no idea how to say it. She wished she had more tact to say things like this.

Will would have known how to tell something like this gently. 'I just, I didn't want you to find this out from someone else.'

He looked up at her. He frowned.

'Will, they aren't going to be pursuing Amber as a suspect in Iz's death.' She felt the words slip out.

He looked up at her slowly. He looked confused.

'Morgan was told from a pretty senior level. They're not pursuing any case against Amber, or Paul either. They're pushing the theory that there's no substantial evidence. I'm really sorry.'

She realised his hands were clenching the tea glass as tightly as possible. She was worried it might break. There was a wild look in his eyes. She had seen it before in the eyes of killers. His teeth were clenched tight. He looked out the window.

'I don't believe it for a second. I promise; I'm going to do everything I can to bring Amber to justice, yeah?' She rested her hand on his shoulder. Her voice was calm and confident. 'She won't get away with this.' She reassured him.

He shook his head absently, lost in thought.

'Morgan and I will fight this. You know that right?' She asked him warmly.

He looked at her, his gaze softened. He smiled sadly and nodded. Then looked at the floor.

She sat there next to him and put an arm around his shoulder. They sat in silence. She tried gently and unsuccessfully to get him to talk. When she eventually left the apartment he still hadn't said a word.

WILL

He wouldn't have been able to sleep. He waited until Beck fell asleep and then snuck out as quietly as possible. His thoughts had been of Amber all day. All he felt was a sick guilt. He barely remembered driving to Beck's, he couldn't remember where he had parked. Eventually he found his car. He didn't know where, but he knew that he needed to drive somewhere.

He rolled down the windows. The cold night air whirled around him as he drove. He left the radio off. The only thing he heard was the sound of the city outside; rubber tires against the asphalt, the constant melody of the pedestrian crossing, police sirens as new crimes were committed, the roar of trains taking people to and from work. He drove down to Cremorne Point Wharf and got out of the car. He looked out across Sydney harbour at the city nightline. He had always thought the city skyline was so beautiful at night. As he looked from a distance, all he saw were skyscrapers jutting up at different heights, illuminated by bright neon of conflicting colours that reflected over the harbour. He thought of all the things that made up the city. The individual lives that were lived and lost every day, and the dreams and hopes and nightmares that came true. Each day out there in the city was the worst of someone's life. And yet, after all that, every day the city would start again. Reborn. Fuelled by the energy of those who dedicated their lives to it. No matter what happened, the city was unchanged. Monolithic and impassive, the city did not care whether it was a good or a bad day. The city would be the same regardless.

He shook his head, remembering the times that he and Iz had come down to that point. The two had sat together, enjoying the view, drinking, smoking, talking. He clenched his fist, feeling anger running through him again. He turned and left.

He drove for a while, aimlessly. He did not know how or why but he ended up outside Amber's house. It looked bright and perfect, immaculate as always.

He had no plan, but he walked to the front gate.

'Sorry, no visitors.' The guard said flatly as he got closer.

'Where is she?' He asked bitterly.

'Who?' The guard looked confused.

'Get Paul out here.' He said, grinding his teeth. 'Tell him it's Will.'

The guard made a quick call. There was movement at the front door as Paul walked outside.

'She's not here, Will.' He said sadly as he opened the gate.

Will marched past. 'I'll look.' He said tersely.

'You're wasting your time.' Paul scratched his head. 'She's long gone.'

Will shook his head as he walked through the door. He walked briskly, scanning the house. He searched for any trace of her.

'Will, I heard what happened. I am truly sorry.' Paul said gently, following behind.

Will shot him an angry glare as he walked upstairs. 'Is any of what you say true?'

Paul shook his head and sighed. 'I'm telling you the truth.'

'Where is she?!' He asked angrily as he swung open every door.

'She's gone.' Paul said again.

Will smirked. He walked to the end of the hallway and opened the door to Amber's room. There was a mess. Clothes had been discarded on the bed. Drawers had been left open. It looked as if someone had raided it already. Will started looking through the mess. He threw clothes and books off the bed, clearing the mess away. He looked for any clue as to where she was.

'Like I said, she's gone.'

'Where?' Will shouted, turning and facing the old man. 'Where did she go?!' He yelled, storming toward the old man. This man had caused so much destruction, committed so many crimes. He was filled with fury.

Paul shook his head.

'Where did she go?!' He roared again and pushed the old man into the wall.

Paul braced himself. As he hit the wall he winced. He looked up at Will with bitterness.

'She killed someone.' He roared. 'Does that mean anything to you?' He shook his head. 'And what, you're just going to cover this up? Hide her?'

The old man looked at him sadly. 'Yes.'

Will shouted in frustration and pushed him against the wall again. He swung a punch that connected with Paul's head.

Paul swore under his breath and held his head. He stood up and glared at Will.

'Where has she gone? Answer me!' Will yelled.

The two guards ran into the room, drawn in by the commotion. They looked at Paul, concerned.

He held his hand up and shook his head. He waved them away dismissively.

They relaxed and frowned. They turned around and walked out of the room.

Will exhaled. It was an unexpected action from Paul.

‘I told you the truth.’ Paul said slowly. ‘I have no idea where she’s gone, but she is gone, Will. She packed a backpack calmly for half an hour and then left for the airport.’ He shook his head. ‘That’s all I know. I have no idea what her plan is.’ He sighed.

Will looked at him with anger. He was suspicious.

‘I’m telling you the truth.’ Paul said frustrated, his hands out. There was already a cut on his forehead where he had been hit.

Will sighed and shook his head. He scanned the room. Her laptop was unplugged and the power cord was gone from where she had left it. All the audio and design equipment connected to it had been left. He walked past her desk, searching through.

‘Her passport is gone.’ Paul said softly. He shook his head. ‘She took out all the money she had in her account a short while ago. I don’t think she plans on coming back, Will.’ He said softly.

Will clenched his fist.

‘I’m looking for her too.’ He said gently.

‘Where?’ He turned to Paul. He shook his head. He asked again, softer. ‘Where did she fly to?’

Paul looked at him and narrowed his gaze. ‘Thailand.’ He said faintly. ‘She bought a one-way ticket to Thailand. Beyond that I don’t know.’

Will sighed.

‘Drink?’ Paul asked gently.

Will nodded silently.

‘I’m sorry for your friend.’ He said sincerely as the two walked to his study. He opened the door and led him inside. He walked to the counter, picked up two thick rock glasses and poured scotch. He walked to Will and handed him a glass. Paul sighed and sipped from his own glass slowly.

‘Amber arranged for Chris to be killed. Chris found something.’ Will said.

Paul sighed, he walked to his desk and sat slumped against it. ‘He found something of mine. Amber heard this. Maybe overheard somehow, maybe from me.’

‘It was never your plan to kill him.’ Will said slowly. He didn’t know if it was a question or a statement.

Paul nodded. ‘I was against it.’

‘She made other plans?’

He frowned, and nodded again.

Will exhaled deeply. He assumed knowing the truth would have made him feel better. It didn’t. ‘I’m going to find her. Then I will kill her.’ He said, his voice thick with anger.

Paul shook his head, disappointed. ‘And then what?’

Will turned and looked at him, confused.

Paul sighed deeply. ‘Nothing will bring back Chris or Isabelle.’

‘Don’t say their names.’ He said between clenched teeth.

Paul ignored the comment. ‘You won’t find her anyway. I can find her much easier than you could. If need be, I will hide her. You can’t compete with the resources I have.’ He said flatly, wiping the cut on his forehead. He seemed tired. His glass was empty. He walked to the counter and poured another scotch.

Will watched silently.

'Do you want to know something I realised a while ago?' He asked absently, sipping at his drink. 'Capitalism is a game. People pay money to play, they put all the money in the pot, and everything is decided by the roll of dice, by the luck of the draw of where they start off. The rules say that everyone is given the same odds, and if they're smart and know probability, strategy, and so on. They will succeed. It's a system in which, say a million people play. They all know that only one of those million people will succeed, and will become rich and safe and get all the money in the pot. If they lose then they face a life of stress and worrying about money and trying desperately to make ends meet. They keep telling each other that they're all better off when someone wins, that it makes everyone else better off as well, but they ignore that those people who keep on winning were lucky from the start, they started at the right point. They ignore that the game is being played with rigged dice, and they ignore that the lucky ones get to play with a few extra dice. Capitalism is a game, but it's played with loaded dice. Yet, everyone is happy to play, because they believe that they could be the one who wins.' He shook his head with a bitter smile. 'Each and every person in that system believes they're better, believes they're different. Believes that it will be them who becomes rich and safe. Because of that, people keep playing. And they're happy to play.' He turned and smiling sadly at him. 'Just remember who the real enemy is.' He said, narrowing his gaze.

'The lucky ones?' He asked with a frown.

'Is that what you believe?' Paul asked with an eye raised. 'Maybe it's the lucky ones? Maybe they could share what they win to those that lose? Maybe they could just give back some of the excess they win? Do you believe it's the lucky ones? What about the ones who decided the rules? How about the people who are allowed to vote to change the rules, and yet they vote the same way each time? And what about the players? Imagine, what would happen if they all decided to stop playing?' He shook his head bitterly. He seemed older than he should be. 'We all have our choices to make, Will.' He said softly, turning his gaze to the window, sipping on his drink.

Will frowned, thinking. He sighed deeply and turned, leaving Paul who continued to sip his drink, staring out the window. Will walked out of the room, passed the guards in silence, and exited the mansion.

LEW

Freedom felt good. He was reborn. He adjusted the silver cufflinks, grinning smugly that he felt the weight of wealth again. He straightened the silk tie, feeling the power run through his blood. He wore a tailor made suit for the first time again. He had needed to abuse the tailor and berated him for only fifteen minutes before he convinced the man to make the suit in a few hours. If he had waited a day it would have only cost a few tens of thousands of dollars, but he refused to deal with these wankers again looking even a cent less than a millionaire. He grinned, thinking of everything he planned to do once the meeting was over. He couldn't wait to get out of the dump. Why they kept on meeting at the abandoned office was a mystery to him. He looked around at the exposed concrete pillars and empty window frames. If it were up to him they would sell the property for one dollar to a mate of theirs. If nothing else it would piss all the poor people off, which was always good for a laugh. He chuckled at the idea.

Fucking peasants, he thought to himself.

He couldn't wait to torture them again. He missed having money and telling everyone what to do. He exhaled and calmed himself down, excited already by the prospect of his revenge.

'Mr Noble.' The old guy with perfect diction said, smiling. He clutched that stupid orange book as always. 'Good to see you without the bars.'

'Don't mention it.' Lew said with a smirk. He disliked the guy who looked like a grandfather, with his wise old smile. The man thought he was far too intelligent. 'Though you took far too long getting everything arranged. If I ever tell you to do something again you better get it done faster.'

'Noble.' The old man said reproachfully with a curious smile. 'Remember, we are partners in this matter. While we appreciate your assistance, we feel we have rewarded you adequately.'

'Don't give me that!' Lew shouted, taking a step closer for intimidation. Just like he had learnt in all the wealth books. 'If I had never delivered the information about Fulton or Martec, you would have never known what they were doing!' He yelled. He spat on the floor, staring the older man down. 'You owe me. I can name my price and you will pay it!'

The old man smiled with excited eyes. 'Mr Noble, you are the very spirit of deregulation. You will be a valuable asset in getting things back to normal. However,' The old man's eyes and voice turned cold in a flash. 'You are aware of your market price. We have rewarded you sufficiently. As it turned out, your information was valuable, but things did not go as planned. Ms Fulton survived, Mr Martec evaded capture, and detectives Sun and Morgan are still a threat.'

The pure cold calculation this man displayed made Lew feel fear as always. He denied the fear and hid it. Just as he had been taught as a trader. Any emotion was weakness and could kill you in a room of sharks. He needed to be the most vicious of the sharks and kill anyone in his way. That was the only way to succeed. He needed to get back to trading in the zone. He needed to kill any emotion he had started to feel during his prison sentence. He spat again and stared the man down. 'You gave me a job and cleared my name. That much was owed me. I took the fall for you. You all stayed free men because of me. You should kiss my feet.'

'Apologies if I don't, Noble.' The old man smiled, narrowing knees. 'Old knees, you see.'

McDermott smirked.

'However, you will be aptly rewarded with a new venture, and yes, I have provided you with *peasants to torture*, as requested.'

He said, stroking his chin. 'Though I disagree with your methods, you achieved excellent results. Thus, you can utilise whatever methods you want.'

Lew smiled with a twisted grin. He felt excited at the prospect of humiliating interns and graduates again. 'Bring on the good old days, hey?' He laughed. 'Fuck. I can't believe what you have been up to since I was in jail. I mean, CDOs?' He roared with laughter. 'I can't believe the peasants tolerated that shit and our banks still exist!'

The old man smiled. 'Now you see our position. There was always the possibility we would end up destroying ourselves in the process. However, our contacts in the government ended up responding to our reward structure.'

'You mean bribes right?' Lew twisted his face into a grin.

'Yes.' The old man shook his head. 'Put crudely. However, these are our men. They are old timers from financial institutions running the reserve and treasury. Their interests are our own. Do not forget that. We need them as much as they need us.' He said reproachfully.

'Whatever.' He waved him off dismissively. He was already bored off these old men. 'We can do whatever we want.'

'Yes, that is true.' The old man pursed his lips. 'It would seem we hold an unprecedented opportunity in our hands gentlemen. We have transgressed and evolved from being businesses and organisations. Gentlemen, our corporations are now the new empires of the world.'

'About time.' Lew grinned excitedly. 'Tell you what, the ones that visited me in conjugal were not the best, I cannot wait to hire some proper women.'

'What, and give them a laugh with that tiny dick they always tell everyone about?' Paul said quietly, shaking his head with a smile.

‘Fuck you!’ Lew roared, flexing his muscles. He presented himself him in a dominant stance to remove any suspicions, just as he had learnt from the business books.

‘Your own activities are your responsibility, Noble.’ Paul shook his head. He was far too soft for this group now. The man used to be the best, now he seemed like a weak excuse for a man. It seemed there was no killer instinct anymore. He worried if the man was too liberal. ‘Keep yourself out of trouble.’ He said with a smirk.

‘Don’t get caught. I know, of course. What about you McDermott?’ Lew said, twisting his mouth in bitterness. ‘I went to jail for your crimes, and now I hear you have been out of the game for almost a decade. What’s the matter? Have you gone soft?’ He said, roaring with laughter. He felt excitement run through him. He had missed abusing people so much. It filled the void in him. ‘Why didn’t you just go to jail then? If you weren’t going to make money?!’

Paul glared at him, narrowing his gaze. There was anger in those sky blue eyes. There was a tinkle in them, a fire. He said everything in that look.

‘There’s that look.’ He grinned. He remembered what he once knew; never to underestimate that man. When he wanted to he could destroy anything and create anything. ‘Good to see the old killer instinct is still there McDermott.’ He said grinning.

‘Speaking of killer,’ The old man said with a wry smile. ‘Your daughter has been quite busy Paul. I find it quite strange that she acted on your instruction in ordering the death of Collins?’ He asked, stroking his chin with curiosity.

‘Franz.’ Paul turned to him. He glared with venom. ‘The way I conduct matters is of no concern to you.’ He responded flatly.

The old man glared at him. No one ever referred to him by name. There was a moment of silence. Then he breathed deeply, his face relaxing. 'It is an interesting situation. Don't you agree Paul?' The old man smiled. 'You inform us that it is not necessary to kill Collins, then order his murder on your own behalf?' He said with feigned curiosity. 'Does that not seem, suspicious? And furthermore, that is an interesting injury you have on your forehead. Would you like to illuminate us on how that occurred?'

'There were extenuating circumstances.' Paul responded, ignoring the second question. He seemed unconvincing.

The old man hummed. 'Regardless, given our actions in cleaning this situation with your daughter up, I feel we have provided you with valuable assistance.'

'Yes.' Paul responded bitterly. 'I'm grateful for that.'

'I mean,' The old man cut him off. 'Not only with dispatching the rogue agent Malceski, before he could give evidence to the authorities. But also, I feel we have been more than valuable with cleaning up the matter at the residence of Mr Martec.'

'As I said.' Paul said with a narrowed gaze. 'I appreciate what you did for Amber, but I never asked you to do that.'

'Mr McDermott.' The old man said shaking his head. 'We are all partners; whatever our shared crimes, we rise or fall together. And I, I shall not fall. We will take whatever measures are necessary to ensured our collective survival from any attacks from the *peasants* as Mr Noble affectionately refers to them as.' He smiled coldly. 'Not only will neither you nor your daughter be investigated, but I am ensuring that our resource within the police is actively pursuing a case against Martec.'

Paul frowned. 'But the weapon had Amber's fingerprints. She left it at the apartment. I thought he didn't even touch the weapon.'

'Not anymore.' The old man said with excited eyes. 'The truth is relative.'

Paul sighed, perhaps realising the position he was in.

‘I think your assistance may no longer be temporary. We have matters to deal with. Fulton, Martec, Sun and Morgan are all still active concerns. So long as they continue to live they present a risk to our sustainable competitive survival.’ He frowned and stroked his cleanly shaven chin. ‘Furthermore, I have been informed that our lady Beaufort has become involved in drafting a rather radical and game changing piece of legislation. She is collaborating with a man named Arnoud. Gentlemen,’ He paused, smiling. ‘They are attempting to reintroduce legislation from before the deregulation era. They are furthermore intending to introduce more complicated regulation to remain competitive with our innovative trading and profit producing enterprises. This will reduce our competitive advantage and create potentially an equal playing field with the average investor. If this occurs, inequality would be reduced. Despite all the rhetoric about relative wage being irrelevant, we know this is not correct. If the relative wage of the masses were allowed to increase, the potential to lead the life of excess, to maintain this standard of living, would be reduced. Significantly. We cannot allow this to occur.’ He said coldly.

‘What is the answer? Kill them all?’ Lew asked bitterly. ‘Fine then. I’ll do it myself if that means an extra dollar for myself.’ He smirked.

‘Why not utilise Andrea now then?’ Paul asked in a calm voice. ‘She is after all, with the company? She’s in a delicate position right now I understand, with her extra marital affairs and pending divorce?’ He suggested diplomatically. ‘Surely we can leverage that to resolve this matter without creating any complications?’

‘Excellent point, and well made, Mr McDermott.’ The old man said with a smile, narrowing his gaze. ‘See, Mr Noble, the true skill in our line of work is to conduct matters in such a way that there is no unnecessary attention drawn. The key is to maintain the status quo, to manage the media. That way we can conduct our business before trading hours open, to maintain profitability.’

‘So you don’t want to kill them?’ Lew asked frustrated. The old man talked in riddles and corporate bullshit that no one used except for job interviews and websites.

‘Not at the moment.’ The old man shot a look at Lew. ‘However, in regards to utilising the Beaufort asset at this moment, you are surely aware of how to play chess, are you not, Paul?’

Paul nodded, eyes narrowed.

‘Then you surely know; you never bring out your queen too early in the game.’ The old man said with a devilish grin.

Lew laughed. He straightened the collar of his jacket. He hadn’t anticipated to enjoy being back in the game so much.

‘What about the vigilante?’ Paul asked. ‘The police have him in custody. Do we kill him too?’

‘Anders?’ Lew asked, he scratched his chin. ‘Used to be a fuckin’ good trader. Can’t believe he turned soft and grew a conscience.’

‘Interesting phraseology, Mr Noble.’ The old man responded. ‘And no, I have far different plans for Mr Sorensen. If we remove him from the game then we run the risk of creating a martyr out of a criminal.’ He paused, eyes twinkling. ‘I plan on destroying him.’

Lew roared with laughter.

‘Gentlemen, we need to resume profitable operations. It is time to *ramp up* operations, as a simple man might say. Our short term interests lie in continuing profitable operations outside of trading hours, while the lay investor continues to believe that profitability can be achieved in the *day trading* markets. I cannot stress the importance of this enough. It is simply critical. If there is any disruption to the transaction fees that are collected by our financial institutions from equity and derivative markets, then the game stops. If those investors stop believing that profitability is possible, then the game stops. And, I am unsure about you, but I rather enjoy this game. I do not wish it to stop.'

'Reckon' it's time to create another one of those motivational speakers? One of those self made millionaires who sell all those books about investing and trading?' Noble suggested.

'Precisely.' The old man said excitedly, a gleam in his eyes. 'And I believe I know the perfect candidate. Mr Noble, how would you like to become a millionaire? Would you be interested in becoming the latest success story, and getting a book series and all the perks associated with motivational investing seminars?'

Lew grinned excitedly. He hoped he might be able to land this deal, much like the other convicted company men before him. 'Sounds bliss.' He said, feeling his slight erection pushing against his trousers. He thought of the revenge he had planned. Destroying his wife who left him. Destroying the lives of all the other soft people who betrayed him. And finally destroying these Azure idiots once he had what he needed. He grinned excitedly. He loved conducting business before the markets even opened.

WILL

Things keep going, it all changes slowly. And then one day you realise you are there. The lowest ebb. Where you are no longer who you started out as. Where the good times are only memories. When you no longer feel. He caught a glimpse of her then in the distance, the hope came back before he could remind himself that she was no longer there. All he wanted at that moment was his sister, but she'd taken her away and he had only himself to blame. Her with the ocean blue eyes, with the long golden curls. The smile, the style, the grace that enchanted and deceived the room. She had taken the life of his friend and his little sister, and then his as well. Everything was lost except the fact he was still alive. There was nothing left to do but walk or stop. He lit another cigarette and started walking. All he heard was the voices in his head.

He snuck into his old apartment, it felt haunted. He packed his previously unused backpacking bag, leaving everything he didn't need. He took only essential clothes; underwear, socks, t-shirts. Any button up shirts, suits, or three quarter jackets would only be useful for the purposes of vanity. He looked around at the apartment. It didn't feel his anymore. It was the product of an obsession with the consumer lifestyle. He owned a lot of comforts he didn't need, to compensate for any meaning in his life. He breathed deeply. The alcohol was sinking in now, he felt dizzy. He had gone back to smoking as soon as he left the mansion. It seemed everyone was going to die now, he saw no point in denying the reality of life anymore. He may as well just go with it. He lit another cigarette inside his apartment, the flame illuminating the cold dark room with a flash of orange. He looked around at everything he was leaving behind; the LCD TV, the gaming console, and furniture like the modern entertainment storage unit and styled black coffee table. He scanned around the room, inhaling the soothing tobacco, looking over all the trivial things he had purchased in moments of consumerist desire. It all seemed so trivial at that point. He didn't need it. He grabbed a small first aid kit he kept in a closet drawer. He had never used it. One purchase that was not pointless. He fitted it into his backpack. He shook his head with a sad smile; clothes and a first aid kit. He realised he had surrounded himself with pointless purchases of comfort to make others believe his life was comfortable. To make others believe he maintained a life of a certain standard.

He realised in that moment he had purchased that useless junk to make himself believe that his life was good enough. That he could tell and show other people what he owned.

He frowned, taking a drag on his cigarette, looking over all the unnecessary items he owned. He smiled bitterly as he slung his backpack around his shoulder. He took one last look at the life he had led. He smiled sadly and exhaled. Someone else would have to deal with the rest of the junk he had accumulated.

There was one last purchase he needed to make. He opened his expensive laptop and took out his credit card.

It was still night when he left his apartment. Dawn would not be for a few hours. There was no one else on the streets. He walked alone through the city until he found a cab. He told the driver to take him to the airport.

AUTHOR'S NOTE

Many thanks for reading!

Keep in touch through my website, henrystokes.org, or through Facebook, facebook.com/thehenrystokes.

www.ingramcontent.com/pod-product-compliance
Lightning Source LLC
Chambersburg PA
CBHW030823310726
48980CB00006B/608/J
9780992548506